Cassidy's Challenge
Russian Amerika
Book 3

Stoney Compton

**NAZCA
PRESS**

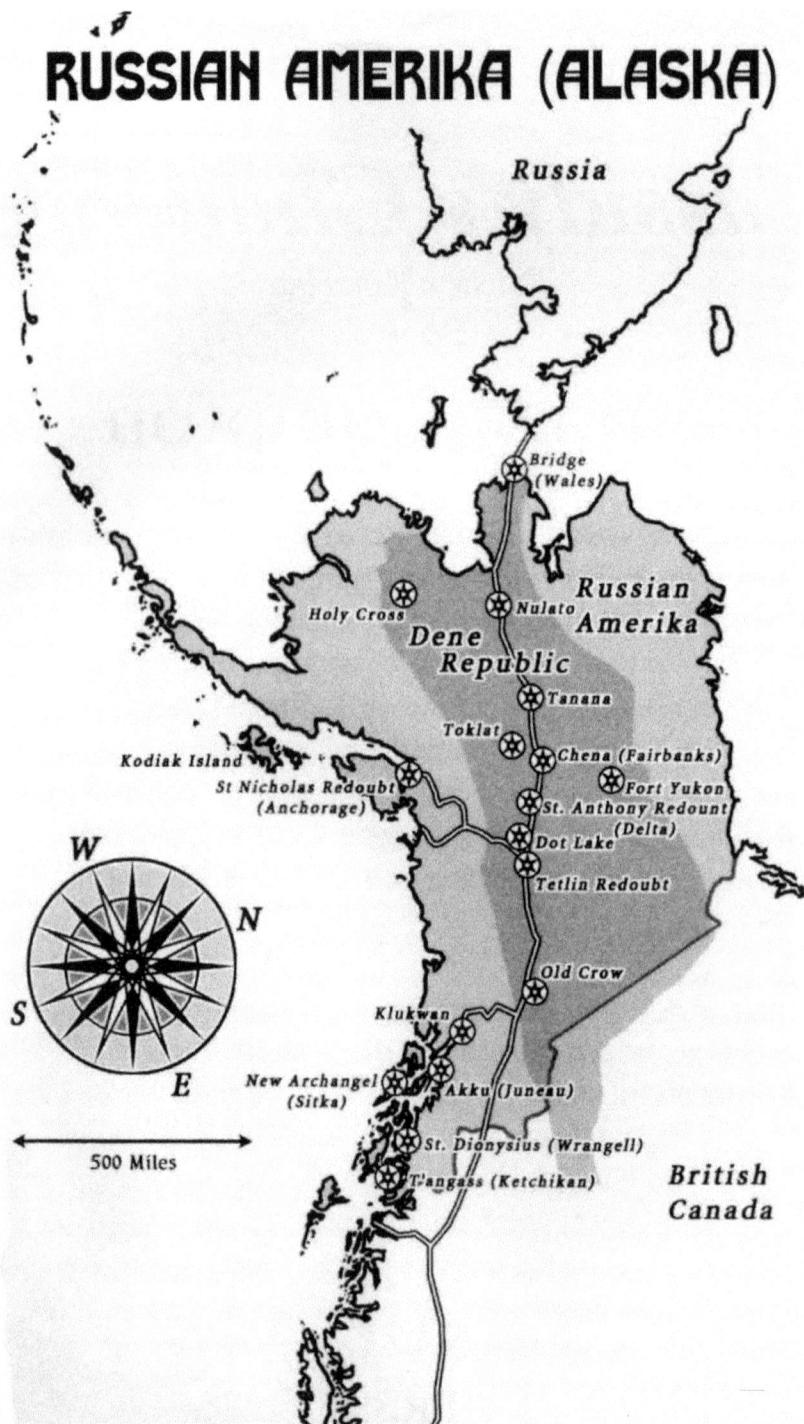

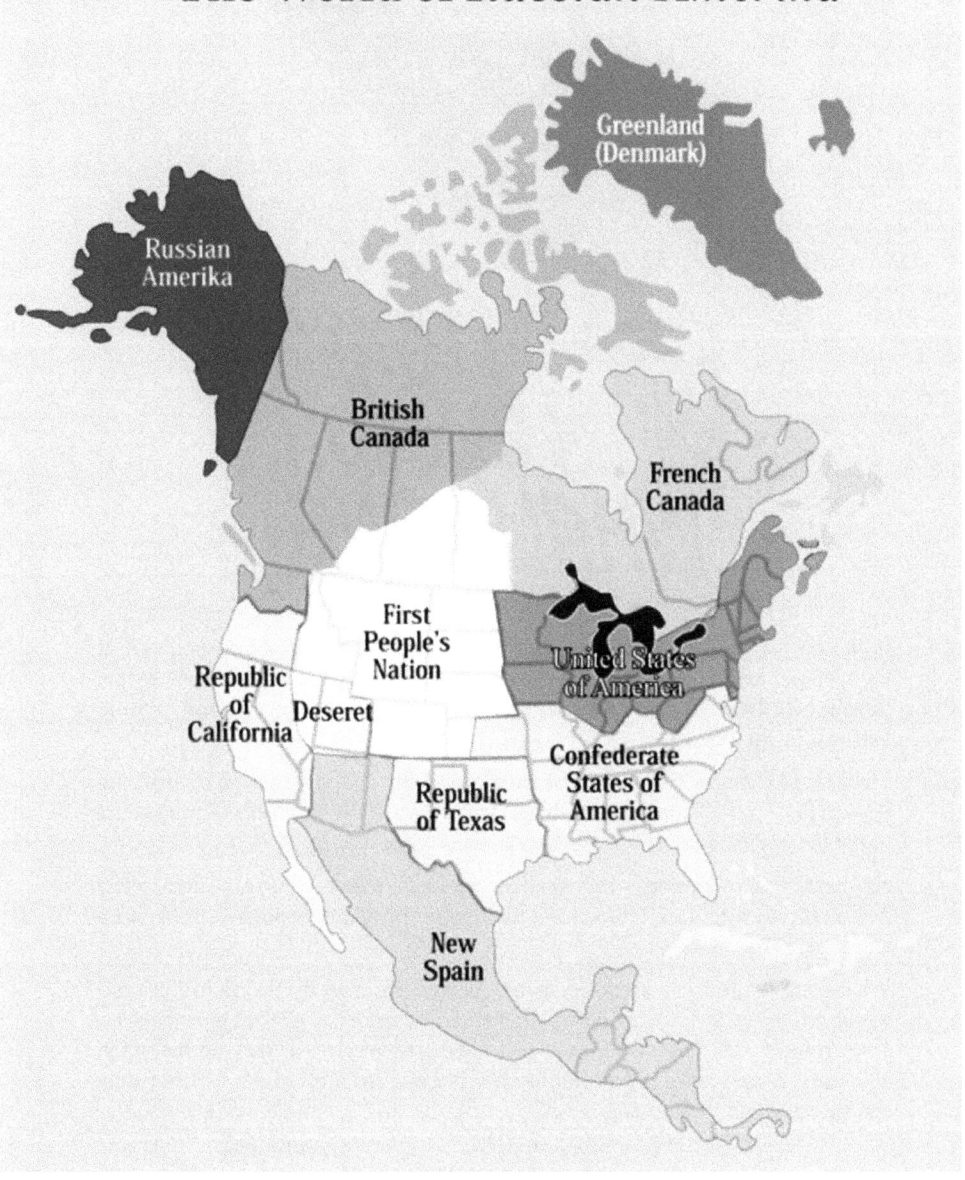

In the years after the stars fell, young Noah Manaluk, an Inupiat Eskimo living at Point Hope, Alaska, eats a piece of possessed seal liver that changes his life. By the time he is 17 he is a shaman who can call game to the hunter's spears and fish into nets cast by the People.

Thinker, a Humpback whale, is the only one of his pod who perceives anything beyond his immediate surroundings. He is aware of the longteeth waiting at the top of the world and cautiously moves to the middle of the pod.

He hears the summons and realizes another exists who can completely communicate with him - something that has never before happened in his life - and it wants to kill him.

Whalesong is the story of two disparate beings, enemies by the nature of their world yet closer in understanding than with any member of their own species. Two creatures that have as much to learn about themselves as they do the other, and come to rely on one another as they begin a journey which will not only change the world, but save it.

Paperback ISBN: **9781963479553** Hardback ISBN: **9781963479584**
eBook ISBN: **9781963479546**

Cassidy's Challenge
Russian Amerika
Book 3

Stoney Compton

This edition published by Nazca Press
A division of Misti Media LLC
Available in both Paperback and eBook Editions
1 2 3 4 5 6 7 8 9 10
Copyright © 2025 by Stoney Compton
Cover Design by Stoney Compton
Cover Copyright © 2025 Stoney Compton and Nazca Press
a division of Misti Media
Paperback ISBN: 9781963479805
eBook ISBN: 9781963479799

Without limiting the rights under copyright reserved above, no part of this publication may be reproduced, stored in or introduced into a retrieval system, or transmitted, in any form, or by any means (electronic, mechanical, photocopying, recording, or otherwise), without the prior written permission of both the copyright owners and the above publisher of this book.

The scanning, uploading, and distribution of this book via the Internet or via any other means without the permission of the publisher is illegal and punishable by law. Please purchase only authorized electronic editions, and do not participate in or encourage electronic piracy of copyrighted materials. Your support of the author's rights is appreciated.

No generative artificial intelligence (AI) was used in any aspect of the creation of this work. Without in any way limiting the author's [and publisher's] exclusive rights under copyright, any use of this publication to "train" generative artificial intelligence (AI) technologies to generate text is expressly prohibited. The author (and publisher) reserves all rights to license uses of this work for generative AI training and development of machine learning language models.

This is a work of fiction. The characters, dialogue and events in this book are wholly fictional, and any resemblance to companies and actual persons, living or dead, is coincidental.

Also in the Russian Amerika Series

Book 1
Russian Amerika

Book 2
Alaska Republik

Dedication
To the memory of
Maisie Rose Verley Reynolds Grandgenette
1899—1972
One of the first strong women I ever loved

CHAPTER 1

20 KILOMETERS WEST OF TANANA CROSSING, ALASKA REPUBLIK

The labouring utility struggled against horizontal sheets of heavy rain carried by an incessant wind.

"How the hell are we supposed to find anyone in this *merde?*" Roland Delcambré yelled, disdainfully. "Let alone someone on foot!"

"Be thankful you're not driving," Yukon Cassidy replied. "Keeping this thing on the road is the hardest work I've done in years."

The rough mining road wound through the boreal forest of spruce and birch surrounded by the ever-present, wind-whipped willow thickets of late spring. The utility swayed heavily due to the sail-effect created by the lodge top bolted to the chassis. The wipers offered tantalizing clear glimpses of the crude road ahead for mere seconds per swipe.

"I would point out that you won't allow me to drive your ancient machine," Delcambré snorted. "But at this moment I am more than happy you are in charge of this disaster in progress."

Wind shrilled around the slightly warped right-hand door, misting them with a fine, cool spray.

"Remind me again why I took you on as an associate."

The small man gave Cassidy a look of contempt. "Because I am your intellectual superior, and you require my keen observation to keep you from harm's way! That's obvious even to a *promyshlennik*!"

"No, that wasn't it. I think it's due to your claim to be a superior navigator here in the new Alaska Republik. Yet we seem to be lost."

"You finally admit you're lost! Perhaps now you will listen to me. As I pointed out at the time, we needed to turn left at that last crossroad."

"It went south. We need to go north."

"Have you ever seen a straight road in Russ—, uh, the Alaska Republik? Roads twist and turn to follow the terrain, not the quickest route from one point to another. You must think you're in the Republic of California!"

"As if you had ever been there yourself," Cassidy scoffed with a wide grin.

"Too true. If I had ever gotten that far south, I would have stayed. But we still should have—"

The utility slammed to a halt as Cassidy stood on the clutch and brake pedals. The vehicle slewed sideways and rocked alarmingly before creaking to a stop in the wind and rain. Thunder rolled over them.

"Do you want my face smeared all over the damned windscreen?" Delcambré yelled, bracing himself on the dashboard.

"It would have been if we'd hit that," Cassidy said, pointing.

Between swipes of the wiper blade a lorry could be seen sitting in the middle of the road. There was not enough room on either side to go around it.

Cassidy and Delcambré glanced at each other. Delcambré touched the boot knife hidden beneath his trouser leg. Cassidy wondered if his friend ever thought about the unconscious preparation gesture.

Since they had worked so well together to put Timothy Riordan behind bars, they had teamed up as bounty hunters. This was their first man hunt and it wasn't going as planned.

"Be careful," Cassidy said as each opened their door, grabbed their weapons, and moved out into the turbulent weather. Both men slowly eased around the lorry. Its cargo sat securely covered by a heavy tarp. Nothing seemed amiss other than the fact it silently blocked the road.

Cassidy peered around in the stinging rain, the barrel of his .45-.70 moved across the landscape with his focus, a third lethal eye. The odor of wet vegetation rode the wind and gave him a frisson of unleashed elements. He grinned in appreciation.

"Damn!" Delcambré said with a snort and pointed.

Two men sprawled in death in front of the lorry. The blood from their wounds created by a heavy caliber weapon had been washed away by the downpour.

"Why were they killed, and their cargo not looted?" Cassidy asked loud enough for Delcambré to hear through the pounding rain and whistling wind.

"Perhaps we interrupted the murderers?"

"Stay where you are. No need to risk both of us."

"Whatever you say, *mon ami*," Delcambré said with a nod.

Both men squinted through the storm. Visibility stretched to twenty meters at best. Delcambré huddled near the abandoned lorry and continued to survey the forest around them. Cassidy cautiously moved down the road, hugging to one side so he could throw himself into the brush if need be.

Abruptly he stopped and called over his shoulder, "Roland, come look at this."

His eyes snapped from right to left in a constant metronome between anticipation and wariness, Delcambré moved forward through the incessant rain. Thunder again rolled across the sky and the rain increased in volume.

"I am soaked to my damned skin. This better be worth it!" Water ran off his wide-brimmed hat in counterpoint.

"You decide." Cassidy nodded toward the body splayed in the middle of the road next to a rifle.

"What the hell?" Delcambré sidled up to the body and closely examined it for a long moment. He looked back at Cassidy. "This is Ferdinand Rochamboux, the *homme* we've been tracking!"

"Thought it might be," Cassidy said in a musing tone.

"Looks like he killed the two back there at the lorry and then someone dispatched him." Delcambré looked up at Cassidy. "That how you parse it?"

"Exactly, my friend. But who killed Ferdinand, and why?"

Delcambré bent down and stuck his hand inside the collar of the dead man's shirt. "Despite the rain, he's still warm. This happened within the last hour."

The rain and wind suddenly diminished, and they both stared around at the dripping, saturated forest.

"Let's do what we must and get out of here," Delcambré said with a snort. "I feel very much like a large target despite my perfect, compact size."

"Check the body and I'll keep watch."

Cassidy surveyed the area and turned his face aside as the wind and rain renewed their assault.

"Yukon, what do make of this?"

Cassidy looked down. Delcambré had rolled the dead man over and a blood-soaked playing card lay on the ground where the body had covered it.

"What is it?"

"The Queen of Spades," Delcambré said with a shiver. "Let's get the hell out of here."

"Grab the card and the weapons. I'll keep watch."

"If you want that card, you grab it! I'll keep watch."

"God's codpiece, Roland. Are you that goosey about a little bit of blood? I thought you were the epitome of a mercenary soldier."

"I have my limits. Touching a Queen of Spades covered in a dead man's blood is beyond them. Do you doubt my courage?"

"Didn't until now." Cassidy smirked. He bent down and picked up the card, wiped it on the dead man's denim pants and put it in his pocket.

"There's no way we could track anyone in this weather. Even our own tracks are washing away." Cassidy felt he was being watched.

The rain slackened again and the sky brightened overhead. They both peered around. The wind kept the foliage moving enough that they wouldn't have heard a tank pass more than twenty meters away.

Delcambré spat on the ground. "I don't mind telling you that this place spooks me. Did you notice what was missing on our quarry, there?"

Cassidy looked at the soaked body. "What's missing?"

"His right ear. The ear they said had a ring in it, one of the means of identifying him."

"Good observation. I missed that entirely."

"Per my assumption. That also means someone else will get the bounty for this miscreant's death."

Rain hammered through the trees and swept over them once again.

"Okay, Roland, let's pack up and get out."

"What about the bodies?"

"You want to bury them?"

"Not if you don't."

"Give it a week and there won't be anything left. Check the other two bodies for identification and weapons. The rest can stay."

Roland quickly went through the pockets of the two victims. "What about this?" He tossed a small bag and Cassidy caught it.

He dumped the contents into his hand. A pile of shiny, newly minted Austrian gold ducats filled his palm.

"These guys are Austrian? What in the hell are they doing in the middle of Rus—ah, the Alaska Republik?"

The wind increased and they had to raise their voices again.

"I thought you were supposed to be the brains of this outfit," Delcambré said with a grin. "Let's get out of the weather. At least we're not walking away empty handed."

The men climbed into the utility and sat for a moment in the dry, quiet cab. Water dripped off them as they stared at the foreign utility. Cassidy divided the ducats, slipped half into his pocket, and gave half to Roland as he stared at the lorry.

"Let's try and sort this out." Cassidy continued staring through the windscreen at the late model Mercedes. "At first I thought we had a simple case of highway robbery. Then we discover some vengeful soul has eliminated a public nuisance, who happened to be our quarry, before departing with his ear."

"Works for me," Delcambré said. "We got paid anyway. Now let's get out of here."

"But if those two are Austrian agents, there's more to this than a simple robbery gone wrong."

"Kismet, Yukon. Can we let it go at that? They happened to come across a bad man who killed them, probably nothing political involved."

"They're from *Austria!* How could this *not* be political?" Cassidy demanded.

"Not everything is political these days, dammit!"

"I wish." Cassidy continued staring at the utility. "What would Austrians be hauling out here in the middle of the bush? And they had to go through either the FPN or British Canada to get that beautiful lorry up here."

"And your point would be?"

"Why didn't either of those nations let us know we had Austrian visitors?"

Delcambré gave him a sidelong look. "You want to examine the load on the lorry, don't you?"

"Now I remember why I took you on as an associate. You're smarter than you look! We *have* to check it. You know that as well as I do."

The capricious rain slackened and slowed to a drizzle.

"No time like the present," Delcambré said. He jumped out of the utility and scrambled up over the tailgate of the lorry. His knife flashed as he cut the lashings holding the canvas flaps together, quickly tied both sides back, and disappeared inside.

"He *is* quick, once you get him moving," Cassidy muttered as he stepped out of the cab. In a moment he climbed into the back of the Mercedes. "What do we have, Roland?"

"Fancier armament than anything I've ever used." He pointed into the long metal box he had already opened. "What the hell is that?"

"It looks like a much larger version of those anti-tank weapons the Austro-Hungarians developed. *Panzerfaust* is what I think they called them. In addition to size, this looks more highly developed than the ones I saw years ago."

"You were in the Austrian War?" Roland asked, respect tingeing his words.

"For a while." Cassidy shrugged. "Are there any manuals with it?"

Roland shook his head. "First thing I looked for after I opened this package."

"There has to be one somewhere in here. However, it doesn't matter. We can't leave all of this sitting here. We have to take the whole thing back to Chena at the very least."

"I came to the same conclusion. There might be a reward. Which vehicle do you wish to drive?"

"You drive this. I'll drive my utility. First we have to load the bodies. There might be evidence or intelligence to be gained from them by someone smarter than we are."

"I'll help load them, Cassidy," Delcambré said, puffing out his half keg chest. "But there's nobody smarter than the two of us together!"

Cassidy laughed. "Thanks for including me in your delusions."

CHAPTER 2

TANANA, NORTHERN CAPITOL OF ALASKA REPUBLIK

"Where are my dress shoes?" General Grisha Grigorievich demanded as he rummaged in his closet. Heavy rain beat on the windows of their apartment for the third day in a row. Spring in the Interior of Alaska Republik tended to be whimsical.

"Where you left them?" Wing Demoski Grigorievich suggested.

"I've worn the damn things once, and that was months ago! How could they go missing?"

"Perhaps you should ask Sergeant Major Tobias about them? Doesn't he know everything about you?"

"Not even remotely!" Grisha snapped. "Are you trying to provoke me?"

Wind slammed rain against the outer wall and rattled the windows. Thunder grumbled in the distance.

Wing reined herself in and smiled at her husband. "Not exactly. There is something I have to tell you and I'm nervous about your response."

"What could you possibly worry about telling me? I love you without reservation!"

"That I am carrying our child?" She looked away for a moment and then faced him. "Does that give you pause?"

"We're going to have a *baby*?" Grisha looked stunned. She had never before seen him this agog.

Wing grinned at him. "Do you know your mouth is hanging open? Yes, we're going to have a baby. Believe me, I was as surprised as you are now when I realized it."

"When?"

"I talked to some of the older women, and they applied some equation. They said the child would be born in the third or fourth week of October."

"Have you seen the doctor?"

She laughed. "We live in a hospital, Grisha! Of course, I saw the doctor. He said everything looked fine and that the baby had a healthy heartbeat."

He dropped his butt onto the bed, staring at her. "This is something I hadn't anticipated. After almost two years of marriage, I thought we couldn't have children."

Wing frowned and her voice grew soft. "Do you *not* want children?"

He grinned, jumped to his feet, and wrapped his arms around her. "Of *course,* I want children! I just thought it was something we weren't going to have together. What are we going to name her?"

"Her? What if she's a he?"

They both laughed. Her mind flew back to the day she married him. He was in the hospital recovering from a leg wound and she was fresh from the battlefield. It seemed longer than two years since the Revolution.

Someone knocked on the door.

"Come in Sergeant Major," they said in unison.

Sergeant Major Nelson Tobias stepped into the bedroom and came to attention. He started to speak and then noticed the obvious good humor on both faces.

"General, Colonel, is there something amiss?"

Grisha opened his mouth, but Wing spoke first.

"We're going to have a baby, Sergeant Major. We wanted you to be the first to know."

"We are? I mean, you are?" His smile shot from ear to ear under his full moustache. "How wonderfully marvelous!" He walked over to Wing.

"If the colonel would permit?" Without waiting for a response, he hugged her tightly to him and spoke quietly into her ear. "You have my undying support, madam. If anyone tries to harm you or that child they will have to go through me first!"

Wing felt sudden tears and a wave of emotion for this complex man. "Thank you, Sergeant Major," she said, returning the hug. "I sincerely appreciate that."

He stepped back and swallowed, turned to Grisha, and shook his hand. "You have no idea how this gladdens my heart, General."

"Thank you, Sergeant Major. Was there something you wished to tell me when you first arrived?"

"I have a communication from First Speaker Haroldsson for you." He reached into an inner pocket on his tunic and handed Grisha a folded sheet of paper.

"Thank you." Grisha opened the sheet and read the contents.

"Colonel, do we know when the blessed event will transpire?"

Wing had to keep from laughing, but Tobias had completely changed from a precise drill instructor to an excited, avuncular parody. "The third or fourth week in October. Do you have any children, Sergeant Major?"

"My life has been blessed with three children. My oldest son served as a lieutenant in the British Army and fell in the Austrian War. My daughter is married to a member of the Australian parliament, and my youngest son is currently in his third year at Sandhurst."

Wing saw the baffled look on Grisha's face and realized she probably mirrored the same surprise.

"I had no idea you were ever married, Sergeant Major!" she blurted.

"Twenty-four years, and then I lost her to an epidemic in India. Edna always had to be helping the unfortunates she encountered, and India has a surfeit of them."

"Do we have a complete record on you, Sergeant Major?" Grisha asked.

"No, General. Do you require one?"

Wing gave Grisha her best "shut up now" look.

"Um, no. You've more than proven your worth and we're glad to have you on our side. Although I'm sure your record would prove fascinating reading."

Wing smiled in agreement. "What does the First Speaker say?"

Grisha looked down at the paper in his hands. "Well, now I know why he wanted to see me today. He wants me to give the army to Paul Eluska and for me to set up a national police force."

"What?"

"He also moved our meeting up. He wants to talk to me in an hour."

"Grisha, he is removing you from the army?" She didn't like the feeling in her chest, especially after realizing it to be anxiety mixed with anger.

"I don't know. I'll tell you more after I talk to him. Sergeant Major, please get my driver. I want to leave in five minutes."

Sergeant Major Tobias stiffened to attention. "Yes, General Grigorievich." He left their residence immediately.

"Grisha…"

"Wing, I don't know anything more about this than you do. As soon as I get an explanation I'll tell you."

"He can't just dump you as General of the Army!"

He stood looking away from her for a long moment as the wind and rain continued to attack the windows. He turned and held out his arms. She immediately went into his comfortable embrace.

Another long moment passed as he held her tight. Then he whispered into her ear.

"He can do anything he wants to. He's the First Speaker. So, we will agree and go along with it."

She pulled away and looked into his face, felt unwanted tears creep down her cheeks. "But that's not fair!"

"Life isn't about fair, my love. It's about reality."

Then he turned and was gone.

She put both hands on her still small stomach and wondered about their sanity for bringing a child into this capricious world.

CHAPTER 3

DOYON HOUSE, TANANA, CAPITOL OF ALASKA REPUBLIK

"Mister First Speaker, General Grigorievich is here to see you."

Pelagian looked up from his desk. "Thank you, Annika. Please show him in."

Pelagian leaned back and knuckled his eyes. His back ached and he hadn't smelled fresh air in far too many hours. Rain clattered against the windows and distant thunder grumbled.

There is so much yet to do.

"Mister First Speaker, you requested my presence?"

He stood and walked over to Grisha. "Thank you for being so prompt, General Grigorievich." They shook hands formally.

The storm outside continued unabated.

"Now let's dispense with the formal crap and talk like the friends we are, okay?"

"Whatever you say, Pelagian," Grisha said through a wide grin. "Why do you want to kick me out of the army?"

Pelagian laughed. "That's how Wing sees it, huh?"

"Yes. How do you see it?"

"From where I sit it's all a fall windstorm and I need to notice every leaf blowing off the trees. There are so many different things I have to deal with in creating a workable government that I almost wish I hadn't won the election."

"Nathan Roubitaux is a good man," Grisha said, "But I am happy you are the First Speaker. Your vision expands beyond the Yukon and Tanana Rivers."

"Because you can say that and mean it," Pelagian said, "is exactly why I need you to create a national peacekeeping force."

"I thought we had an army."

"What we have is a reserve army if we need it. Most of the men and women who fought to get us this far have all made their goodbyes and gone home. Damn near every one of them said, 'If you need me again, just let me know.'"

"How many stayed on?" Grisha asked, realizing he should be the one answering that question. The thought flashed through his mind that perhaps he wasn't doing as good a job as he thought.

"I don't know about down in Sea Alaska Province. Here in Doyon Province, we have almost as many officers as we do enlisted. The army group up at Bridge has a couple hundred effectives, but that's a long way from here.

"The positive part is we are training the Dená Rangers you created and have one class already in the field. They all enlisted for four years' service, and I considered giving them police duties, but it felt too much like Cossacks to my way of thinking. Our new government is already divided over this issue."

"What issue?"

"A standing army. One faction, the smallest at the moment, wants us to keep a standing army at all times. The traditionalists want to keep things the way they are."

"We can't afford a standing army unless they will work for free. How are we going to keep everyone happy on this one?"

"We aren't," Pelagian said. "I find it amazing how people with the same backgrounds can differ so extremely on issues."

"Paul Eluska and his people are in Bridge right now?"

"Yes."

"Holy crap, then we're a sitting target for anyone who wants to walk across the border and mess with us. Why the hell haven't I realized this before now?"

"You've been as busy as the rest of us. Like me, now you're getting the picture." Pelagian's grin vanished quickly. "I'm torn about this thing and I hope that creating a police force will silence some of the arguing."

"I have a military background. I don't know the first thing about being a policeman."

"The hell you don't. You have military *command* experience. You know how to choose men and women to do a job whether they like you or not. You are a keen judge of character, and you are the only damned option I have."

"Well, since you put it that way…"

They both broke into laughter.

"Seriously, Grisha, you are the only man in this new nation that could pull it off for the very same reason you were the only man who could command an army of Inuits, Yu'piks, Dená, Russians, Kolosh and whoever else came down the road. Nobody would trust anyone other than you."

"When the hell are you going to give me something easy to do?"

"Want to hear your new title?"

"You're having way too much fun with this!"

"Grisha, I am honored to have you as a friend, I am doubly honored to have you as a supporter, and it is with utmost trust that I appoint you as head of national security."

"What's my title?"

"Chief Peacekeeper. You are the final word in security after me. I know that most questions will never reach my desk about this subject, and I thank you in advance for that."

Grisha took a deep breath.

"Only because I want to see this nation thrive do I agree to this, Pelagian. If I fail, you can't hold it against me. Understood?"

"Understood, my friend, and thank you."

"What laws do we follow and enforce? Where do I get the people we'll need? How many can I hire, and how much can I promise we'll pay them?"

"In reverse. From three to seven California dollars per day. Hire as many as you can find. We need people all over the Republik. But they have to be trustworthy and take an oath to the Alaska Republik. The laws are fundamental, for now it's how we handled the election; no clubs and behave yourself."

"No other rules?"

"Not yet, Grisha. If you do the best you can I know that it will fill the bill. Here's how I envisioned the organizational structure…"

CHAPTER 4

CHENA,
ALASKA REPUBLIK

Cassidy drove up to the rebuilt hospital and stopped in the emergency parking area. Two men hurried out into the steady rain.

"What's the emergency?" the first one asked.

"No emergency," Cassidy said. "We have three bodies the coroner will want to see."

"What coroner?"

"Coroner, doctor, it doesn't matter to me. Ask General Grigorievich. He's the one who sent us out in the first place."

"Wait here, I'll be right back."

Both men retreated into the building.

Roland jumped out of the lorry parked behind Cassidy's utility.

"What's going on? Who were those *hommes*? Are we going to get rid of the carrion in the back of the lorry?"

"They went to get someone who is in charge."

"I knew we should have left them there!" Delcambré said with a snort.

"A little patience, my compact friend, is all I ask."

"Don't patronize me."

Someone in rain gear hurried out to them.

"Yukon Cassidy and Roland Delcambré, just the men I want to see!"

"Now that's more like it!" Roland said with a wide smile.

"General, we have three bodies–"

"Don't worry, Yukon. Someone will take care of them. Come inside where we can talk and get you some hot food."

He turned and hurried back into the hospital.

"Who the hell was that?" Delcambré asked. "I couldn't see him."

"That was General Grigorievich. I wonder what he's doing out of

Tanana. He mentioned food."

They ran through the rain into the building. Cassidy relished being out of the weather. General Grigorievich stood dripping in the hallway, giving them both measuring looks.

"You mentioned food?" Cassidy said.

"I thought you both might be hungry."

"Why is the General of the Army waiting on us?" Cassidy asked, "Not that we don't enjoy your company."

"We need to talk. I had the cooks put together some steak and potatoes for you. Is that enough?"

"What kind of steak?" Delcambré asked.

"Beef, from California. Is that acceptable?"

"Absolutely! I am so sick of moose meat that I could–"

"We appreciate the change in diet, General," Cassidy said, while elbowing Roland. "How is it you are in Chena and treating us with such solicitude?"

The general grinned. "I was told nothing got past you, Yukon. I have a proposition for you both, but it can wait until after you've eaten."

They went inside the hospital and the general led them to the large dining area. Intoxicating aromas of cooking food filled the air. A woman stuck her head out of a doorway.

"How do you two want your steaks cooked?"

"Medium rare," they said in unison.

A different, younger woman brought a large pot of coffee and three cups. "Anyone take cream or sugar?"

"I'd love some sugar," Delcambré said through a leer.

"For your coffee, right?" she answered with a smile.

"If that's all I can get."

Cassidy interrupted, "That's all he needs, miss. Thank you." He turned to the general. "So why don't you tell us your proposition before Roland gets us thrown out before we get to eat."

"My job title changed about four hours ago. The First Speaker asked me to be Chief Peacekeeper for the whole Alaska Republik."

"Chief Peacekeeper. Like a gendarme or something?" Roland asked.

"Exactly, Mr. Delcambré. I have been tasked with creating an organization to provide security for the people and the republik. I had the army fly me down here because I want you two to be the first of my officers."

"This would be a full-time job, with pay and all that?" Roland asked.

"You even get a badge. Not that we have them yet, but this will all be official."

"Well, it beats bounty work," Yukon said. "By the way, all three of the men in the back of my utility were killed by someone else."

"I know. She brought in the ring ear of Rochamboux late last night."

"*She?*" Roland blurted before Cassidy could speak.

"Solare is also a bounty hunter and a very good one. For the record she only killed Rochamboux. He killed the two strangers."

"Why have I never heard of her?" Cassidy asked. "I thought I knew all the people in that line of work here in the Alaska Republik."

"She's new. She came up from California with a letter of introduction from a man I implicitly trust."

Roland snorted into his beard. "Some *fille* just bounces into the country, tracks down, and kills a man of Rochamboux's stature in a few days?"

"She's not exactly a little girl, Mr. Delcambré. She is a very effective agent with an impressive record of successes behind her."

"Why does this bother me, General? Other than the fact she didn't discover the strangers were gunrunners and Austrian." Yukon said.

"They were? This puts a whole new perspective on the situation."

"Roland discovered their origins. I would have missed it too, General."

"Please, call me Grisha. Solare had been on Rochamboux's trail for over a year. He was wanted in California, the First People's Nation, British Canada, and even his own home country, French Canada."

"I'll wager she gains a lot of bounty money off that ear," Roland muttered.

"No wonder he came to Alaska," Yukon said. "He had nowhere else to go. Is this Solare a California Peacekeeper?"

"No, she's a free agent."

Delcambré cleared his throat. "So are her actions legal in the Alaska Republik or is she going beyond the law in killing a fugitive?"

Grisha made a wry smile and spread his hands out. "You have a knack for cutting to the pith of the situation, Mr. Delcambré. The reward warrant did stipulate 'dead or alive' and it was signed by a judge."

"Please, Grisha, call me Roland."

The wry smile disappeared. "It's probably not a good idea to piss on the boots of your new boss."

Delcambré bristled and he stuck a pose. "Have I agreed to take this job? Or for that matter, has Mr. Cassidy, here? I thought we were still negotiating and therefore still equals."

"Roland," Cassidy said, "Mind your manners." He grinned at Grisha. "Really, I can't take him anywhere!"

"Are you comparing me to a child, Cassidy?"

"Only when you act like one."

"So, are you fellows interested in the job or not? We have no time to waste in either direction." Grisha's tone firmed.

"Explain the hierarchy, and where we would fit in," Yukon said before Roland could open his mouth. He hadn't missed Grisha's evasion of Roland's question. *Obviously the legality of the situation isn't as important as the results.*

"Truthfully, I'm still sorting this all out, so nothing is set in stone. We have fourteen different provinces in this nation, some are of a single ethnicity and others are a mixture of everything we have to offer.

"The constitutional convention is currently working out the overall legal framework this republik will employ. So right now, we are out on a limb, yet it's obvious something has to be put in place immediately. What's the cargo in that lorry you two brought in?"

"It's loaded with rocket launchers a single man can handle. They look something like the Panzerfaust the Austrians used against us in the war, but fancier."

"You were in the Austrian War?" Grisha suddenly looked haunted. "I was in the Troika Guard under Prince Dimitri's Imperial Expeditionary Force at the Battle of Bou Saada in French Algeria."

"Didn't that unit suffer heavy losses?" Roland asked in a respectful tone.

"Indeed. We lost our commanding officer and over 3,000 officers and men. I lost sixty percent of my outfit before the retreat ended. I was one of two Troika Guard officers who survived and they gave me a court martial for just staying alive."

"Do the Russians always hang the commanders of lost battles?"

Cassidy asked. "I didn't stay in the fight as long as you. I was hit in the invasion of Calais, evacuated back to Britain and invalided out as soon as I healed enough to walk. They wanted me gone, before I could beat up some senior officers."

"You were in the *British* Army?" Roland said.

"I was in the FPN Regiment. That was back when we thought the British might treat us like equals if we took their side. Instead, they used us as a cheap diversion so they wouldn't have to sacrifice their own troops."

"You were a Dog Soldier?" Grisha asked.

Cassidy nodded and tightened his jaw muscles.

"I thought they were wiped out," Roland whispered.

"They were. Only those of us who were hit early enough to be evacuated lived through it. We had 100% causalities."

"No wonder your people ripped through British Canada this last time," Grisha said. "And I thought *we* had been poorly used!"

"We all were. It was a worthless war between kings, kaisers, and czars. People like us were just pawns on the chessboard of Europe and Africa. I'd like to get back to the matter at hand if you don't mind. I'll have dreams as it is."

"The rockets," Roland prompted gently.

"I think they might be for shooting down aircraft," Cassidy said. "Which begs the questions; what were two Austrian nationals doing in Alaska Republik, and to whom were they delivering the weapons? I thought the Treaty of Paris stipulated against the Austrians ever meddling in another nation's affairs."

"Have you told anyone else about what you found?" Grisha asked.

"You're the first person we've talked to since we found the bodies and their rig," Cassidy replied.

"Good. Let's try and keep this a state secret. We have to find out where they were going. This is exactly the reason we have no time to lose putting the Peacekeepers in action." Grisha stopped and stared hard at the wall.

"By the way, Grisha, I accept the offer," Cassidy said. "I know you're a good boss."

"Yeah, me, too," Roland said. "Sorry if I was a bit abrupt before. Must be hungry or something."

As if on cue the woman who had brought them coffee now delivered two plates of steak, potatoes, and something green.

"What's that?" Delcambré asked.

"Broccoli, it's a vegetable, and it's good for you."

"I'll try anything once," Roland said.

"Just what a girl wants to hear," she said and winked.

He looked up at her. "Roland Delcambré, soldier of fortune, warrior, and lover of women. At your service!"

"Laura Jack, woman of unknown depths. Pleased to meet you."

"May I visit with you later?" Roland asked, rising to his feet. Laura was no more than two inches taller than him.

"That might be interesting. Please do." She nodded at the other two men and vanished into the kitchen.

"I think I'm in love," Roland declared, sinking back into his chair.

Cassidy snorted. "Now *there's* a challenge!"

"Thank you both," Grisha said in a rush. "I feel that we now have a chance to fulfill our mission. Here's what I want you to do first…"

Thunder rumbled somewhere over the Tanana River.

CHAPTER 5

FORT SELKIRK,
FIRST PEOPLE'S NATION

Captain Dumont briefly but firmly locked eyes with every man in the large room. He strived to infuse every man with Gallic *orguiel*. Pride would carry a man much further than any other emotion. After a long pause he spoke.

"We have been awarded the mission. Because of our successful service, the Legion knows we are *tres* formidable. We must not fail. Do you all understand?"

All thirty-nine heads nodded in tandem.

"*Bien!* I agree with the opinion that this new upstart republik is ours for the taking. Remember the stakes and do not let your fellow legionnaires down." He snapped his hand up in salute.

Every man sprang to his feet and returned the salute.

"We are the Phantom Legion, and we shall prevail!"

Every man in the room shouted, "We shall prevail!"

"Officers and senior enlisted to me. Everyone else is dismissed. See to your equipment."

Stubbornly cold spring winds moaned around the weathered barracks.

Within seconds only five men remained in the room. Standing at attention.

"At your ease, as the Brits say." He awarded them a thin smile and nodded toward the chairs. As one the five sat.

"The Alaska Republik has yet to formalize their method of government, let alone their order of battle."

"They seemed to have done well this far without one, Captain Dumont."

The captain smiled at his first sergeant. "Emilé, you are correct. However, that may actually be a weakness."

"Sir?" Lieutenant Klein rumbled in his ruined voice.

"They will believe they are nearly invincible due to their political victory over Imperial Russia. We know European politics won the day, not the rebellious Dená Separatist Army. Wait until we turn their politics against them and beat them in the field at the same time."

Ensign Meté allowed a feral grin to cross his face. They all nodded.

"We will travel by inflatables from the drop point. Ensure all have extra ammo. We will live off the land."

All but quivering in anticipation, they stared at him.

"We leave in six hours. Make good use of the time. Dismissed."

They silently hurried from the room.

Captain Dumont hoped Ferdinand Rochamboux would not let him down. Their successful operation hinged on his abilities, and the weapons he would provide. Not to mention they would have to go through hell to even reach him.

CHAPTER 6

CHENA,
ALASKA REPUBLIK

Lieutenant Alex Strom, late of the International Freekorps, sat in his cell wondering how much longer they were going to wait to run him through a bogus court and then hang him for war crimes. He could hear birds singing to the world through the small window, and smell the earth shedding ice while embracing green.

"Damned Riordan," he muttered.

He had no doubt that the actions initiated by his former commander would get all of them a noose, or a firing squad. He ruminated on which he preferred, finally decided he'd just as soon pass on both, and die quietly in bed many years hence.

What a hell of a way to end up!

A key turned in the lock on cell door and he stood at attention. They might kill him, but he would go out like a professional.

The heavy door swung open and Strom blinked.

"Delcambré? What the hell are you doing here?"

"Changing your life, perhaps?" The small man strolled into the cell and grinned at Alex.

Another man walked in behind Delcambré.

"Ain't you the *homme* that captured Riordan, twice?"

"You have a good memory, Lieutenant Strom. Which will probably work in your favor."

"I don't know why you're both here, but please, don't play with my mind. If you're going to put me in front of a firing squad, let's get at it. I'm ready for anything and sick to death of this damned cell."

Delcambré glanced at Cassidy who nodded.

"What would you say to complete amnesty, citizenship in the Alaska Republik, and an honorable, *paying* job to go with it?" Roland asked.

Strom blinked, glanced back and forth between their faces, seeking mirth or cruelty. "Is this some sort of test, or trick? Why would you offer me something out of a dream?" His knees wanted him to sit, so he dropped his large frame back onto the bench.

Cassidy walked over and sat down beside him on the rough wood. "Because we have thoroughly examined your record with the Freekorps, taken testimony from other troopers who served with you, and listened to what Roland, here, has said about you. This is neither trick nor test."

"So, what's the deal?" Alex suddenly found it difficult to breathe. Hope slowly stole into his mind and took root.

"We want you to work with us. Would you like to be a Peacekeeper?"

"I don't know what that is, and I don't care. If I would be working with you two, and doing something worthy of a soldier. The answer is yes!"

"Welcome aboard," Cassidy said, sticking out his hand.

Alex shook hands with both men. This had all happened so fast after weeks of staring at the wall of this cell it nearly made his head spin. *Have I just made a huge mistake?*

"So, what exactly is a Peacekeeper?" he asked, looking from Delcambré to Cassidy.

Although he knew the man was seemingly fearless, Cassidy was mostly a cipher to him. However, Delcambré had fought at his side. He knew the small man had courage to burn. When they stood next to each other Roland Delcambré only came up a bit higher than his belly button. Still, he trusted the small fighter implicitly; always had.

"The best part, *mon ami*, is that you will represent everything that Riordan loathes," Delcambré said with a wide smile.

Alex grinned back. "Oh, I like the way this sounds already! When can I start?"

"You're on the clock when you walk out of this cell," Cassidy said.

Wearing a wide grin Alex strode out through the cell door, a free man. Finally, he could hear birds calling to him.

CHAPTER 7

FORT YUKON, ALASKA REPUBLIK

"What do you have for me?" The speaker sat in a dark room, visually no more than black on black. Ryan Hemingway knew the small cabin offered little space yet felt a vast emotional distance around him. The stifling air smelled of leather, wool, and recent cooking.

"I was promised payment..." If he didn't pay his subcontractors, they would kill him.

"You will be *paid*, Mr. Hemingway, according to the *worth* of your performance." Steel lay beneath the surface of the dark man's tone.

"Well, the shipment was hijacked. We don't know who has it."

"How much security did you provide?"

"The two were experienced agents who assured me they didn't need anyone else. They didn't want to split the bonus."

"And you allowed that?"

Hemingway didn't like the implicit admonition in the remark. After a decade of manipulating humans and events, he knew his business. But this was one of those situations where success was not guaranteed, and the dark man should understand that.

"They were Austrian agents. It has been my experience one does not question professionals with the credentials these men possessed."

"Perhaps *you* don't," the dark man said. "But I may have."

"Are you insinuating that I have failed you on purpose?"

"No, I am only noting that you have failed me. To make matters worse, the shipment has been discovered by others and is now in the hands of the Alaska Republik."

Hemingway's guts went hollow with apprehension. So many questions. How did the dark man know who had apprehended the shipment? Ryan didn't know that, and he had hired Rochamboux.

Who else did the dark man have in the field besides himself?

"Are you sure?" Hemingway had to turn this conversation around, his fee, reputation, and very life depended on it. According to what little he had heard, the dark man did not easily forgive, but paid well for success.

"Are you insinuating that I don't know what I am talking about?"

"Of course not, Boss! I am merely surprised that you have received knowledge that I have not. It was a mere slip of the tongue."

"You are not to speak my title! Have you lost your edge, and therefore value, as an agent for me?"

"I have experienced a setback, I admit. But I am still very much in control of the situation I manage for you."

Sweat beaded on his bald head and brow, ran down the side of his face. As much as he wanted to, he couldn't wipe it away.

"Come now, Ryan, we both know that is not the case. You have failed in a most fundamental way, and changes must be made."

"Changes?" he said. His voice came out as a squeak due to the abrupt restriction of his vocal cords. He instantly regretted saying anything.

"I *am* sorry."

He didn't feel the garrote until it suddenly cut into his throat. Speech went first and he felt the wire sever his windpipe. His final sensations were blood pouring down his chest and urine down his legs.

CHAPTER 8

CHENA, ALASKA REPUBLIK

"Here's the deal," Alex Strom said as he surveyed the ten men in the room. "You can get full pardons, full citizenship, and a paying job if you play your cards right."

"Who we gotta kill?"

Alex laughed. "I like your spirit, Dahlke. You always were ready to go for the throat. It's this simple, guys; the new Alaska Republik needs Peacekeepers, same thing as cops, gendarmes, flics, police. Need I go on?"

"You're hiring *us* as *coppers*?" Danny Casey said in a disbelieving tone. "Seriously, do the Dená know you're doing this?"

"They told me to find people that I trusted. I have fought beside each and every one of you, and none of you ever turned tail or considered surrender until you were told by your officers to put down your weapons. Every man in this room has proven his worth to me many times over. Do you accept or do you want to go back to a cell?"

Casey stood up and looked around the room. "You make some good points, but the options are kinda bleak."

"True, that. Keep in mind that you were led here by an incompetent asshole that threw you into the arms of his enemies so he could escape. Those adversaries have recognized your collective worth as potential useful citizens and make this offer through me.

"I accepted the offer and feel like I now have the opportunity to actually make an honest living. What you decide is completely up to each of you. But if you turn this down you are responsible for your part in the crimes perpetuated by Major Riordan and, frankly, I wouldn't advise that."

"Where are Riordan and N'Go?" Kelsey asked.

"Don't know, don't care. There at the last, people were deserting left and right. I don't remember seeing Rasputin again either, dead or alive."

"You're already part of this thing, Alex?" Sergeant Langbein asked.

"Yes, Fred, I am. This new country needs a police force. They call them Peacekeepers, and I like that."

"So, how long do we have to serve before we can quit without landing in the stockade again?" Sergeant Harris asked.

"They didn't cover that, Dennis. Was there something else you were more interested in?"

"Of course not. I always read the full contract before I sign anything, that's all."

"So far they don't have a contract. This is all being done at face value and sealed with handshakes."

"You can sure tell these people aren't Scots."

Everyone in the room laughed.

Alex waited and let them talk among themselves. All were individuals and all were willing to fight for a cause they believed in. Maybe even a few they didn't believe in, if the pay was good. They were pragmatists and all would keep their word if given freely.

"The winters up here are really tough," Casey said.

"Yeah, I vividly remember. But I plan to be part of the community and have someone to snuggle up to for the whole eight months." Alex flashed his grin and saw it reflected throughout the room. He knew he had them.

"Will that be in the contract?" Harris asked.

CHAPTER 9

CHENA,
ALASKA REPUBLIK

Trying to ignore the summer breeze wafting through the window, Peacekeeper Major Yukon Cassidy sat in his small office trying to figure out what the memorandum from Pelagian's office meant. Someone knocked on his door.

"Oh, for the love of God, please come in!" he cried out in relief, dropping the paper on his desk.

A woman stepped in and shut the door behind her.

"Hello, Major Cassidy. I am Solare."

For a few moments he assessed her looks and build. Despite himself, he had built numerous images of her in his head. What he saw wasn't any of them.

So much for that.

He took a deep breath. "The free agent bounty hunter?" he asked, feeling inane.

"The same."

Her short, dark red hair capped a face that broadcast intensity and yet appealed to something in him. She stood perhaps a third of a meter taller than Roland Delcambré with a slim build and looked wiry enough to wrestle a man twice her size and win. A hard competence radiated from her.

Her eyes looked to be turquoise one moment and then a deep green the next. He found her both attractive and off-putting at the same time. Not sure which predominated, he felt his pulse quicken all the same.

"I am pleased to meet you, Solare. General Grigorievich has spoken of your skill and persistence. Congratulations on your apprehension of Ferdinand Rochamboux."

"I didn't apprehend him. I killed him from a distance of fifty meters with a high-powered weapon. Then I took his ear, left my calling card, and departed. Why should you congratulate me for what was essentially murder?"

"Because you got to him before I did."

"By less than a half hour. I watched you and the dwarf examine the area from where I shot Rochamboux. I could have killed you both easily."

"Are you here to gloat, or what?" Cassidy asked.

"In Alaska Republik?"

"No, in my office."

She nearly smiled. "General Grisha asked me to introduce myself to you. Why, I'm not sure."

Cassidy felt totally at sea. *Why did Grisha send this nail-hard harpy to me? Does he want me to enlist her in the Peacekeepers?* He made a mental note to have a daily conference with his direct superior.

"Well, first of all, Roland Delcambré is not a dwarf. He is merely of small stature but solid as a brick. Secondly, I think Roland and I were in no real danger, as I wager that you don't kill anyone who does not offer you gain of some nature. Thirdly, I suspect that the general thought you a prime candidate for the Peacekeeper unit we are currently creating; and I think he was mistaken."

Her face finally creased with a quick smile that vanished instantly. However, that flash of amicability gave him a glimpse of what might be created with this woman, and he felt another snag in his mind.

What the hell is wrong with me?

"I think he was, too," she said. "Do you always rush to judgment like this?"

"Where am I wrong in my observations?"

"Those weren't observations. They were opinions, and biased at that."

"Where was I biased?"

"Like you, I have killed for sport."

"When–, where–, I have *never* killed for sport!"

"Grand Prairie, 1979, in the land of the Pawnee. You shot a man by the name of Jimmy Hits Twice. You could have brought him in, but you killed him instead. If that wasn't sport, what was it?"

"How did you... he killed a kinsman of mine. That was honorable

30

tribal revenge! Where did you get your information?"

"You know revenge is an empty meal. It changes nothing; therefore, it falls into the category of blood sport. The general wanted me to introduce myself so you would know who I am should ever we meet again in the course of our duties."

"What duties do you have yet to perform in Alaska Republik?" Cassidy realized his tone was less than cordial, but this woman had surprised him, and hit in places he didn't know were vulnerable.

"There is another, the man behind Rochamboux and the two men with the lorry, who constitutes my next quarry." She flashed her beguiling smile again. "Unless you get to him first."

"Will you share your intelligence with me? It might work to our mutual benefit."

She allowed her features to soften as she stared at him. He found himself fantasizing and suddenly realized he might do stupid things to win her approval.

"So, what are you thinking, Mr. Yukon Cassidy? And how did *Wayne* get changed to *Yukon*?"

"Damn, woman! Is there anything about me you don't know?"

"Perhaps," she said in a purr. "But I bet I can find out."

He nearly bit a hole in his tongue to stop his first retort. She knew more about him than did most of his friends. She had thoroughly investigated his background; that was stingingly obvious. However, why, and how?

"The question stands; will you work with me?"

"As a Peacekeeper or as a free agent?"

"I would prefer as a Peacekeeper."

"Answerable to who?"

"Me."

"Then the answer is no."

"General Grigorievich?"

"Perhaps."

"What would be your caveats?"

"*Caveats*, yet! You possess more education that you show."

"Did you think you were the only one who does? Please answer the question."

"I would become a Peacekeeper if I reported directly to the general. I would share intelligence with whomever he so directed, but it would completely depend on a need-to-know basis. I haven't worked all these years building an intelligence network to just give it away to the first Dog Soldier I ran across."

Cassidy wanted to slap her down verbally, dominate her intellectually, and possess her sexually. All three of those desires died unborn since there was no possible way to achieve any of them now.

This woman is fascinating!

"I agree to those parameters. Go talk to the general."

The smile flashed across her face like heat lightning on a prairie summer night. "I already have. He said he would abide by whatever terms you and I made."

Anger, lust, admiration, and defeat whirled though him in a maelstrom of emotion and relief. He felt exhausted. He also felt titillated; something he hadn't felt for a very long time.

"Very well. Let's start by you telling me what you know about this situation."

She smiled again and he knew he was doomed. This was a challenge he hadn't expected.

CHAPTER 10

CHENA,
ALASKA REPUBLIK

"So, what are we looking at, Sergeant Williams?" Grisha asked, staring at the missile on the bench in front of them.

"It is the most modern weapon I've ever seen." He glanced around the three people in the room. "And I was trained by the top munitions experts down at the Presidio in California."

"How is it different than what you saw down there?" Cassidy asked.

"This has a fancy trigger assembly that I've never seen before. I removed the explosives section before I touched that trigger."

"Isn't that pretty fundamental?" Roland Delcambré asked drily.

"Of course, it is. But with anything we've got I could make the explosives inert without going through all that."

"So how does the trigger work?" Grisha glowered at Delcambré who ignored him.

"I don't know, General Grigorievich. This thing is years ahead of our remote munitions. I don't know exactly what it does, but I do know how to deploy the weapon."

"Did you discover a manual?" Delcambré asked.

Sergeant Dexter Williams curtly replied, "There are aspects I don't understand *yet* about this weapon, but it's easy to operate."

"Can you show us?" Grisha asked.

Sergeant Williams stared hard at the missile before facing him. "Not within two miles of the town of Chena. I have some theories about what will happen, but I don't want to endanger civilians."

"Why haven't you been commissioned, Sergeant?" Grisha asked. "I've known captains who are less knowledgeable than you."

Williams grinned. "Thank you, General. They already tried talking me into being an officer, but I love being a sergeant, okay?"

Grisha laughed. "Of course. Do you know where a safe place would be to deploy this thing?"

"Yes, sir, I do. First, I would like to point out the features I don't understand on this thing."

"Like what?" Cassidy said.

"These markings. What do they mean?" He handed Cassidy a large, hand-held magnifying glass and pointed just above the fin assembly.

Cassidy peered through the lens. "It's in German, probably Austrian made. You'd think they'd get the message that they don't own the fucking world!"

"Major Cassidy, are you ill?" General Grigorievich asked in an official tone.

"Sorry, Grisha. No, I'm venting anger I thought had dissipated long ago."

"Not to worry, Yukon. Sergeant, how new were the weapons you trained with in California?"

"I was down there nearly a full month and got back to Alaska Republik two weeks ago. They believed they had examples of *all* the field armament in the Austrian armory." He looked down at the missile. "I think their spy has been made."

"I'll make sure they are alerted. We are sending one of these down on the next supply plane. So where do you want to light this off?"

"The moose meadow two miles upstream is perfect."

"Gather what you need and let's go."

✪

Cassidy worked hard at suppressing his grim memories as they rode out to the site in an armored personnel carrier. The faces of friends who had fallen in the line of duty flashed through his mind and his anger and angst fed on each other. Grisha had brought along an infantry sergeant and ten people from his platoon all in full combat gear.

I hope these kids don't hurt themselves, he thought with a frown. He was immediately pissed at himself. *Get yourself together, dammit. Quit wallowing in it!*

Just when he thought they had traveled five miles the driver pulled over and stopped on the edge of the RustyCan Highway. The infantry sergeant deployed his troops and saluted Grisha. "The area is secure, General."

"Thank you, Sergeant. Make sure they stay alert despite our distractions."

"As you say, General." The sergeant made a ghastly grin and hurried off.

Sergeant Williams already had the launcher assembly and missile ready to go. He turned and spoke with a teacher's mien.

"I asked Sergeant Haroldsson to have one of his men light a flare."

"Wait," Grisha said. "Haroldsson is not a common name in Alaska. Is the sergeant related to the First Speaker?"

"You'd have to ask *him*, General," Williams said, trying not to grin.

"Very well. Why the flare, Sergeant?"

"I have a theory I want to test. It will be worth the wait."

"I have no doubt, Master Sergeant Williams."

"General, I am a technical sergeant."

"Not anymore."

"Thank you, General Grigorievich!"

"You've earned it. Are you sure you don't want to be an officer?"

"Quite sure," he laughed. "Now, if you'll excuse me." He picked up his field glasses and peered toward the far end of the meadow where a flare could be seen.

"Good, all the troops are away from the flare. "Major Cassidy, would you like to do the honors?"

"Happily!" Yukon grabbed the assembly and squinted through the sights. "Do you want me to aim at the flare?"

"No, sir. Aim at the trees about twenty meters behind the flare."

"Any particular one?"

"That clump of three, see it?"

"Got it."

"Fire when ready, Major."

Cassidy peered through the sight and pretended he saw an Austrian panzer. He pulled the trigger and the missile surged from the tube and streaked toward the trees before abruptly nosing down into the flare. The missile shattered on impact and knocked the flare spinning into the woods.

"Fuck!" shouted Cassidy. "We've started a forest fire!"

"Don't worry, Major," Master Sergeant Williams grinned as he picked up the field phone. "I anticipated this. Hey, this is Williams.

Go put out the fire. Thanks."

The crash truck from the airfield screamed toward the small fire and the crew had everything drenched within minutes.

Cassidy spent the whole time trying to figure out why the test ended as it did. The rockets they had used in the war flew straight and tended to hit the target. When he finally looked at the master sergeant, Williams all but laughed at him.

"Just believe what you saw, Major. They've developed a heat-seeking missile that figures out the trajectory *immediately*! We need to hoard these things like they were made of gold. I hated using one on this demonstration, but I knew it was the only way you'd believe something so fantastic."

"I agree with the general. You should be an infantry officer."

"I have other plans, sir."

CHAPTER 11

CHATANIKA CROSSING, ALASKA REPUBLIK

"Captain Easthouse, there's been a lot of vehicle traffic through here." Sergeant Ben Titus glanced around the heavily wooded area. The last time he had passed through here in his scout car the trail was overgrown, and he had to cut down a sapling growing in the middle of the rough road. Now he found himself staring at ruts and new cut roads.

"Through here, Sergeant Titus? Where could that many vehicles be going clear the hell out here?"

"Maybe mining, sir? I don't know. This is very un–"

Bullets ripped through the scout car. Captain Easthouse's forehead suddenly spewed a stream of blood as his body slammed against the passenger door and then bounced against the back of his seat. Sergeant Titus swept up the field radio and threw himself out of the vehicle just ahead of the rounds that tore through the operator's seat he had occupied.

He lay behind the roadside rocks and thumbed the set alive. "Chena command, this is Staff Sergeant Ben Titus. We are under attack in sector eight. Captain Easthouse has been killed. I have no idea where the enemy is. Do we have any aircraft in the area?"

"Stand by, Sergeant, we're checking. From which direction did the fire originate?"

"Directly in front of us. North of the scout car."

"Get away from the vehicle if you can."

Ben Titus rolled away from the scout car and thanked the spirits when he fell into a creek channel created in wetter times. More heavy weapons fire hit the scout car and the vehicle exploded into flame. The firing slackened.

For a long moment all remained still in the solstice heat.

"Chena, this situation is going to get very personal and quickly!"

"Hug the ground, Sergeant. Deliverance has arrived."

A P-61 Eureka screamed over, and in the forest where the enemy fire had originated trees blew into whistling shards, splinters flying everywhere. Another P-61 screamed over and the wooded hillside behind the first target zone erupted into fire and destruction.

Some of the dry underbrush caught fire but beyond that total silence reigned.

"Sergeant Titus, are you still with us?" the radio operator asked.

"Yeah! How'd you get planes here so fast?"

"They were on a training mission no more than ten miles from you. We have dispatched a helicopter with a ground force to assist. Reconnoiter the area with extreme caution."

"Copy that. Titus out." He clicked off the radio. He didn't want it to give away his location, and he might need the battery strength later.

Ben didn't look at the scout car or the charred body of the captain. This wasn't the time to dwell on the loss, that would come later. He wished he had his carbine but it remained in the burning scout car, its rounds cooking off in muffled pops.

All he had was his service .45 automatic as he crept into the woods adjacent to the target zone. A P-61 buzzed over him again, but he didn't look up this time. Sunlight glinted off something approximately thirty meters ahead of him.

He eased down into the brush and watched the spot as he quietly pushed the safety off on the pistol. There was at least one man alive in there and he wanted to change that as lethally as possible.

Those bastards didn't give us a chance and I'm going to return the favor!

The P-61s whined away into the distance and only crackling flames broke the stillness. Directly ahead of him a lean man in camouflage stood up and looked around. Only sharp angles comprised his thin face.

"They've gone!" he shouted.

"We're lucky to be alive," another man said as he lurched to his feet. "That bloody concussion about deafened me!"

Others stood. Ben shrank down into the bushes around a clump of willows and black spruce. He counted them as they emerged from their cover. Sixteen dazed men shuffled toward the man who had first shouted.

"This is all? We had *sixty* troopers!"

"How'd those blokes know we were here?" another asked.

"Anyone here close to a hundred percent?"

"I am, Captain Rawls." A man emerged from the forest off to Ben's right.

That makes eighteen.

"Go check out that scout car. See if there are two bodies in it."

"Hell, Captain, we caught them injuns flatfooted. They didn't know what the hell hit 'em."

Ben stared hard at the tall man who last spoke. He wanted to remember what he looked like.

"You can't take anything for granted, Peacock."

One of the other men stumbled, fell flat on his face, and ceased all movement.

Now we're down to seventeen.

"Did Doc make it through that attack?" Captain Rawls asked.

Silence. A muted pulse, more felt than heard, gained in strength.

"Captain!" the man checking out the scout car shouted.

"Quinault?"

"There's only one in here but looks like two rifles. We have an unfriendly out here somewhere."

"Captain," another man yelled, "...we also have an inbound helicopter!"

The beat of fast moving blades rose increased in volume in the heavy air and dominated the attention of all living things.

Ben did a careful 360-degree visual of the scene. The captain carried an automatic weapon and at this point was closest. He heard movement behind him and turned to see Quinault searching the ground as he quickly closed on Ben's position.

Damn, this guy is good! And he's carrying heavy firepower.

"Take cover," Captain Rawls shouted. "We'll pull an ambush on them."

Ben cupped his left hand under the butt of the .45 held in his right hand. His right elbow rested on his knee and he sighted on Quinault's chest as the man picked up his pace without giving up the hunt. Quinault was no more than two meters away when he looked up and stared straight at Ben.

Quinault's eyes widened and he opened his mouth to shout. Ben pulled the trigger.

His shot hit Quinault between the eyes and blew the back of his skull to pieces. As soon as he fired Ben broke cover and raced for the dead man. He snatched the assault rifle off the ground where a still quivering Quinault had dropped it, and crashed into the nearest brush, rolling for two meters before stopping.

The others had frozen when the .45 went off and seemed dumbstruck at the sudden flurry of activity. Ben snapped into kneeling position and fired a sweeping volley into them. Three men went down in the boneless collapse only the instantly dead or severely wounded achieve.

Captain Rawls had the presence of mind to immediately hit the ground and return fire. Ben keyed the radio on.

"I'm alone down here! There are at least a dozen highly trained bad guys around me, so look out!"

"Thanks!"

The beat of the rotors changed pitch and the helicopter sat down somewhere behind him. He hoped they would get here soon enough to help. Bullets ripped through the saplings just above his head. They were firing high. That would change in moments.

Ben flattened and tried to sink into the ground. A bullet snapped past his cheek. A hungry mosquito hovered around his face.

A heavy machine gun stuttered to life and he thought he was doomed. Abruptly he realized the sound was coming from behind him. He lifted his head and saw sustained bursts tearing through the enemy position.

Who is the enemy?

All fire ceased and he could hear the helicopter blades swooshing at idle somewhere behind him.

"Sergeant Titus, you still with us?"

The voice sounded familiar which came as no surprise. He knew damn near everyone in the Republik's Northern Army. He watched the area in front of him carefully as he shouted back.

"Yeah! I'm still here. Did you get them all?"

"Let you know in a few minutes. Stay down."

Ben hadn't made sergeant by being stupid and didn't bother answering. He caught movement on both sides of his peripheral vision and quick glances found Dená Rangers moving steadily forward without unduly exposing themselves.

Immediately he felt better. The concept of regional ranger units was a masterstroke ordered by General Grigorievich two days after the First Speaker was inaugurated. All of the slots in the ranger units were avidly sought after and they only took the best.

The United States and the Republic of California had both loaned them training NCOs who knew their craft. The first group of local graduates now moved through the forest around him.

Even though he had not made the first cut, he was on the waiting list. Ben felt sure the Dená Rangers had more battlefield experience than any of the quarry. At any rate he hoped so.

Shots rang out ahead of him and six rangers rushed forward.

"I surrender, dammit!"

"Me. too!"

"We have twelve prisoners, Sergeant Titus," someone yelled. "That all of 'em?"

"How many dead you got?" he shouted.

"Three."

Ben stood up and walked back to where Quinault lay sprawled. "Here's number four. I saw seventeen of them."

"We're missing one."

The rangers had rounded up a group of men and Ben walked over to the guards.

"Who's in charge here?" he asked.

"I am, Sergeant Titus, why?"

Ben stared into the face of Lieutenant Gus Hildebrand, his second cousin from Nulato.

"Because I want to deal with the asshole who laughed about ambushing the captain and me."

"Laughed?" Gus' eyes went hard and brittle.

"Yeah. His exact words were 'we caught them injuns flatfooted. They didn't know what the hell hit 'em.'"

"You have my permission, Sergeant. Do what you will."

Ben turned and stared at the tall man called Peacock.

"Hey, there was nothing personal in that, Sergeant!" Peacock said. His face shiny slick with sweat and fear. "I'm an unarmed prisoner of war. You can't–"

"We are not at war with anyone, you piece of shit coward. You are not soldiers. You are bandits. Not ten minutes ago you were laughing about murdering Captain Easthouse."

Peacock's eyes rounded and he blurted, "Our orders, we couldn't allow anyone to see us–"

Ben lifted his .45 and shot Peacock through the head. The dead man fell like a cut tree.

"He wasn't in charge, was he?" Gus asked.

"No. Someone named Rawls. They called him Captain."

Lieutenant Gus Hildebrandt looked over the prisoners. "Anyone admit to that name?"

"He's not here, Gus." Ben felt stupid for being distracted by Peacock. "He's still out there."

"Attla, Huntington, find him. Bring him back alive," Lieutenant Hildebrandt ordered.

Two men immediately moved into the tree line next to the nearly extinguished fire caused by the aircraft. Two rangers checked the prisoners for weapons. The remainder rushed over to help with the fire.

"Good thing those assholes had a lot of water," Gus said absently.

"Yeah, or we'd all be in the middle of a forest fire." Ben gave his cousin a level look. "Sorry I let that get personal."

"I liked Captain Easthouse, too. Don't worry about it."

"But what if that Peacock asshole had all the answers?"

Gus looked around at the prisoners and grinned. "Oh, I think all of our answers are right here, eventually."

"Can I help?" Ben asked.

"Yeah. They have three lorries hidden in the brush, away from the firefight. I could use another driver."

"Happy to help, cousin." Ben felt a wave of grief. "Uh, can you have someone collect Captain Easthouse's remains? I don't think I–"

"We got it, Ben. You take off now and drive the first lorry to Chena, okay? We'll haul the prisoners back in the helicopter."

CHAPTER 12

NEAR CHATANIKA CROSSING, ALASKA REPUBLIK

Captain Dumont watched the helicopter depart the combat zone through his Zeiss binoculars. Lieutenant Klein, towering next to him, lowered his binoculars but continued to stare into the distance.

"Has the savages' fledgling air force just made our job easier, Captain?"

"Excellent question. I think yes. However, why did the mercenaries fire at a Dená patrol to begin with? And how am I to parse my belief we were the only group in this area?"

"Our scouts are good but, had the mercenaries been closer we would have known. We keep our pickets closer to the main body to prevent infiltrators." Klein waited while Dumont considered his response.

Dumont knew he had made his point. Further admonishments would be counterproductive.

"Send Corporal Kahn. I want to know how many died there and how many didn't. He will search for rations and ammunition that fits our weapons."

Dumont killed a mosquito on his arm.

Klein grinned. "He will be able to write a book about the site when he returns."

"We know nothing about the Dená Army. They may have left sentries."

"Remember, he comes from a long line of Gurkas."

"Warn him anyway. I wonder how many helicopters they have?"

"That was an old Imperial Russian troop carrier. It can hold over twenty people." Klein peered through his binoculars again, moving them across the terrain.

"The Russian mission in Alaska was inferior and deficient. I would wager they didn't leave many functioning aircraft when they retreated, else they would have used them."

"Good point, Horst. I wish I knew more about the war they fought here."

"They fought it with a great deal of help, else they would have lost."

CHAPTER 13

TANANA, ALASKA REPUBLIK

"We need to set up a postal system," Bodecia said as she walked unannounced into Pelagian's office.

He pulled his eyes from the stack of reports on his desk, looked at her, and smiled. "Who would want to send us letters?"

"The First People's Nation, for one." She held out a slim, creamy-white envelope to him.

After opening the seal with an old skinning knife he used as a paperweight, he frowned down at the calligraphy on the single sheet of paper. "How was this delivered?"

"Through our embassy in the Republic of California. It came in on the last plane from San Francisco. What does it say?"

"The FPN wishes to establish formal diplomatic relations with Alaska Republik, as well as build an embassy here in Tanana."

"That seems a positive thing."

"This is something that would be decided by a full session of the House of Delegates according to the constitution currently being considered. However, since the constitution hasn't been ratified by that chamber, I suppose this burden would fall on me." He grinned at her.

"Why are you making faces at me?" She walked over and opened a window. "It's too damn stuffy in here."

"This is my first official international act as First Speaker. I don't have to ask anyone's permission to accept this, and I know that very soon I will no longer have that right. Who has a decent hand for calligraphy here in Tanana?"

"Not you!" Bodecia snorted. "Let me ask around." She left the office.

Pelagian stared at the letter. "I wonder who they will send?" he mused aloud. "I know it will not be an idiot."

CHAPTER 14

CHENA,
ALASKA REPUBLIK

"Since we have a lot of area to cover, we will be sending three-man units to various places in this province of the Alaska Republik." Grisha stopped and licked his lips. He could almost taste the smell of unwashed bodies, leather, and gun oil.

Cassidy and Delcambré had done a superb job of finding recruits for the Peacekeepers. That most of them were former mercenaries didn't bother him for a moment. He knew they would be loyal to their paychecks first and sentiments second.

Or, if not, I'll fire them.

Besides, he had spent many years in the Troika Guard and that was as close to mercenary as Russia fielded in the old days. He visually assessed the recruits carefully. All were alert, quick-witted, and physically fit.

He had listened to the exchange between Lieutenant Strom and the group he had enlisted. None of these men were soft in head or spirit. He would lead any and all into battle in the next ten minutes if necessary.

Although I might have the sergeants keep an eye on a couple of them.

"The subunits will consist of a sergeant and a trooper. When our manpower increases, we will be adding personnel where needed to fulfill the mission. There will be up to four subunits to every sector, with up to four sectors to each province depending on size."

He drew more lines on the chalk board. Most gave it a courteous glance.

"Each sector will be led by a lieutenant who will report to the province captain and all the captains report to Major Cassidy who in turn reports to me. This is obviously still a work in progress. I'm sure we will be adjusting for many months to come, but we need to start somewhere.

"We haven't had a lot of time to evaluate each and every one of you as much as we would have liked. So, suffice it to say that you all will be critically assessed as you perform your duties. Your first allegiance is to the Alaska Republik, your second is to the Peacekeepers, and your third is to the people with whom you serve."

Grisha stopped, caught his breath, and drank some water. He sat the glass down hard enough to make some of the men flinch.

"Allegiance works in two directions. If you uphold our laws and serve honorably, I, personally, will guard your back to the death. You have my word on that. Always keep in mind we are creating tradition."

Grisha coughed and looked down at his hands, tried to unclench the fists with which he had just gestured. He again wondered if he really was the right person to be leading these people. He looked up at them.

"Any questions?"

Lieutenant Strom stood and waited to be recognized.

Grisha had heard much about this large man and had been impressed. It didn't hurt the man's reputation that he was Cassidy and Delcambré's unanimous first choice for the Peacekeepers.

"Lieutenant Strom, what is your question?"

"General, you hear a lot of things in a situation like this. Well, you know, about sorta wild stuff you didn't see personally but hear about later?"

"Around the campfire talk, you mean?"

"Yes, sir, exactly that."

"So, what is your question?"

"Is it true that you were going to parachute into an active combat zone by yourself?"

"A very unadvisable decision, I want you to know." The men all grinned and Grisha felt the blood flame in his cheeks. "But, yes, I did request to do that. I was extremely fortunate that a few hundred Republic of California paratroopers decided to go with me, or I probably wouldn't be here to talk about it."

Everyone laughed and Grisha felt the reserve, of which until now he hadn't been aware, melt away and suddenly they were all colleagues.

"Any other questions?"

A grinning Lieutenant Strom had already sat down, and they all waited.

"Very well. Sergeant Major Tobias will read out the assignments in a moment. First, I want to welcome you all into the Peacekeepers, and I want to personally thank each and every one of you for volunteering to keep this new republik safe.

"This will be the hardest job you've ever attempted and probably the best work you'll ever do. You will be proud to tell your grandchildren that you were one of the first Peacekeepers. Once a Peacekeeper, always a Peacekeeper!

"My door is always open to all of you, singly and collectively. I will back you to the hilt."

Every man stood and saluted. Grisha felt his face grow even warmer as he returned the salute. He nodded to Sergeant Major Tobias and left the room.

✪

The sergeant major stood and grinned as the men slowly ceased their applause. When the room quieted and all found their chairs again, he said in a cheerful tone, "It's probably all downhill from here."

He elicited a few chuckles and felt gratified they all seemed seriously intent on him.

"For the next week you will all be put up in the hospital where you will live and receive classroom training. We will also interview each of you to determine where in our shaky structure you would fit best. In time you will be moving into the old Russian redoubt at the other end of town. It received major damage in the opening battles of the revolution, and we have a crew repairing and modernizing it.

"We have uniform coats for you that won't be worth a damn once winter sets in, but it will give our citizens the visual concept they are being protected. I will be conducting many of the classes and would be most grateful to all of you if you make use of the showers adjacent to each room. This is going to be an interesting experiment and all eyes are on you.

"Dismissed."

CHAPTER 15

FORT YUKON, ALASKA REPUBLIK

"Even without any enacted laws, the ersatz government is sending what they call Peacekeepers to all the regions. Some are to be stationed here."

"Do you think this is something we have to worry about, Number Three?"

"I don't know, Boss. The information we received is that most of them are former mercenaries from the International Freekorps."

"That was very clever of the First Speaker to hire former enemies," the man in the dark room said in a musing tone, "Not that he got *all* of them. They see themselves as a national police unit. The whole thing is so new I feel they still lack a complete view of their duties. That could benefit us.

"Try to recruit the people they send here, either with money or promise of other gain. They served for money in the past so why would that change?"

"All I know is that they took an oath to serve the Alaska Republik," Number Three replied.

"They also took an oath to the International Freekorps and see how well they lived up to that one. There will be weak links in this new chain. Find them, you know who they are. In the meantime, observe all they do, and why."

CHAPTER 16

TANANA, ALASKA REPUBLIK

Grisha stared through the one-way glass at the man sitting behind the interrogation room table. The man could only see himself in a mirror. The window was yet another gift from the Republik of California.

He idly wondered when and what they would ask for payback. With a shake of his head, he banished those thoughts and concentrated on the prisoner. This Rawls person had led sixty armed men into the Alaska Republik to do something, killed one of its most promising officers, tried to kill a sergeant, and nearly escaped.

Why are they here, and what did they want to do?

Thus far they had learned nothing from the other prisoners beyond their names. Grisha wished for a brief moment that the new republik allowed the use of torture.

He shook his head, knowing they would lie to stop the pain, so torture really didn't work.

With a sigh he walked to the door and entered the small room. Rawls stared at him with total lack of expression. Grisha maintained eye contact as he pulled out the chair on the opposite side of the table and seated himself.

"What is your rank, Mister Rawls?"

"May I have some water?" he said in a raspy croak. "I haven't had anything to drink in hours."

Grisha pushed a button on the side of the table and Sergeant Major Tobias immediately opened the door.

"Sir?"

"Bring Mister Rawls a carafe of water please, Sergeant Major."

"Very good, sir." The door closed.

"Your rank?" Grisha repeated.

The door opened again, and Sergeant Major Tobias entered and sat a carafe and an empty glass in front of the prisoner, nodded to Grisha, and exited.

Rawls drank a full glass of water without stopping for breath. He wiped his mouth with a sleeve and regarded Grisha.

"Thank you. I thought you might withhold water as an inducement."

"Torture, you mean?" Grisha said with a slight smile.

"Exactly."

"It was an oversight, and you have my apologies. Now would you please tell me your rank?"

"I'm a captain."

"In the service of what country?"

"I'm a mercenary."

"What outfit?" Grisha kept his questioning conversational.

"The International Freekorps." He delivered his automatic answers smoothly and sincerely. They were almost believable.

"*Captain* Rawls, you are a liar."

"You arrive at that conclusion how?"

"I had you vetted by a former lieutenant in the FI, and he says he never saw you before today."

"Probably lying to save himself from the noose."

"He's not facing a noose. He is a member of our organization now. You, on the other hand, *are* facing a noose. You will hang tomorrow morning as a bandit unless we can perceive some worthy reason to keep you alive."

Rawls poured another glass of water and drank half of it. His flushed face belied his aloof posture.

"I thought this was a republic. Don't you people have laws that protect people accused of crimes but have yet to be convicted?"

"Not yet, we don't. The constitution's ratification is still underway. Besides, you were captured in the field with blood on your hands as it were. We have a witness."

Rawls swallowed and his complexion lightened measurably.

"I don't believe you would really hang me. This isn't the eighteenth century." His voice had tightened.

Grisha looked at the mirror window, "Sergeant Major Tobias, please bring in the death warrant for this man."

The door opened immediately, and Sergeant Major Tobias entered the room, placed a single sheet of paper in front of the prisoner and departed.

Rawls leaned forward and stared at the warrant. His face paled even more.

"This is not legal," he said in a monotone. "I have had no trial, no counsel, and faced no accuser."

"Where do you think you are, Mr. Rawls? You invaded the Alaska Republik wearing no uniform, where you took the life of one of our military officers in an ambush. You also tried to kill one of our non-commissioned officers. What makes you think that we owe you anything other than a rope?"

"When you put it that way, I suppose I have no options."

"You do realize that we will have your execution witnessed by the survivors of your unit. I have no doubt that one or more of them will happily tell us what we wish to know once they see you kicking your life out on the gallows. So, your death will not safeguard intelligence that any other member of your group possesses."

"You're a real bastard, you know that?" Rawls snapped.

"And don't you ever forget it."

"What kind of a deal can I cut here?"

"What do you believe you deserve?"

"To get out alive, safe conduct to a neutral country, and maybe even some living expenses?"

Grisha abruptly stood so quickly his chair crashed backward to the floor. His countenance darkened and his voice rumbled with anger.

"You *may* avoid death at our hands if you are forthcoming. But beyond sparing your greasy life there is nothing else offered nor implied here. Do you understand me?"

"I just wanted to know where I stood."

"Lower than whale shit, and that's at the bottom of the ocean."

"You drive a hard bargain, General."

"How did you know my rank?"

"We didn't just walk into Russian Amerika–"

"It's now referred to as the Alaska Republik," Grisha said heavily.

"Uh, yeah, Alaska Republik. We knew who did what and if things hadn't gone tits up by that little stream, we would have accomplished our mission."

"Which was what?"

"Damn, I'm a dead man no matter how I cut this. You give me safe passage to the border, and I'll tell you everything."

"Which border?"

"British Canada."

"There's not much of that left."

"All the more reason to change the political map, no?"

"So, you are a British agent, leading a paramilitary band into our country to do what?"

"Do we have a deal or not?"

"I think you just answered my question. That being the case, I believe you are far more valuable as a political pawn than as a repentant secret agent. I also believe that your country will expect you to maintain your silence all the way to the grave, but we covered that nonsense earlier."

Rawls quivered and Grisha could smell fear on him.

"How about we keep you safe, and away from your men. They won't know if you betrayed them or not. Therefore, a number of them might be eager to tell us everything you won't."

"Keep us all safe as prisoners of war, and you have a deal," he said quickly.

"I'll agree to that. Now tell me what you came here to do, who sent you, and why you believed you would prevail."

"I'm a captain in the Special Air Service of the British Empire. We were sent here to connect with someone who would provide weapons previously smuggled into Alaska. We would then create an incident that appeared to be a conflict between one of the factions in your country and the Republic of California."

"So that's where the surface-to-air missiles were going!"

"You *know* about them?" Rawls blurted.

"We *have* them. Why does the British government wish to disrupt our alliance with the ROC?"

Rawls gave him a surprised look. "You don't look mentally deficient. How can you ask such a stupid question?"

Grisha glared at him. "You're not safe in the slammer yet, Captain Rawls. Don't piss on my boots."

"We lost heavily in the recent conflict, troops, equipment, and territory. My superiors are not happy nor are they quiescent. Of all our adversaries you are the most vulnerable. It was decided we could prevail if we struck quickly."

"You do realize this is an act of war?"

Captain Rawls smirked. "You have a small army, no navy, and a fledgling air force. How are you going to stand off the British Empire?"

"We have friends out there in other parts of North America. They will back us."

"But at what cost?"

"What do you mean?"

"General, you people are already in hock up to your collective asses. If the Californians or the United States puts any more of their people or equipment into this subcontinent you will never be free of them. They already outnumber you."

Grisha wanted to shoot the bastard on the spot. Unfortunately, the bastard had a point. They were close to the end of gratuitous aid, if it had ever been that freely offered. He knew Pelagian was waiting for the diplomatic bills to arrive, and this could push the debt even higher.

"So, who were you supposed to link up with, and where?"

"What makes you think we were meeting anyone?"

"Answer *all* my questions or the deal is off!" Grisha snapped.

"Somebody called 'the Boss' near Fort Yukon. We were traveling at night on your crappy roads to avoid discovery. Your patrol stumbled onto us."

"The Boss? How were you to contact this person?"

"We were supposed to camp three miles north of Fort Yukon, off the edge of the old Russian mining road, and flash a battery lantern three times precisely at midnight."

"Sounds like a pulp fiction novel to me," Grisha said with a snort. "What then?"

"Someone with the right password would contact us."

"What's the password?"

Rawls looked away, staring at something only he could see, then he stared back at Grisha.

"Troika. The password is Troika."

CHAPTER 17

ON THE RUSTYCAN HIGHWAY

Captain Dumont quietly walked around the small, cold camp where they would spend the night. In this part of the world *night* was more concept than reality. Even with the solstice gone for well over a month, the sun refused to stay away for enough hours.

He knew his men were weary of traveling through the mosquito-clouded bush rather than taking the road. So was he. Unfortunately, their security demanded it.

One roadblock, one official question, and they would have to fight for their lives first and complete the mission second. He much preferred the other way around. Once the sun dipped below the horizon the air became chilly and for security's sake they could not use fire.

This had best be worth the cost of admission, he thought.

Ensign Meté walked slowly toward him, looked up into his eyes, and saluted.

"Anything unusual out there?" Dumont asked as he returned the salute.

"Not that I saw, sir. I have the guard tonight. Why don't you get some sleep?"

"Thanks, François. Unfortunately, the mosquitos seem to find me when I stop moving even though the air has chilled."

"I have some pyrethrum powder I can share with you."

"Thank you, but not necessary. I'll sleep with my netting up for a change."

"Are we going all the way to Tanana, sir?"

"We are to disrupt the revolution here. Tanana is the current capitol where all their politicians are in one tidy spot. Cut off the head and the snake is much more manageable."

"Brilliant. If I may, to whom do you report, sir?"

"Sorry, François, you may not; that's classified."

The ensign blinked. "What happens if you are killed or captured? How do we know whom to turn to for further direction? *Most* importantly, how do we get paid?"

Dumont laughed. "Your pay is already in the Banque de France in an account under your name and billet number. Every one of us has an account growing every month this mission takes."

"That's brilliant, sir. However, if *you* get killed, what do *we* do?"

"Follow Lieutenant Klein's orders. He will fill you in if I am no longer in action."

"I don't mean to sound pedantic, sir, but what if you are *both* killed or captured at the same time?"

"Then you will be notified by a superior officer, Ensign Meté. Do continue your patrol."

With a crisp salute, the ensign moved on.

CHAPTER 18

TANANA CROSSING, ALASKA REPUBLIK

THE STATION DOOR SLAMMED OPEN and a loud voice bellowed, "Who's in charge here?"

Sergeant Fred Langbein's attention jerked away from the report he was slowly composing. He successfully stifled the impulse to pull his sidearm on the large Black woman who had just scared the crap out of him. *No, she's not large. She's statuesque.*

"You might try knocking, next time, Miss…"

"Skip that 'miss' stuff, pal, so far, I haven't missed anything!" She slammed the door behind her and stomped over to his desk.

Fred slowly stood and straightened his blue tunic with the three chevrons on each sleeve. "Your name, please?"

Damn, but she's beautiful!

"My name is MacKenzie MacDonald."

"I am Sergeant Fred Langbein of the Alaska Republik Peacekeepers. How can I help you?"

He looked up to make eye contact. Physically looking up at a woman happened rarely enough to be remarkable. He idly wondered if her height made her bust seem larger.

"Tell me where I can find Ferdinand Rochamboux."

"Are you a friend of his, Miss MacDonald?"

"For the record, I'm not *Miss* MacDonald; I'm *Mack*, okay? If you want to be my friend, you treat me like I have a brain along with everything else."

Her voice has a fascinating resonance!

"As you say, Mack. But why are you asking about Ferdinand Rochamboux?"

She laughed. "I was told yesterday that he was dead. Can I see the recently departed? I have to make certain Rochamboux is no longer with us."

"I see," Langbein said. "But why are you so intent on him being dead?"

"Let's just say I have a vested interest. That okay with you?"

"How do I know you weren't in league with him?"

"You don't. Will you please show me the body?"

"It isn't here. It's in Chena if they haven't buried him already. Why are you so intent on this man if you weren't involved with him?"

"He murdered my husband, you little shit. Is that enough reason?"

"Uh, sure." Fred suddenly felt as if he stumbled around in waders and the bottom of the river dropped from beneath him. "How far have you been tracking him?"

"From Iowa, down in the USA."

"You tracked him *that* far?" Fred said, doubt evident in his tone.

"Yes. I even lost his trail for about two weeks and picked it up again down in the First People's Nation."

"A virtual odyssey, it seems." He was impressed with her doggedness.

"Are you mocking me, Sergeant? I'm not real keen on mockery."

"Absolutely not!" Fred made a mental note to curb his propensity for theater until he knew for certain he had an appreciative audience.

"Sure as hell sounded like it!" She gave him a scowl that shriveled him in places he didn't want mentioned.

"I assure you, uh, Mack, I mean no levity whatsoever."

"You can dump those fancy words, too. I appreciate plain English."

"Of course. Would you like directions to where your quarry lies in state?"

"You said he was in Chena, right?"

"Yes."

"I don't need directions. There are only two ways to go out there on that road and Chena is one of them, right?"

"Absolutely true."

"Then I'll be leaving. But I have a suggestion for you, Sergeant."

"Oh?"

"Don't be so damn condescending in the future. It pisses people off."

"Thank you, I'll keep that in mind."

"See that you do."

She slammed the door behind her, and Fred sighed in relief. After a moment he decided that perhaps the sector office might want to have a heads-up on this person. He picked up the newly installed telephone and started dialing.

I'm certain she is the first dark-skinned woman with blue eyes I have ever met, he decided.

CHAPTER 19

CHENA, ALASKA REPUBLIK

Alex Strom wore a lieutenant's silver bar again. The fact that he didn't have to worry about getting paid would take some getting used to, as would the fact he was now a gendarme rather than a mercenary. He decided yet again that he liked both new developments and the trust of General Grigorievich was a definite plus.

"The part I don't like," he said to the empty room around him, "is this sitting behind a desk stuff!" Once the crew of laborers finished rebuilding the damaged portions of the Russian redoubt, Alex's office would be moved there as well as a contingent of Dená Rangers and other army types.

Until then the Peacekeepers would use this small cabin. It had been a storehouse for the Russian Amerika Company back when they held a total monopoly on trade in Alaska. There were still some intriguing cases of goods with Russian labels gathering dust on shelves in the other room.

He had almost decided to investigate their contents when the door slammed open and a huge man filled the frame, effectively blocking all the light behind him.

He bellowed something in Russian and Alex gave him a level stare.

"The official language here is now English. But I speak passable French if needed."

"You are new government official in this place?" The gravel-on-iron-plate voice issued from behind a massive dark beard that stretched to his belt line. He wore a fur hat; his animal-hide clothes were basic, and much repaired. The odor of old leather and sweat enveloped him like an invisible tent. Not even the fresh air from the door could dissipate his need for a bath.

"In a manner of speaking, yes. I am a Peacekeeper and sworn to uphold the law. Is that what you mean?"

"Da! Yes, that is my asking. I have need of your justice making or I must kill this person."

Alex pointed to the chair on the other side of the rough table that served as his desk.

"Sit, tell me about your problem."

"No time. Must come now or he steals, takes, my work, property?"

"Oh, what the hell," Alex muttered to himself as he grabbed his hat and fancy jacket, "I was bored shitless anyway."

The telephone rang.

Both Alex and the huge man started in surprise.

"By God, the damn thing works!" Alex said, grabbing the handset. "This is Lieutenant Alex Strom, Alaska Republik Peacekeepers."

"Alex, this is Fred down in Tanana Crossing. How are things in the big city?"

Alex reflected on the small village of Tanana Crossing and smiled. "Yeah, I guess compared to where you're at this is the big city. Look I got a *homme*, a client, to deal with. Is this official?"

"It could be. I just had a very, um, *statuesque* Nubian warrior woman in here demanding to see the body of this Ferdinand Rochamboux guy. I told her that you had him up there in Chena and she's on her way to your office. So, when she bursts into your office, be sure to call her 'Mack,' okay?"

"Why does she want to see a dead body?"

"Ask her. I'm just giving you an alert—she is rather formidable, about your size but more far more interesting. She has intense blue eyes."

"Thanks, Fred. All you've done is confused me. Which isn't too hard to do, but right now I have more immediate fish to fry. Thanks, I think."

"You're welcome, Lieutenant." An exaggerated kissing sound issued from the phone and Alex slammed it down.

Rules need to be made about telephone protocol in the very near future.

The large man stood staring at him as if waiting for a sleight-of-hand trick to be finished.

"What is your name?" Alex demanded.

"Dimitri Kaspartin, promyshlennik of repute."

"From what I've heard that's a contradiction in terms."

Dimitri frowned. "Please?"

"Never mind. Who is stealing what from you?"

"Trader. Come please."

Alex matched Dimitri's giant stride as they moved down River Street toward the hulking mass of Chena Redoubt. Even the bright summer afternoon couldn't make the redoubt look inviting. On either side of the street shops of all descriptions plied their trade and many people nodded to Alex while frowning at Dimitri.

After a five-minute walk they entered a small building, whose large front window boasted advertisements in four languages. The window also displayed a variety of pots, pans, firearms, and manufactured clothing. "Gorki" was painted in bright yellow across the top of the window. It was the only thing that looked new.

Dimitri threw open the door and bellowed in Russian.

"English, please!" Alex said, poking him in the back.

"Justice to be served!" Dimitri shouted in a joyous tone.

"Right. Calm down." Alex peered around the dim room redolent of combined odors and stinks. Two customers stared back at both men with obvious apprehension. The counter was barricaded with stacks of shirts and trousers, piles of pans and pots, all jammed to the point it left only a small, clear space for commerce.

Behind the counter stood a skinny, hunched man with a face like a rat. Alex immediately disliked him and then realized he had to be fair. *It's my job, after all.*

Alex grabbed Dimitri and swung him around. "So, what is this guy doing to you?"

"Not pay for furs. Say he not required to give me money."

Alex nodded and turned to the proprietor. "Do you owe this man money?"

"No. He is Russian. We are finished with Russians. They are not in charge in this new day."

"Did he give you something you have not paid for in money or trade?"

"Is of no consequence! He is Russian. No more pay Russians."

Alex turned back to Dimitri. "What did you give him? Do you have a list?"

"Six wolf pelt, five fox pelt, seventeen beaver pelt, thirty-five muskrat pelt, forty-four rabbit pelt, one bear skin." He blinked and stared at Alex. Dimitri's voice went from aggrieved to rumbling earthquake, "This man say he owes me nothing because I am Russian."

Alex held up his hand and turned back to the proprietor.

"What is your name?"

"Gorki, Boris."

"Did this man give you the pelts he just listed?"

"Matters not. He is Russian. I have been told that Russia is not here now. New republik."

The two customers edged out the door.

"That does not mean you don't owe him for his goods. You're Russian, too, aren't you?"

"Am new Alaskan!" He puffed up his thin chest for all of ten seconds.

"So is Dimitri! You can't cheat him because he is of Russian birth! That is stealing."

Boris Gorki regarded him coolly. "Who are *you*?"

"I am Lieutenant Alex Strom of the Alaska Republik Peacekeepers. I am the head of justice and law in Chena until a magistrate is appointed. You do *not* want to piss me off!"

"You are new Cossack?"

"Just once do you get to call me that without you losing teeth," Alex growled. "I administer the law here. Nothing more, nothing less. Do you understand?"

The door opened and another man entered. Alex suddenly felt relief of sorts.

"Yes." Gorki glared at him for a moment before shifting his glare to Dimitri. "I only count forty-two rabbit pelts."

"Count again. I know how many I skinned and cured."

Alex sighed. "Sergeant Dahlke, come here, please!"

Sergeant Dahlke moved away from the door with a wide grin on his face. "Yes, Lieutenant?"

"Go with these men and count the number of pelts you find. Be sure to differentiate between species."

Dahlke's grin vanished. "I wouldn't know a horse hide from a fox pelt, lieutenant. How am I–"

"They'll show you. And you are the final authority of what you find, understand?"

"I understand, but–"

"You'll be fine. I'll see you back at the office. Carry on."

The three men watched him leave in silence, each eyeing the other two with suspicion. As he shut the door behind him, Lieutenant Alex Strom decided sometimes rank was worth having. The day seemed brighter than he remembered.

Now he had to watch for a big titted Black woman with blue eyes. *There are worse things to anticipate!* he decided with a wide grin. A fragrant breeze came off the Chena River, rustled the trees, and the summer day promised quiet and order.

CHAPTER 20

TANANA, ALASKA REPUBLIK

Wing violently vomited into the porcelain toilet bowl and ruminated while her body, seemingly chastened by the spasm, settled back into its normal routine.

My body has been invaded by an alien being! When do I get to be in charge again?

At that moment a small force thrust itself against her stomach so sharply that she nearly gasped. She smiled, marveling at the symmetry of the situation. She washed her face and pulled on the housecoat Grisha had given her. She grinned, remembering when he gave it to her she had complained it was much too large.

"Tell me how it fits in six months," was all he said. It had only been four months and it already felt tight on her. She focused for a moment on her husband, feeling an almost overwhelming urge to weep.

She felt so lucky, had no doubts that he loved her beyond any other, and knew that her hormones were making a total wreck of her. The realization struck her that she should resign her commission until the child was born. It was only fair to the country.

Wing thought of nothing other than the life within her, and she liked it that way. All the military, security, and political crap boiled down to just that: crap. Never in her life had she been this focused.

Was it a boy or a girl? Did she care? Did Grisha care?

Would he tell her if he did care? Would it matter? I want mother to be here.

The last thought made her pause. Her father had passed many years ago and her mother had not approved of Wing's first marriage. So, she had turned her back on what little family she possessed and devoted herself to her new husband. Then came the night of the Cossacks.

She forced herself to focus on the memory and realized it no longer hurt, caused pain, nor anger. In some odd way she felt liberated but could not define why.

Her thoughts moved back to her mother. She went to the apartment door and opened it.

"Sergeant Major Tobias?"

He was there so quickly she suspected he had been loitering in the hall waiting for her summons.

"Colonel?"

"I want my mother."

"Very good, ma'am. I'll see to it."

CHAPTER 21

TANANA AERODROME, ALASKA REPUBLIK

"CADET ANAROK, WITHOUT LOOKING AT YOUR checklist, after you have inspected your aircraft, what is the first thing you do once you're in the cockpit?" Lieutenant Colonel Jerry Yamato tried not to sympathize with the pilot trainee when the young man immediately looked blank.

"Uh, strap me in?"

"You've already done that. What's next?"

Peering past Jerry's head and squinting into the distance, Cadet Anarok slowly recited the exact wording of the engine warm-up.

All nine of the trainees laughed. Jerry barely smiled.

"I trust you can read it faster than that. You can't take as much time to do preflight as it took you to tell me about it."

"Oh, I don't Colonel." He said with a smile. "It is more difficult for me to remember the words than to do the preflight. I know all the things I must do and what order to do them."

"Show me, Cadet."

Anarok climbed up the wing and settled in the cockpit. Jerry stepped up on the wing so he could clearly watch. Without a fumble or wrong move Anarok surveyed the cockpit and quickly had the prop spinning. After a final instrument check, he turned and smiled at Jerry.

"This is when I close the canopy and take off, sir," he yelled over the engine noise.

Jerry nodded and gave him the cut sign. As the engine died Jerry jumped to the ground. The cadets all stared at him.

Anarok jumped down and joined them.

"Is that how all of you do this?"

Every head nodded.

"Pretty much, Colonel," Cadet Roger Titus said. "It becomes automatic, sir."

"Of course, it does. It's supposed to. You're all doing well. The problem is how do you translate mechanical problems if you don't know the correct words? Mechanics are good at what they do, but they need to fully understand the problem."

This first class of aviation cadets had started with twenty people, three of whom were women. Five weeks into what was designed to be four-month course had already whittled their number to nine. Eight men and one woman stood staring at him with somber faces.

"There will be a blind cockpit familiarization test on Friday. Any cadet who scores lower than eighty percent will be washed out. Any questions?"

After thirty seconds of silence the class snapped to attention until Jerry exited the area.

He heard their instant buzz of conversation behind him. In his former life as a cadet and then pilot, he had not dreamed of what an ordeal the situation must have been for his instructors. Every washout tore at him. He was not a trained instructor and felt he must be depriving these earnest young warriors of the wings they probably deserved.

However, his two chief instructors, both seasoned combat pilots, had agreed on every elimination.

"Colonel, we are saving their lives and saving an aircraft by washing them out," Major Merritt said one night in the ready room after some excellent California brandy.

Merritt was the best female pilot in the RCAF; always had her mission straight, had never been caught flatfooted by any situation, and was always respectful of the cadets.

The understanding brown eyes in her warm chocolate face could turn to rock when angered. Cadets only crossed her once. After that if she said, "jump," they gained altitude.

"Aisha's right, boss," Major David Marx said. "It's our job to either make them good pilots or to change their military occupation specialty. Anything else would be murder."

Dave Marx was the tallest friend Jerry had in the RCAF. At 6'4" he towered above most of the other pilots. Alisha Merritt was within an inch of Jerry's medium height. Both were dear friends and had immediately requested posting to Alaska Republik after Jerry asked them for their help.

"It wasn't that long ago that I was in their shoes," Jerry said with a shrug.

"Did you forget that I was there with you?" Aisha asked.

"Never. You helped me when I thought I was going to get washed out."

"You thought!" She laughed and rolled her eyes. "You had better grades than any other cadet. It was your self confidence that was lacking."

"Which is what's lacking right now," Dave said. "You don't have time for self-doubts and what-ifs. You have a big job ahead of you and no time for recriminations."

"I've always felt that the individual was due all the latitude they deserved," Jerry said, feeling somewhat unnerved by his friends.

"We are giving them all the same classes, the same problems, the same tests," Aisha said. "If they don't make the grade that's their problem, not yours."

"I concur," Dave said. "Do you have a second class of aviation cadets lined up?"

"Of course we do. I told my admin people to cut the number at 30 and we have 73 applicants."

"Make the initial tests more difficult," Aisha suggested. "You'll probably get more graduates out of those who make the cut."

"Are you writing this stuff down?" Dave asked with a laugh.

CHAPTER 22

TANANA AERODROME,
ALASKA REPUBLIK

"GENERAL GRIGORIEVICH, THE First Speaker is on the phone for you."

Grisha looked up from the pile of paper work that seemed to grow higher every day.

"What the hell does he want now?"

"He didn't say, sir." Sergeant Major Tobias said with a wide grin. "Do you want me to tell him you're busy?"

"Christ, no. He already knows I'm busy. This must be important."

Grisha grabbed the phone.

"Mr. First Speaker, how may I help you?"

"Grisha, we have a stunning opportunity sitting in our lap, and you are the man I need to make sure it receives a proper reception."

"Damn it, Pelagian, I'm neck deep in the all the crap you've already dropped on me, in addition to the plot to overthrow the republik. Can't someone else handle this emergency?"

"Give me a name and I'll consider it." The First Speaker's tone became more subdued.

"What's the situation?"

"In the recent unpleasantness the Japanese lost a destroyer to the Russian forces defending Sitka. The Russians have departed along with their Japanese prisoners of war. But they left the destroyer."

"It was sunk, wasn't it?"

"Yes, and no. It ran aground on the shoals off Sitka. It's still there."

"Above the waterline?"

"Most of it."

"By the Metropolitan's beard!"

"The Tlingits are beginning to make noises about taking command, refloating it, and patrolling the Alexandr Archipelago. I don't have a problem with that, but this has to be a Republik vessel and perhaps the beginning of the Alaska Republik Navy. They might need a careful diplomatic reminder."

"I'm on my way, Mr. First Speaker."

"You have me at your back. You declare it and it will be so."

"Does that include my pay scale?" he asked in a humorous tone.

"I gave you a raise two days ago. Ask Wing about it."

"I was joking! Thank you, sir. I'll be in touch."

Why didn't she tell me?

Grisha slammed the phone down and looked into the face of Sergeant Major Tobias.

"Pack my gear and yours. We're going to Sitka. Be sure you include rain gear."

"Very good, General. Will the colonel be accompanying us?"

"No, she won't. She's too pregnant and forgetful."

Sergeant Major Tobias' grin widened. "Very good, General. I'll see to the details at once."

CHAPTER 23

FORT YUKON, ALASKA REPUBLIK

"So, what kinda money they paying you?" Ray Mingus asked in drunken confidentiality.

"Making about CD90 a month. Not bad for around here. Why you asking, Ray?"

"Thought I might apply to be a Peacekeeper, that's all, Dan."

Sergeant Danny Casey grinned. "If you do apply, tell them I sent you. I'll split the fifty dollar bonus with you."

Ray displayed his lack of teeth in a quick grin.

"Y'know, I heard there's this guy who's willing to pay for advance notice on what you guys are plannin'."

Casey's brain ordered his mouth to choose his words carefully. *This might be what Grisha had warned all the sergeants about.*

"Whattya mean, Ray?" Casey took a long pull from the pint he had been sipping. Ray had matched him two beers for every one Casey had downed. This was his third and Ray's sixth.

"Whatever comes up, y'know? What sort of cases are being investigated 'n' things."

"Why would this guy give a damn? You ready for another one?"

"Yeah, another one would be nice, thanks. I dunno why he would care. But if you agree to tell him things you get a hunnert dollars, California."

Casey waved at the bartender and drank from the glass of water he always ordered along with the beer. John, the owner of the pub, brewed his own ale and knew his craft. Getting the ingredients sometimes took up to half a year but he never scrimped nor substituted any part of his recipe.

John had built on to the original cabin and then bought the larger cabin next door. In the four years of operations, he had doubled his business and hired a cooper to make beer barrels so Borealis Brewery could sell up and down river. The pub was the nicest Casey knew of.

His "Earthquake Stout" was the best Casey had ever drunk, and he had a long list for comparison. It contained seven to eight percent alcohol by volume and only took a few pints to put one under the table. Ray was about to slide out of sight.

Grisha had told him to watch for someone called 'the Boss' who supposedly hired foreign agents. As far as he knew, Casey hadn't seen hide nor hair of the person. Might this be the quarry?

As casually as he could, he asked, "Who is this guy?"

Ray opened his mouth but caught himself before uttering a sound. His eyes changed, became crafty as only a drunken man could achieve. Casey knew his next words would be a lie.

"I dunno his name. He's just this guy I see ever now and then, y'know?"

"Where do you see him?"

Ray suddenly looked trapped, and Casey waved his hand.

"Ah, what the hell. It don't really matter. How much do I have to tell him to get money?"

Ray blinked and greed took over again. "Just something that he will see happen pretty soon. Then he'll get an idea of what you're worth to him."

Casey wondered if the unknown person had approached any other Peacekeeper with this proposal. Some of the younger men were already getting restless and a proposition like this might appeal to them. The image of Sam Demientieff, his solitary Peacekeeper trooper, flashed through his mind.

Grisha had hired Sam, and Casey was still getting to know him. At the moment, he was off in the tiny village of Chalkyitsik, sorting out the resurgence of an ancient feud between two neighbors. So far, Sam had proved reliable and honest.

"Well, we're all looking for whoever was working with two dead guys we found."

Ray looked blank. "How d'ya know they was working with someone?"

"They had a lorry full of rockets, the kind that shoot down planes. That's not something you buy a bunch of and try to sell door to door. Know what I mean?"

Ray frowned. "Yeah. That could really be important, huh?"

"I sure as shit think so." Casey finished his beer and waved to John while rubbing his fingers and thumb together. John nodded and moments later brought the bill over to their table. Casey signed it and John vanished.

"I've got to get back to the office, Ray. Good talking with you. Let me know what this guy says if you see him again."

"Hey, yeah, Dan. I'll do that. Thanks for the beers."

Casey quickly left the pub and crossed the street to where a lorry sat. The driver was helping unload his cargo at the old Russian Commercial Company.

"Georg, do you mind if I sit in your cab for a few minutes?"

The driver grinned and wiped his brow. "Buy me a beer later and you can sleep as long as you like, Danny."

"It's a deal."

Casey swung up into the cab and scrunched down until he could just see the pub door clearly. Three breaths later Ray Mingus staggered out into the daylight. He peered up and down the street, then leaned against the wall for a moment.

Casey was afraid the man would pass out. Ray lurched upright, walked slowly and deliberately down the street. Fort Yukon wasn't all that big, but this was the only truly straight street it boasted.

The rest of the village had been built haphazardly and by whim to Casey's way of thinking. He wasn't surprised when Ray turned at the next building and vanished from sight.

Casey jumped out of the lorry and hurried down the street until he could get a clear view of Ray's last turn. Two women walked toward him but other than them the small lane between the cabins lay bereft of humanity.

"Damn!" He quickly covered the two blocks back to his office. He needed to write a narrative of the event as soon as possible so he wouldn't forget anything. He wondered why Grisha thought he could do this thing all by himself.

CHAPTER 24

TANANA AERODROME,
ALASKA REPUBLIK

"Is everything in order?" Grisha asked as Sergeant Major Tobias hurried into his office.

"Our personal effects are at the aerodrome, General. Major Cassidy has been fully briefed on all pertinent situations of which we are currently aware." Sergeant Major Tobias took a deep breath.

"And your mother-in-law just arrived."

"My what?"

"Colonel Wing asked me to locate her mother, so I put the word out. The lady in question arrived fifteen minutes ago."

"Why was I not told of this request?"

"Well, General, I thought the colonel had already spoken to you about it. It did not occur to me to question her on a private matter."

"What is she like, my mother-in-law?"

"Much like her daughter, I must say. Quite formidable."

"Do lead the way, Sergeant Major."

"To the plane, or to your mother-in-law?"

Grisha sighed. "To my mother-in-law."

✪

After eight years, having her mother in the same room with her had nearly unhinged Wing initially. She wasn't even sure she had meant the comment she made to Sergeant Major Tobias in the first place. If *she* couldn't differentiate between a comment and request, how could she expect it of others?

Eleanor had always been a force of nature. She observed, took command, and solved the problem at hand. Wing and her mother were far too much alike to ever agree on the correct man for Wing to marry.

Wing's first husband, Aaron, didn't measure up to her mother's expectations.

"Can he even field dress a moose?" she had demanded. "Or build a fire with wet wood?"

"He's a schoolteacher, mother, not a *promyshlennik*. His strength is relating subjects like history and literature to students."

"Is he even a little bit Athabascan?"

"Does it matter?"

"I would never marry a Russian."

"He's half Russian and half British Canadian."

After two hours of Eleanor's unwavering belligerence, Wing had simply gone to her room. There she packed the clothing she would need and a few personal items into a rucksack. She put on her outdoor gear, threw the pack over her shoulder, walked past her mother in the small living room, and left the house forever.

Neither of them had said goodbye.

She married Aaron in Chena at the home of a rabbi. They had two wonderful years teaching together at Holy Cross and were planning a family when three drunken cossacks broke in one winter night. They killed Aaron and raped her.

In her struggles, one of them slashed at her throat with a knife and missed, but opened her left cheek from jaw to ear. The blood ran down onto her throat and the drunk thought he had killed her. They finally left, and she stumbled to the cabin of friends where they hid her and nursed her back to health.

She still remembered the feeling of power when she joined the Denà Separatist Movement. Aaron had thought it too dangerous to become involved with an anti-government group. There were too many spies in Russian Amerika.

More than once she reflected on the grim irony that if they had been trained, Aaron would still be alive. So would the three Cossacks. She hunted them down and left all three of them naked, tied to trees in the forest, shrieking in pain as they bled out from having their genitals sliced off.

So much has happened, she thought. Rescuing Grisha and the others had led to the death of her second love, beautiful Alex. Were it not for Grisha she would have surrendered to madness long ago.

Eleanor had arrived that morning just after Grisha left for his office. When someone knocked on the door, she thought it was Sergeant Major Tobias.

"Come in."

Her mother stood in the doorway. "Someone told me you wanted me to come and visit." Eleanor glanced around the room. "Is that true?"

"Come in, Mother. Welcome to our home."

"Isn't this the old Russian hospital?"

"Yes. Still a hospital. No longer Russian."

"You certainly went farther in the army than I did. I understand you're a colonel now?"

"Yes. I didn't know you were in the army. Did you see action?"

"Yeah. Paul Eluska promoted me to sergeant after the Battle of Bridge because I was a good shot. It took me awhile to realize we won that war. We were so outnumbered."

Wing leapt to her feet, rushed over, and hugged her mother. When Eleanor returned the hug Wing burst into tears.

"It is so good to see you again," they said simultaneously.

"You've had a long trip," Wing said into her mother's ear. "Let me fix you some tea."

"I'd like that. Got anything to put in it?"

"Honey or whiskey?"

"Yes!" Eleanor said with a wide grin. "Tell me about this *creole* you married." Eleanor's grin widened.

"I think you'll like him. But it won't matter if you don't." Wing took a sip of honeyed tea.

Eleanor laughed. "No, it won't matter a damn bit. It never really did."

Wing pondered her words for a long moment and decided to let it go. "And how is Auntie Ida?"

Before her mother could answer, the door opened, and Grisha entered.

"We have a guest?"

Wing gave him her best smile. *Dammit, he's supposed to be working!* "Grisha, this is my mother, Eleanor Laughlin. Mother, this is my husband, Grisha."

Eleanor got to her feet and looked up into his face. She nearly matched him in height. "You're better looking than I thought you would be, General." She grinned and he grinned back.

Grisha glanced at Wing and then to her mother. "You're a total surprise. Until five minutes ago I didn't know you existed!" He gave her a wide smile. "But now I do and please call me Grisha."

"Even if I'm in uniform, Grisha?"

"Are you in the army?"

"Sergeant. I'm a sniper."

Wing loved the look of utter surprise on his face.

"Sniper! Did you have to shoot anyone?"

"Didn't *have* to, but it seemed like a good idea at the time."

Grisha laughed and Wing knew there wouldn't be any problems between them.

How times change.

"What are you doing now?"

"Well, since there's no more war, I went back to sewing moose hide mukluks and teaching kids how to write and spell."

"She does lovely work," Wing said. "Her beadwork is flawless."

"Once we have a grandchild for you, are you looking for something more exciting than that?"

"More exciting than beadwork and teaching? Like what, Grisha?"

"Being a Peacekeeper."

Her smile went wary. "What's that?"

As Grisha explained, Wing watched her mother's face light up with interest, and recognized the toss of her head as a sign of approval. She knew her mother would do well as a Peacekeeper, but the job would put her in a great deal of harm's way.

She just helped win a war! She'll be fine. Wing sighed.

"What?" Eleanor said, looking at her daughter.

"I didn't say anything." Wing decided to be invisible.

"So, I would be bossin' other Peacekeepers down river in Nulato?"

"Exactly," Grisha said.

"Who hires the other peacekeepers?"

"You do. You will be entered on the rolls as a lieutenant in charge of the Nulato Sector. You will have four units under your supervision; Ruby, Galena, Koyukuk, and Kaltag, in addition to your home base of Nulato."

"How many staff in each unit?"

"A sergeant and a trooper."

"I'll be the boss of *five* sergeants and *five* troopers?" She grinned.

"If you'll take the job."

"I get *paid* to do this?" The grin grew wider.

"Of course. It isn't much but–"

Eleanor grinned at her daughter, "You found a keeper, all right!"

Wing laughed.

"Is that a yes?"

"It sure is, Grisha. You sure know how to get a party going."

Grisha grinned at Eleanor and then shifted his gaze to Wing. His eyes told her she wasn't going to like what he said next.

"I'm afraid I'll miss the rest of the party. The sergeant major and I need to fly to Sitka, and the plane is waiting."

"Sitka! What the hell for?" Wing blurted. She didn't like him going somewhere without her.

"It seems we have the beginnings of a navy. If we can get to it first."

"Bon voyage," she said with as much empathy as she could generate.

CHAPTER 25

FORT YUKON, ALASKA REPUBLIK

SERGEANT DANNY CASEY DIDN'T BEGIN to feel apprehensive until after lunch. He knew Ray didn't get up until noon or later and for a good hour was rarely in any shape to do anything other than moan. At three he wondered if Ray even remembered their conversation.

He sure as hell wasn't headed home. He lives in the opposite direction. How could I lose a man in a village this small?

Casey wished he had something to do other than dwell on the possible actions of a drunk. This job hadn't turned out to be as exciting as they had described it. *At least I'm getting paid for sitting on my ass.*

The door swung open, and Ray walked in, looking anguished.

"Ray, how's the head?"

Ray frowned and glanced over his shoulder at the man who followed him through the door.

Casey had never before seen the man, but being new here he had not met everyone in the village. Nevertheless, he knew a rough character when he saw one and this guy fit the description. He looked Russian or Canadian.

"How're you?" Casey said lightly, sliding open a drawer. He slipped on his brass knuckles behind the cover of his desk, and silently closed the drawer again.

"I'm interested, that's how I am," the man said heavily. "Where'd you get your information?"

"Who are *you*?" Casey asked. "And why do you think I would tell *you* anything?"

"Because if you do, I'll give you money. If you don't, I'll beat the shit out of you." He smirked.

Considering his history of a brutally rough childhood, and his love of a good fight, it took much less than that to ignite Danny Casey. He laughed as he shot to his feet, used a small stool as a launch point, and dove over the desk onto the man, swinging fast and hard. The third time he hit him, the man lost consciousness.

Casey felt electric. He jumped up and faced a very wide-eyed Ray. "Who is this guy? Tell me right now or you're next!" Only when he raised his hands did he see the blood dripping off the brass knuckles.

Ray had already noticed. "His name is Strada," Ray said, his words coming out in a rush. "He's one of the Boss' men. You shouldn't a done that!" Shock widened his eyes and he seemed ready to bolt.

"Go sit on the bench," Casey said, nodding toward the back wall. *"Now!"*

Ray sat, regarding Danny as if he were a stranger. Casey reached down, grabbed Strada's collar, and dragged him to the cell next to the bench. A smear of blood marked their progress. After confiscating two revolvers and a knife, Casey wiped the blood off his hands on Strada's shirt. He slammed the cell door and locked it.

"Who's the 'boss', and how many more toughs does he have here?"

"I don't know his name. I've only been in the same room with him once."

"What's he look like?"

"There's no light in the room. I don't know what he looks like."

"No light at all?"

"No. And they didn't use any names other'n mine."

"How many people do you think were in there besides you?" Casey shook off the brass knuckles and jotted down notes. He didn't want to forget anything.

"I dunno, maybe three. I was scared the whole time. Wasn't worried about anything other'n gettin' outta there alive."

"Did they threaten you?"

"Fuck yeah, they did! Said if I told anyone about 'em they'd kill me. You gotta get me outta town, man."

Casey grabbed the phone and waited ten seconds before realizing it was dead. He slammed it down and unlocked the steel box holding his Kalashnikov. He pulled the weapon out and made sure it had a full clip.

"Go lock the door and then get over here behind the desk!"

"Wh–"

"Do *not* argue! They're coming for us!"

Ray ran to the door, his eyes flicked back and forth. "I ain't stayin' in here to die!" He jerked the door open and stepped out into a barrage of bullets that knocked him over backward.

"Shit!" Casey said to himself. "He even left the fucking door open!"

"You're next, asshole," Strada, said groggily from the cell, wiping blood off his face. "Once they're done your own mother won't recognize you." He wiped again at his still gushing nose and glared at him over a deep smile.

Casey knew Strada would alert the people outside to anything he tried for defense in here.

They started the fight. This asshole is a liability.

"Thanks for the tip. See you in hell." Casey shot him in the head with his .45 automatic.

"Strada!" a shout from outside bellowed. "You in there?"

"He can't come to the phone right now," Casey shouted. "It doesn't work anymore!"

"You must be Sergeant Dan Casey." The voice evolved into something resembling conversation. "You are out-numbered. Your position is hopeless."

"Who are *you*?" Casey asked. The voice sounded distantly familiar.

"That doesn't matter. Suffice it to say I hold all the cards in this little game."

Movement caught Casey's peripheral vision and he glanced out the station's side window and saw Trooper Sam Demientieff carrying a rifle, and edging around the next-door cabin a few meters from theirs. Hope blossomed in his chest.

"So how many of you does it take to fight me, Mr. Flannel-Mouth?" he shouted.

"Enough to do the job." The voice was loud. Unless he was using a megaphone, the *homme* had to be close.

The first day Casey accepted this job, he had carefully examined the immediate neighborhood. Knowing your terrain was classic military doctrine Riordan had pounded into their heads.

Say what you will about the man, he knew his shit.

Twenty meters directly in front of the station sat a small, locked cabin used for storage. It had a pitched roof, so nobody was up there. The cabin's back wall featured one window that had been boarded shut from the inside.

To the left of the storage cabin was Old Elmer's place. He lived alone and was well into his eighties. He wasn't fond of bathing and Casey didn't think there was anyone in the world that would spend time in there if they didn't have to.

On the right was Auntie Simon's place. If anyone had barged in on her, Casey would have heard her cussing them out. She was quite loud when provoked.

Flannel Mouth wasn't worried about a defensive position. He was in attack mode. Casey pursed his lips as he considered all the ramifications and decided he had the advantage. He knew they could see Ray's body bleeding all over the floor.

He sidled over to the cell and quickly unlocked and opened the door, pleased he had oiled the hinges not two days ago when he was bored. Casey dragged Strada's body over against the wall before edging up to the opening. The fresh air smelled sweet over the stink of Ray's blood and effluvia; he took a deep breath.

"So whattya want from me?" he shouted.

He leaned his Kalashnikov against the wall and with both arms hoisted Strada erect as if he were standing. Next to the door hung his collection of elastic tie-downs.

"I just want to *talk* to you." The condescension in the tone enraged Casey.

I hate it when people think I'm stupid.

Pushing Strada's corpse against the wall with his left arm, he tossed his longest strap over the center beam holding the five trusses bearing the roof.

"About what?"

Two more tie-downs and he had Strada supported in an uptight position. The benefit of elastic tie-downs was their ability to stretch briefly before pulling back.

"I want to know about the rockets. Tell me what you know, and I'll let you live."

"You must think I'm as stupid as Ray was."

"Ray failed me. He knew the consequences."

"You won't kill me if I come out?"

"No, I won't."

"Okay!" He shoved Strada far into the doorframe as he peered out from the edge.

Strada immediately took seven rounds to the chest. One of the rounds took out the strap holding him upright and he collapsed. Casey saw the triggerman on the far side of the storage cabin.

When Strada fell to the floor, the shooter automatically lifted the muzzle of his weapon. Casey leaned over and put three rounds into the man before jumping back.

"You lied to me!" Casey bellowed.

"He acted on impulse! That wasn't supposed to happen! I swear it!"

Casey backed up to the bars of the cell and sprinted toward the door. He shouted, "Now, Sam!" and dove over the body in the door, rolled once and landed on his forearms in order to roll over again and assume a defensive position.

Bullets blew more pieces of the doorway to flinders before a different weapon boomed three times in quick succession. Casey rolled over and raised his weapon, searching for targets. Quiet settled over the scene.

"Where are you, asshole?" Casey shouted.

Silence.

"Sergeant Casey, I got one of them," Sam shouted.

"Stay where you are. Do you see anyone else?"

"No."

Casey crawled over to the man he had shot. The stranger had been killed instantly and Casey felt a glow of satisfaction. *Fuck with me, will you?*

He glanced up at the storage cabin window. Two boards had been removed. Casey eased around to the front and saw the door standing ajar, a broken lock lay on the ground.

I wish I had a smoke grenade, he thought wistfully.

He looked around his position and found a rock that filled his hand. He threw it through the door. Nothing.

"Sam!" Cassidy shouted. "Did you see anyone leave this cabin?"

"*Which* cabin?"

"Storage place in front of the station!"

"No. But I can't see the front of it, either."

"Come on out, I think he got away."

Sam edged around the corner of Old Elmer's cabin, his rifle at the ready. "You okay, Danny?"

"Yeah. You?"

"Sure. I think I just killed a guy."

"Thanks for that. I got three dead men over here."

"What the hell is going on, man?"

"It'll take some time to explain it all. But first, how'd it go in Chalkyitsik?"

Sam glanced around at the bodies and blood, then gave him a puzzled frown.

"Are you serious?"

CHAPTER 26

SITKA, ALASKA REPUBLIK

"This is a nice transport," Sergeant Major Tobias said. "But we seem to be losing a great deal of altitude and I have yet to spy a landing strip. All I see is water and forest."

They had flown from Tanana to St. Nicholas in a Republic of California cargo plane. From there they had boarded a *Gidro Samolyet Transportnaya*, a large seaplane undergoing extensive maintenance when the war started and left by the Russians in their retreat. They were the only passengers in the aircraft and the four-man crew would take them wherever they wished to travel for the next week.

"You didn't know we'll have to bail out?" Grisha said, struggling to keep a straight face.

"Nice try, General. I wasn't bounced off the potato wagon yesterday. This is one of those amphibious birds, isn't it?"

"Why can't I ever fool you?"

"Because you're not old enough."

The plane dropped and flew no more than thirty meters above the North Pacific Ocean. Sunlight sparkled off the water and a wall of distant firs ascending a mountain slope made for a memorable image. Grisha had requested a flyby of the destroyer and the pilot clicked onto the comm channel and said, "The vessel is dead ahead on the starboard side, uh, the right side of our plane."

"Thank you, Captain." Grisha pointed to the right and both he and Tobias pushed into the Plexiglas blister that could hold a .50 caliber machine gun. The plane slowed and dropped another ten meters toward the water.

They both stared avidly as they passed the destroyer.

"That's a lot of boat!" Tobias muttered.

"It's a ship, not a boat," Grisha said.

"Begging your pardon, General, but what's the difference?"

"You can carry a boat on a ship, but not the other way around."

"Good to know. What I know about the navy can be contained in a teacup."

"I used to own a boat. Her name was *Pravda*."

Tobias glanced at him. "*Truth?* That's an odd name for a boat."

"She was the only truth I knew." *I wonder if Alexi still works at the fuel dock in Ft. Dionysus.*

Tobias was right. It was a lot of boat. Smaller boats crowded around it and people walked the level decks.

The Tlingit Navy, he thought.

"I think I now understand the First Speaker's anxiety," Tobias said with a grunt. "I'm glad he sent us, General."

"Why?"

"Those lads down there will listen to you. I don't think they would listen to anyone else from Tanana. Also, I get to *watch!*" Sergeant Major Tobias grinned.

As they taxied up to the floating dock Grisha saw a crowd waiting.

"We're either getting a nice reception or a very bad one."

Tobias laughed. "Isn't that always the case, General?"

"Yes, Sergeant Major, but we aren't armed."

Tobias gave him a knowing grin and Grisha decided not to push it.

The port engine died first, and when both had ceased turning, the main hatch in the fuselage opened. Grisha squared his hat, and bending over to get through the hatch, stepped out onto the dock. A bosun's pipe shrilled and a large man in naval uniform bellowed, "General Grigorievich, arriving!"

Eight men formed in two facing ranks all brought rifles up to present arms. Standing between the two ranks was a navy captain who immediately saluted Grisha.

"Welcome aboard Alaska Republik Naval Base Sitka, General Grigorievich."

Grisha returned the salute.

"I am Captain Didrickson. I am honored to be your liaison during your unexpected visit."

Grisha smiled. "So, you got the honor of keeping me out of

trouble and busy. Who did you piss off?"

Didrickson grinned back. "Actually, I asked for the privilege. I wanted to meet the man who saved my brother's life at Bou Saada."

"That's why your name is familiar! Your brother was a first lieutenant in the Troika Guard. How is he?"

"He is well, prosperous, and would like to have you to dinner if time allows."

"Superb. We'll make sure that happens. What do we do now?"

"Admiral Soboleff is waiting for you and your party in the wardroom."

"My party, yes. Allow me to introduce Sergeant Major Tobias. He keeps me honest and motivated."

The sergeant major saluted. "It is my honor to meet you, Captain Didrickson."

"We've heard your name also," Didrickson said as he returned the salute. "What you people did up in the Interior gave the rest of us the determination to get into the fight. Now we must attend the admiral. He wants to know why you're here."

Grisha laughed and followed the captain. He nodded to the sailors as he passed.

Admiral Soboleff proved to be tall, slim, and very fit. His face bore deep smile lines, which Grisha thought promising.

"So, I finally get to meet the Hero of Chena!" he boomed and held out his hand.

Grisha shook and said, "All I really did was break my leg. I was here about a year ago and met a General Soboleff…"

"My brother, Vincent. We chose different services. My given name is Ross, and you are Grisha, yes?"

"Yes, Ross. Thank you for your warm reception."

"May I offer both of you a drink?" He indicated a bar where a chief petty officer stood. "This is Chief Petty Officer Freeman Dundas. We have served together for decades. He is an excellent bartender."

Dundas nodded without smiling.

Grisha smiled. "I would love a cold beer."

Sergeant Major Tobias stepped over and shook the chief's hand, said something to him and the two men grinned. Chief Dundas opened a beer, poured it into a glass and handed it to Grisha.

Admiral Soboleff already had a glass in his hand. "So why did our new First Speaker send you clear the hell down here when you have so much on your plate in Chena?"

"He doesn't know Southeast like I do. He is working his ass off trying to unite our new republik, and is worried that old cultural divisions will turn into new political problems. That beautiful destroyer out there is more of a symbol than a defensive war craft, but its potential worried him."

"You know him pretty well, don't you?"

"I guess so, why?"

"Does he trust the Tlingits and Haidas in his new country?"

"I'll answer that in reverse. First, *he* doesn't have a country. *We* do."

Grisha hesitated a beat and continued, "Second, he trusts people he knows, has fought with, and some that he fought against. He's not a young man and he knows it. He has dedicated the majority of his adult life working to make life better for the Peoples of Alaska.

"Also, for what it's worth, I trust him implicitly."

Admiral Soboleff gave him an appraising look. "Well, you *are* the commanding general of the Alaska Republik Army, so of course you are loyal to him."

"He didn't give me that rank. The War Council of the former Dená Republik did. He's not a schemer, Admiral; he's a worrier.

"He's First Speaker by the will of the people. He and a lot of other people are trying to create a workable constitution to bring order that favors no one clan or division."

Soboleff frowned and knocked back the drink in his hand. "Thank you, General. You have reiterated everything I know about the man from your viewpoint. I value that very much.

"A lot of us feel outside the fire circle down here. I know for fact that the Aleuts feel the same way. However, all of us support this new nation. We *have* to as there are *no* alternatives!"

"Ross, we know there are foreign agents trying to spread discord and division in Alaska. We are a weak baby republik and still on Mama California's tit while Auntie United States changes our nappies. Alaska Republik is physically huge and politically vulnerable, and we have to work with that.

"And you are correct. There are no alternatives. The more we can do for ourselves hastens the day we ask our allies to remove their troops and aircraft squadrons. I'm sure you can appreciate how distant that day is, and how easily other nations could ally themselves with a faction here in Alaska."

"Grisha, we have a long road ahead of us. Tell the First Speaker he has only loyalty and determination down here and out on the Chain. Nobody hates the Russians more than the Aleuts."

Grisha knew what the admiral said was fact. The Russians had decimated the Aleut people in their lust for sea otter pelts. Before a wiser person took over the Russian-Amerika Company, their factors had killed off sea otters to the point of extinction, and more than halved the Aleut population.

If the Aleuts are loyal, Pelagian has nothing to worry about.

"I agree with you on that one, Ross. Thank you for your words. The First Speaker can move something off his mental plate and worry about other things."

"Did you really doubt us?"

"I never did, but I wasn't about to turn down a trip to Southeast."

Admiral Soboleff laughed. "I think we should all go get some decent food. That includes you, Master Sergeant Tobias, but the chief probably already told you that."

"Indeed, he did, Admiral. Thank you."

CHAPTER 27

TANANA,
CAPITOL OF ALASKA REPUBLIK

"I NEED TO TALK TO General Grigorievich as soon as possible," Yukon Cassidy gasped, chest heaving from his dash to the second floor.

The corporal standing in the door said, "The general is in Sitka for a few days. Is there someone else you can talk to?"

"Who's in command here, right now?"

"That would be Colonel Smolst, the general's chief of staff."

"Please tell Heinrich that his old comrade, Yukon, needs to speak to him immediately."

"Please come in and have a seat, sir. I will let him know you are here."

Cassidy was still trying to figure out the corporal's village when Colonel Heinrich Smolst hurried into the small room.

"Yukon, so good to see you!" The handshake was quick. "What's on your mind?"

"Are you up to speed on the rockets we found?"

"Yes."

"Sergeant Danny Casey, the chief peacekeeper in Fort Yukon, was attacked yesterday by at least four men with automatic weapons."

"*Schiess*! Is he wounded?"

"No. Between him and Trooper Demientieff they got three of them. They wanted to know what Casey knew about the rockets."

"The one who escaped is the cause of concern, correct?"

Cassidy grinned. "I love talking to you, Heinrich. You're always one step ahead of the conversation. Yes, we think it's the 'Boss' the British captain told us about."

"What do you need from Tanana?"

"A plane large enough to hold three passengers and a pilot to fly it."

"I have just the people for you!"

"People? I just need a pilot."

"This is the perfect solution for you. Trust me."

As Heinrich hurried back through the door Cassidy shouted, "I *never* trust you when you say, 'trust me'!"

CHAPTER 28

ST. ANTHONY, ALASKA REPUBLIK

Captain Georgi Fedorov rushed into his twin brother's room. "Rejoice, we have another exciting mission!"

"Promise me you won't get shot," Ivan said looking up from a book.

"Stop that. It's your turn to get shot if anyone does. Get into your gear. We're going to Tanana. Colonel Smolst's orders."

Within minutes both pilots walked out to their patched helicopter. The ground crew had the main rotor turning lazily and both men ducked as they hurried under it. Georgi tried to hide his permanent limp. He had been wounded during the war while flying reconnaissance drunk.

The day looked perfect for flight. Very few high clouds and a mere twelve-knot warm breeze out of the south bearing scents of plant life and promise.

Georgi strapped into the pilot's seat while his eyes ran over the gauges in front of him. He could fly better than he could walk. Ivan plugged his headset into the console.

"So, what is this exciting mission?"

"We are to stop in Tanana to board a team and transport them to where they desire."

"The Republik of Hawai'i, for instance?"

Georgi laughed. "I fucking wish! I have heard incredible stories about that place."

"When you were drunk, yes?"

"Ivan, you used to be entertaining. What happened?" As soon as the words left his mouth he wished he could call them back.

"I got my twin brother wounded because I was inebriated in combat."

"We were *both* inebriated! I'm the one who was hit, and I don't care!"

"But it was *my* fault," Ivan insisted.

"You were a lot more fun as a drunk." Georgi went to full power and they lifted off.

He maintained a 100-meter altitude as they followed the road toward Chena where they would refuel before flying on to Tanana. Georgi glanced at his brother.

"Do you not enjoy flying anymore?"

"I am self-apprised of my mortality and the prospect disturbs me. You nearly died yet you are as carefree as a stripling."

"We are no longer in a war. Nobody is shooting at us."

Ivan stared down at the passing road. "Please to turn around for a moment!"

"Why?"

"There is person waving. They may need assistance."

"We have a mission—"

"Please to turn back, my brother!" Ivan shouted.

The helicopter rolled to port as they reversed course. Georgi stared intently down at the road.

"You are correct. They appear to require assistance. However, there is no place to land, and it could be a trap."

"Two excellent points. Please continue to Chena."

"Ivan, *I* am the pilot. *I* am in charge, *nyet?*"

"*Da.* My apologies, Captain Pilot."

CHAPTER 29
AKKU,
ALASKA REPUBLIK

"The last time I was in this place I was a prisoner and a pawn." Grisha looked at the faces around the banquet table and smiled. "This is a wonderful homecoming. Thank you."

The group applauded as he sat down.

Piotr Chernikoff, Grisha's cousin, stood and raised a glass. "I would like to propose a toast to our distinguished guest."

All stood but Grisha. He sat with a reddening face and waited for all the formality to end. He had work to do.

At long last everyone sat down and ate. The meal surpassed superb. He had forgotten how much he loved halibut and fresh caught King salmon.

Eventually they all sat back in their chairs and Rebecca, Piotr's wife asked, "Did you accomplish all you wished down here, Grisha?"

"Not yet. One of the main reasons for my trip was to offer a lot of people jobs."

"Doing what?" she asked.

"Let me tell all of you about the Peacekeepers..."

✪

An hour and a half later Grisha sat with his cousin in a corner sipping French brandy while watching Sergeant Major Tobias hand out applications to Peacekeeper recruits. Some of the men and women took two or three in order to give them to friends and family. A few old questions swam to the top of Grisha's mind.

"Piotr, is Kazina still in town?"

His cousin gave him a troubled glance and nodded. "Yeah, she is."

"She still with the former Russian commander?"

"Naw. He left right after the war started up north. Got called back to St. Petersburg."

"She didn't want to go with him?"

"He didn't want her to go with him."

At many earlier points in his life, he would have taken pleasure in his ex-wife's comeuppance, now he felt sorry for her.

"Is she working as a clerk again?"

"I don't think so. Do you wish to see her?"

"I would like to observe her. I have no reason to speak with her."

"Let's go for a walk. The town has changed somewhat since you, ah, left."

"I'd like that. Let me tell the sergeant major."

"I'll get our rain gear."

Grisha walked over to Tobias who was deep in a conversation with two young women.

"Sergeant Major, may I interrupt you for a moment?"

"Of course, General. In fact, I would appreciate you answering the questions these young ladies have."

"If I can." He gave them his full attention. "What would you like to know?"

"Can Peacekeepers transfer to other locations in Alaska Republik?"

"Yes, once they have been through training and there is a need for people in another sector. Where did you wish to go?"

"We're not sure yet, sir," the larger woman said. "But we want out of SeaAlaska Province."

Grisha glanced at Tobias who gave a slight shrug.

"Why is that? This is where you would have to train."

The younger one looked embarrassed and turned her head away from them.

"I am General Grisha Grigorievich. Who are you?"

"Tatliana Dundas," the first one said. "And this–" Grisha held up his hand.

"She can tell me who she is," he said kindly.

"Anastasia Long." The smaller woman looked into his eyes. "We want to see more of our new country, sir. Would it be possible to go elsewhere for training?"

"I'll look into it. This is the first time we have heard a request like this. I promise I will get back to you, okay?"

"Thank you, Grisha," Anastasia said.

From across the room Piotr said, "Come on, Grisha."

He looked at the sergeant major. "I'll be back in a few hours, Tobias. Not to worry."

"Very good, General."

Once outside and walking down the steep street towards the commercial district, Grisha said, "Care to tell me what the story is with those two women?"

Piotr made a small laugh.

"One of them thinks she's a man and the other one likes it."

"Lesbians, yes?"

"That's one word for them. What we–"

"I don't care what you call them, cousin. A homosexual saved my life and the lives of many others, and nearly died in the process. They are people who have different needs in life than you, or I."

"You condone that–"

Grisha stopped and turned to face Piotr.

"Here's the thing, cousin." He couldn't keep the edge out of his voice. "There are no laws against loving whom you wish in Alaska Republik, and there never will be as long as I live. You don't have to understand it, but you *do* have to accept it."

Piotr nodded and they continued toward town.

"Talked to any priests about this subject?" Piotr asked in a conversational tone.

"No. We're taking a page from the United States' constitution. Separation of church and state."

"You have changed," Piotr said. "You were pretty devout when you were younger."

"A lot has happened since then. Where are we going?"

"St. George's Pub."

Grisha laughed. "I damned near used to live in there. Does Gallagher still own it?"

"He sold out to a woman from T'Angass. She runs the place."

They walked through the door. People filled the place, mostly fishermen from their odor. Two barman poured and pushed filled glasses into eager hands while grabbing money.

"Damn, it hasn't changed a bit, has it?"

Before Piotr could answer, a familiar voice said, "Grisha, is that you?"

He turned and smiled at Natalia Fialkoff, an old friend from T'Angass.

"I wondered if it was you that bought this place. Why'd you change locations?"

She grinned and kissed him. "Good to see you, too. I moved to get away from Dixon's Entrance. Too many British Canadians in the neighborhood."

"Ah, I take your point. Would you be willing to answer a few questions about the situation down there?"

"Not right now!" she laughed. "I've got a business to run."

"After breakfast, then?"

"Sure. Do you want to come by," she winked, "or stay here and I'll wake you?"

He held up his hand and displayed his ring. "I'm happily married with a child on the way. But I sincerely appreciate the invitation."

"You've changed, Grisha," she said. "It looks good on you. Your drinks are on the house." She patted his cheek and vanished into the crowd.

"Would you like another drink, Piotr?"

"No. I think we should leave."

"Hello, fellows," a familiar voice said, "buy a girl a drink?"

Grisha turned and stared into his ex-wife's face. "Hello, Kazina."

Her eyes widened and she put her hand to her chest. "Grisha! You're alive!"

"So, it seems." He wished they hadn't come in here after all.

"They told me you had been killed up in the Interior."

"In a way, they were correct. The old me died up there and what you see now is the improved version. How are you?"

"I get by," she said evasively. "Are you moving back to Akku?"

"No. I live in Tanana now, on the Yukon."

"Don't the nights get pretty cold up there?"

"So do the days during the winter. I have a wife to keep me warm." He again held up his left hand and displayed the gold band on his ring finger.

"Congratulations. What do you do up there?"

"I'm in the military. I seem to have a gift for it."

"Aren't you going to ask me what I do for a living?" Her voice had gone brittle. In the old days that had signaled an impending argument.

"No. I don't really care."

"You don't have *any* questions for me?"

"Just one."

"What?"

"What happened to *Pravda*?"

"The government seized it and auctioned it off."

"Good seeing you, Kazina. I have to go."

Her face worked for a moment, then she turned and walked away through the crowded pub.

"Let's get out of here, Grisha," Piotr said. "I shouldn't have brought you here. Sorry."

"I asked, and you showed me. After you, cousin."

They went out into the rainy evening.

CHAPTER 30

CZAR NICHOLAS HIGHWAY, ALASKA REPUBLIK

M<small>ACK</small> M<small>AC</small>D<small>ONALD</small> <small>WATCHED THE HELICOPTER</small> thwap away in the cloudless sky.

She snarled, "Those bastards saw me. Why didn't they help?" Her silent utility didn't answer. She felt bereft enough to cry.

"Fuckers!" she shrieked. The empty road made no comment.

She returned to the utility, wished she had taken better care of it. Mack had regarded it as just another tool. *Maybe more complex than a hammer or an axe, but still, just a tool.* Yet when it stopped running, she had felt betrayed to the point of tears.

It had let her down. *I haven't pushed it any harder than I have pushed myself.* The thought sobered her, and she took stock.

She peered down at the engine wishing she understood it even half as well as she understood weapons and people.

"Dammit, Jimmy. I've almost finished this journey. As soon as I see his dead ass, we can both move on to other things. *Fuck*, but I miss you!"

She jiggled the radiator hose and it resisted perfectly.

"People think I'm crazy because I talk to you. *Fuck* 'em. They don't understand that you *can* hear me. I miss you so much, Cuddle Bear."

She glanced around to make sure nothing living had heard her other than the trees and tundra patches. Birds called from behind leaves, and the breeze brought the fresh, invigorating bouquet of flowering plants and budding trees to her nose.

A distant mechanical noise invaded her space. She reached into the cab and grabbed her 9mm pistol. After a few seconds she decided it was a land vehicle coming from the direction of Chena. Mack relaxed and hid the pistol in the shoulder holster under her jacket.

Appearing to be a damsel in distress was going to be difficult enough without flashing a pistol. At 5'8", full-bodied, coffee-au-lait skin, and a thick braid of hair so black it sometimes gleamed blue hanging down to her fanny, made for a formidable looking woman. She sighed. She wasn't a convincing victim.

She squinted and discerned the vehicle was a truck of some sort. As it neared her, it slowed and finally stopped beside her. It was a tow truck.

The helicopter did help! She grinned.

The driver grinned back at her as another man swung down out of the cab. When she got a good look at him, her heart made a small flip. He could have been Jimmy's brother.

She bit her lip and reminded herself of the dangers of transference. He might remind her of her dead husband, but that's probably where the similarity stopped.

"We were notified by radio that you needed assistance. How can we help, ma'am?"

"The name's Mack, okay?"

His eyebrows shot up. "Oh, you just came from Tanana Crossing!"

"How the hell did you know that?" she blurted.

"My sergeant down there said to expect you."

"Who the hell are *you*?"

He grinned beneath his moustache, squared his shoulders, and bowed. "Lieutenant Alex Strom, Republik of Alaska Peacekeepers, at your service."

She laughed. "He warned you, didn't he?"

"Sergeant Langbein is an excellent Peacekeeper. He keeps me informed of everything I should know about and doesn't bother me with crap. Do you have any idea how rare a man like that is?"

"So, he thought you should know about me, huh?"

"I'm keeping a body in the cooler so you can look at it. If Fred hadn't called, Ferdinand Rochamboux would have been buried yesterday and it would have cost you money to dig him up again."

"I appreciate Fred's efforts and your response, Lt. Strom." She worked hard to sound contrite.

"Please, Mack, call me Alex."

From beneath the hood of her utility the other man said, "I think the thermostat has crapped out on you, Mack."

"Sorry, I forgot to introduce Scott Burgett, mechanic extraordinary."

"Pleased to meet you, Mack. Your rig could also need some tuning up and probably new spark plugs."

"Nice to meet you, too, Scott. How much would all of that cost?"

"We'll put it on the Peacekeeper's ticket," Alex said. "You're up here on Peacekeeper business, right?"

"I am now." She grinned.

CHAPTER 31

NEAR TANANA, ALASKA REPUBLIK

Captain Dumont peered through his binoculars as the helicopter landed in Tanana.

This is something I didn't expect. I wonder how many troops are aboard that fat bird?

"This changes things, *ja*?" Lieutenant Klein asked as he glared through his binoculars, standing shoulder to shoulder with his boss.

"I am not certain, however, until we know for sure we will stand down from the operation."

Klein nodded. "Perhaps we need an infiltrator to make an assessment."

"Good thinking. Send Private Babcock to me."

"At once." Klein left the observation post.

I'm always amazed how such a large man can move so quietly.

He heard Babcock's approach from twenty meters.

"You wanted to see me, sir?"

Dumont glanced at the private first class. The large man panted from the exertion of walking up the ridge but still maintained his mocking smile.

"I want you to go into Tanana and assess the military presence. If you have to talk to anyone, tell them you are a mechanic looking for work. I want to know how many troops came in on that helicopter."

"Where should I say I am from?"

"Where *are* you from?"

"Massachusetts, down in the United States."

"Tell them that if you must. Do not offer information and answer as briefly as possible when asked."

"How long do you want me to stay?"

"As long as it takes you to obtain the information. Twenty-four hours at the most. I wouldn't send you down there if I had another way of obtaining intelligence. Don't forget your oath to the Phantom Legion. Try not to attract attention."

"Not to worry, *mon Captain*. I shall leave at once." He grinned and tossed off a salute that Dumont didn't return.

"Don't forget that we are all counting on you, Private Babcock. Our lives depend on your success as much as your life does."

Babcock sobered and snapped to attention, rendered a precise salute.

Dumont returned it. "Good luck and be careful."

"Thank you, sir. I will, sir."

CHAPTER 32

FORT YUKON, ALASKA REPUBLIK

Solare pushed back strands of grey hair from the wig and watched the second man casually walk into the cabin. This one she had seen before. She continued to hobble along the dusty street trusting that her old woman disguise would keep her anonymous. She hated the stink of the cosmetics she wore.

"Auntie, are you looking for someone?"

She looked up into the earnest face of a young man.

"No, thank you. I'm going down river and thought I would look at your town." The strain of making her voice sound old and tired was more difficult than she thought it would be.

"Oh, you're from upriver? Which village?"

"Twenty Kilometer Village," she croaked. "I must go."

He frowned at her and smiled. "If you need help, just ask anyone, okay?"

"Thank you, young man." She continued her shuffle down the street. More than anything, she wanted to look back and see if he still watched her.

Pushing the interruption out of her mind she concentrated on her findings. Three different men had entered and departed the suspect cabin. She knew one of the men was a felon by any nation's standards.

He even had a price on his head, which marked him for capture or death once she located her main quarry. In two days and brief nights of watching, she had not seen anyone else leave or enter. Yet on both mornings she had seen wisps leave the smokestack at a time when it logically stood empty.

Someone is having breakfast.

The urge to just walk in took real effort to suppress. Someone's grandmother might live there. She grinned at that. Not one of those wolves would do anything for their grandmother unless money was involved.

The other possibility, which she put at ninety percent, was that the person in that little, out-of-the-way cabin was an extremely dangerous individual who didn't want to be seen, and kept a loaded Kalashnikov at hand.

Weapons fire had drawn her to the battle at the Peacekeeper Station. She was ready to break cover and fire on the attackers when a second ally materialized and evened the score. Still, Casey's flying attack out of the station had been a thing of beauty.

He's good at carrying the fight to the enemy, she mused. *Unfortunately, he is far too fond of a good fight.* That deleted him from her mental list of possible partners. She had admired how well Cassidy and Delcambré worked together and realized having a trustworthy partner could be a good thing.

Her predilection toward Irishmen had pulled her attention away from the storage cabin door and she missed seeing who fled. She still wanted to slap herself until the anger dissipated, but what good would that do?

She moved slowly and purposely toward the edge of the village and her camp spot. As she neared the end of the street, two men stepped out of the shadows and stood in her path.

"I'm Sergeant Dan Casey and this is Trooper Sam Demientieff of the Alaska Republik Peacekeepers. Who are you and exactly what are you doing in Fort Yukon?"

CHAPTER 33

TANANA,
ALASKA REPUBLIK

Yukon Cassidy chafed at the amount of time the helicopter pilots needed to refuel their craft and themselves. He grudgingly agreed that a helicopter was perfect for his mission and further agreed all tanks must be topped off to insure a successful outcome.

Unfortunately, I am going mad with impatience! Communications with Fort Yukon had yet to be repaired.

"What's taking these *hommes* so long?" Roland Delcambré growled as he edged up to Cassidy. "I could have cooked a meal for six, served it, and still beat them out here."

"I know exactly how you feel. It's all I can do not to go in there and drag them out by their ears. At this rate we'll have snow before we get a ride."

The objects of their discussion ambled out of the cafeteria. Before they could go anywhere else, Cassidy hurried up to them.

"If you both are ready, we would like to get on with the mission."

"At your service, Major Cassidy," one of them said. Without Georgi's limp Cassidy couldn't tell them apart. "What is the nature of our mission on this beautiful day?"

"Let's walk as we talk, okay?" They walked with him, and he held out a map. "The red x is where I want you to set us down outside Fort Yukon. Don't circle, just go in and land. Sergeant Casey needs a bit of back up."

"Is good," one of the pilots said. "We are making this trip just for you and," he glanced down at Roland, "him?"

"Captain Delcambré is a one-man squad. However, we are also taking Corporal Dalhke and Trooper Bennett." He nodded toward the helicopter where both men waited next to their packs and weapons.

"Is good. Ivan, my talented and professional brother will be pilot. I am Georgi, and will serve as copilot and navigator."

"Have you ever been to Fort Yukon?" Cassidy asked Georgi.

"This will be maiden voyage to new place. Not to worry. We have flown far down on Yukon River when rescuing Colonel Yamato last winter."

Cassidy felt mollified and nodded his head. Georgi hurried ahead and opened the side hatch. Dahlke and Bennett loaded their gear and climbed in. Cassidy and Delcambré followed them.

The metal-framed web seats were barely more comfortable than sitting on the deck. The four of them checked their weapons, making sure they were empty and with ammo at hand. Roland nested four hand grenades into the pouch hanging on his harness.

Cassidy didn't like wearing a harness. They caught on every damn branch he passed, and Alaska was full of brush and trees. His grenades nestled in a canvas pouch no longer needed by an unknown Russian soldier. The helicopter lifted off and headed north.

"Who made this thing?" Cassidy asked Delcambré.

"It's a Russian Mi-17. They seem to crash a lot."

"Why the hell did you have to say that?"

"Because it's true!"

Cassidy glanced out the door window. They seemed impossibly high. He knew how wide the Yukon River was and from here it looked like a ribbon.

"You're frightened of heights, aren't you?" Delcambré asked through a wide grin.

"I don't like to fly, okay?"

"Well, it certainly is easier than going by boat." Delcambré glanced out the window. "It would have taken us forever to get to Fort Yukon otherwise."

"How much longer is this flight going to take?" Cassidy shouted at the pilots.

"Hour and half, more or less," Georgi yelled over the engine racket. "Relax and enjoy scenery."

Cassidy gritted his teeth and endured

CHAPTER 34

FORT YUKON, ALASKA REPUBLIK

"Boss, I just got word from an informant that the Peacekeepers are closing in on this location."

"Initiate the retreat, Number One."

A trap door was lifted in the darkened room and a small dim red light clearly showed the ladder leading downward. N'Go walked over to his escape hatch.

"Don't forget to arm the welcome, Number One."

"I won't forget, Boss," the man said with a chuckle. "I hope they don't wait until the battery goes flat." He went to the back of the cabin and clicked the switch on a large, gray metal box.

He could see the tiny red security dot attached to the doorframe three feet above the floor. If one worked, so did the other. He hurried over, grabbed his weapon, and went down the ladder, pausing only to carefully shut and secure the hatch above him.

The circumstances called for retreat.

CHAPTER 35

FORT YUKON, ALASKA REPUBLIK

"I'm giving you one more chance to tell us the truth before I kick this whole thing upstairs," Sergeant Danny Casey grated in his best tough cop tone.

Solare rolled her eyes. "Dammit, Sergeant. You said you had fixed your phone. Call your commander! I'm not telling you anything until I get to talk to him!" She had washed her face and pulled off the mop-like wig.

"You're really sticking to that story," he mused, beginning to feel doubt gnaw at his gut.

"So fucking *call* him, you cretin!"

"You have a real way with words, lady." He reached for the phone.

"I'm no damn lady!"

"I know that. I was just being polite. It's part of my job."

Trooper Sam Demientieff snickered from where he sat by the door.

"Who's this, please?" Casey said into the phone.

"Oh, hi, Corporal Titus. This is Sergeant Casey at the Fort Yukon station. Yeah. I need to talk to General Grigorievich right now."

Corporal Titus responded, "Are you calling from the Peacekeeper Station? We heard the line was down."

"Yeah, we fixed the cut wire."

"Good to hear. This might take a few minutes. The general just returned from a trip and is with his very pregnant wife. However, he gave specific orders that if any of you folks called, he would talk to you."

Casey felt impressed. He wasn't used to superior officers who did what they promised. He glanced over at Solare. Despite her eyes continuing to burn a hole through him, she wasn't hard to look at.

"Sergeant Casey, what can I do for you?"

"Oddly enough, General, I have a prisoner who wants to speak to you. Here she is."

As he passed the phone to Solare he could hear the general laughing on the other end of the line.

"It's me, Grisha. Tell this fool to leave me alone. What? That wasn't part of–" Her eyes continued to burn at Casey and it was beginning to piss him off.

"I have a strong inclination to quit, here and now. Why can't I? *I signed that?*"

Although he wasn't sure why, Casey was beginning to enjoy himself, but knew better than to show it.

"Fuck! Sure, why not?" Solare held the phone out arms-length to Casey. "He wants to talk to *you*."

"General?"

"Sergeant Casey, this is not going to be easy for you, and I know that before anything else happens."

"Sir?"

"Solare is a Peacekeeper who takes orders only from me. It's in her contract."

"Very well," Casey said dubiously.

"The thing is, she's worth the trouble, and she can definitely be trouble. I told her she has to work with you, and you both have to agree on strategy. She's going to be hostile."

"*Going* to be?"

"Danny, she's worth the anguish, I promise you."

"Okay, Grisha, I–"

"Oh, one more thing; Major Cassidy and three other peacekeepers are on their way to your station by helicopter."

"We have a helicopter?"

"I have to go. Keep me in the loop."

"Yes, sir. Welcome home from your trip."

"Thanks!" The phone went dead.

He replaced the handset and looked into her eyes.

"How about we start over?" He extended his hand. "I'm Peacekeeper Sergeant Danny Casey, pleased to meet you."

Her demeanor softened and she nearly grinned. She took his hand and shook it.

"Call me Solare, Sergeant Danny Casey. I believe we are both on the same side."

"Yeah, we all work for Grisha. This is Trooper Sam Demientieff." They nodded at each other. "So, what have you discovered?"

"I need a cup of tea. Is that possible to obtain?"

"Absolutely. I'll put on the kettle. He went to the small hand pump next to the small sink and filled a teakettle. "We killed three of them yesterday."

"I know, I saw part of the fight. But the Boss got away, right?" Solare asked.

"Who?" Sam asked.

"He calls himself the Boss. I haven't yet discovered his real name." Solare gave Sam a slight smile.

"He's trying to take over the Alaska Republik?" Casey asked as he filled three cups with steaming water. "Do you take anything in your tea, Solare?"

"A dollop of honey if you have it. Yes, as near as I can deduce, he is working in league with the British to weaken what little cohesion we have up here."

"Are you from Alaska?" Sam asked.

"I am now."

"Me, too." Casey set down steaming mugs on the small table Sam had cleared of reports. He dropped into his chair and sighed. "By the way, Yukon Cassidy and three other troopers are on their way here."

"Did I hear you say *helicopter*?" Solare asked.

"Yeah. They should be here any time now."

"Okay. Here's what I think we should do—"

"Won't Cassidy be in charge of the operation?" Sam interrupted.

"Stay on my good side, Sam, and don't ever do that again." She gave him a level look before continuing. "I think we should divide the area up into sectors and search for–"

"Do what?"

Solare jumped in front of him and yelled into his face, "Don't *ever* fucking interrupt me; *that's* what!"

"Oh." Raising his eyebrows, Sam looked away and took a sip of tea.

"–and search for anything abandoned or rarely visited within a hundred meter radius."

"Of what?" Casey said, confusion clouding his face and mind.

"Of his cabin, of course."

"You know the location of his cabin?"

"Yes. But if he is at all intelligent, and I believe he is, he will be long gone by now. He will also leave a trap for anyone who finds his former hideout."

Casey opened his mouth and then squinted at the wall for a moment. "What kind of trap?"

"Nasty, as brutal as he can make it. Remember how frightened you said Ray and Strada were? There's a reason for that fear, and you don't want to test it. You want to outguess it."

He was beginning to really like her even if she did seem to be a step or two ahead of him all the damn time.

"Yeah, I think you're right." He pulled a out map of Fort Yukon and said, "We're *here*. Where's his cabin?"

She echoed his finger tap. "Right there."

"That damn close?" Sam said. "Shit!"

"So how would you handle the next steps?" Casey asked, staring into her off-green eyes.

The door flew open and Yukon Cassidy, panting as if he had completed a long race, stood in the door, his .45-.70 clutched in his fists. "Are you people okay?"

All three of them burst into laughter. Roland Delcambré pushed in past Cassidy and glanced around. He looked at his boss, "We can now stop with the running, *non*?"

"*Oui,*" Cassidy wheezed.

CHAPTER 36

CHENA,
ALASKA REPUBLIK

"That's the son-of-a-bitch," Mack said staring down at the corpse. "Who killed the murdering bastard?"

"A bounty hunter, name of Solare."

"How the hell did she beat me here? I sent her on a wild goose chase down in the FPN."

Lieutenant Alex Strom wisely kept his silence. *I wonder what this Solare is like.*

"Thank you, Alex. I appreciate the help. Now I can get on with the rest of my life."

"Do you have someplace to stay?" he asked. "Being new here and all."

Her eyebrows went up and he mentally hurtled through the possible connotations of his question and winced.

"No, I didn't mean it like *that!*"

"What *did* you mean?" She asked with a grin.

"There is an excellent roadhouse here in St. Anthony. The Peacekeepers rent a room there full time to house witnesses, traveling Peacekeepers, whoever. There's nobody scheduled for the room tonight and you can stay there if you wish. It even has a private bathroom."

"A bathroom! Alex, you really know the way to a girl's heart!"

"That's a good thing, right?" he asked, trying not to sound as totally at sea as he felt. He could tell she enjoyed his discomfort.

"Do they serve food?"

"Excellent food. Would you be my guest for dinner this evening?"

"Thank you, yes."

"So, what time—"

"Does that mean you have a key to this room?"

"Ah, yes, I do."

"May I have it?" She glanced at the clock on the wall. "Is that accurate?"

"Yeah," he said, handing her the key.

"Tell me where to find this place and call for me at seven."

He grinned. "Down this little street to the main road, and it's the fourth building on your right. It faces the Tanana River."

She winked at him. "I *definitely* have worked up an appetite."

CHAPTER 37

FORT YUKON,
ALASKA REPUBLIK

"You're sure that's the place with all the traffic?" Yukon queried.

"For the fourth fucking time, yes!" Solare hissed, daggering him with her eyes. She cursed herself for not reading the contract with Grisha more carefully. Never again would she agree to 'assume other duties as necessary'!

"Okay. Don't get pissy. My neck is the one on the block here, not yours."

"Don't tempt me, Cassidy!"

Cassidy, Solare, and Roland all sat on wood rounds behind a meter drop-off visually sheltered from the cabin in question by a clump of bushes. Dahlke and Bennett sat on the ground fighting to stay awake in the August sultry shade. Sergeant Casey and Trooper Demientieff manned the office.

"It's too quiet," Cassidy muttered.

She nodded. "For once I agree with you. There was a steady stream of people in and out of that door two days ago."

"Define steady."

"In the time we've all been sitting here, there would have been at least two people in and out. He's gone."

"I agree with you. But we have to find out for sure."

"Don't risk any lives, okay? If you have to go through the door, push it open with a very long pole."

Cassidy turned to his troopers. "Dahlke, Bennett, do a complete loop around this area. Stay out of sight of this cabin and warn off any pedestrians. We have no idea what we're going to find in there or what reaction we'll get."

"We're on it, Major," Dahlke said. They scrambled to their feet and hurried away.

"This isn't that big of a village," Roland said softly. "Why would someone planning the overthrow of a nation do it from *here*?"

Solare felt impressed. *The midget actually has a brain.*

"It's off the road system but on the river," Cassidy mused. "There's a military grade runway here, too. There are probably other cells out there, maybe even in Tanana and Chena."

"I followed Ferdinand Rochamboux from an equally quiet cabin on the edge of Chena," Solare said in a low voice. "He moved faster than I thought he would, or you would have never found his body down at Tanana Crossing."

"How long did it take for you to physically find him?" Cassidy asked.

"Two weeks. You found him less than an hour after I finally caught up with him. I thought he had been trying to elude me." She snorted.

"He didn't even know I was after him," she continued. "Whatever else the bastard was he was a good field agent until he got hooked up with the Boss. He ignored things he shouldn't, and that's what killed him, with my help of course."

"Wait a minute," Roland Delcambré said. "The two *hommes* we found at the lorry had Austrian gold. Lots of it."

"They *did?*" Solare blurted. She silently cursed herself for not examining the bodies more closely. *I'm learning too many new lessons this afternoon,* she thought.

Roland laughed. "Yes. *But* the point is this: the captured British commando said he was seeking the Boss. Rochamboux was working for the Boss. Why would he kill fellow operatives?"

Solare grinned. She had done much the same thing in less lethal situations.

"Because the Boss is working them from two sides. "He's buying the goods from one and then increasing the price before selling it to the other while posing as a factor between them."

Cassidy said, "How do the Austrians fit into this? Purely as salesmen?"

"That's an assumption–"

A man hurried up the small street, glancing back over his shoulder every fifth step.

"Not one of ours," Cassidy murmured.

"He's going to the cabin," Solare said. "He must not have gotten the word."

The man turned and ran to the door, pushed in.

"Get down, you idiots!" she yelled.

Cassidy and Roland hit the ground as the front of the cabin

exploded. Debris flew over them to smash into the neighboring buildings.

"Thanks," Cassidy said. "I think you just saved my life." There was something new in the way he looked at her, and she didn't like it.

"Road apples. You were already dropping before I said a word."

Roland jumped to his feet. "Come on you damn fools. We have to put out this fire!"

Flames raged through the structure and curled up to the roof from both wrecked windows and the shattered door. The town fire alarm went off and groups of people appeared. Three of them rode in a utility pulling a wagon comprised of nothing more than a tank on wheels.

As men and women hooked a hose to the tank. A generator racketed into action. Two men carried a large hose up from the Yukon itself and hooked to the other side of the tank. The racket changed pitch and river water shot out of the hose.

Universal consensus decided the cabin to be a total loss. They kept the fire from spreading rather than trying to put it out. Eventually the structure collapsed into a heap of debris and the firefighters saturated it. The stink of wet ashes hung in the air.

A middle-aged man came over to Cassidy.

"I'm John Bifeld, the village chief. Any idea what happened here?"

Cassidy shook the man's hand. "It's an honor and a pleasure, Chief Bifeld. So very few people know what a magnificent job you did of keeping the airfield operational and unnoticed in the early days of the resistance."

Bifeld grinned. "Hell, I'm surprised *you* know about that."

"I was aircrew, working for the US on some of the weapons drops."

"That have anything to do with this?" He nodded at the destroyed cabin.

"It might. Come on over to the office and I'll fill you in. I would have done it before now, but I just got this job and have been overwhelmed since."

Solare watched them walk away. While people were paying her no mind, she slipped away toward the river.

I think there's a tunnel under that cabin. I think it heads toward the only road in these parts; that big wet one down there.

CHAPTER 38

CHENA, ALASKA REPUBLIK

Lieutenant Alex Strom didn't know if he was in trouble or not. He had taken Mack to dinner. Then they had decided to have a couple drinks at the bar. Their dinner conversation had been more casual flirtation than actual personal information exchange.

She was easy to talk to, and he appreciated that. After comparing a few war stories, he realized she had seen as much shit as he had. He also realized he *really* liked her.

"What are you going to do now, Mack?" he'd said over a nearly empty pint glass.

"I have no reason to go south again. Jimmy's murderer is just as dead as he is."

"No other family?" Alex said.

"Somewhere down there I have a brother, but no idea where. Our parents both died in a car crash years ago. I hadn't planned two minutes past catching up with Rochamboux, so here I am."

"What do you think of our new little republik?"

"Little it ain't. Everything people down south takes for granted are luxuries up here. I understand it was even tougher under the czar."

"Wouldn't know," Alex said. "I was following an insane man around killing people he pointed at."

"Damn, you didn't have any trouble with that?"

"Yeah, I did. I had a lot more trouble finding work that didn't demand I ignore my humanity. It's a tough world out there. You know that."

"Yeah, I do know that. So why are you paying attention to me?" She grinned and sipped her drink.

That caught him off guard. He shrugged mentally and told her part of the truth.

"I'm a direct person. I try to be polite because it's part of the job. Sometimes those two things overlap and I usually just stick with direct. That's what I know best."

He hoped he hadn't pissed her off.

"So be direct, it beats lying or exaggerating."

"I think you would make a hell of a Peacekeeper and I really want to recruit you. You have resilience, aggressiveness, and a strong sense of honor. You would make a great Peacekeeper."

"What if I'm not interested?"

Alex grinned. "C'mon, you have to admit that a job offer is a good thing. I have no doubt of your abilities. You would be good at this."

Please, please don't say, no! he thought.

"Would I be working with you?"

"At first, then you might be transferred to another sector."

How far apart are the sectors?"

"It's all still being thrashed out."

"How far is the closest one?"

"Well, that would be–"

She leaned forward on her bar stool, grabbed his ears, pulled him toward her, and kissed him.

I think I'm in trouble! he thought, and then concentrated on what he was doing.

He pulled away, completely at sea.

"Did I just mess up my chances for a job by kissing you for rescuing me?" she asked.

Alex took a deep breath and grinned.

"No. Not this time. And for the record you're welcome."

CHAPTER 39

FORT YUKON, ALASKA REPUBLIK

S<small>OLARE HURRIED TOWARDS THE RIVER</small>. Every north-south lane in the village ended there. Still slow at this point in its descent to the sea, the Yukon River appeared to be an inland ocean populated with brush-filled islands large and small.

Thickets of brush and small trees extended to river's edge and sheltered the many landing places for boats. The bank dropped gradually to the water and Solare didn't think a tunnel could end any closer than the last line of buildings bordering the village. The brush muffled sound as well as hemmed in one's view.

She found a large log high on the bank left by a previous flood and settled down into a cleft offering a view of the long bank. A close examination of the nearby buildings didn't reveal any clues. A number of boats lay near various cabins, most of which were turned over and looked heavy enough to require two strong people to right them.

One boat suddenly lifted as if by magic, revealing a man who poked his head up from a hole and looked around.

Alarms went off in her brain. *People as clever as these seem to be wouldn't just pop up in broad daylight without–*

She sensed movement behind her and, before she was able to move, a stunning blow knocked her senseless.

✪

Roland Delcambré glanced around. Cassidy and Chief Bifeld minutely discussed the situation while Sam Demientieff carefully cleaned his rifle. Dahlke and Bennett leaned drowsing against the outside wall. Casey sat behind his desk and listened to the conversation.

Where the hell is Solare?

Roland repeated the question out loud.

Cassidy looked up, irritation writ large on his face, and then he grinned. "How the hell would I know? Go find out what she's up to."

Roland hurried out the door before Cassidy could change his mind. He had long ago realized that in a new situation Cassidy tended to speak first but reconsider quickly. The first time would state the obvious course. The second time would be tempered by a variety of second thoughts that only impeded the solution.

Roland stopped and regarded the smoking ruins of the cabin, trying to see it as Solare would. A number of villagers stood chatting and staring at the destruction. Roland wondered who owned the building.

"She said there was always someone in the cabin." He tended to think out loud when alone. "If they could manage to stay hidden for any amount of time, they would need a way to escape. These people were arrogant, but not stupid."

He regarded the smoldering cabin floor.

It's too hot to check, but I know it's there. Where would it lead?

Pivoting to his left he saw, not more than a hundred meters away, the wide Yukon River sliding past in its eternal journey to the Behring Sea. He hurried toward the river, knew there existed many access points to the water, but would bet on the most direct to be his goal.

I hope this is the same path she took. The thought nearly brought him to a halt. *What do I care about that arrogant wench?* He answered himself. *She's a peacekeeper, idiot.*

He reached the bank and glanced about. Where the next street over ended at water's edge three men awkwardly carried a body over the runneled beach toward a boat being held by a fourth person. Roland felt positive the inert form was Solare.

He cursed himself for not bringing his rifle. All he had was the Yankee Colt .45 revolver on his hip. He jerked it free of the holster and using both hands aimed at the man holding the boat.

Thank the deity he's standing still.

The revolver recoiled when he fired, and the man shouted in pain and collapsed into the aluminum river boat. The boat began to drift out toward the main channel. Delcambré cocked the weapon again and watched as the men dropped Solare and ran toward their salvation.

One stopped, turned, and leveled a rifle at Roland. He dropped behind a clump of brush as the round cracked over his head as the accompanying report echoed out across the Yukon. He jumped up to see all four men in the boat as the motor roared to life and they curved out into the wide river, heading west with the current.

Out of range.

In moments he knelt next to a moaning Solare. A quick inspection found blood and matted hair at the back of her head. He still wore his canteen and pulled it out to rinse off the damaged area. He didn't seem chilled anymore.

"Wha, who…" she slurred.

"Be still for a change, *mon ami*. Allow me to minister to your wound." He spoke gently, knowing that loud noises would increase her pain.

She blinked and started to shake her head.

"Ah, *fuck!* That hurts!"

"Someone hit you with something very hard," Roland said in a low, soothing voice. "Give me some moments and I will have you back to your acerbic self."

"No time!" she said and tried to stand. "They'll get away."

She would have fallen on her face if he hadn't caught her and lowered her to the ground.

"I regret to inform you they have already departed Fort Yukon. If you can squint you might see them rounding the first large island out there. They were trying to take you with them."

Solare stared into the distance, then shifted her gaze to his face. "You *rescued* me, Delcambré?"

"That is so. I cannot lie."

"Oh great. There goes my reputation." She moaned and held her head in her hands for a moment before looking up at him. "Thank you, Roland. I owe you one."

He shrugged. "You would have done the same for me, *non*?"

"*Oui*," she tried to smile. "But I probably wouldn't have been as nice about it. I *do* know my limits."

The air chilled and the sky slowly filled with gray, moisture-pregnant clouds.

An open top utility roared up. Cassidy, Casey, Sam, and Chief Bifeld jumped out, weapons in hand.

"Roland, what happened here?" Cassidy said as he hurried over. "We heard gunfire."

"I think I killed one of the men who were trying to abduct Solare."

"Solare?" Cassidy said glancing at her. "Why did they try to do that?"

She held up her hand and they helped her into the utility. "Take me back to the office. I need tea and whisky. Now that it's too late, I'll explain everything."

CHAPTER 40

TANANA, ALASKA REPUBLIK

General Grisha Grigorievich and Sergeant Major Tobias burst into the headquarters portion of the hospital.

"Somebody update me!" Grisha yelled. He hurried down the corridor to their quarters and burst into living room. The apartment sat empty.

"Omigawd!" he blurted and rushed down the corridor to the medical unit.

A nurse looked up in alarm when he came through the door.

"General–"

"Where is she?"

In the delivery room!" she pointed down the hall.

He ran to the door and stopped, breathing heavily. He didn't want to cause alarm. He pushed into the room.

"It's about damn time you got here!" Wing shouted from her bed. "Get over here and hold my hand!"

A nurse and a doctor were peering anxiously under the sheet draped over Wing's elevated legs. Her mother sat on the far side of the bed and an empty chair waited on the side closest to him. The smell of viscera surprised him.

How did she know I would get here in time?

He went to the bed and grasped her wet hand. Sweat covered her face and dampened her gown.

"When did the contractions start?" he asked, trying to sound knowledgeable.

"Ha–half an hour ago."

"Right after her water broke," Eleanor said, and smiled.

"Did the conference with the Tlingit Peacekeepers pan out?" Wing asked as her eyes flicked over his face and she suddenly knotted up and grimaced. "Oh, *damn* that hurts!"

He waited until she relaxed. "Yes. We have a growing force of Peacekeepers in Sea Alaska Province. My cousin Piotr is the colonel in charge. I so loved giving him rank, even if he was a shit when we were kids."

"Why would you reward that kind of attitude?" Wing asked between shudders.

"He and his brother made me mad enough to show them what I could achieve. So, I joined the Troika Guard. It's all been a sleigh ride from there."

Wing laughed and immediately went rigid in pain.

"Doctor," snapped the nurse peering under the sheet, "she's at ten centimeters and I see the head!"

The doctor dropped the chart he had been reading and hurried over.

Grisha didn't remember seeing this man before and wanted to ask about his credentials but time had run out.

Wing shuddered, squeezed her eyes shut, and screamed, "Auuggg! That hurts, dammit!"

"You have to push, Wing!" the doctor said in an urgent, commanding tone.

Grisha wondered if she would argue. He knew his wife well.

"I'm, trying!" She became rigid and arched her back." Ahh, ahh, fuck! Damn that hurts!"

"Push hard, dammit!" the doctor yelled. "Now, right now! Push!"

Wing audibly ground her teeth and her face clenched shut. "Uuunnng!"

"I have the head," the doctor said to the nurse. "Get the disinfectants ready!"

The nurse looked at the doctor and Grisha had to turn his head away to keep from laughing at her expression.

"Doctor, everything was ready before you came into the room."

"Sorry," he said. "This is my first delivery."

"What!" Grisha, Eleanor, and Wing simultaneously shouted.

"That did it!" Silence reigned for a long moment, then a thin squall broke the quiet.

Wing relaxed into the bed, tears running down her face. "We did it, Grisha. We did it!"

He leaned over and kissed her, said gently, "You did most of it."

She opened her eyes and gave him a feral grin. "And I'll never let you forget that!"

The doctor cleared his throat. "General, Colonel, would you like to meet your daughter?"

He laid the impossibly tiny, wrapped form on Wing's breast.

"Have you decided on a name? Eleanor asked.

"Yes" Grisha said. "This is Cora."

CHAPTER 41

OVER THE YUKON RIVER,
ALASKA REPUBLIK

"There are so many places to look all at once," Georgi complained. "And I'm worried about the weather that's moving in!"

"Stick to your sector, Captain Fedorov," Cassidy snapped. "And stop chatting!"

In the pilot's seat Captain Ivan Fedorov grinned at his brother. Georgi *always* talked incessantly when he was nervous or excited. He had since they were boys. Ivan enjoyed having someone else tell him to shut up for a change.

Ivan held the helicopter to two hundred meters above the widespread and meandering Yukon River as they slowly flew west-southwest searching for the riverboat filled with criminals.

That's what Major Cassidy called them, he thought. He wondered why they had tried to kill the Peacekeepers. *If it were me, I would merely avoid them.*

"I see something at four o'clock," Sergeant Casey said. He lifted binoculars to his face for a moment before letting them drop on his chest again. "Never mind. It's just a log."

Roland Delcambré searched the shore for sign. "How can they disappear like that? There is no place to go, is there?"

"How much fuel do we have, Captain Fedorov?" Cassidy asked.

"Enough to fly another hundred kilometers before going somewhere to refuel."

"Take us down to a hundred meters above the water."

"*Da!*"

The helicopter rolled to starboard and went into a wide spiral. Ivan grinned as the audible distress increased over the intercom.

"Not so damn fast, please!" Delcambré growled.

"I'll second that!" Cassidy said. "Unless you want to spend hours cleaning up back here."

Ivan slowed the decent. He didn't enjoy pulling the noses of non-aviators enough to spend time cleaning up their vomit. They always puked all over everything. He slowed some more.

He glanced at his brother. Georgi's face held a wide smile and Ivan knew he was inwardly laughing at all of them. He leveled out above the river and flew as slowly as he could.

"Which direction do you wish us to go?"

"Go back toward Fort Yukon. This is the perfect speed, by the way. Well done."

Cassidy's words perked up Ivan. "Thank you."

Georgi rolled his eyes and stared out at his sector.

✪

"They are returning at much lower altitude, Boss!"

The man wearing a thick mesh mosquito hat and dressed in black motioned the others back into the heavy brush.

"You've covered the boat completely, so they won't see anything. Bring Rosaine's body back to the trees."

"Are we going to bury him, Boss?" Selkirk asked, slapping a mosquito.

Rasputin snickered. "So that someone may find him? We leave him out in the open. In five days, there will be nothing left except his skull and a few bones. With any luck those will be carried off by animals." Mosquitos flew around him but didn't land.

Selkirk stared at the small dark man with horror writ large on his face.

"What if it had been *you* that was killed?"

"I would expect nothing less than this. There's nothing in there anymore. His spirit has gone to the bardo."

"Enough!" hissed the boss. "Get down."

The helicopter flew past less than two hundred meters away from their hiding place at an excruciatingly low speed. Sunlight flashed off the windows as well as the lenses of binoculars.

"Everyone freeze! Don't make any motion at all," Boss ordered.

The helicopter moved on up river.

"Wait until we can't see them—then they can't see *us*."

"How long do we stay here, Boss?" Rasputin asked.

"Until three hours after we hear no more motors of any kind. They do not have unlimited fuel or endurance. They all have to sleep."

"D'ya want I take first watch?" Selkirk asked, waving mosquitos away from his face.

"No," Boss said. "I'll take the first watch, you take second, and Rasputin will take third if needed."

"Aye." Selkirk pulled a ground cloth from his knapsack, lay down on a patch of sphagnum moss, and rolled the ground cloth around him to sleep and escape the desperate mosquitos.

Rasputin glanced at the spindly trees and went five meters away from the already snoring Selkirk. After surveying his surroundings carefully, he leaned against his knapsack and closed his eyes.

Boss moved his gaze across the horizon and back. He wondered if they had hung Riordan yet. He hoped so.

CHAPTER 42

TANANA,
ALASKA REPUBLIK

G̲r̲i̲s̲h̲a̲ ̲a̲m̲b̲l̲e̲d̲ ̲i̲n̲t̲o̲ ̲t̲h̲e̲ ̲l̲a̲r̲g̲e̲ ̲c̲o̲n̲f̲e̲r̲e̲n̲c̲e̲ ̲r̲o̲o̲m̲ in the hospital. He felt a bit out of place since history was in the process of being made. He occasionally came by to briefly bear witness. Fifty-five people sent here by their constituents were hammering out the ratification of the Alaska Republik Constitution.

Deliberative yes: quiet no.

"We don't have adequate communications to unite a land as diverse and huge as Alaska!" a delegate yelled at the moderator. "A vice president from both areas could advise the president on all national matters."

"Advise, or would he have to sit and arbitrate spats between two people of equal political power? That's not a good solution, sir. If we trust a person enough to make them First Speaker then we should allow them to do the job."

"What if the wrong person gets elected?" a woman asked. "Do we just allow a dictatorship to take over?"

Grisha quietly left the balcony where no more than a dozen visitors watched or recorded the proceedings. He pulled out his pocket watch and realized he had two minutes to get to Pelagian's office. He all but ran through his boss' door.

"Grisha! You're on time. I am deeply impressed. When Magda was born I didn't know the time of day for over two months in the beginning. How is little Cora?"

"Thank you, Mr. First Speaker. I admit to a good deal of distraction. Cora is beautiful and demanding, takes after her mother." He dropped into the chair in front of Pelagian's desk, and allowed himself to relax.

"What do we know about the lorry full of missiles at Tanana

Crossing, as well as the situation in Fort Yukon?" Pelagian asked.

"Less than I'd like at this point." *So much for relaxation!* He related events in Fort Yukon, ending with, "Six Peacekeepers are on the job. I expect results soon."

"Do you want to keep our pact with Captain Rawls?" Pelagian asked. Grisha found his face completely unreadable. Something he had never encountered.

"You mean let him go? Hell no. He stays until we have this Boss person in the cell next to him. I want to listen to the conversation."

Does the First Speaker want to release this man? he wondered.

"I have received intelligence that we might have more than the British to worry about."

"The Freekorps has been neutralized," Grisha said, and thought fast, but could only respond with, "Who else is there?"

"We border on two countries besides British Canada."

"That leaves French Canada." He hesitated before continuing. "Or the First People's Nation. I cannot fathom considering the FPN an enemy."

"Nor can I. However, I've noticed that one of our dead men had a very French name."

"That's true, Pelagian. However, I know a lot of good people with French names from here to T'angass and none of them are traitors. Some are Peacekeepers."

"I'm not saying they all are traitors. I'm saying a spy or provocateur made the mistake of pissing off too many people."

"Rochamboux was a thief and a killer. He ambushed and killed two men carrying Austrian gold. They were driving a lorry full of modern weapons. As far as we know he acted out of greed, not patriotism or sectionalism of any sort. Unless he was being paid by the French."

"Dammit, Grisha, quit pissing on my boots." Pelagian grinned. "I think you are correct, old friend. Why would the French get involved this far north?"

"Territory, domination," Grisha said. "If they had Alaska Republik, they would effectively wall off British Canada from the rest of North America. I hope the British aren't insane enough to piss off the Republic of California."

"I hope you're right about that. I already gave you a raise this month, didn't I?"

"I don't want a raise. I want to find the people messing with our new nation. I no longer pledge my life to just any flashy outfit."

CHAPTER 43

ARAF AERODROME, TANANA, ALASKA REPUBLIK

"Cadets, follow me!" Lieutenant Colonel Yamato said over his intercom as he went to full power and released the brakes on *Satori*. He lifted into the bright Alaskan sky and glanced out over the landscape in appreciation. Thousands of birch trees sported gold leaves and contrasted with the dark firs and evergreens creating a stunning landscape.

The Yukon ribboned out ahead of him and he checked to left and right before making a wide swing to the north and circling back over the eight aircraft struggling to achieve formation.

"Form on me," he ordered. "Remember, this is more than a training flight. We're also searching for bad guys."

Nine comm clicks signaled understanding.

"As soon as we pass Beaver, we will commence searching the Yukon for any boats with three or four people in them. Our quarry is armed and dangerous. You all have live ammo, so be careful. Keep in mind that with one exception every boat we see will be citizens of the Republik and maybe even kin or friends."

Jerry Yamato flew lead, Major Marx flew two thousand feet above everyone else to monitor the situation, and Major Merritt followed at the rear of the flight. Jerry switched frequencies and radioed Tanana.

"Search Flight One to Control. Do we have any further traffic from Major Cassidy?"

"Negative, Search Flight One. Will inform you if situation changes."

"Roger, out."

He switched to the instructor's frequency.

"We still have nothing from the Peacekeeper end of things. I thought we were out here to assist *them*."

"They had a long day yesterday, Boss," Aisha said. "Perhaps they got a late start."

"We had to do a training flight anyway," Major Marx said. "I love flying over the Yukon. It's so serene. There's the village of Beaver if I'm not mistaken."

"Okay, I'm going to take them down," Jerry said. He switched to the training frequency. "Search Flight One, follow me."

He put *Satori* into a shallow dive and dropped to 300 meters above the river.

"Spread out. Maintain station. Be aware of your wingman."

The flight buzzed over a six-meter riverboat and the two surprised occupants waved madly. The river seemed vacant of any other traffic. Jerry knew they wouldn't be able to search the riverbanks at their speed. The fall day promised a clear sky and temperatures near 60°F while the sun shone.

He missed sitting out at night, drinking beer, and talking with friends. In Alaska Republik once the sun went down the air chilled. *No sweaty nights in the Land of the Midnight Sun!*

Perfect flying conditions, Jerry thought. *The cadets should all be fine.*

CHAPTER 44

ON THE YUKON RIVER, ALASKA REPUBLIK

Boss and his men watched the Eurekas fly past. Selkirk and Rasputin shrank down even more, eyes wide with fear.

"They can't see us," he said and spat to the side.

"Yeah," Selkirk snorted. "Mebbe not, but I remember what one of those fuckers did to us last winter. They d'nay have ta see us ta kill us. I lost me best mate."

"He's probably up there right now," N'Go said grimly. "I'd love to shoot one of those bastards down."

"Why don't we?" Selkirk asked, his eyes gleaming.

Rasputin gave the Scotsman a contemptuous sneer. "Because if we did, they'd kill us all, you fooking idiot."

"Aye, they probably would now that I stop and think about it."

Rasputin watched the planes disappear to the east. "Boss, what do you want to do now?" He slapped at a mosquito.

"Move farther back into the brush and make a cold camp. We'll use jellied fuel for cooking. Pull the boat up the bank and into the trees, then cover it with anything that makes it look like the rest of the forest."

"Yes, sir," Rasputin said. "I thought the ROC squadron left Alaska."

"I shared that misconception. However, I didn't see the California Bear rondels on any of the fuselages. Perhaps this is a new addition to the problem."

"You didn't hear anything about this before they let you go?"

"*Obviously* not." Boss let his tone go glacial. *Rasputin always has to push the parameters.*

He helped them drag the boat up into the brush and cover it. He stood watching the river while his men built camp. Traveling in the dark would be a dubious proposition. The Yukon hid death traps in the form of sunken trees that bobbed just under the surface.

Hit one of those preachers and we're all dead. The water temperature can't be more than 40°F.

His thoughts went darker than the night. Years ago, Riordan had ordered them to attack a military post that he had erroneously believed to be a simple laager and trading post down in the FPN. At that point Boss knew he needed to have an exit from the International Freekorps. Fortunately, he had previously groomed a lieutenant to help him create that alternative.

Rasputin hailed from West Africa just like himself. His grasp of English hadn't been all that good in the beginning but his loyalty to Boss and extra money proved exemplary. Both Rosaine and Selkirk were likewise recruited. Rasputin's quick grasp of English worried him.

Trying to kill Danny Casey hadn't bothered him. Casey had turned him down when he tried to recruit him for his "special squad". At that point Boss knew one day he would have to eliminate the short-tempered Irishman.

I'm pissed that I didn't already succeed. Maybe next time.

He had recognized Delcambré back there on the bank of the Yukon. He knew the little bastard was a good shot with a rifle, but he hadn't dreamed he could shoot that well with a .45 revolver. Of his three men Rosaine was easily the most expendable.

That's why he was holding the boat, he mused with a sardonic grin.

Not once had he regretted bailing on Riordan. After all, the man had abandoned the majority of his men. *Except for me: he needed me more than I needed him. He's still in jail and I'm not.*

Once again he hoped they had hung Riordan. The son of a bitch deserved it.

Two P-61s flew over them, heading back to their base. No sooner had the sound of their engines faded when he heard the beat of rotors moving toward them. His adrenaline spiked.

"Get under cover. Make sure none of our gear can be seen from above. If they see anything suspicious here, we'll all be dead."

All three of them huddled in their camouflaged hides as the rotors thundered toward them.

CHAPTER 45

CHENA,
ALASKA REPUBLIK

"*W*HERE THE HELL AM I BEING POSTED?" Mack MacDonald shouted.

"Tanana Crossing, and it's considered impolite for a trooper to shout at a lieutenant."

"Isn't that where that litt–"

"Sergeant Fred Langbein is currently station chief there, but he's being transferred to Tanana. You will be working with Sergeant Bekai Konteh, the new station chief."

"Sounds African."

"He is. You have a problem with that?"

"No more than with any other man. Besides, who am I to make judgmental remarks about skin color? Are there any women station chiefs?"

"Yeah, down river in Nulato."

"How far is that from here?"

"About 300 miles in a straight line."

"I'll go nuts in a little place like Tanana Crossing."

"This isn't happening right away, Mack. You've got to get through three months training here first. Who knows, things might change."

"Isn't Tanana the capital of the Republic?"

"At the moment, yes. That's just it, everything in Alaska Republik is in flux. We're all making stuff up as we go along."

"Then why do I have to transfer somewhere else after training? For that matter, when does the training start?"

"Grisha said something about 'allocation of personnel' to places where not many people are signing up. As for your second question, you're already an expert in field work so the training is less physical and more mental."

"You're full of shit."

"You're not supposed to speak to officers like that, Trainee!"

"Okay. You're full of shit, *Lieutenant*."

"Trooper MacKenzie, you are out of line. Do you hear other troopers speak to me like you do?"

"No, sir. I don't."

"So why do you?"

"Because I see you as an equal, not a superior. That's not meant to be a negative attitude, sir."

"No," he said slowly, "I can see that."

She had a strange glint in her eyes. He wondered if she was going to quit. He hoped not because he really liked her.

"I apologize for my attitude, Lieutenant Strom."

He grinned. "I keep forgetting how independent you are, and have been for a long time. Probably longer than I've actually been completely independent."

"You're not going to sack me?"

"Hell, no! I would be stupid to do that."

"Good to know. I'll try to work on my professional discipline."

"I can't ask for more than that." *Well, I can, but I won't.*

CHAPTER 46

OVER THE YUKON RIVER, ALASKA REPUBLIK

"They've got to be down there," Sergeant Danny Casey said, peering through binoculars. Nobody heard him over the engine and rotor noise in the cabin.

Sixteen people besides him surveyed the slowly moving land and river beneath them. A cold draft of air flowed through the cabin and kept everyone chilled. He watched a large piece of brush-covered bank fall into the river and slowly move downstream.

The inclusion of twelve trainee Dená Rangers and their three drill instructors bolstered the mission. Any time now Major Cassidy and Captain Delcambré would come downstream in a riverboat with at least three more searchers.

We're going to find this son-of-a-bitch, Casey swore to himself. *Using Fort Yukon as a base of operations limits his avenues of escape. It doesn't make sense.*

The helicopter slowed and hovered over a meadow. The drill instructors finished rigging up to a winch on the overhead of the compartment. One instructor lectured while her two subordinates demonstrated the machinery.

The sloping aft deck of the helicopter yawned open and more cold air whipped into the cabin. Casey was happy he had worn his parka. Two of the trainees walked backward to the lip of the open deck ramp, stepped off, and disappeared.

He tried to ignore the training even though he was intensely interested in the procedure. Many years ago, he qualified for ranger training in the U.S. Army but hadn't gotten far. Not for the first time he wondered how his life would have been different if he hadn't tried to kill his lieutenant.

Riordan hadn't had any helicopters but he had money for people with military training. Casey shook his head and peered out of the window. The sun reflected off the Yukon and numerous small lakes and ponds.

This whole country looks like a sponge from up here. Movement upriver caught his eye and he quickly lifted his binoculars to discern Major Cassidy and Delcambré in a long, aluminum riverboat with three other people. He wondered if Solare was with them.

Cassidy had told him that he and Roland would do a careful search as they went downriver to Tanana. Cassidy had other irons in the fire he had to deal with. Casey knew they would do a careful search.

"You're getting distracted, Sergeant!" he said aloud to himself. With all the cabin noise he wasn't worried about being overheard. He glanced back at the trainee group.

Only four remained in the aircraft. The rest were already on the ground or descending a rope. Master Sergeant Searby motioned the last two trainees out as he watched.

Without hesitation they backed out of the lowered ramp and dropped from sight. Searby and Staff Sergeant Burnett removed their headsets, secured them to the bulkhead, and followed their people to the ground. Two minutes later the winch whined into motion and retracted the rappel ropes. Soon the hatch lifted against the fuselage and clicked into place.

The lack of cold wind created the illusion of warmth in the cabin. With the rangers deployed the helicopter slowly followed the river. One of the crazy Russian pilots yelled at him, motioned him to put on his headset. Giving him thumbs up, Casey obeyed.

"We have information from troops on ground!" one of them said.

"How–"

"Sergeant Casey, this is Searby on the ground." Her clipped voice carried all the softness of a saw blade.

"Yes, Master Sergeant Searby."

"We found their laager, but they're gone. No fire to check. Took everything with them except their slit trench."

"So, there's no way to figure out how long they have been on the river."

"Affirmative. Pilot Captain Fedorov, please return to the meadow and land. Keep your rotors turning and drop the ramp. We will all load in under a minute."

"As you say, Master Sergeant," Ivan boomed loud enough to make Casey wince. He thought the cloud cover was lowering and hoped a storm didn't move in while they were still airborne.

He wasn't enamored of flying to begin with.

CHAPTER 47

TANANA, ALASKA REPUBLIK

"Excuse me, miss. Can you direct me to a store or trading post?"

Solare, leaning against a store front, looked up from her notebook and tapped her pencil on her teeth. Tanana wasn't all that big and she had never seen this man before. He was attractive enough that she would have remembered him.

Big, sure of himself, practiced liar, and he thinks I'm stupid. She grinned. *This might be fun.*

"There's a small food market just down the street there. You must have passed it at least once."

His grin didn't waver. "Yeah, I saw that one. I thought there might be another."

"Are you collecting them?"

"No. I'm looking for work." His grin sagged into a smile.

"Store clerk?"

"Mechanic."

"To my knowledge, most food stores don't require mechanics."

His arrogance abruptly fled, and he glanced around. "Storekeepers usually know what's happening. I'm sorry to have bothered you, ma'am." He turned away.

"I do know where they need a mechanic, but it's not a food store."

He turned and looked at her, wariness writ large in his eyes. "Where?"

"Over at the aerodrome."

"Who would I ask to see about the job?"

"Ask for Sergeant Major Tobias." She put a touch of honey into her voice.

"Do you live here?" he asked.

"I live where I choose. Where do you live?"

He shrugged and glanced around. "Nowhere right now. I'm traveling."

"What's your name?"

"Ba—, uh, Babcock. Bill Babcock. What's yours?"

"Sally. Such a silly name I always thought."

"No," he grinned. "Not at all."

"Where are you from, Bill Babcock?"

"Massachusetts, a long time ago. Where you from?"

"Iowa."

"What are the odds, two U.S. natives meeting on a village street in Russian Amerika?"

"I believe they call it Alaska Republik these days."

"Yeah, for the moment." He shrugged again and glanced around.

He's looking for something in particular. A person? Is he another bounty hunter?

Her smile dimmed and she allowed a tiny frown as she considered his response. "I don't understand. What do you mean, 'for the moment'?"

Babcock's obvious incipient lust instantly evaporated, and fear briefly flashed in his eyes. "Turn of phrase. New republiks are usually pretty unstable, right?"

"Interesting observation, sir. What have you seen that seems unstable?"

He glanced around and shrugged. "The lack of troops here in the capitol for one thing."

"They won their independence from Russia. Why do they need an army now?"

"You wouldn't understand," he said in a tone as mocking as his smile.

He's no drifter. I would tag him as a mercenary. He hasn't missed any meals, so he's a working mercenary. She frowned at him.

"Why on earth would you say that?"

He grinned. "You're from *Iowa*."

"You're the one wandering around asking stupid questions, Mr. Massachusetts. Try me. Answer my question. With your help I'm sure I'll figure it out." She struggled to keep her tone lighthearted and not shatter his larynx.

"Look, I'm sorry I said anything at all. I–"

"Why does the Republik need an army?" she snapped, her voice sharp and menacing before she could rein it in.

Babcock turned and walked quickly in the other direction.

"Dumb shit. This could have been easy!" She wasn't sure whom she was talking to as she sprinted after him. Just as she closed, he twisted around into a defensive stance.

Karate? she wondered as she leaped up on a bench, pushed herself higher, and came down on his head with her left foot. She suspected he was slow to react to her charge because until it was too late, he thought she would stop.

"Dumb shit!" she yelled and kicked him in the head. He collapsed on the boardwalk. She landed on her feet and glanced around.

They had attracted an audience. Solare pointed to a young boy.

"Would you please go find a Peacekeeper and bring them here?"

With a nod the kid ran off.

"I think this man is a spy," she said to the other five people gathered around. "The Peacekeepers will figure it out." One man walked away, three women and a man stayed to watch. Tanana lacked entertainment.

Solare looked down at Babcock. *Whom do you serve? It can't be the British, and I know it isn't the International Freekorps.* Someone ran toward her and when she saw it was Cassidy, she grinned.

CHAPTER 48

PEACEKEEPER STATION, TANANA, ALASKA REPUBLIK

"Why'd you have to kick him so hard?" Delcambré said as he put a dressing on the prisoner's head. Now that he had finished stitching up the tear across the man's scalp, Roland wanted to know who he was.

They hadn't been back in the office from their trip more than an hour when a kid breathlessly reported that a lady was killing a man down the street. Cassidy had laughed and said, "It has to be Solare."

"He was going to hurt me, so I hurt him first." Solare gave Delcambré a hard look. "Do you always wait for the other guy to swing first?"

"Of course, he doesn't," Cassidy said from the other side of the table where he held down the man's shoulders. "Roland has his knife out before the other guy knows he's in a fight."

"Why didn't you take him to the hospital instead of here at your station?"

"Because the doctor wouldn't allow me to question the prisoner until he had gotten some rest. I don't believe we have that luxury."

Roland nodded in agreement and held the smelling salts under the man's nose.

"I already know his name," Solare said.

"You do?" both men said in unison.

The prisoner twisted away from the vial and shook his head once before going very still.

Solare started to say something, and Cassidy held his hand lightly against her mouth.

"We know you're awake. You might as well stop pretending."

"His name is Babcock, and he thinks I'm stupid," Solare said in a flat tone around the side of Cassidy's hand.

Babcock's eyes opened and he stared at her. "I was the stupid one, and I know it. Now can I leave?"

"Not until you answer my question."

He continued staring at her. "What question?"

"Why do you think Alaska Republik needs an army here and now?"

"That's not what I–"

"You inferred it, mister! Now answer before I kick in the other side of your head!"

Babcock's eyes wandered over to Delcambré. "She can't do that, can she?"

"She's already done it once, *homme*. Do you require a second demonstration?"

"I mean, can she do that *legally*?"

Cassidy pressed a bit harder on Babcock's shoulders.

"We're still working out all the legalities of the Republik at this point. I'm Chief Peacekeeper and I don't have a problem with it. Who are you and what are you doing here?"

"I'm a mechanic looking for work!" Babcock's voice nearly went shrill. "She attacked me."

"You're either a spy or an active mercenary, perhaps both," Solare spat. "Either one will get you a rope in Alaska Republik. Am I correct, gentlemen?"

Delcambré nodded in unison with Cassidy. *She's quick on her mental feet,* he thought.

Babcock paled and clamped his mouth shut. A tear slid from the corner of his right eye down across his cheek.

He thinks we are going to kill him no matter what, Roland realized.

"Unless he cooperates with us, of course," Roland suggested.

"That is a possibility," Cassidy said, still holding down Babcock's shoulders.

"Okay, I admit it. You're a good-looking woman and I wanted to get chummy. I pulled that comment out of my ass trying to break the ice with you. I don't give a crap if you people have an army or not. I'm looking for work, and I end up with my head kicked in by a *fille*. What else can I say?"

"He's convincing, isn't he?" Cassidy said.

"His eyes say he is not telling us the truth," Delcambré muttered.

"What's wrong with you people?" Babcock shouted.

"Let's send him down to the prison in Chena for a month," Delcambré said.

"Do what you want. I'm not saying another word." Babcock's mouth snapped shut.

Solare snickered.

"I'm going to let you up," Cassidy said. "You're going to walk back to that cell and sit down. If you try anything exotic you'll get hurt. Understand?"

Babcock nodded and winced in pain.

Cassidy released his shoulders and Babcock slowly sat up. Cassidy saw him eye the door on the other side of Solare before rolling off the table and shuffling to the cell.

Delcambré grinned at Solare. Cassidy hoped the damn fool wouldn't make a pass at her. He had enough on his hands as it was. He locked the cell.

"You really should let me go," Babcock said easily.

"Why?" Cassidy asked.

"Because you're making a fatal mistake keeping me in here."

"How could jailing an itinerant mechanic be a fatal mistake?" Roland asked.

"I'll tell you after it's too late to save your ass," Babcock sneered.

Cassidy picked up the telephone and dialed three numbers.

"This is Major Cassidy. I need to speak to General Grigorievich or First Speaker Haroldsson immediately! We don't have time for niceties, Corporal. If you value your job and your life, connect me to one of those men, now!"

Both Solare and Delcambré stared at him as if he had suddenly sprouted horns.

"Pelagian, this is Yukon Cassidy. The capitol is in danger of coming under attack any time between now and two days from now."

"Do I—of *course* I really believe that. Someone wants to do the Republik great harm. I don't know who, or why, yet," he shot Babcock a murderous look, "but I will soon. In the meantime, get hold of whoever is in charge of the garrison and put them on alert around Doyon House."

The others could hear the First Speaker's voice from across the room.

"I'll do it. But if this turns out to be a waste of time—"

"Pelagian, my friend, have I *ever* bullshitted you? Of course not. I truly feel this is an immediate threat that could change our young history for the worse. Perhaps end it."

The voice on the other end of the line lowered.

"I have no idea how many. I just know they are a real and immediate threat. Get the Dená Rangers back here as quick as humanly possible, okay?"

✪

Cassidy put the phone on the cradle. He stood and walked back to the cell, pulled up a chair and sat.

"This is official. I believe you are a spy for a belligerent. I don't know why your people are a threat, but I *know* that is what we are facing." He glanced at Solare and Delcambré and frowned.

I wish they were not here to witness my actions, he thought. He turned back to Babcock.

"Your group represents a direct threat to me and a lot of people I *deeply* care about. I would be derelict in my oath to the Alaska Republik if I did not do *everything* and *anything* to secure its safety and future." Cassidy leaned over and glared at the prisoner. "You have *one* minute to tell me what I want to know, or I am going to maim you for life."

Babcock glanced at Delcambré and Solare before refocusing on Cassidy.

"I can't tell you anything! I don't know—"

Cassidy looked at his two subordinates. "I want both of you to leave this area. Right now."

"Mon ami," Roland said. "You cannot—"

"I said leave now."

They both looked into his eyes and Solare shuddered.

"C'mon, Roland, you really don't need to see this." She walked out the door.

Roland frowned, looked from Cassidy to Babcock and back again. He followed Solare and the outer door shut with a slam behind them.

Cassidy pulled out his skinning knife and put the key in the cell lock with deadly determination evident on his face.

"Wait!" Babcock screamed. "I'll tell you!"

"You'll tell me what?"

"I am a member of the Phantom Legion. We're all specially trained French Foreign Legionnaires. They'll kill me for telling you."

"Why are you here?"

"We have a mission. That's all I know."

"You were sent by the French government?"

"I have no idea. Only the *capitaine* knows. We do what he says." He put his hand to the bandage on his head and winced before pulling his hand away.

"How many of you are there?"

Babcock hesitated and Cassidy loudly turned the key in the lock, and pushed the cell door open.

"Sixty, including me." Babcock fell back on the cot, a stricken look on his face. "Jesus, I am going to die for this."

"Only if they win," Cassidy said with a smile. "When do they plan to strike?"

"They were going to hit you day before yesterday, but that troop carrier helicopter came in and we needed to know your strength."

Cassidy threw back his head and burst into manic laughter.

"Why the hell are you *laughing* at me?" Babcock asked in a bewildered, wounded tone.

"We have been given needed time by an empty helicopter. Even you must find that grimly humorous, Mr. Babcock." He turned and yelled, "Roland, Solare!"

They burst through the door, anxiety, and fear on both faces. After quickly surveying the scene, they stopped as one.

"What do want us to do?" Roland asked.

"I want everyone in full combat gear in ten minutes. Alert our other stations. If French Canada is coming for us here, there will be other actions, especially on the road system."

CHAPTER 49

DOYON HOUSE, TANANA, ALASKA REPUBLIK

"So, have we ratified a constitution, people?" Claude Adams' smile beamed around the room. The fifty-five delegates and the spectators all milled in the chamber, laughing, and shaking hands.

Standing next to Claude, Nathan Roubitaux gave him a somber nod. "Yes, but we all lost closely held beliefs to make it happen."

"Only the political ones, Nathan." Claude didn't lose his smile. "Our culture and our people have spoken through the delegates in this room. We have a ratified constitution."

Someone slapped Claude on the back and they began a lively conversation.

"If we *all* can keep it," Nathan said and turned away so as to not glare at his one-time friend. He gathered his things from his desk where had fought so valiantly for his cause. Claude's mental waves of victory made his guts roil.

Claude was too excited to notice as Nathan quickly made his way out of the building. He saw two soldiers chatting in the small courtyard, but they didn't seem to be guarding anything. He glanced around. There *had* to be a courier or else all was lost.

"Mr. R?"

Nathan whirled and beheld a serious young man sporting a military haircut. *Subtle!*

"Yes, hello." Nathan smiled widely and held out his hand. When the man glanced at his hand and hesitated, Nathan growled in a low voice, "Shake my hand, you damned fool, or we're both dead!"

The man grabbed his hand and for the next ten seconds his eyes never once fell on Nathan's face as he tried to look everywhere else at once. He radiated fear. Nathan released his hand and grabbed his shoulder to make him walk beside him.

"What's your name?" he asked as gently as he could. The fellow was as wary as a feral cat.

"Lawrence Dabney, sir."

"Call me Nathan in public. Is Major Dumont in place with the rest of your people?"

"Yes, si–, ah, Nathan. The major wants to know how many troops are present here at this time."

"Ten, maybe twelve, I think. Nobody in this building is worried about armed conflict."

"We saw a helicopter land and then leave again. Did it deliver any troops?"

"Not to my knowledge." He wondered why the helicopter had been here at all. He was always the last to hear what the military was doing.

"Tell the major he is to execute Plan B at once."

"Execute Plan B at once. I understand, Nathan." He turned and walked purposefully up the boardwalk toward the beckoning forest.

Even though his watch read 4 PM the light already faded from the sky. Nathan smiled. He felt safer in the darkness.

CHAPTER 50

HOSPITAL CAFETERIA, TANANA, ALASKA REPUBLIK

Magda walked into the cafeteria desperate for coffee. She hurried over to the large samovar, grabbed a cup, and turned the ornate handle. Four drops coalesced in the bottom of her cup.

"Damn!"

"May I be of service?"

Magda looked over to where a red-haired woman sat at a table with a carafe in front of her.

"Yes, if there's more coffee in that thing."

"There is. Please grab a cup and join me."

Magda snagged a cup as she went to the table, instantly assessing this woman she had never seen. She stopped at table edge and nodded.

"Thank you so much. I am Magda Haraldsson Yamato. I'm afraid I've become addicted to coffee."

Solare waved and smiled. "Do sit and partake. I am Solare. You have a fascinating name. Are you related to Pelagian?"

"He's my father," Magda said as she poured. She added milk and took a tentative sip. "Ah, ambrosia! Thank you again."

"So, you're married to the colonel in charge of the air force?"

"Yes," Magda said after her second sip. "Actually, Jerry is a lieutenant colonel and I think it is high time they promoted him."

"And what do you do while he's off playing with planes? Do you have children?"

"Not yet." A dark shroud seemed to envelope her for a long moment. Magda believed in omens and realized she and Jerry would never have children. The knowledge devastated her.

"Are you crying, Magda? Whatever is wrong?"

She wiped the sudden tears and tried to laugh.

"I'm fine, really. I just had this premonition that made me sad."
"You believed it?"
"They've never yet been wrong. What is you do?"
"I, ah, kill people for profit."
"Say again?"
"I'm a professional bounty hunter. Right now, I'm working with the Peacekeepers, which I suspect may have been a mistake."
"In what way?"
"Do you know Yukon Cassidy?"

Magda laughed. "Since I was twelve. He's like an uncle to me. Why?"

"If you don't mind me asking, how old are you?"
"Twenty-one, and why again?"
"You just seriously aged me, Magda. It's been some time since I was so vividly aware of my years."

Magda felt alarm shoot through her. "I haven't given offense, have I? I didn't–"

"No. Not at all. You seem much wiser than your years. I'm used to contending with people who are the exact opposite."

"According to my mother I matured early and never looked back. What she doesn't admit is I had to; due to her lack of parenting skills."

"She tied you down?"

"Quite the opposite. She always said 'yes' to my dumbest requests. When I would fail miserably, sometimes painfully, she would say, 'Perhaps you need to think before you speak.'"

Solare laughed. "It sounds to me like she had excellent parenting skills. She allowed you to learn from your mistakes. Do you have any idea how rare that is?"

"I do now. It took me far too long to appreciate her methods."
"What do you do while your husband is off flying?"
"I wait."

CHAPTER 51

DOYON HOUSE, TANANA, ALASKA REPUBLIK

Yukon Cassidy hurried towards Pelagian's office, wondering if he had missed something important and was about to get slapped. He couldn't think of a thing. Coming to a halt outside the door, he checked to see that his blue Peacekeeper tunic was in order, and knocked.

"Enter!"

Cassidy grinned when he heard Pelagian's voice. It held no anger. Despite the heightened security status, the First Speaker sounded happy. He entered the room.

"The message said you urgently needed to see me, First Speaker."

"Relax, Yukon. I thought it only proper that you be one of the first to welcome the First People's Nation Ambassador, Blotahunka Medicine Bull." He nodded to Cassidy's right.

Not believing his ears, Cassidy's heart skipped a beat and he turned to look at the grinning tall man dressed in ceremonial regalia. "Uncle?"

"It warms my heart to see you have achieved great rank here, Napayshnea. I knew you would go far."

"As have you, Uncle! I apologize for not keeping better contact over the years, but…"

"You were leading a life of adventure and many coups. We all understood."

"Any news of my father?"

"No. Last I heard he was still doing an excellent job of running the hospital. Your mother still teaches tradition to young women. You should send them a message now and then."

"I will do that, Uncle. I promise."

"It is good to see you, Nephew. May I call on you to interpret should I need that?"

"Your English is excellent, Uncle," Cassidy said with a slight frown.

"Diplomatic interpretation may be what I require."

Cassidy glanced at Pelagian and then nodded. "Of course, Ambassador Medicine Bull. It would be my honor. I will be as forthcoming as I can under the circumstances."

"I can ask no more than that."

Pelagian laughed. "This is going to be fun!"

CHAPTER 52

NORTH OF TANANA, ALASKA REPUBLIK

"Listen up," Captain Dumont said to the two rows of men circling him. "We're going in without full intelligence of the situation. Dabney found no sign of Babcock or additional troops. I have decided to hold half of you in reserve. If twenty-nine of us can't handle a bunch of flabby, untrained civilians we probably should seek other work."

Most of the men ginned at the thought.

"If they have Babcock, they will know all about us within two hours. Their little kangaroo court just ratified a constitution, and we need to change their minds. Lieutenant Klein, how long until we have snow here?"

"I can smell it in the air, Captain. No more than eight hours away, probably less."

"That's what I thought, too. We have no more time to waste. Staff Sergeant Okappo, prepare Anatole Company to take the field within the hour."

"Sah!" Okappo stood to his full 6' 3" and saluted smartly. His Zulu heritage and training had cast him as a warrior from the age of eight. Shouting for his squad to assemble, he left the circle with them.

"Staff Sergeant Gellatly, you and Berthe Company will remain in reserve. Be ready to move out immediately if we message you. Speed will be of the essence."

"Aye, sir. T'will be done," the wiry Scot said. "Ye heard him, laddies!" More of the group melted away.

"Staff Sergeant Vaston, prepare half of Célestin Squad to take the field within the hour. I leave it to you to decide who goes and who waits with Sergeant Gellatly."

The burly Chek nodded and swung his right hand in a circle over his head before pointing to an empty spot near their camp. His troops silently moved as one and assembled where instructed. He rapidly sorted men into two groups.

Dumont stood with Lt. Klein, Ensign Meté, and First Sergeant Emile Good. The three of them regarded their boss.

"Klein, you take Célestin Company. Meté, I want you to remain with Gellatly. Listen to him if he has questions about your orders. He's been doing this stuff longer than you and me put together."

"Yes, sir," Meté said with little enthusiasm.

"First Sergeant Good, I want you with Anatole Company. I will range back and forth as needed. We've already talked this through."

"Sir," Good said. "How long will we have to infiltrate the perimeter?"

"Twenty minutes should be ample, don't you think?"

"If they are as unaware as we believe, that should do it."

"Excellent. One more thing, and make sure every man under you hears this from your lips; if any of you meet either a man named N'Go, or a man named Nathan, treat them like gold and protect them as if you are related."

"Yes, sir," the three said together.

"Excellent. Now deploy."

CHAPTER 53

NORTH OF TANANA,
ALASKA REPUBLIK

Solare picked her way through the willow thickets and brush as slowly and quietly as possible. *Things that make noise become prey*, she thought. Birds in the canopy above carried on conversations and arguments, all giving her a sense of safety.

The cold breeze carried winter on its breath. The leaden sky burgeoned with heavy gray clouds. She knew they carried moisture and imminent snow.

She moved on. Less than five minutes later she heard a noise that shouldn't be there. She stopped, eased the camouflaged hood on the cape over her head while slowly sinking down on her haunches. Having already streaked her face with black and dark green war paint, she allowed her face to extend beyond the hood. She wanted to see and hear *everything*.

She heard the noise again and labeled it a slither, a *large* slither. Moving only her eyes, she carefully searched everything she could see. A quarter mile behind her sat the village of Tanana and beyond flowed the mighty Yukon River. When Grisha and Cassidy started arguing on what to do next she had slipped out and started her own recon.

Although she had done reconnaissance and surveillance in many places in times past, she also knew every time was different. Four meters directly in front of her, a black man wearing combat gear rose up from invisibility and signaled with his hands. He pointed and nodded prior to making more signals.

Solare slowly eased to her knees and allowed her eyes to follow his orders. Mercenaries filled the forest around her. For less than an eye blink part of her brain panicked at nearly being discovered while the other part marveled at the professionalism the group exhibited.

Her training kicked in and she pulled her double-edged killing knife from its sheath in her left boot. *The boss won't be difficult to take, but if anyone else sees...* She squelched her imagination, sank even lower, and allowed her animus to rule.

Inch by inch she pulled the hood farther out to conceal her face from the sides and watched the boss ease toward her. The birds still sang in the canopy.

I won't trust them again!

When the man started turning his head toward her Solare slowly lowered her face and stared at the ground. Her steady right hand held a 9mm pistol fully loaded with seven rounds, and her left hand clutched the boot knife. If they discovered her she would go down fighting.

She tensed her muscles, ready to spring up as quickly as possible. There wouldn't be time for introductions, only flashing steel and sudden bullets.

The man walked slowly past her. Less than a meter away he stopped behind her. He sniffed.

Solare never wore scent of any kind and was fastidious in her personal grooming. *Does he smell my soap?* The irony could be terminal.

He muttered, "Something died out here!" and moved on toward Tanana.

She sampled the air and mentally agreed with him. In her stealth mode, smell only registered if it threatened. It had been a while since whatever stank had last breathed.

Solare didn't think the smell came from a human; it wasn't sweet enough. Other mercenaries passed her in their slow, careful advance. She continued staring at the ground, listening for indications of discovery.

The thin third rank brought up the mercenary rear; far more alert to the woods behind them than what lay ahead. All Solare could think about was getting word to Tanana before it was too late. She slowly pivoted and raised her head.

The men, unsurprisingly she had seen no women, were spreading out into attack formation. *I have to do something! But what?*

CHAPTER 54

DOYON HOUSE, TANANA, ALASKA REPUBLIK

"What did the army say?" Cassidy asked.

"The graduating group is an hour into a thirty-mile hike. They've been ordered to drop gear and return as fast as they can," Grisha said. "The good news is that we have a full platoon just down the street. They're saddling up as we speak."

"That's what, twelve guys?"

"Twenty, including their commanding officer and his sergeant."

"Grisha, we're talking about sixty highly trained mercenaries who could attack us five minutes from now!"

"Fifty-nine, Major Cassidy. We have one of them in the brig."

"I still want to get outside and see what's going on."

"Concur. Sergeant Major Tobias!"

"Yes, General Grigorievich?" Tobias said, looking up from his clipboard.

"Please alert Colonel Yamato to the fact we need a combat air patrol over the capital as soon as he can make it happen."

"Yes, sir." He hurried out of the room.

"Are there any other troops we can get within two hours?" Cassidy asked.

"No, and I don't think we have two hours. We need to get all of the delegates into a secure place right now."

"Where? We don't have a basement."

"Wherever is in the center of this complex. Come on, this is going to take both of us."

Cassidy followed Grisha and yelled to Delcambré over his shoulder. "Stay here and direct people, Roland!"

"Oui!"

Grisha and Cassidy hurried down the hall and approached two

nervous guards.

"Any problems, men?" Grisha asked.

Both snapped to attention before Grisha could wave them off.

"Nothing so far, general," one said.

"The delegates sure don't like being told what to do," the other man said with a smirk.

"I'll bet. Get yourselves some cover in here. Turn over a table or a desk, something you can safely get behind."

"Yes, sir!"

Cassidy followed Grisha through a double door where delegates, their assistants, and staff members all stood in groups talking. Everyone in the large room went quiet and stared at Grisha and Cassidy.

"Ladies and gentlemen," Grisha boomed, "we are about to come under attack–"

Everyone began speaking at once.

"Be quiet!" Grisha bellowed. "We have guards around the building, more troops on their way, as well as a combat air patrol from our air force. In a very short time, there is going to be an attack on this building. The attackers want to kill *you*. All of *you*. We don't yet know who is financing these mercenaries, but we *will* find out!"

"What do you want us to do?" Claude Adams asked.

"Yukon and I are going to lead you all to the armory. We need everyone armed and ready. Does that meet with everyone's approval?"

"Hell yes!" Waterman Stoddard boomed. "I would have brought my bear gun if I had any idea this shit would happen!"

Cassidy followed a grinning Grisha out a different door with all the delegates behind him. Listening to the delegates, Cassidy didn't worry as much as he once had.

"Who are these people and why would they want to kill us?"

"–don't give a muskrat's ass what they want. They fuck with me and they're dead!" Blue Bostonman snarled.

"They must be crazy to be attacking us! Don't they know we all just won a revolution?"

"I hope I can get a machine gun!"

"Have these fools looked around them? Winter is going to happen any day!"

CHAPTER 55

ON THE YUKON RIVER, BELOW RAMPART
ALASKA REPUBLIK

"There's more ice in the river, Boss," Rasputin snarled, pulling his coat tighter around him. "You *do* have somewhere in mind that is warm and has food, *don't* you?"

Snowflakes drifted out of the leaden sky as if by accident. The dried brush providing them camouflage limited their movement inside the boat and offered no other comfort from the cold. They hoped that from the air they looked like any other clump of floating brush.

"Do I hear doubt in your voice, old comrade?" A wide smile creased the man's dark face.

"You must admit," he said in Kongo, their native language, "it has taken much longer achieving this goal than you first boasted."

Selkirk glared at them. "Speak something civilized or I'll think yer plotting again' me!"

N'Go looked at his friend, second in command, and subordinate. He spat. "Shit happens, as the yanks say. I can't foresee every damned thing under the sun."

Rasputin glanced up at the trees on the riverbank losing definition in the increasing snow and growing darkness. "There isn't much of that left, either!"

"Start the motor!" N'Go said.

Selkirk, sitting on the last bench, complied. "An' where ta?" he asked, raising his voice in the cold afternoon.

He pointed. "Over there, where that second creek comes out. Go slow. There may be ice build-up by now."

The aluminum riverboat, which Rasputin considered a fat dhow, skimmed over the water shedding small clumps of camouflaging brush as they went. Bits of ice bumped and thudded hollowly against the sides. In another two weeks the great river would be ice from shore to shore. A month after that it would be frozen to a depth of three meters or more.

Rasputin seethed with anger. His friend's grandiose plans had gone over the hill. They were reduced to just the three of them. And he was doomed to spend another damned winter close to the Arctic Circle.

The boat entered the mouth of the small creek and immediately began hitting thickening ice. Selkirk increased the throttle to compensate. Within three minutes the outboard was screaming and they weren't moving.

"Kill the motor!" N'Go glanced around a couple of times and then pointed. "That way. Break the ice with the paddles until we get to shore."

All three smashed at the surface ice in the shallow creek and pushed the boat against the bank. They climbed out, stretching their legs, and working feeling back into numbed feet.

"Pull the boat into the trees and follow me." N'Go looked about slowly.

"D'ya want we should cover it again?" Selkirk asked.

"No. Nature will take care of that."

Snow gradually lightened the dark shore and woods as it filled the air.

Rasputin hefted his gear out of the beached boat. The only things he had left were his knapsack, weapons, and ammo.

We're out of food, he thought angrily. He followed anyway. All other options were now less substantial than the cold mist surrounding them.

They trudged behind N'Go for a quarter mile before Rasputin smelled wood smoke. Rounding a clump of trees and a low wall of strategically fallen logs, they came upon a sturdy single story cabin with light shining through its solitary window.

N'Go walked up to the door and knocked three times, waited a moment, then knocked twice more. The door swung open spilling light out into the darkness. The figure in the door lowered a large rifle.

"I'd given up on ya!" the large man boomed. "Ya know what I'm saying?"

They all trooped into the warmth and Rasputin realized exactly how cold he had been. Automatically he assessed his surroundings. Four sets of bunk beds ran around two walls and the small kitchen claimed the remaining wall and a half. Rasputin nodded silent approval.

N'Go turned to his followers. "This is Rock. He's one of us."

"So, what happened up in Fort Yukon?" Rock demanded.

Rasputin had never before laid eyes on the large man and wondered where N'Go had found him. The fellow had biceps as large as Rasputin's waist and had cut his hair down to a stubble. He appeared physically competent.

Despite himself, Rasputin felt impressed with this snug bolt hole. "Unfortunate events, Rock."

"I sent Prevo up with a message. Did you get it?"

"Make us some food. We're starved. When did you send him?"

"Been at least a week." Rock opened a trap door in the floor, easily lifted out a moose hindquarter, and laid it on the counter.

"Damn," Rasputin spat.

"You don't like moose, my friend?"

"I love moose! I think Prevo may have triggered the alarm."

"What kind of alarm?" he asked as he sliced off thick steaks.

"A bomb," N'Go grated. "The dumb bastard set off a bomb I had rigged for the Peacekeepers."

The knife stilled halfway through a cut. Rock stared into N'Go's eyes.

"Prevo?"

"...was standing in front of the bomb. It totally atomized him."

"Fuck! Why didn't you warn him?"

"We were all in the escape tunnel. We had been made by the Peacekeepers," N'Go said, disgust eroding his words.

"That's the second time you've said that word. What are Peacekeepers?"

"The new national police for the *Republik*," Rasputin snapped. "Many of them used to be with us in the International Freekorps. Now they're flics."

"I'm glad none of them know *me*," Rock said with a grin. "Ya know what I'm saying?"

"I don't know you, either," Rasputin said in as light a tone as he could muster. "Where exactly did you serve?"

Rock glanced at the Boss before losing his smile and saying,

"That's none of your business, fellow."

N'Go laughed. "Stand down, both of you. Rock, this is Rasputin, and that's Selkirk."

Both men nodded to the large man.

"Rasputin has been my right arm for many years now, and I find him invaluable. Selkirk is a canny soldier who seemingly knows no fear."

Rock continued cutting meat and listened.

"Rock is someone I met two years ago prior to the IF's northern sojourn. I arranged for his future, and ours, by hiring him to build this lovely cabin and stock it with enough food and supplies to keep eight men, including him, alive for four months. Therefore, it should keep four of us in comfort for eight months if need be."

Rasputin frowned and said, "But what if–"

"Of course, the problem will be," N'Go said without pausing, "...if we can keep from killing each other."

Rasputin knew when to shut up. Meat sizzled in the large cast-iron frying pan and gnawing hunger eclipsed all other thought.

CHAPTER 56

OUTSIDE DOYON HOUSE, TANANA, ALASKA REPUBLIK

Snow drifted from the darkening sky. The temperature dropped below freezing at ground level. With the light fading, Solare could see her breath.

She waited until the mercenaries spread to their fullest extent and decided they held high opinions of their abilities. That aided her immensely. She quietly stole up to the nearest man directly in front of the closest access to the building, sure that he had no idea of his importance or peril.

In one quick movement, she grabbed his mouth with her left hand, and as he stiffened, slit his throat with the knife in her right hand. He collapsed and gurgled as he died. She plucked the automatic weapon out of his spasming hands and moved in tandem with the others advancing toward Doyon House.

Ten meters from the structure a man to her far left held up his clenched fist and everyone else stopped moving.

Solare sprinted for the building. Confusion behind her lasted less time than she had hoped. Automatic weapons fire blew chunks out of the building as she scurried around its corner.

She kicked open the door and found three men with weapons pointing at her.

"No!" Yukon Cassidy bellowed. "She's one of ours!"

She grinned and sank to the floor, spent. "They're right behind me. Twenty-nine by my count."

"That's nearly half of them. They must have lost one," Cassidy said, peering though the door.

"Yeah," she said wiping off her blade on her pants. "I suggest you get farther back into the building. Ricochets are notoriously indiscriminate."

"I agree," Cassidy said. "Fall back."

The two men with him didn't argue and pushed back into the hallway of Doyon House. Solare turned and peered past them. A number of people stood beside doors leading into rooms with windows. All of them carried arms and looked ready to fight.

Automatic weapons fire sounded outside. People pulled back as rounds smashed into the wall opposite the open doors. A thud sounded from inside the closest room.

"Grenade!" Cassidy shouted. Someone closer slammed the door shut and jerked away from it. Smoke streamed around the door. More smoke billowed through other doors into the corridor.

"Shut the doors. They're trying to make us come out into the open," Solare yelled. "They're gonna rush us in a minute. I'd bet on it."

Cassidy laughed. "It's interesting seeing you in a firefight, lady. You get more elemental—"

The outside entrance door blew off its hinges and fell into the arctic entry. The two men who rushed in were surprised by the second set of doors.

They're not from around here, Solare thought. *But they're gonna die here.*

Five or more people in the corridor fired through the doors, shattering them and the men in the entryway.

Gunfire erupted at the other end of the building. Solare ignored it. For a split second she popped her head around the doorframe of the nearest demolished office. The smoke finished venting through the broken windows, leaving only wisps.

"Cassidy, they're not coming through the windows yet. I need back-up." She turned and lunged into the room.

CHAPTER 57

OUTSIDE DOYON HOUSE, TANANA, ALASKA REPUBLIK

Captain Dumont frowned. *Not only did they not leave the building, we should be finishing them off by now. I thought these were politicians!* He signaled First Sergeant Good to deploy the assault squad.

Staff Sergeant Vaston led his men with his signature ferocity. The dusky man came from somewhere in the Balkans where he had killed his first soldier at the age of seven years. He had never stopped killing.

All of Assault Company enjoyed their work. They tossed two of their members though a gaping window and waited as gunfire sounded and rounds buzzed out over their heads. Vaston waited for a ten-second count and then threw a grenade through the window.

All the remaining window glass blew out over their heads. Two seconds later two more of Vaston's men were lofted though the window. Another explosion blew debris and an arm out the shattered opening.

Gunfire raged throughout the building yet none of the defenders tried to flee.

This isn't good. Our intelligence was insufficient, Dumont thought, trying to suppress the flash of panic lancing through him.

A cacophony of weapons fire issued from the building and two of his men waiting in reserve grunted and fell as bullets hit them.

Eight down and we have achieved nothing.

"Sound recovery!" Dumont shouted. *We were here for a quick strike, not a damned siege!*

Two whistles blew a quick tattoo and his men turned and streaked for the forest. Three dropped in death and another went down howling with a leg wound. Increasing fire from the building put wings on his feet and he sprinted for the forest, stifling tears of frustration.

We'll have to use the rockets.

CHAPTER 58

INSIDE DOYON HOUSE, TANANA, ALASKA REPUBLIK

"Cease fire!" Grisha screamed. He hoped the indiscriminate fire hadn't hit any civilians. He smirked as he realized all those delegates were probably happy to have a violent outlet to dispel the frustration of beating a constitution into being.

The attackers had fled. Through the remains of a window, he saw men in familiar battle fatigues dash towards the woods. The Dená Rangers had arrived.

"Anyone hurt?" he yelled.

"Oh, I think I have a cut!" A female voice said.

"I think one of them ricochets hit my thigh, here," a male voice muttered.

"Pass the word. We need a medic in here!" Cassidy shouted. "Grisha, should we join the pursuit?"

"No. The Rangers know what they are doing. They know who is on their side, and anyone they don't know could get shot. Besides, they're a lot younger than we are and have more energy."

Cassidy grinned and kicked the broken glass off a spot on the floor. He leaned against the wall and slid down to sit. "Sounds good to me."

Grisha regarded Solare. "How did you know they were going to attack?"

She told them what she had done.

"That was a gutsy thing to do, Solare," Cassidy said.

"It was stupid. I didn't know what I was up against in terms of numbers and ability. Those bastards are good at what they do."

"It seems their reconnaissance was worse than yours," Grisha said. "They lost at least a third of their attacking force and gained nothing other than breaking our windows. They have also put us on alert and rangers are tracking them as we speak."

"I know they're here to kill our delegates, but why would French Canada want that badly enough to send their mercenaries and not their army and air force?" Cassidy asked.

Grisha had been wondering the same thing. Thoughts flew about in his mind like little brown bats. One of them had part of the answer, but it wouldn't land.

"The French don't want this to be more than a simple, little coup. This is the most vulnerable we'll ever be, I promise you that, and we've already eliminated the English."

"Why wouldn't they just attack and be done with it?" Delcambré snorted.

"Entangling alliances," Solare said as she examined the weapon she had acquired. "If any national entity openly sends in their military, they'll have a at least a two-front war on their hands."

"They'd send in better units, Grisha said, thinking out loud. "This group sacrificed good reconnaissance for stealth. If Babcock is the best spy they have…"

Cassidy interrupted, "Grisha, I need to speak alone with you at once."

Grisha grumbled to his feet. His leg didn't like cold weather. He nodded toward the hall.

Cassidy led and Grisha followed him into an intact office.

"So, what's on your mind, my friend?"

"I think we're dealing with a traitor."

CHAPTER 59

NEAR RAMPART, ALASKA REPUBLIK

"Have you kept the batteries charged, Rock?"

"Of course, Boss. It was part of my daily routine after my helper was gone."

"What helper? I authorized no helper! If you have–"

"Once we got the place built and operational I eliminated him. He was too much of a security risk."

"Now that is impressive. What about him didn't you like?"

"He talked too fucking much. He'd read lots of books and was always trying to teach me shit I don't need. Ya know what I'm saying?"

"I can see how that would irritate you," N'Go said. "Set up the radio now, please."

After removing a section of log wall, Rock lifted out a Telefunken transmitter-receiver of impressive size. He brought out a large battery and hooked cables between the two units. Finally, he picked up a wire protruding from the cabin wall and hooked it to the back of the machine.

"There you are."

"Impressive, Rock, truly impressive," N'Go said as he made his way over to the unit and sat in front of it. He lifted a set of headphones off the radio and put them on.

After turning knobs and waiting for tubes to warm, he pulled out a small microphone nestled in the mechanism's frame. He tapped it once and then said, "Are you there, Phantom?"

Unbroken static issued from the small speaker.

N'Go frowned, checked his setting, and repeated the question.

A slight crackle broke the static.

"Check your settings, Phantom! I cannot hear you."

"–read you loud and clear. This is Phantom. Who are you?"

"The Boss."

"Where are you? We have been looking for you. We need the rockets."

"Who is this?"

"This is Ensign Meté."

"I want to speak with Captain Dumont."

"He is leading the attack on Tanana. I am not sure when he will return."

N'Go released the transmit button and sat back in the chair.

"This is not good. They are already attacking Tanana. I told them to infiltrate and wait for an opportune moment."

"Perhaps the opportunity arrived much faster than you thought is would," Rasputin suggested.

"Perhaps." N'Go bent to the microphone again. "Ensign Meté, when Dumont returns have him contact me at once."

"Yes, sir."

"Boss, out."

"Phantom, out."

When N'Go sat back in the chair, Rock asked, "How long do we wait?"

"Until he, or his successor calls. Why?"

"Keeping the battery charged is not easy work."

N'Go gave him an appraising glance. "You don't appear to be wasting away from the labor."

Rasputin snickered.

"Wha' rockets daes the mon refer ta?" Selkirk asked. "Tha three we brought w'us?"

"We were supposed to have possession of a lorry full of surface-to-air missiles, but our man failed to deliver. If I ever find him, he will die a very slow death."

"There's someone out tha w' the balls to cross *you*?" Selkirk said with a ghastly grin. "Or is it a wee lack o' brains?"

"That's yet to be determined."

The radio abruptly came to life.

"Boss, this is Dumont! Over!"

"Boss here. Your tone indicates much stress, Captain. What is the situation?"

"Your assessment of the fighting abilities of the *politicians* in

Tanana was well off the mark. I have lost nearly a squad of men and we are now being hunted by land and air."

"I thought you were all legionnaires, Dumont. How could a handful of civilians outfight you?"

"Are you mocking me?"

"Sorry, I suppose I was. Will your *Phantom Legion* be able to extract itself from this situation?"

"I don't know. Where are the weapons you promised? This would be an excellent time to produce them."

"It seems we have been left standing at the altar of Mars. Our man with the weapons failed to deliver. We have three of the weapons with us, but not the three-score we were promised; and *paid* for in advance."

Dumont chuckled. "I'd hate to be that poor bastard when you find him."

"He's a *rich* bastard at this point. Can you exit the area?"

"We're trying. Where do we go if we succeed?"

"Upriver, halfway between the RustyCan and Rampart. You're going to have to cross the Yukon to get to us. Don't trust the ice. It's still far too thin to support you."

"We have two SAMs; I plan to use them if I can. We'll see you in a few days if we're still alive."

"Good luck and good hunting! Boss out."

"How many of them are there?" Rock asked.

"Plan for forty."

"Where am I gonna get grub for that many people?"

"Maybe you should go hunting." N'Go turned away. *Everything is turning to shit!*

CHAPTER 60

CHENA REDOUBT

"What are we looking for, Jerry?" Aisha asked.

They both led three cadets each. He had asked Dave to stay with the rest of the class at Chena.

"Armed mercenaries stormed Doyon House today. We think they wanted to kill all the delegates. Fortunately, we had enough weapons to arm those folks and the attack was unsuccessful."

"They were dumb enough to attack people who hunt to stay alive?" Aisha laughed.

"We also believe they're not local."

"Not too professional, either," she observed.

They flew widely spaced at five hundred feet altitude. The terrain grew darker by the minute. Light snow on the ground gave the trees enough contrast to appear black.

After flying over Tanana, they had gone north for five miles without seeing anything. Jerry knew a man on the ground merely had to remain stationary to not be seen by aircraft. He decided they were wasting time and fuel.

"Okay, return to base. We aren't doing any good–"

A brilliant flash on the ground surprised and alerted him

"Rocket! Take evasive act–"

The explosion destroyed the tail of *Satori*. Instantly he threw back the canopy as he ripped off his straps. With all his strength he threw himself up and out of the cockpit and pulled his ripcord.

The parachute deployed and snapped him still for an instant. The trees came up at him far too fast.

✪

Major Aisha Merritt recognized the flash and immediately dove at the location, all guns blazing and wishing she carried her own rockets. She realized she was now in command and had to take care of her chicks.

"All birds back to base, now!"

Six comm clicks calmed her somewhat. She saw Jerry's chute catch in trees and didn't know if he was injured, on the ground, or anything else.

"Tanana command, Colonel Yamato is down in sector 2-2. Do you copy?"

"We copy, ma'am. The Dená Rangers are closing on his position."

"Is he okay?" She wanted to scream.

"Wait one."

Automatically her eyes went over her gauges and then did a 360° scan of the area. No threat to be seen.

"Combat Air Patrol. We have Colonel Yamato, and he is alive and well."

"Thank you, Tanana command. I could kiss you for that."

"You know where to find me," the man said with a chuckle.

Aisha increased her speed and flew toward Chena.

CHAPTER 61

CHENA
ALASKA REPUBLIK

"Lieutenant Strom, may I have a word?"

Alex looked up from his report.

"Trooper McKenzie, what is it?"

"I'm bored as hell."

"That goes with the job. You've got the paperwork end of things figured out pretty well. Let's do some more outdoor training and field test our new patrol utility."

She grinned. "Can we run the siren?"

"*Very* briefly, just to make sure it works."

Alex glanced over at a grinning Willie Kimura.

"What's so funny, trooper?"

"You two are fun to watch."

"That's not part of your duties, Trooper Kimura. Manning the office *is* for the next four hours. We are going to patrol north to the sector boundary."

"Enjoy!"

"We will," Mack said, pulling an automatic weapon off the rack. She went through the door into the half-built garage attached to the station house portion of the massive redoubt. The local crew who had been working on it had all taken leave to go moose hunting. They had their priorities.

She slid into the driver's seat and pressed the start button. *Why they built it without key start is beyond me*, she thought. It wasn't the first time it had crossed her mind.

Alex slid into the gunner's seat and shut the door tightly.

"Commence the patrol, Trooper." He turned on the heater and modulated the fan. "What a wonderful utility!" he exclaimed. "This job just gets better and better."

"I'm very happy I can train with you, Alex," Mack said as she drove north on the Russia-Canada Highway. "And this is one sweet rig. It makes my old utility look like shit. I especially like those little fender mirrors that show the whole side of the machine."

Snow fell from the sky and lightened the ground.

"It's not your utility's fault you deferred maintenance for as long as you did. That's a good machine you own. It merely needs some care and repair."

"I was obsessed with my mission. The utility was a tool and nothing more."

"What do you call it?"

"A Fargo utility, for crissake. What else would I call it?"

"You didn't *name* it?"

"Are you nuts, Lieutenant Strom? It's a *machine* not a living thing."

"Wrong. This patrol utility and your personal one are both very complex machines that have personalities and quirks. I truly believe they are sentient to a degree."

"I think you spent too much time alone in that cell."

"When I was a kid down in the Nation, I–"

"You're from the First People's Nation originally?"

"Not necessarily. Anyway, I had an old '56 Shasta Avalanche I just loved. Had scores of adventures in that thing. I called it Sancho after the character in *Don Quixote*."

"Never heard of him," Mack said stiffly.

He recounted several escapades involving Sancho and several other youthful delinquents. "We had a great time. Some of those guys are dead now. I was lucky."

"You went to college, huh?" She checked her watch and felt surprised they had been on the road for an hour. The snow had thickened, and the road ahead became a bright ribbon in the deepening afternoon gloom.

"No, we couldn't afford it. I just read a lot. We had a librarian who suggested titles she thought I would enjoy. I read some pretty strange books, but I learned something from all of them." He looked out the window at the fading light on the forest.

"She must have liked you. You were lucky."

"Yeah, I can hold my own in a conversation."

"What's that?"

"I said—"

"No. I heard what you said, but what's that?"

Alex finally looked where she pointed ahead of them on the previously empty road.

"It looks like an armored personnel carrier like the military have down in the States. Why the hell is it blocking the road?"

Mack brought the utility to a stop. "So, what's its name?"

"Who?"

"This utility. I know you well enough to know you've already named it."

Alex laughed.

The gunner in the APC blocking the road traversed his machine gun and centered on them. An armed man in combat gear waved them forward.

CHAPTER 62

NEAR THE TANANA AND CHENA SECTORS BORDER, ALASKA REPUBLIK

"There's a vehicle coming towards us, Sergeant Okappo." Private Adamo announced.

"Damn! We can't leave any witnesses."

Staff Sergeant Okappo felt torn. Since shooting down the plane all the remaining Phantom Legion had force marched until they reached the RustyCan Highway. From that point on they *requisitioned* every vehicle they came across.

Encountering a bivouacked Alaska Republik Army Recon squad had been the ultimate stroke of luck. The dumb bastards were dead before they knew they were in trouble. The long night stretched into this exhaustingly long day and all the men now pushed against their limits.

Okappo glanced at his watch. Dumont and the others had left the road forty minute earlier. He, Adamo, and Corporal Kahn being the rear guard, were to follow after an hour had passed.

With what seemed to be a late model patrol utility bearing down on them, Okappo wondered if their stroke of luck had been a bad one. He knew he was delaying the inevitable.

"Block the road, stop them. We have to give the captain and the others time to get away."

He stepped out of the armored personnel carrier and waved Corporal Kahn forward with him.

Okappo raised his right hand and smiled. Out of the side of his mouth he said, "As soon as I shoot the driver, you take out the other one."

Kahn nodded. Okappo had never seen the man smile.

Okappo walked up to the window as the driver cranked it down. It gave him pause when he realized the driver was an attractive

Black woman. *No matter. This must be done.*

"Good day to you. Where are you folks going?" His waist now hidden below the door window, he undid the loop on his holster, and started to pull his pistol free.

He was still wondering why her eyes never ceased moving when she lifted an automatic pistol and shot him through the head.

✪

The utility threw rocks as it roared backward and Mack screamed, "Shoot that sonuvabitch. They ain't *our* army!"

Alex sprayed the corporal and the armored car with the Kalashnikov he had lifted onto his lap when they were stopped. The corporal went down. The gunner in the APC returned fire.

Mack snapped the utility into a tight turn and slammed on the brakes. Before they stopped sliding, she straightened the wheels and stomped on the accelerator. They roared down the RustyCan toward Chena.

"You really know how to drive!" Alex said in wonder.

Bullets hit the road next to her side and three rounds came through the back window, one punched through the windscreen. She immediately steered to her side of the road as the gunner miscorrected and fired where they had been.

Alex sighed in relief that the gunner hadn't used the cannon. By comparison the machine gun seemed minor.

"Do we have a smoke grenade?" she snapped.

"No. Pull into the trees! They started this fight!"

She drove off the road and bounced across the tundra into the trees.

"Cover me while I call in!" Alex said and grabbed the microphone and yelled, "Peacekeeper Station Chena, come–, ah, shit!"

"What?" Mack said, peering at the road behind them.

"They hit the damned radio! We're on our own."

"Fine," Mack said as she grabbed her backpack and weapon. "Let's go teach these bastards some manners!"

CHAPTER 63

TANANA
ALASKA REPUBLIK

"The only mercenaries here are dead, General Grisha," the Dená Ranger captain said over the radio.

"How many dead?"

"Three, sir."

"Did they bleed out or what?"

"All three have a bullet in the forehead, sir." The captain's grim tone strengthened the image.

"Too wounded to make it out on their own. Damn that's harsh. That makes a total of eleven dead. I wonder where the hell they went."

"I have people tracking them. As soon as I hear anything I will notify you at once."

"Thank you, Captain Williams."

Two clicks came through the speaker and the radio went silent.

Grisha surrendered the microphone to the radio sergeant and glanced around at the others. All were deep in thought.

Sergeant Major Tobias came through the door. "Begging the general's pardon, but we have a visitor."

Lieutenant Colonel Jerry Yamato entered wearing a rueful smile and a ragged flight suit. A large tear in the right side of his suit revealed a fresh bandage. He came to attention in front of Grisha and started a salute.

Grisha stood up and hugged him. "I'm so glad to see you in one piece, Jerry."

"When I dropped into a group of guys in uniform, I thought it was all over. They turned out to be your Dená Rangers. If they hadn't wasted time helping me I think they would have caught up with the mercenaries."

"They're on the trail right now."

"Grisha, may I call Magda? I'm worried she'll hear about the rocket and…"

"By all means. Sergeant Major Tobias will set you up on my private line. Please come back after talking with Magda, and tell her I send hugs."

✪

The initial ring didn't finish before Jerry heard Magda's voice over the line.

"This is Magda!"

"Sweetheart, it's me."

"Are you injured?"

"Just a couple of nicks where parts of Satori went through my flight suit at high velocity. Only scratches. They hardly bled."

"I think I heard about your plane getting hit before you even reached the ground. Aisha is beside herself with angst. She keeps saying she wasn't watching close enough."

"Tell her none of us expected them to have rockets. You sure have a fan club up here. Captain Dexter Williams asked me to say hi, and Grisha sends you hugs."

She laughed. "Good friends, old friends. We're sending the helicopter to pick you up in the morning, Colonel Yamato. I trust that meets with your approval."

"Tell them not to leave until it gets light out. That gives me time to eat, clean up, and debrief before flying away."

"I'll pass the word. Thank you for calling. I love you. Now go eat." She hung up before he could respond.

"Here he is," Grisha said as Jerry walked back into the room. "Sit down. We have food coming."

"Good, I'm starving." He grinned at Yukon, "Congratulations on your promotion, Major Cassidy. Delcambré's eyebrow lifted marginally.

"And congratulations to you, also, Captain Delcambré. They have finally recognized your worth."

"Are you running for political office, Colonel?" the unknown attractive woman asked in a husky voice.

"Don't let her fool you, Jerry," Grisha said, "…she is only pulling your leg. This is Solare, one of our field operatives."

She gave him a wide grin and held out her hand to shake his. "I am honored to finally meet you, sir."

As she shook his hand, her eyes assessed his face and body. He felt sure she missed nothing. After he dropped her hand Jerry glanced at his to make sure he still had all his fingers.

The radio burst into life. "Tanana Control. This is Ranger One, over."

"We read you loud and clear, Captain."

"We tracked them to the RustyCan. They stole three vehicles and headed toward Chena. Advise you warn Chena and mount motorized patrols."

"We'll make it happen. Excellent work, Captain Williams."

Jerry grinned and yelled, "Magda says, *hi*."

Williams laughed. "You're a lucky man, Colonel. General Grisha, my men are beat. With your permission we're going to bivouac here at Hammock's Roadhouse."

"Good choice. Tell Dave to put a round for all of you on my tab. We'll have transport for you in the morning."

"Thank you, General Grisha. Ranger One out."

"Tanana Control out." Grisha put down the microphone. After a moment he picked up the telephone. "Get me Colonel Smolst. Grisha here, Heinrich. Were you monitoring the radio? Good. Have you notified Chena?"

Food arrived and was deposited on the conference table. Everybody filled plates and Sergeant Major Tobias made one up for Grisha. Jerry was so hungry he thought he might faint if he'd had to wait much longer.

The steak wasn't moose, but it was delicious. The ambiance of the room gave him a certainty the Republik would survive.

"Thank you, Heinrich." Grisha returned the phone to its cradle. "We think they're going to attack Chena."

Jerry nearly choked. "Has the airfield been warned?"

"Everyone we can reach has been alerted. Two of my Chena Peacekeepers went north on a patrol who haven't returned and can't be contacted by radio. The army can no longer reach a motorized training patrol they have out.

"I'm going to have the Fedorov brothers pick up Captain Williams and his men before starting an air search. As soon as you all eat, turn in and get some sleep. You're going to be glad you did."

"General, I'll notify my command and have them in the air at first light."

"You saved me from asking, Jerry. Thanks."

CHAPTER 64

YUKON BRIDGE
ALASKA REPUBLIK

Lieutenant Alex Strom crept along the tree line until he spotted the APC. He stayed back in the woods where very little snow had fallen to reduce chance discovery. The road and the brush lay covered with a skein of snow as more drifted down out of the dark sky.

He stared at the armored personnel carrier but could detect no movement. *Time to up the ante*, he decided. He wondered if Mack was in position and glanced at his watch.

Watching where he stepped, Alex circled behind the machine. The near total darkness was both a benefit and a curse. He couldn't see if the gunner still stood behind the machine gun.

The still-warm bodies in the road lay dark and stark as the falling snow melted on their splayed forms. Alex shook his head. He thought Mack had gone nuts at first.

After they stopped, he shouted, "How did you know they were going to hurt us?"

"I watched all my mirrors. The fender mirror on my side reflected his whole body. He was pulling out his pistol when I shot the bastard!"

I was worried about her?

Now she was back there in the woods on the other side of the road. He slowly moved toward the APC, ready to fire back, dive out of the way, or just endure. This close to the machine he examined it critically.

That's a M113! He grinned. In his past he had been the gunner on one of these U.S. arse kickers.

The machine gun alone makes victory a near-guaranteed thing. Maybe they didn't know their vehicle too well. Did they have a large enough crew to adequately field the machine?

The rear hatch was swung open and clicked into the catch. The interior looked empty, and he shrugged. In two steps he was in the APC ready to kill anything that moved.

He jumped back out and in a normal tone of voice said, "It's empty. The *homme* hauled ass."

Mack stepped out of the brush no more than five meters from him.

"I'll start tracking him. Look for anything in there that can help us understand what happened."

Alex nodded, pulled out his small torch and went over the deck, seats, and driving compartment slowly and carefully. Nothing other than some sticky blood on the deck with boot tracks over them. Lots of boot tracks.

Out in the night a single shot sounded.

That was heavy caliber. What was Mack carrying?

He followed her tracks until she stopped walking on snow. The darkness made it impossible to follow on tundra.

If she fired the shot, she would go back to the APC.

In minutes he arrived at the quiet machine. Nothing. He tried not to think of Mack.

"What did you find?"

Alex jumped in surprise. "Goddammit! Don't sneak up on me like that!

"Sorry, luv," she said in a heavy British accent. She stopped grinning when she made out his face. "Seriously, Alex, I thought you knew I was there."

"S'okay. All I found was a lot of old blood. People died in here and I don't think *we* killed them. Who did you shoot?"

"The gunner who thought we was invincible. I gave him the opportunity to surrender and he went for a weapon. I'm not one to fuck around, so I shot him."

"Is he dead?"

"Of course, he is. There's a small road out there, not much more than a trail," she said nodding behind her. "Any idea where it goes?"

"How far have we come on this patrol?"

She frowned and said, "We've traveled a bit over a hundred miles. We're pretty close to the Yukon Bridge. If you want, we can make Tanana before dawn. So, where does the little road go?"

"Weird name. Never been there, but it always reminded me of a castle—Rampart, that's it! That's where that trail goes."

"Why the hell would a mercenary want to go to there? How big is it?"

"Trooper McKenzie, I just told you I've *never* been there. How the hell would I know the population?"

"The point is it can only be a hiding place. There's nothing else there and not many locals, *maybe*."

"Good points. I think you just made corporal. Now why would three mercenaries—your description, not mine—hijack an armored personnel carrier just to block the road so we couldn't get by? I'd love a sane answer."

"They were a rear guard," she said. "Good thinking there, Lieutenant."

"I have my—"

"Stand tall and don't move!" a hard voice said in the night. At least five safeties clicked off around them.

"You're the boss," Alex said and dropped his Kalashnikov on the deck, pissed at himself.

Mack dropped her weapon. "Do you know who we are?"

"No. I just know you're standing in a hijacked armored personnel carrier that nine of our people died defending."

Alex cleared his throat, "Send a couple of your people down the road about fifty meters and they'll find the bodies of at least two the men who killed your comrades. A third one is out there in the woods. I am Lieutenant Alex Strom of the Peacekeepers, and the corporal here is under my command. Any idea who these people are?"

A soldier ran up the ramp and whispered in the ear of the man holding the automatic rifle. Alex watched the leader's face and knew when they had slipped off the hook.

"Sorry, Lieutenant. We're all tired and pissed off to boot." He dropped the barrel of the weapon and stuck out his hand. "Captain Williams, Dená Rangers."

Alex grinned as they shook. "Lieutenant Strom of the Alaska Republik Peacekeepers. This is Corporal McKenzie."

"Yeah, we are following about forty to fifty mercenaries. They ambushed one of the training patrols, killed everyone, and made off with four vehicles, including this one. The other three are back toward Tanana, out of fuel. When we saw you, we naturally thought—"

"I would have done the same thing. Any idea which mercenary outfit?"

"They call themselves the *Phantom Legion*. Ever heard of them?"

Alex made a low whistle. "Shit, yeah, I have! They're not mercenaries. They're all French Foreign Legionnaires fresh out of prison or headed for one. Think of them as highly trained, expendable pawns. They only do things the Frogs don't want to deal with responsibly."

Captain Williams frowned at him, "So?"

"They are not anyone you want to go up against with," he glanced around, "...what, six guys. The PL is only sent out for high priority targets because they guarantee results or they go back to prison, so they are extremely motivated. What the hell are they doing up here?"

"That's a good point, Lieutenant. They tried to kill a lot of our leaders. It didn't go too well for them and we're going to make it much worse."

"Please, call me Alex. This is Mack."

"Dexter, but please keep it official. I need to keep my people sharp."

"Understood, Captain. We want to help with your mission if you'll have us."

'Hell, yeah. We can always use more people."

"Do you have a radio? I seriously need to report in to my station. These assholes shot up ours. Ask the corporal what *she* discovered."

Alex followed a ranger who waved him back to a radioman. He looked again, radio*woman*. Behind him Mack was explaining about the road to Rampart.

The woman carrying the radio said, "I've got him right here, sir, please hold." She pulled the headset off and handed it to Alex. "It's for you, sir."

Alex frowned, donned the headset, and said, "Hello?"

"So, tell me what happened out there, Lieutenant Strom."

"Good evening, General Grisha!"

CHAPTER 65

TANANA
ALASKA REPUBLIK

Yukon Cassidy sat in Grisha's outer office staring at a map of the province when Roland Delcambré grumped through the door.

"As if we don't have enough to deal with already!" Delcambré rumbled.

"What's the new problem?" Cassidy continued staring at the map.

"Riordan has escaped."

Cassidy clamped his eyes shut in response to the sudden blinding headache screaming through his head.

I don't need this! "Did N'Go escape, too?"

Roland laughed. "As it turns out, yes. Over two months ago. They let him walk."

Cassidy shot out of his chair. "*Who* did, and why?"

"The *authorities* decided he was only a dupe. Since they had Riordan to atone for all the problems he instigated, they let N'Go walk. I thought intelligent people operated this new government."

"What authorities? Who *exactly* signed the release form?"

"The clerk in Chena didn't say and I was too upset to ask. Why is it so important?"

"Call him back. Find out who signed it."

"*Her*, the clerk is a young lady with a beautiful voice–"

"And you think you're in love. I know. Call her back right now."

"You are bereft of romance and passion, Cassidy," he said, dialing the number. "Hello to you, Patricia. This is Roland, of course. Yes… yes… I know you are busy!"

Roland's ears turned pink first, then his cheeks. Cassidy grinned.

"*Allow me*, madam. My supervisor wishes to know a very simple thing. Yes, not to worry. Yes. He needs to know who signed the release papers for the prisoner N'Go. Yes, I will wait."

With clenched jaw Roland stared at the office wall.

Cassidy couldn't stop grinning. "What happened to your romance, Roland?"

He turned to face Cassidy. "You have no more class than she–, yes, Patricia, I am still here."

The small man listened intently. "I see. There is a new investigation into this matter. Please forward the document to Peacekeeper Headquarters in Tanana."

Cassidy nodded. *Wish I'd thought of that.*

"No, you are not in trouble. You are doing your job and quite well. Yes, I'm sure. That is fine. I understand. Goodbye."

He hung the phone up with finality.

"You already knew who signed it, didn't you, Yukon?"

"I have a strong suspicion."

"Who?"

"Nathan Roubitaux?"

Roland nodded his head slowly, as if passing judgment.

Grisha walked into the room and dropped onto a chair. "We know where they are. We just don't know why."

Cassidy leaned against the wall.

"We know why, and we know the name of our traitor."

Grisha straightened to his full height, his face suddenly ashen. "Tell me any name except Nathan Roubitaux."

"See," Delcambré said. "Everybody knew but me."

CHAPTER 66

TANANA
ALASKA REPUBLIK

"Won't there be patrols out there?" Dez Pitkov asked. He was new at the mercenary business.

"Not yet. Too much is happening for them to understand it all yet," Nathan Roubitaux replied. "Stop for a moment and think. Do you have all the food, ammo, and gear you'll need for the next three weeks?"

Charley Bastrop snorted. "All of us couldn't carry the food I'd need for that long. I figure we'll have the opportunity to hunt, right?"

"I can't guarantee that."

"Shit, Nathan. At this point you can't guarantee anything," Billy Hood said with a laugh.

"Is everyone ready to go?" Nathan gritted through clenched teeth. It didn't require a clairvoyant to see this bunch was only here for a fee.

"Shoot and holler shit!" Charlie yelled. Nathan could smell vodka on him.

"Drive," he ordered.

Ben Kirkpatrick nodded and let the clutch out. The squad-cab utility lurched and roared out of the parking area and pulled onto the Russia-Canada Highway. The vehicle's weak headlamps kept them at a moderate speed.

"Ben, you need me to keep you awake?" Charley asked.

"I need you to shut up so I can concentrate on driving. Go to sleep."

"Keep it between the ditches, son." Charley settled back and closed his eyes.

"Do you know where the Rampart Cutoff is?" Nathan asked. He

knew worry permeated his tone, but he couldn't help himself.

"That's why you had me drive, remember? Hell yes, I know where it is. I lived there for a year and a half."

"Why'd you leave?" Billy Hood asked.

"None of your fucking business."

"Please, everyone, either get some rest or watch out for potential problems," Nathan said. He wished he could fall asleep as easily as Charley had. Exhaustion and anxiety fought a war for his mind, and he hoped exhaustion would eventually win.

If only I could get them out of my head!

The snowy road stretched empty ahead of them. Nathan would have been surprised and worried had there been traffic at this time of the morning. He felt sick in his heart.

How could they have bungled such an easy mission? When they demanded a substantial deposit in gold, they assured him they would succeed, or he would get his money back. *And I was naive enough to believe them!*

"Boss, what happened at Doyon House yesterday?" Dez Pitkov asked. "I thought—"

"I thought so, too, Dez. You can bet I am going to question those people closely."

The vehicle lost speed.

"Why are you slowing?"

"Nathan, there's an armored personnel carrier up there blocking the road."

"How the hell can you tell in the darkness?"

"Would you fucking look! They have it lit up like a damned Christmas tree!"

If only I hadn't been so tired...

"Stop! Turn around! Everyone wake up and check your weapons. Make sure you're fully loaded, and your safety is off!"

Ben turned the utility as tight as possible but had to back up to complete the turn.

Three men in combat gear stepped into the headlight beams and leveled their weapons at the utility. A sharp rap on the door window brought Dez's attention to the gun muzzle pointing at his head.

"Turn off the engine or you are a dead man. *Now!*"

Nathan wanted to cry.

CHAPTER 67

NEAR RAMPART, ALASKA REPUBLIK

Captain Dumont worked at controlling his anger. After a frigid trek to this tiny cabin in the wilderness they were faced with inadequate shelter. The fabled Mr. Roubitaux had failed to materialize and this former mercenary with delusions of grandeur had tried to give him and the Phantom Legion orders.

"One more unnecessary word from you, Mr. N'Go, and I will put a bullet in your brain."

The man shut up immediately. Dumont glanced about and pointed at the angular man with thinning red hair. "What's your name?"

"Selkirk."

Dumont nearly laughed. "We spent some miserable days coming down a river by that name so that we might arrive in this laughable republik unobserved."

"Are ye braggin' 'r' complainin'?"

"Explaining why we are less than overjoyed at this situation. Our employer neglected to mention any of you when he provided these coordinates. If you had not mentioned his name, you would all be under the ice on the Yukon."

Selkirk didn't alter his expression. "So, what is it ya want?"

"Shelter and food for my men. *All* of my men!"

"Then ye best be getting them busy adding on ta this cabin. As ye can see, this one tain't near big enough. As fer grub, poor Rock there is working hard as he can to feed yer boys."

Dumont struggled to stay awake. They had hiked all night through the cold and snow. They were exhausted to a man, but they didn't dare trust the four men they found here at the rendezvous point.

The cabin was too small for all of them, so they drew straws for the right to go into the warmth or help build a camp.

Where the hell was Roubitaux?

CHAPTER 68

NEAR RAMPART, ALASKA REPUBLIK

"I don't understand your actions," Pelagian said, trying to keep the pain from his voice. "You *paid* strangers to murder your friends and fellow delegates?"

Hands and legs shackled, Nathan Roubitaux stood in the middle of the room where a week ago their new constitution received ratification. He appeared unmoved by the First Speaker's words to the point of boredom. Cassidy and Captain Delcambré flanked the prisoner.

Nathan shook his head and a hint of a smile played on his lips. "You're all so pathetic. You believe all of this is going to remain just because you *willed* it."

"We fought for it, we bled for it, and far too many died for it. Did you feel it was all a sham because *you* were not elected First Speaker?" Pelagian thundered in his reach-the-back-rows voice.

"That was merely the culmination of a long trail of witless moves. Do you people believe this farce will hold up to all the assaults the world will throw at it?"

"Obviously you don't. What would you have done differently?" Pelagian said.

"This republik contains more square miles than any other country in North Amerika. All of our neighbors look at us with avarice in their hearts. We need a strong army and you let them all go home. *You* should be in prison, *not* running the country."

"Do you think you were cheated out of the First Speakership, Nathan?"

"I have given my adult life and personal fortune to the Dená Separatist Movement. I was its provisional president, and this is the thanks I get–"

"You never *once* carried arms or engaged the Russians except with your mouth!" Pelagian roared. "Hundreds of our people died to make this nation what it is today. You stayed safe behind walls and orchestrated diplomacy and planning without ever attaining first-hand knowledge of the situation—for that you depended on the rest of us!"

"I worked day and night to help the revolution! I paved the way for you to become First Speaker!"

"My black ass you did! You fought the people every step of the way. You didn't even want a constitution!"

Pelagian realized he was screaming in the prisoner's face and that he should be more circumspect. He willed the anger out of his voice, replaced it with acid.

"You did your worst to make every election go your way, right down to hiring thugs to intimidate voters. You were aghast when the delegates voted in Grisha instead of you. But you know what? None of that really matters."

"Then why are you bringing it all up?" Nathan yelled. His face had gone red with suppressed rage.

"To put your arrest for treason in perspective, that's why. To have a fighting force, maybe two fighting forces, in place prior to the election for First Speaker. You had to have been planning it for over a year."

Nathan's face suddenly lost color and his mouth quivered. He stared into Pelagian's eyes and grated, "If I had won the election, there would have been no crime."

"Because you already had a standing army ready to do your bidding!" Pelagian knew his voice quivered, but he silently vowed to hold his temper as best he could. "A mercenary army possessing more modern weapons than did the Alaska Republik Army." Pelagian paused and took a deep breath. "You wanted to be a fucking dictator!" He couldn't help screaming the last sentence. He felt he needed to vomit.

Nathan looked away first.

"Who are they, your little army? Tell us about them or I'll hang you with them!"

"You will anyway." Nathan's voice lacked life. He nearly mumbled his words. "The British SAS didn't cost me anything more than a guarantee of favored nation status. The Phantom Legion, who were anything but, cost me a lot of gold if they survived. N'Go came to *me* with an offer."

"While he was still a prisoner?" Cassidy snapped.

"Yes. We came to an arrangement. He could obtain modern weapons for gold. So, I had him released."

Pelagian now wanted to weep. *It's one thing if he just wanted to beat me politically—but to shit on our people so he could be a Caesar!*

"Nathan Roubitaux, I formally charge you with treason, armed rebellion, and murder. You will have the opportunity to plead your case in a court before a jury of your People. Please lock him up, Captain Delcambré."

Roland grabbed Nathan's arm and swung him around to leave. "No shit!" he muttered.

CHAPTER 69

NEAR RAMPART, ALASKA REPUBLIK

Lt. Alex Strom and Corporal McKenzie huddled into the hillside. Captain Williams and his six Dená Rangers strung out in a wide arc in the woods. They all watched the large cabin with its surrounding tents and huts.

They had spent the night advancing on the village through the trees on either side of the road. Despite the falling snow, the road surface attested to the passage of many people on foot. Who knew when they were coming back, or what ordinance they had left behind.

The trackers didn't use the easy path. The rangers on the left side of the road picked up a large trail heading toward the river. At that point Rampart lost status as a target. Alex had been worried about the villagers if a firefight started. A weight lifted off his back.

The snow continued to fall heavily. He knew that was a positive. The temperature wouldn't drop more than a few more degrees and it was cold enough already.

Good, we've only got bad guys in front of us!

They came to a halt when they heard sounds of chopping and banging. Captain Williams sent two scouts forward and everyone else rested while they could. Less than five minutes later the scouts returned.

"They're building a camp around a large cabin," the scout whispered to all of them in a huddle. "They don't look happy about it. They are not maintaining any military discipline we could see. No pickets, sentries, or patrols at all."

"We make a line and infiltrate to the point we can see them," Captain Williams ordered.

"Good call," Alex muttered.

It took them an hour. Then they hunkered down in place so they would lose less body heat.

These PL assholes give mercenaries a bad name. Alex felt disgusted. He also felt cold.

Snow had fallen steadily all night and seemed to be thickening. They had been there so long that from the camp nobody would be able to see them due to the covering of snow they all wore.

Someone edged up beside him. Mack.

"Lieutenant, are you warm enough?" she whispered.

"I would welcome a roaring fire and a steak, but I'm okay," he whispered back.

"I brought an extra scarf just for the hell of it. Here, put this on."

Alex wanted to argue but the scarf sounded wonderful. He took it and threaded it around his neck without moving the hood on his parka. It nicely covered the one spot his parka didn't and he felt warmer.

"You trying to make sergeant?" he whispered with a chuckle.

"Just trying to keep you alive. That okay?"

"Far more than okay. Thank you, Mack."

"Now tell me what we are waiting for, the bad guys to get fully rested?"

"We're waiting for orders or reinforcements. Hopefully both. There aren't enough of us to take on that many guys who know how to fight."

"Good point. I'm glad help is on the way. Be careful, okay?"

"You, too," he whispered through a smile.

She slowly returned to her position eight meters away. Alex wondered if the sun would ever again show its warm face. The ranger on his left side eased over to him.

"Lieutenant!"

"It won't happen again—"

"Not why I'm here," the ranger chuckled. "Captain Williams said to tell you there will be air support as well as ground reinforcement as soon as it's light enough to fly."

"How the hell does he know that? He's been out here with me all night," Alex hissed.

"We have radio communication with Tanana. Don't you?"

"Not yet. But are they broadcasting in the open?"

"I don't know, Lieutenant. Why is that important?"

"Because they have a fuckin' radio! See that antenna sticking up behind the cabin?"

"Oh, shit!" the ranger blurted. "We didn–" He bent his head down but Alex could hear him.

"Turn off all radios, now!"

Alex heard a small click. The ranger stared with ashen face at the cabin again, looked at Alex and said, "I suggest you find cover right now," before he scuttled off.

✪

"Are we sure they are within sight of our laager?" N'Go asked.

"I, I don't know," Rock said. "I'm no radio expert."

N'Go regarded Dumont. "Do you have a radio expert among your men?"

"Of course. I've already sent for him." His disdain was obvious to all, N'Go decided. The radio expert came into the cabin and immediately went over to the barrel stove glowing with heat.

"Nice. Why aren't we rotating people through so we can all be *equally* warm?"

"It's in the works," Dumont said curtly. "Now tell me how far away these transmissions are."

The man put on the headset. "I don't hear an–" His head bent forward, and he slightly turned a couple of knobs back and forth before looking up into Dumont's face.

"They are within a kilometer, perhaps closer! It's those *verdammnt* rangers and they have us surrounded!"

"Get a grip on yourself! If we are surrounded, then why are they not already attacking?"

The radioman took a deep breath. "Sorry, sir. You're correct. Do you want me to monitor them?"

"That's why you're here in the nice, warm cabin, Corporal."

"I highly recommend you rotate the men through, Captain. Even a half hour's warmth can make a difference."

"I have Sergeant Dupre working on a rotation roster, Corporal Neville. Now please tell me what the indigenes are doing."

Neville listened for a few minutes and broke into a grin.

"They are between us and the road, sir. There aren't that many of them yet. Once there's adequate light, they have aircraft coming for us."

"Why does that make you grin, corporal?"

"We have at least three hours, sir. We can take them out right now."

CHAPTER 70

ST. ANTHONY, ALASKA REPUBLIK

"This is Colonel Romanov." He listened for a moment and frowned. "Are you absolutely sure, Lieutenant? Can you bring me physical proof, perhaps a prisoner?"

He waited while the caller hemmed and hawed.

"Lieutenant Kirov, even a few photographs would be enough. Good. Report back to me as soon as you can." He slowly replaced the phone on its cradle, deep in thought.

"I must contact Tanana," he said to the room. After nearly a minute of ringing, someone answered.

"This is Colonel Stephan Romanov at Suslov Field. Yes, St. Anthony. I need to speak to a senior officer; I don't care who. In regard to a very serious matter. Now please do as I ask."

✪

Grisha quietly surveyed the damage from the attack on Doyon House. He wondered if the building had received serious structural damage. Sergeant Major Tobias stepped into the room.

"Colonel Romanov down at St. Anthony would like to speak to you, sir."

Grisha frowned. "Any idea what it's about?"

"He insisted it was serious and would only discuss it with a senior officer." Tobias shrugged and smiled. "You're the only one here what fits the description."

Grisha laughed and hurried into his office and grabbled the phone.

"Put Colonel Romanov through, please. Stephan, this is Grisha, what can I do for—" He waited for the torrent of words to register in his mind before responding, "Stephan, are your men absolutely positive?"

While listening he scribbled a note, turned to the door, and held his hand over the speaker. "Tobias!" he hissed. He continued listening to Romanov.

Sergeant Major Tobias stepped into the room and raised his left eyebrow. Grisha handed him the note and he instantly vanished back through the door.

"We have most of our people north of you chasing a large band of mercenaries, but if you require assistance–, of *course* we can get some planes in the air. I'll get back to you as soon as I know more. Please do the same."

"Sergeant Major Tobias!"

The sergeant major puffed into the room. "General?"

"Is Colonel Yamato still here?"

"Yes, General. Do you wish to see him?"

"As soon as possible."

✪

Engrossed in *History of the Peloponnesian War*, Jerry was startled by the brisk knock on his door.

"It's open!"

Sergeant Major Tobias opened the door and leaned in. "Pardon the informality, sir. General Grigorievich would like to see you as soon as possible."

"I'm in my pajamas, should I—"

Tobias grinned. "He won't mind if you don't, sir."

"Lead the way, Sergeant Major."

Jerry had never seen Grisha so agitated. "Did the mercenaries get away?"

"They are suddenly small potatoes, Jerry. Stay with us, Sergeant Major, but shut the door."

Jerry dropped into a chair, as did Tobias after Grisha's nod.

"I just had a call from Colonel Romanov. One of his roving motor patrols caught sight of a large group of people moving toward them on the RustyCan. They took cover and surveyed through binoculars."

"More mercenaries?" Jerry asked.

"The scouts swear it is the French Canadian Army, complete with armor. We have heard nothing official from the French in weeks and we have been attacked by their clandestine forces. So, we have to treat this as an invasion."

"Grisha, wouldn't they have their air force lead the way if they were invading?"

"Well, you and I think alike on this, Jerry. I would think so, but we have no idea what the situation actually is. I need your birds in the air at first light for reconnaissance."

"They already have a combat mission, general. Do you want me to divert some planes to check this out?"

"Absolutely. If it is the French, we have a war on our hands. Feel free to use the communications room, Jerry. Then get some sleep while you can."

CHAPTER 71

DOYON HOUSE,
ALASKA REPUBLIK

"Mr. First Speaker, may I have a quick, unofficial word with you?"

Pelagian raised his eyes from the distressing allocation table of too few troops, relieved for a distraction.

"Ambassador Medicine Bear, my door is always open to you. How may I be of help?"

"I believe it to be the other way around, sir. I have just received notice from my government that a small French Canadian force has entered your country after transiting through ours."

Pelagian felt his good will fade. "Did they transit your country with an official blessing from the Great Council?"

"I asked the same question," more wrinkles appeared on Medicine Bear's forehead as he looked down at a small card in his hand, "…and wrote down the answer. 'French Canada is a longtime ally of the First People's Nation and therefore we answered their transit request in the affirmative." The old Cheyenne frowned and attempted a smile. "I felt I should make you aware of this."

"Are we still allies, your country and mine, or is this a declaration of war from both you and the French?" Part of Pelagian's heart still felt empathy to the point of kinship for the ambassador.

Medicine Bear shook his head softly and muttered, "I don't *know*." He appeared on the verge of tears. "Why would they send me here if they knew this was on the horizon, and give me no warning? Do they think I will honor my oath as a dog soldier, pin my robe to the earth with my sacred arrow, and fight to the death?"

Despite himself, Pelagian snorted. "Calm yourself my friend. I know exactly why they sent you here. I deeply appreciate their brotherhood."

"You do? Please, sir, share your mind."

"They chose an honest man in order you would unofficially tell me this thing *without breaking a treaty.*"

Medicine Bear grinned, bearing more predominant wrinkles. "Of course! How insightful of them." The smile faded in a breath. "But you have had no time to prepare. The French are here!"

"You have given me more time than I would have had otherwise. Thank you. Now I have much to address."

"Your cause is worthy. If you have need of a dog soldier, please let me know." He nodded and left the office.

CHAPTER 72

NEAR RAMPART, ALASKA REPUBLIK

Staff Sergeant Abe Canless moved among the men laagered around the cabin where N'Go held sway, much to his chagrin. He stopped at a shelter-half rigged to reflect the heat of the campfire in front of it. Five of his legionnaires sat warming themselves. All looked up at him at the same time.

"Whatever you do, do not stare up at the forest between us and the road. We are being observed by several Dená Rangers who plan to attack us at daylight." The sharp, cold air caused the heat of his words to puff out and lose their warmth to the night.

"Why are they waiting for light?" asked a shivering African.

"They will have aircraft to assist them and perhaps reinforcements."

"So, we're just going to sit here and wait for them to kill us?" Private Charleston blurted. His breath vanished in the cold air.

"No, Buzz. You all are going to attend to your weapons. Make sure they are clean and free of snow, fully loaded."

Buzz nodded, his eyes darting from side to side as if willing his peripheral vision to locate the threat.

"After I have talked to the rest of the men, I will blow my whistle. At that point you all turn and fire into the woods and they will shoot back. There's about ten of them and over forty of us."

"I like the odds," Private Jones said, the feral grin in his sharp-planed face advertised missing teeth.

Canless went on to the next campfire. By the time he had spoken with each group, an hour had passed. Despite the low temperature, his hands felt slick with sweat, and he wanted a glass of scotch more than anything else in the world.

Making his way back to the edge of the cabin, Canless put the whistle to his lips, and tilted his head back as his chest expanded.

An arrow flashed through his throat and severed his spinal cord before stopping. He toppled as would a cut tree.

Private Buzz Charleston, wide-eyed and poised for the whistle, saw it happen.

"What the fuck! They're using bows and arrows!" he shrieked.

All the men threw themselves into defensive positions and poured fire into the dark forest. Their heavy fire would prove murderous to anyone in the field from the myriad ricochets heard careening about. "Cease fire!" an authority-laced voice bellowed.

Quiet descended as men stopped panting and blood pressure returned to normal. They waited. Nothing. No return fire. No cries of the wounded. Just dead silence.

"We had to have hit *someone!*" Corporal Kandinsky said, speaking for all. The lull in hostilities expanded, pregnant with anticipation.

The cabin door swung open, and Dumont hurried out followed by Rock, both carried weapons.

"Did you get them all?" Rock said with a wide grin.

An arrow thwacked into the middle of Rock's forehead. His eyes instantly stared wonderingly up at the quivering shaft as he crashed full-length to the ground. Again, the night erupted with weapons fire.

"Cease fire!" Dumont screamed from where he had taken cover. "There's only one or two out there. The rest have gone."

"Why?" someone asked as men kicked their campfires to embers and darkness returned.

"I don't know why they left, but there will be planes here in the morning and we would be wise to be elsewhere. I want three volunteers to go up that hill and find the archer."

"We'll watch," a voice said. Chuckles mixed with derisive laughter came from all directions.

"A month's pay bonus for any man who volunteers." Nobody laughed and Dumont grinned.

CHAPTER 73

CHENA AIRFIELD, ALASKA REPUBLIK

Engine revolutions already at maximum, at first light Major Aisha Merritt released her brakes and lifted into the air with full flaps. Five new second lieutenants followed her. Major Dave Marx taxied to the runway and turned into the wind. In moments he also was airborne with his flight of fledgling pilots climbing into the sky behind him.

I'm nervous as a cat in a rocking chair factory, he thought as he craned his head around to check his people. They all faced a quandary as old as close air support. Keep their people on the ground alive without getting shot out of the sky, not to mention doing reconnaissance on a possible invasion.

At least they had daylight this time. In his mind's eye he imagined the missile scorching up to hit Jerry's bird. When the report came in, he thought he had just lost one of his best friends.

I really like that little guy, he reflected.

Today will be different! His people would support the ground troops on the Yukon, and Aisha's people would look for invaders. Dave hoped the invaders didn't have air support.

Three planes following Aisha peeled off and fell into formation behind Dave's group. He was Strike Leader, and she was Recon One. At morning roll call, with light slowly eroding dark, Major Merritt had explained their orders.

Dave now glanced around his airborne formation and spoke into his microphone, "Tanana Control, this is Strike Leader. Please advise as to location of target, over."

"Strike Leader, this is Tanana Control. Make note of these coordinates."

As the voice slowly read off numbers, Dave wrote them on a pad taped to the leg of his flight suit and knew the rest of his pilots were doing the same. He peered at the map on the back of his clipboard and blinked.

"Hell, that's in the middle of nowhere!" he exclaimed.

"Strike Leader, be advised there are no friendlies in the area, only hostiles. Over."

"Roger, Tanana Control. We'll be over them in fifteen minutes. Strike Leader out."

Major Marx glanced at his map. He keyed his microphone.

"Here's the deal, people. We're going to come in wing-to-wing. Keep your heads on a swivel and look for targets to take out on our *next* pass. Got it?"

They got it.

Major Dave Marx surveyed the land beneath him.

Even in the winter this country is spectacular!

✪

Major Aisha Merritt cut across country, glimpsing the RustyCan off to the side and finally flying above it again near Tanana Crossing. The scout report had placed the leading elements of the bogie force this side of Old Crow.

She didn't know what to expect, which worried and pissed her off at the same time. They said a ground force had been confirmed, but nothing was said about *enemy* air support.

I sure as hell would have air support if I was invading someone.

"Recon flight," she said into her microphone. Two clicks answered. "We're going to swing wide a few miles and cross the RustyCan north of Old Crow. You will both maintain station four miles away while I bisect the road. Keep your head on a swivel. There are potential bogies out there."

Again, two clicks.

When she decided they were four miles out, she radioed, "Maintain station here. Keep your eyes peeled." She registered the comm clicks but her thoughts ranged far ahead of her.

From a thousand meters altitude she could see the snowy road empty of traffic of any sort. She flew south to Old Crow and spied a total of two utilities roaring in different directions and showering the white, pristine road and landscape with plumes of dust.

"Recon Flight, no contact between the intercept point and Old Crow. I am now flying the highway north. Maintain station."

As she proceeded, she wondered if the scouts had been drinking or indulging in hallucinogens. She also wondered how Dave and the strike force fared. She changed frequencies and heard, "Break right, break right! It's on your tail!"

✪

Major Dave Marx dove toward the burning cabin and strafed it a third time. Pissed wouldn't touch how he felt. It had started out as a textbook recon...

Strike Force flew over the cabin and Dave first thought it a mistake in navigation. In his rearview mirror he saw the missile scream up and hit one of his people. The P-61 disintegrated in a huge fireball.

"Break formation! Missiles!" He pushed the stick over hard and came back around at full throttle.

When his sights lined up on the cabin, he squeezed the trigger button hard enough to bruise his hand. People on the ground ran for cover and he dropped as many as he could. The forest seemed to leap up at him and he pulled out of the dive.

At 1500 meters he rolled over to survey the situation. Out in the middle of the Yukon the major debris of the downed bird burned. Melting ice had already snuffed out some of the flames.

I wonder who we lost.

A heavy machine gun near the forest fired at the planes. He snarled and went into a steep dive, guns blazing.

"Strike Leader, this is Courtney. My bird is hit and losing oil. Headed for Chena!"

Another missile torched up straight at him. He jinked to port and the weapon passed so close he imagined he could feel heat from the propellant. In his mirror he saw it curve around and chase him!

"What the hell. They can't so that!"

Someone screamed over the radio, "Break right, break right! It's on your tail!"

Dave released the trigger button and pulled up, giving his bird, *Turner* every ounce of throttle he could. The missile tried to follow but burned out and exploded.

"Strike Leader, this is Tanana Control. We have ground troops advancing into the area. Break off your attack. I repeat, break off your attack."

"Roger that, Tanana. Strike Force, retire now."

Six clicks responded.

"Who'd we lose?"

"Annette Eluska," someone said with a catch in his voice.

Not our only woman pilot! "Head for home," he ordered, willing away the tears leaking from the corners of his eyes.

✪

Aisha heard the name at the same time she saw vehicles on the RustyCan. She flew over and rolled to the left to get a good view. At first glance it looked like a military column.

No armor other than an APC, no weapons in view at all. What the hell is this?

She came around, dropped to a hundred meters, and flew over the vehicles. The leader was a limousine of some exotic make and both the French tricolor and a white flag flew from the front fenders.

"Tanana Control, this is Recon Leader. I have what looks like a French diplomatic mission approaching Tetlin. Please advise."

"Recon Leader, please repeat that transmission."

She complied, then rattled off her coordinates, and flew back to her lieutenants.

"Recon, our mission here is finished. Now we are part of the Strike Force. Follow me!"

They flew toward Rampart.

CHAPTER 74

TANANA
ALASKA REPUBLIK

"Why didn't they contact us first?" Pelagian muttered as he paced his office wall-to-wall.

"Perhaps they tried and were unable to find our frequency," Claude Adams suggested.

"I love you, Claude," Pelagian said, "I truly do. You are the only person I know who finds the possible benefit in any situation."

"So, you agree?" Claude asked in evident surprise.

"No. The French have never done anything without analyzing it to the point of ineffective. This is no doubt a diplomatic exchange of some sort, but it is also a well thought-out ploy."

"I agree. What are you going to do?"

"Appoint you Minister of State and make you take care of it."

Claude laughed. "No, seriously, what are you going to do?"

"I *am* serious. Will you accept the portfolio, as I believe it's called?"

"Pelagian, I have never directed anyone other than myself. To run a full department–"

"Which *you* would build with nobody looking over your shoulder."

"Really? Seriously? *Nobody* looking over my shoulder? What if I do not agree with all your positions?"

"Then I would expect a cogent, well thought-out rebuttal which I would give full consideration. This trail runs in two directions, Claude. I know you and I trust you, otherwise I would not make the offer."

"I accept, Mr. First Speaker. Do I get a limousine?" he asked lightheartedly.

"If you can find one in Alaska Republik, it goes with the office."

CHAPTER 75

CHENA
ALASKA REPUBLIK

Lieutenant Colonel Yamato exited his office and stopped behind the podium in front of two rows of pilots standing at attention. Behind them was a growing number of civilians who listened attentively.

"Please be at ease. We have lost one of our own. Second Lieutenant Annette Eluska served her country and her people with enthusiasm, professionalism, and love."

He studied his audience as he spoke. Every eye glistened and tears leaked down numerous cheeks.

"There is no doubt in my mind that had she been given an even chance in her last flight; she would have prevailed. In essence, she was shot in the back. Our first combat sortie ended in grief, but with honor."

Aisha dabbed her eyes with a tissue, and Dave audibly swallowed.

"There will be a closed casket funeral tomorrow and I hope to see you all there to honor Annette. The only lesson we can take from this sad event is the knowledge that it could have been any of us in the air that day. Pilots rely on professionalism first and luck second; her professionalism was evident. It was her luck that ran out."

He regarded the somber faces before him and felt at a loss. Words couldn't bridge this situation. He knew what might help.

"There will be a wake tonight in the ready room. I will be there and I hope to see all of you. You are dismissed."

✪

When Jerry and Magda entered the ready room five hours later most of the others ranged from tipsy to smashed.

"You didn't wait for me?" he asked Aisha.

"Well, *I* did. But then, I don't drink." She gave him a wide smile.

"This is the perfect antidote to their grief. Good work, Jerry."

"C'mon, Aisha. This was my *only* option and you know it."

"Yeah, Dave and I knew it, but nobody else did. Go get a beer, Colonel. Magda, thank you so much for the hen party last week. All of us enjoyed it."

Magda smiled. "Thanks, Aisha. Annette and I were friends when we were growing up. I had hoped to catch up on all her adventures, but that is not to be."

"Hen Party?" Jerry nudged.

"Women only," Magda said firmly. "No regulations were broken."

"We only have five regulations at most."

Dave Marx nudged his elbow and handed him a beer. "Surrender, Jerry. You will lose no honor and gain peace in your house.

Jerry nodded to the women, "Ladies, if you'll excuse me." He turned to Dave and they wandered toward the bar at the back of the room. "Haven't you been divorced twice, Dave?"

"Your point, sir?"

"I guess you earned that bit of wisdom the hard way."

Dave laughed and tossed back the drink in his hand. "Of course, I did."

"I think Grisha was pissed that we didn't leave anyone alive at the cabin."

"Anybody who was alive got the hell out of there fast. Besides, the Dená Rangers took a prisoner this morning."

"Why didn't I already know that?"

"You were busy, *sir*. We didn't bother you with it since it didn't affect us."

Jerry drank more beer. "Yeah, I can see that. What's the prisoner's name?"

"Take your pick; he's either the Boss, or N'Go."

"N'Go's in the stockade!"

"As I understand it, he was released months ago due to the command's conviction he was not a criminal but a tool of a Major Riordan." Dave said. "So, what's the big deal about this guy?"

Dave and Aisha had come to Alaska Republik some months after the capture of the two men and had no idea of the circumstances.

"He and his boss planned to assassinate Pelagian on Election Day. Grisha and Yukon Cassidy captured them. I never felt that Riordan was the commander he thought himself to be."

"N'Go?"

"Was his second-in-command in the International Freekorps."

"Jerry," Dave said gently. "Drink your beer and forget all the other bullshit for an evening. You deserve it as much as anyone else in this room."

"Excellent idea, Major. I concur."

Jerry talked to every person in the room in the next four hours. After he finished his beer, he filled the bottle with water and went about consoling his people.

✪

Solare walked into the hanger next to Yukon Cassidy, who was nearly asleep on his feet. She heard about the woman pilot being killed and wanted to pay her respects despite the fact she had met none of the aviators other than Lieutenant Colonel Yamato. Magda Yamato saw them, grinned widely, and came over and hugged Cassidy.

"Thank you so much for coming to this sad event, Yukon."

"Magda, I want you meet Solare. If she has a last name I don't know what it is. Solare, this is Magda Haroldsson Yamato, the lieutenant colonel's partner, and all-around warrior woman."

Both women smiled. "We've already met, Yukon, but thank you," Magda said.

"He has a real way with words, doesn't he?" Solare said.

"He's dependable, keeps his word, and has aided my father more times than I can enumerate." Magda's smile widened. "He is a family member as far as we are concerned."

Solare glanced at Cassidy who had grown quiet and somewhat red in the face. "We are still new acquaintances, so I will take you at your word, Magda."

"Ask my parents," she said, looking over Solare's shoulder, "they just walked in with someone. I didn't even know they were in Chena."

Solare turned to see the First Speaker and two small women closing on them. She elbowed Cassidy and they turned toward the new arrivals.

"Major Cassidy, how good to see you here," Pelagian said with slight smile, "and Miss Solare. May I present my wife, Bodecia, and Naomi Eluska, our fallen warrior's mother."

Solare immediately went to the mother and hugged her tightly. "I am so sorry for your loss, Naomi. She died a hero and will not be forgotten."

Naomi stiffened briefly and then softened into the hug. "Who are you, again?"

"My name is Solare, I am a Peacekeeper. If there is anything I can do for you, please tell me."

"Thank you, Solare. You remind me of my daughter."

Solare pulled back and realized everyone else in the small group had been watching her. Magda also hugged Naomi while speaking quietly into her ear.

"Did you know Annette?" Bodecia asked Solare.

"No, ma'am, I did not."

"Please, my name is Bodecia, Solare. We women bearing only one name need to stick together."

Solare blurted a little laugh. "I heard you were an ass-kicker of the first water. Even though I didn't know her, I wanted to honor Lieutenant Eluska. She proved she was tough as any man. Flight school isn't for shrinking violets."

"You've been?"

"Yes, a long time ago. I am told you are a *midew*."

Bodecia pulled back a few millimeters, and her smile flattened a few degrees.

I shouldn't have said that! Solare thought.

"You are part Chippewa?"

"How did you know that?"

"They are the only people who use that term for *healer*. I happily accept either term, or the many others I have heard over the years."

"So how do we nullify the French, English, and the Austrians at the same time?"

"I'm so happy you are one of us, Solare! We take them one at a time in the order of threat. Right now, the French are fucking with us."

"What did you say, dear?" Pelagian asked.

"I was not speaking to you, sir," she snapped.

He grinned. "I know, but I overheard the word, *Austrian,* and I am sadly lacking in intelligence about their motivations here in Alaska."

"I only meant the source of the missiles, sir." Solare said.

"I'm sure. From now on please call me Pelagian. This position is not everything I am."

Solare laughed. *I like these people!*

"We need to know if the Austrians are merely selling weapons to other countries, or are they part of what we must anticipate."

"I have some contacts in Europe, very few; but some."

"I may call on you, Solare."

"I would be honored, Mr. First Speaker."

CHAPTER 76

NEAR RAMPART, ALASKA REPUBLIK

N'Go crept through the forest. He could not remember being this cold before in his life. He was a son of Africa, not the Arctic where greed had lured him. A distant buzz penetrated his thoughts and he knelt down as yet another P-61 buzzed overhead

Damn those things to the Bardo, he thought.

Ahead of him, Rasputin edged through the brush, his automatic weapon at the ready.

How many times have we done this? he thought. *Just once could one of these wild endeavors go as planned, or is that too much to ask?*

Far behind them the intense gunfire ceased, and he knew they had limited time before the damned rangers would track them down. They had followed Six Mile Creek down to where it emptied into the Yukon. Both creek and river lay covered with snow over bank-to-bank ice.

Bone-chilling wind whistled over the Yukon and into the mouth of the creek. Despite the layers of clothing covered with an Athabascan parka, N'Go shivered. He hated cold almost as much as he hated Nathan Roubitaux.

When I find that pig I will–

"Boss!" Rasputin hissed.

"What?"

"Listen!"

Helicopter. That damned helicopter. I knew I should have brought the last SAM with me!

"Hunker down. Don't look up!" Rasputin said as he demonstrated.

N'Go did the same, fuming. *He is getting above his station. Lucky for him that I find him necessary.*

Both men curled into the tufts of partially covered, withered beach grass and reeds. The helicopter flew 25 meters above the ice, using the Yukon as a guide. It plodded along at low speed.

They're searching for us. N'Go wanted to look up so badly he felt a pain behind his eyes.

The helicopter continued north toward Rampart.

Where will we go? Rampart was their last hope. Stephan Village was too many miles beyond Rampart to be a realistic destination.

Rasputin moved over next to him.

"Okay, Boss, you always have an answer. What now?"

"I don't know. If they don't stay in Rampart they will leave at least a squad of rangers. They are sure to capture us unless we change direction."

"And go where?"

"Do you *want* to be captured?"

"At this point it's better than freezing."

"Rasputin, they will hang us. We have killed too many of them. They view us as bandits."

"Perhaps, but not immediately. They will want many answers before they try us. Much can transpire before then."

He's correct. They will want answers, and he has all of them. He brought his rifle up and shot Rasputin through the chest.

The small man fell backward and stared up him with a puzzled expression.

"N'Go! W, wh, *why?*" he gasped. Blood bubbled between his words.

"You're a fast learner. Think about it. And call me *Boss.*"

He trudged east into the wind toward Rampart. The cold permeated his bones, and he knew he wouldn't make it to the village on his own. *What a stupid way to die!*

CHAPTER 77

NEAR RAMPART, ALASKA REPUBLIK

Although Claude wasn't impressed with the Spartan luxury of the armored personnel carrier, or the permeating stink of diesel fuel, he thoroughly appreciated the security. Nine Dená Rangers, all wearing combat gear and carrying weapons shared the minimally heated compartment. Captain Dexter Williams, his old, recently promoted friend, commanded the rangers.

Another APC filled with rangers followed theirs. Most of the rangers had fought the French Foreign Legion near Rampart, routed, and captured the survivors of the aerial attack. The prospect of dealing with more Frenchmen didn't deter them in the slightest.

"Colonel Romanov has his people at Tetlin," Dexter said. "They have APCs blocking the RustyCan. One way or another, that's where we're going to meet these people."

"I'd like to meet them standing in the middle of the road with no weapons showing," Claude said.

"They would think us weak, Mr. Minister of State."

"And perhaps, civilized?" Claude grinned. "We've been friends far too long for you to call me anything other than Claude, and if I have to enforce it, I'll call it an order."

Dexter's quick grin appeared. "As you say, Brother."

"They're not going to form diplomatic relations by killing us," Claude continued. "They've been on the road for at least two days, and they want something from us. I'm not sure what, but I have my suspicions."

"Care to share?"

"Be very aware of what the quiet ones are doing. The loud ones will be politicians."

"You got it, Claude."

"I would like to be in Tetlin before this delegation arrives. We have to deal with them away from civilians. Is that possible?"

"Give me a few minutes and I'll let you know, Brother." Williams moved next to the female radio-talker.

Claude knew Dexter would do everything in his power get him to Tetlin as soon as humanly possible. Their friendship went back to childhood when they both attended the Priest's School. They constantly incurred the wrath of strict nuns who were long on discipline and sadly lacking in non-secular imagination.

That was nearly thirty years ago. How quickly the time has passed.

Dexter returned and dropped onto the bench next to him.

"We just passed Chena and have at least five, maybe six hours before we can get to Tetlin in this thing." He slapped the side of the compartment. "But I have a helicopter meeting us in about an hour that will carry all of us to Tetlin in an hour."

Claude grinned. "See, you are still the wizard you always were."

✪

Claude watched out the helicopter window as it sat down on Suslov Field. The rear ramp yawned open and four rangers were the first out to ensure all was as it should be. One nodded to Dexter, who said, "Okay, Mr. Minister of State, you're up."

He helped Claude to his feet and they quickly embraced.

"You got nothing to worry about as long as I'm here," Dexter said into his ear.

"I know that. Thank you."

Colonel Romanov stood at attention with an honor guard of six troopers of whom at least two were Claude's cousins.

"Please, Colonel Romanov, dispense with the pomp and circumstance. We have far too much to do." Claude extended his hand. "It's Stephan, isn't it? I'm Claude."

Romanov shook his hand. "I appreciate the informality. After twenty years in an organization comprised of ritual and ineffectiveness, it is a distinct pleasure to be in one that attacks the issue at hand."

"Perhaps *attacks* is not quite the word I had in mind," Claude laughed. The realization that these people would instantly do his bidding, no matter how absurd, weighed on his soul. He understood he was representing the Republik but the full awareness of the dimensions of his rank finally hit him. He nodded to both cousins who grinned as they nodded back.

He looked around and beheld an old limousine. "Oh, my word, what a beautiful machine!"

"General Grigorievich said you would be pleased. It is a 1948 Daimler DE 36 in perfect mechanical condition, and it now belongs to the Ministry of State."

Dexter stepped next to him. "Claude, our scouts have the column about half an hour out."

After staring at the automobile a moment longer, Claude smiled at his old friend and said, "Okay. Here's what I would like…"

CHAPTER 78

NEAR RAMPART, ALASKA REPUBLIK

Yukin Cassidy slogged through the deepening snow and saw a lone figure moving toward them in the gloom. *That's got to be the Boss.*

"Raise your hands or you will be shot!" Cassidy bellowed.

The figure stood still and followed instructions. Two rangers hurried up on either side and grabbed the quarry. Cassidy hurried up to them and peered at the man.

"Pull your hood down." The man complied. "N'Go! What the hell are you doing out here? You could have reached California or Asia by now."

"Mr. Cassidy, how nice to see you again."

"Where's Riordan?" Cassidy demanded in a hard voice. Wind whipped off the Yukon River and snow stung his face.

"*Riordan*? How the hell would I know? I hoped you fools had hung him by now."

Cassidy realized he wasn't lying. "So why did you stay if not to help him?"

"Do you really think I am going to tell you anything without some sort of deal on the table first?"

"You haven't changed a bit, N'Go," Delcambré said, standing off to the side. "Perhaps if we believe you know nothing of Riordan there would be no reason not to execute you as a murdering bandit right here and now."

"Then you wouldn't find out what I know, or why I stayed."

Cassidy grinned. "Would the name *Nathan* have anything to do with your presence?"

The constant icy wind numbed Cassidy and he shivered despite himself.

N'Go's face fell, and his attitude lost definition. He licked his chapped lips. "You could use me as a witness."

"How about as a co-conspirator?" Cassidy asked. He looked over to the radioman. "Call the helicopter, I think we're all tired of walking, and I'm freezing my ass off."

CHAPTER 79

NEAR TETLIN,
ALASKA REPUBLIK

Cold wind whipped his clothes as well as the heavy brush on both sides of the RustyCan Highway. Claude stood in the middle of the road and tried to relax as the lead vehicle roared toward him. The French tricolor snapped in the wind on the front right fender while what appeared to be a white sheet was mounted on the left. An armored personnel carrier followed the car with three lorries bringing up the rear.

Some invasion, he thought. He quickly scanned the sky for aircraft. Nothing.

The car slowed and came to a stop ten meters from Claude. The driver quickly jumped out and opened the back door on the limousine. A man of rotund proportions dressed in a three-piece suit adorned with a collection of medals emerged, walked over to Claude, and held out a rolled paper to him.

"Premier François Mitterrand sends his complements and requests that I, Jacque Velade, be accepted as his ambassador to your newly birthed country. To whom do I have the honor of speaking?"

"Claude Adams, Minister of State for Alaska Republik. I find your arrival interesting."

Keeping his arms at his side, Claude did not accept the roll of paper, nor offer to shake hands.

"How is it you are standing in the middle of the wilderness, Minister Adams?"

The wind picked up and blew new snow over them.

"We wished to know your intentions out here rather than in a populated area."

Velade grinned.

"All by yourself?"

"Not by myself." Claude whistled his deckhand blast and rangers rose out of the brush and snow on both sides of the road. Four APCs pushed through the trees and brush behind them, machine guns manned.

"We were trying to be polite."

Velade looked amused and impressed at the same time. "*Bon!* That was very illuminating, Minister Adams."

"I hate formality. Please call me Claude, okay?"

"Of course. I am Jacque, *oui?*"

"Yes, Jacque. Our major question is, why didn't you call ahead? This is a new nation in turmoil, and you chose to initiate diplomatic relations by roaring into our country with military vehicles."

"But we signaled our peaceful intentions, *non?*" He gestured at the white flag flapping in the now constant wind.

"Does the French nation wish us to believe diplomatic relations are treated as an afterthought or is this a calculated attempt to test our borders?"

"Minister Adams, please. May we discuss this somewhere a little more benign in terms of temperature? As the Yanks say, I am freezing my ass off."

"Of course. Follow my car." His limousine eased down the road and stopped. He turned and got into the back seat. Dexter was at the wheel.

"What do you want us to do, Claude?"

"Turn around and drive to the base at Tetlin. Go slow enough they can keep up."

"You're the boss."

Colonel Romanov and twenty troopers stood at attention when the convoy followed Claude through the gate of the former Russian redoubt and stopped in front of them. Claude hopped out and nodded to Romanov. "Very snappy," he said with a wink.

The French vehicles pulled up next to each other on the parade ground. The Alaskan APCs pulled in behind them and troopers deployed to form a perimeter around the French machines.

Ambassador Velade waited for his driver to open his door before emerging from the car. He stood and brushed himself off as he glanced around.

"Do you fear treachery on our part, Minister Adams?"

"Fear it? No. Prepare for it? Yes."

Velade's wide smile lost wattage as he searched Claude's face for information.

"You are a belligerent new nation, I see. France offers you diplomatic recognition and you respond as if attacked."

"Have all the *independent* nations you entered in this manner become part of your colonies?"

"Are you trying to insult me?" The remnants of Velade's aura of goodwill evaporated.

"Not at all. I am pointing out that *you* have intentionally insulted *us*. We *do* have diplomatic channels through the United States and the Republic of California."

Claude put more frost into his voice. "Please tell your Premier François Mitterrand we would be happy to open nation-to-nation relations if we are treated as an equal. Please don't be insulted while our security forces escort your convoy back to the border of the First People's Nation."

Velade didn't seem chilled any longer. His face flushed red with anger.

"I have never been so insulted–"

"How you deal with it is up to you, sir," Claude said firmly and nodded. "Good day."

He turned and walked into the administration building with Colonel Romanov.

They heard doors slam and engines rev as Romanov shut the door.

"Did I just start a war, Stephan?"

"If you did, Claude, at least we will see the knives. I have never seen arrogance so admirably dealt with before in my life. I am in awe."

Claude laughed. "I'm glad you approve. We've had mercenaries with missiles, subgroups of enemies we thought subdued, and British agents trying to kill us in the cradle. This was the most hubristic attempt yet." He plopped down onto a chair.

"What now?" Romanov asked.

"I need to speak with Pelagian. This isn't over."

CHAPTER 80

TANANA
ALASKA REPUBLIK

CASSIDY AND DELCAMBRÈ TRUDGED INTO THE CAFETERIA AND COLLAPSED onto the first chairs they found. The mingled scents of floor wax and simmering meat wafted past. They shrugged out of their parkas and simultaneously groaned with pleasure from the heat in the room.

Laura Jack stepped through the kitchen door. "I thought I heard someone out here."

Roland smiled up at her. "How wonderful to see your beautiful face again, my dear."

She bent over and kissed his cheek. "I thought you had forgotten me. You haven't come to see me in two weeks."

"Blame me for that, Laura," Cassidy said. "I've kept him in the field doing our jobs. Is it possible to get something to eat?"

"We have a caribou stew simmering. Would that do?"

"Yes!" they said in unison.

She laughed and went back into the kitchen. Grisha walked in and grinned.

"There they are!"

"Oh *merde*," Roland murmured. "What does he want now?"

"Good afternoon, General Grigorievich. How are you?" Cassidy smiled.

"I am fine. I have a new daughter that I see far less than I wish. I also have a huge problem that I believe the two of you can help me with."

"And that would be?" Roland asked.

"You speak French flawlessly, yes?"

"*Oui!*"

"I think we're going to need your skills, Roland. If I'm any judge of military minds, we're going to be at war before the day is out."

"With whom?" Cassidy blurted.

"French Canada."

"Por quoi?" Roland asked.

"We're monitoring a situation down at Tetlin." He related Claude's day and finished with, "Our scouts are *escorting* them to the FPN border. I don't believe they will get that far for a while."

"Who, General Grisha, do you mean when you speak of not getting there; the French or our scouts?" Roland asked.

"The scouts."

Laura Jack came in carrying a wide tray and sat it on the table next to them. She put a steaming bowl in front of Cassidy and Delcambré and tipped the tray onto the table scattering utensils and bread.

"General, can I get you anything?" she asked.

While he watched his friends grab spoons and bread, he shook his head.

"Thank you for asking."

CHAPTER 81

CHENA
ALASKA REPUBLIK

Captain Dexter Williams rode in the forward APC following the French delegation. The rearmost French vehicle was a large lorry with a canvas cover over the cargo deck. He hadn't liked the looks of that lorry from the first moment he saw it.

We got no idea what they have in there. No matter how hard we tried, I and my people couldn't get a glimpse of their cargo.

"Corporal Titus, are you monitoring their radio?" he asked the radioman.

"Yes, Captain. They're getting traffic from somewhere in front of them and the people we're following just said *strike force!*"

"Sergeant, how much farther to the border?"

"About fifteen kilometers, sir."

"George, reduce speed. Put about 300 meters between us and them."

The driver nodded and reduced speed. The lorry ahead of them also slowed.

Dexter keyed his microphone, "Everyone disperse! Get off the road, now!"

George drove them across the left hand ditch and into the brush.

Dexter kept his eyes on the lorry. The canvas jerked up and back revealing a twin barreled 20mm gun mount. The gunner swiveled the muzzles toward Dexter's APC.

"Get the fuck out of here, George!" he screamed.

George stomped on the accelerator and the machine plowed into willow thickets fast as a frightened moose. The ground behind them erupted in a series of dirt and brush geysers. Gunfire thundered around them.

"Go right, George! Get in front of them!" His enraged need to show these bastards they had messed with the wrong people nearly overwhelmed him.

George smashed thickets and bushes for a hundred meters, the APC tracks throwing vegetation, rocks, and snow in twin fountains behind them. He steered to the right and popped out of the brush no more than 30 meters from the middle lorry. Figures in combat gear poured out of its rear ramp.

"Fire!" Dexter screamed.

The fifty-caliber machine gun mount on the APC raked the men on the ground and then blew the lorry to pieces. Blood glistened on the snow before melting in, leaving streaks that slowly turned pink. Dená Rangers scrambled out the back hatch of the APCs and advanced on the personnel and vehicles still on the road.

The 20mm on the rear lorry erupted in an explosion. Everything went quiet.

Dexter switched the channel to the loud hailer on the front of his APC.

"If you want to live, come out with your hands up. Two minutes from now we will kill anything that moves between here and the border."

Ten seconds later men walked toward him, hands in air. Some supported obviously wounded men between them.

"Medic!" Dexter shouted.

Sergeants Helen Anton and Anna Frank hurried forward and began ministering to the wounded.

"Captain, I'm picking up incoming aircraft!" Corporal Danny Titus shouted.

"Whose?"

"RCAF and they're coming fast!"

"Californians?" Dexter said aloud. "What the hell are they doing here? Is *everyone* attacking us?"

"Sir, do we fire at the aircraft?" Sergeant Yaske asked in a tight voice.

"No. The last I heard they were our ally."

"I sure as hell hope that's still true," Yaske said as a spread-out flight of seven jet aircraft shrieked over them.

"So far, so good," Dexter said.

"Captain," Corporal Titus yelled. "They want to talk to you, sir!"

God, I hope this isn't bad news!

CHAPTER 82

CHENA
ALASKA REPUBLIK

"Colonel Yamato," Staff Sergeant Martha Frank said crisply. "We have a message for you from the Republic of California Air Force."

"What is it?"

"Request permission to land at Chena Airfield."

"Why, are they here?"

"Sir, they are overhead!"

"Permission granted."

Staff Sergeant Frank vanished. Her running footsteps faded quickly.

Jerry grabbed his telephone and pressed the red button.

"General—" a female voice said.

"This is Colonel Yamato. I need to speak to Grisha now!"

"This is Gen—"

"Grisha, Jerry here. I have a flight of RCAF jets landing here as we speak."

"Why?"

"Hell, I hoped *you* would know. Has the Republic of California contacted you at all?"

"No. Keep me posted. Get out there, now!"

Jerry forced himself to stop running when he reached the outside door. He hadn't even slowed enough to grab his coat. He stepped outside and came face-to-face with Colonel Shipley, his old boss, and commander of the RCAF squadron.

"Colonel Yamato," Shipley said through a wide grin as he pushed Jerry back inside. "I'm freezing out here! Why haven't they made you a general yet?"

Jerry laughed. "What are you doing here, Colonel Shipley?"

"To keep our favorite ally from getting sucker punched."

"Who's going to do that?"

"French Canada and British Canada."

"I thought they were belligerents."

"They don't know about each other. Can you put me through to Grisha, so I only have to go through this once?"

"You bet your ass!" He turned and shouted, "Sergeant Frank, I need you!"

CHAPTER 83

TANANA
ALASKA REPUBLIK

Grisha grabbed the phone before the first ring completed. "Jerry?"

"Yes, sir. I have Colonel Shipley here. He wants to explain the situation to both of us at the same time."

"Excellent! Put him on."

"Grisha, good to talk to you. I won't wait for responses from you; too much to say. We've been monitoring both British Canada *and* French Canada military communications.

"Alaska seems to be the coup de jour for nations with acquisitive proclivities. Both have agents in your country as we speak. There is a FCAF Mirage jet squadron out of Moose Jaw on its way to Tanana right now. At the same time, with no idea of what the French are doing, British Canada is keeping its powder dry waiting for word from someone already in Alaska."

Grisha blinked.

"Colonel Shipley, thank you. Some of this we have already neutralized, but you just gave us more to investigate. How long do we have before the French squadron attacks?"

"We have them at fifty-four minutes out of Tanana. As your ally, do you wish us to engage them?"

"I appreciate the offer, and yes, we do. But let us have first response, then we will send the message; 'you are free to engage'."

"Roger that," Shipley said with a laugh. "We're standing by."

Grisha depressed the cradle and then pushed one of the buttons.

"Yukon, ask Delcambré if any of the FI people have surface-to-air-missile training." While he waited, he waved at Sergeant Major Tobias and scribbled a note. The sergeant major hurried off. Cassidy came back on the line and gave him an answer.

"Where is this man? We need him in Tanana in half an hour. Is that possible?" A moment passed.

"Thank you, Yukon!" He hung up the phone. Sergeant Major Tobias came into the room and opened his mouth to speak.

"No time! Find Corporal Harris of the Peacekeepers right now! He's *here* in Tanana somewhere! We need him."

Tobias flashed away.

CHAPTER 84

TANANA
ALASKA REPUBLIK

"Dennis!" Cassidy yelled as he burst into accounting where his quarry sat in an otherwise empty office.

"Dammit, Cassidy, you nearly made me crap myself. What do you want?"

"You've been trained to deploy surface to air missiles, right?" he spoke fast and with urgency.

"Well, technically–"

"Follow me, right now! We have no time to waste!" Cassidy thundered down the hallway.

"Oh, fer crissakes!" Dennis Harris scrambled to follow.

Cassidy stood in the building exit. "C'mon, dammit. We don't have much time!"

Dennis slowed. "I didn't grab my parka. I'll freeze out there!"

"We have more parkas. Get out there, now!"

Cassidy pushed him into the back of a sedan, and they roared away down the snow-packed road. The interior of the car was warm without a coat.

Cassidy must be cooking in here. Good!

"Is this a secret mission or do I get to hear everything before it happens?"

In less than twenty seconds Dennis heard all about English and French perfidy and attacking French jets.

"What kind of SAMs do you have?"

"They're Austrian and heat-seeking." Cassidy looked worried.

"Oh good. They're not the usual junk they give us up here. Save the lecture, you know what I'm talking about."

"Yeah, I do. Have you trained with these?"

"I need to see them, Major Cassidy. Afterward, I can answer your question."

"Follow me." The car stopped and Cassidy flew out the door. Dennis rushed to keep up.

"If I fall on the ice and break something," Dennis bawled at Cassidy, "I won't be any good to anybody!"

Inside the large, *unheated*, supply shed Cassidy pointed to a well-lit bench where a missile system lay gleaming with promise of malice. Dennis focused on the weapon and hurried over to inspect. Someone put a preheated parka over his shoulders, and he grunted appreciatively.

Where the hell did they get this? he wondered.

"What we have here is a Krupp *Toter-Engel* 88H. They only have one newer model, but it's not allowed outside the Austrian Empire yet." Dennis swiveled his eyes to Cassidy. "Now what?"

"Can you fire the dammed thing?"

"Of course, I can. You could, too if you'd read the fucking instructions. They dumbed them down so a *conscript* can fire one," Dennis said matter-of-factly. "Who tore this down? They know their stuff."

"A sergeant that transferred to the Dená Rangers. He's a captain now. We need ten people able to fire these things in less than ten minutes."

"Well, where the hell are they? Someday I want to meet that sergeant."

"Behind you."

Dennis turned and finally saw the soldiers in a semi-circle watching him and Cassidy.

"Oh, okay." He grabbed the launcher and began talking as fast as he could. He did his best to ignore asides, as well as technical flaws since they didn't matter at the moment, and demonstrated everything except actually firing the missile in seven minutes.

"It's very elegant. You're lucky to have a weapon this superb." Dennis grinned at Cassidy as he finished. "Do I get to play, too?"

"That's up to you. From this moment on, you are the Chief Armorer with the rank of major. Do whatever you like."

"Outstanding." He grabbed one of the armed launchers and hurried after the others.

I wonder if I should have told him I've never fired one of these in combat? He cackled and increased his speed.

CHAPTER 85

TANANA
ALASKA REPUBLIK

"General Grisha, we have our people deployed," Cassidy gasped, trying to catch his breath. "Colonel Yamato has a bird up for observation purposes only. His P-61s are no match for Mirage jets."

Cassidy took some deep breaths and willed his heart to slow. His lungs ached from the cold. He had just run from Major Harris' position over to the road where Grisha huddled with three others behind an idling APC

Grisha nodded. "I trust the pilot has a camera with him?"

"Yes, a 16mm loaded with infrared film."

"You're getting good at this, Yukon."

"I'm blessed with an intelligent crew. Some of it had to rub off. I'm going out there. I wouldn't miss this for the world."

"Lead on, Major. Please remember that the other guys have weapons, too."

The minimal dusk had fallen and the *Aurora Borealis* danced across the sky. Chief Armorer Dennis Harris had deployed the troops a hundred meters apart in a line along the frozen Yukon River from one end of the town to the other end. Cassidy felt impressed.

"There they are!" Someone shouted. "Straight out of the southeast!"

Cassidy squinted his eyes but saw nothing. "Where? I–"

A jet shrieked directly over his head and was gone before the violent blast from the smashed sound barrier knocked him to his knees. Someone lifted him to his feet, but he only had eyes for the missiles climbing into the air and *following* the screaming jets.

A jet exploded down river and the missile exhaust streaks created a cat's cradle for the *Aurora*.

Another jet roared over them and a portion of the riverbank where the missile launch site had been located erupted in an explosion. More jets thundered over, firing ordinance at Tanana. A cabin two hundred meters from the river blew into whistling wood splinters that cut down half a dozen people.

Another SAM burned into the air and found the tailpipe of an attacking jet. The aircraft exploded and burning debris rained down on the Yukon. The remaining jets disappeared into the darkness.

"The chickenshits aren't coming back!" Dennis howled into the night.

"No," Grisha said. "But they are still in our airspace!" He motioned to the radiowoman standing next to him. "Tell Shipley to engage!"

Wind whistled off the frozen Yukon River, driving most to more protected locations. Their part of the battle seemed to be finished.

✪

"Linebacker Leader, this is Linebacker 4. I have confirmation of target and firm lock. Your orders, sir?"

"Engage, Linebacker 4. All Linebacker elements, fire at will."

Colonel Shipley had flown to a higher altitude to witness the fight and perhaps save one or more of his pilots.

"Splash one bogie!"

"They won't turn and fight! What the fuck?"

"I got one! He ejected over coordinates Charlie nine, and fifteen delta."

"They're running away. Do we pursue?"

"Linebacker Leader here, negative! Do not pursue. We've made our point. Linebacker 3, patrol the area for an hour and then return to base. All other flights immediately return to Suslov Field."

CHAPTER 86

TANANA
ALASKA REPUBLIK

"Are we at war with France?" Grisha asked Pelagian.

"I hope not. We have yet to receive an answer in response to our message."

"Which message is that; the three jets shot down, or our 'why did you kill fifteen of our people?' query, or 'we have a bunch of your people in prison'?"

"Any of them." Pelagian looked tired, worn, and grim. Grisha wondered if he was getting enough rest.

Someone knocked twice on the door and entered the room.

Bodecia glanced at Pelagian and then smiled at Grisha. "How goes the latest war, General?"

"You'll have to be more specific, Bodecia. We seem to have at least two."

"Well, I know about the French. Who else?"

"We have a collection of British Canadian elite commandos sitting in cells here in Alaska Republik. They wanted to create armed chaos between us and our allies. Someone in their government sent them. We're still waiting for an answer to our diplomatic queries weeks after the fact."

"Why haven't I heard about this?"

"Because it's a state secret, my love." Pelagian said. "And you're not on that committee."

"Well, I *should* be!"

Grisha laughed despite himself. "I agree, Bodecia. You should be."

"Were those the *mercenaries* who killed Captain Easthouse?"

"They weren't mercenaries," Pelagian said. "They were British SAS which makes their attack an act of war."

"That's what they want and that's what the French want, a

declaration of war. Then they can bring all their military might down on the Alaska Republik and turn it into yet another European colony!"

"She's right. They're trying to provoke us," Grisha said, "I am embarrassed I didn't think of that already."

"You've both been busy responding," Bodecia said with a shrug. "And now we need to do just that."

"How would you proceed, love?" Pelagian asked.

"Send an official letter through each embassy in California stipulating that if they don't claim their own people within one week, we will hang the prisoners as bandits. If neither government responds, carry out the stipulation."

Why do people think women are the weaker sex? Grisha wondered.

Snow laden wind whistled past the window, echoing the tone in the room.

"Are you willing to pull the lever that drops the scaffold's trap door from beneath them?" Pelagian asked.

"Damn right, I am. And so should you!" she spat. "Have you been boxed up in this building so long that you forget you lead a wolf pack? You taught me more about this than all my other teachers put together!"

Pelagian rubbed his bald head. "Maybe I have. Grisha, do you agree with my beloved wife?"

"I think I voted a few minutes ago. Yes, I agree with her. It's obvious they are provoking with stinging overtures we can easily defeat if we have our heads on straight."

Pelagian grinned. "They came close to doing us great harm here and for that I would hang them all."

"So why did you throw that 'lever' moose shit at me?" Bodecia asked in a sweet tone.

Grisha had always enjoyed their interactions. He thought of both as masters playing an emotional chess game.

"Because I knew your answer would be both worth hearing and straight to the crux of the situation. I was correct. Thank you yet again."

"One of these days your fast mouth won't get you out of a mess you made." She smiled and winked.

"If and when, I will gladly pay the piper. Captain Langbein, would you please bring in the drafts we spoke of earlier?"

Langbein pulled papers out of the valise he held in his left hand. "Here you are, Mr. First Speaker. I thought you might want them."

Grisha cleared his throat, "Ah, *Captain* Langbein, when did you resign the Peacemakers to join the army?"

"Day before yesterday, General Grigorievich. I gave Major Cassidy the paperwork."

"I hope I get it before you outrank me. Congratulations, by the way."

Fred grinned and nodded. "Thank you, sir."

"Okay, Fred," Pelagian said. "Send these to their embassies and copy each hosting country. The ball is in their court."

Bodecia frowned at her husband. "You shit! You had already come to the same conclusion."

"I needed your boot in my ass, love. Thank you."

CHAPTER 87

CHENA
ALASKA REPUBLIK

Solar looked up from the small stack of papers and glanced around. Nothing moved in the cramped office at the back of the silent trading post except her. She thanked several deities the wind had finally stopped.

I have never understood why someone would keep a record of the crimes they committed, but he did a beautiful bookkeeping job, she thought.

She kept most of the papers and slid them up under her bulletproof vest. The remainder went back into the small safe where she found them.

Once outside the trading post, she ambled down the street under thick falling snow. Her eyes constantly moved from left to right, searching for what wasn't right. *If I hadn't known what I was looking for, I would have missed most of these.*

Movement flickered on both sides of the board walk and she instantly had her .45 automatic centered on the fastest one. Two armed men stopped their advance and frowned at the pistol, but made no move to drop their weapons.

She shot the first one through the chest and snap kicked the weapon out of the second man's hands.

"Stand tall or you are as dead as he is!"

He looked down at his companion and then frowned at her with a puzzled, hurt expression.

"This wasn't personal. It was just a mission." His accent wasn't local.

"Your mission was to *kill* me! That isn't *personal*? Who sent you?"

He hesitated.

"Who sent you?" she all but screamed, letting her finger tighten on the trigger. "Tell me or I swear I'll kill *you*."

"I'm unarmed. You can't just shoot me." His crisp enunciation triggered a suppressed memory of agents she worked with in Austria.

Oh, this isn't a good thing.

"You and your buddy there were going to kill me in cold blood. You bet your ass I can, and *will*! *Who* sent you?"

He glanced down at the machine pistol in the snow.

"Go ahead, try for it. If doing that will make you more easily accept death. *Who* sent you?"

He kicked his feet behind him and landed on the pistol. Solare shot him once through the head.

"Stupid shit," she said to the dead man whose feet continued to move for another thirty seconds. "You died for nothing and now I've got a three-foot stack of paperwork to do."

Two people ran up to her. "Peacekeepers! Don't move! We've got you covered. Drop your weapon."

She turned her head and stared at the speaker.

"Cassidy, did you study to get this stupid or did it come naturally?"

"Oh hell, I should have known! Roland, call the Army duty office and get an ambulance over here."

Delcambré ran toward the nearest door showing lights, rapped on it, and after carrying on a quick dialog with a muffled voice inside, entered.

"Who are they?" Cassidy asked.

"I don't know." She relaxed, slid her .45 into its holster, and smiled at him. "They were arrogant and stupid enough to ambush me without making sure I wasn't armed."

She knelt and pulled the would-be assassin's weapon from beneath him. She glanced up at Cassidy. "Check the other one, okay?"

"Ah, sure." Cassidy went over to the first dead man.

Solare squinted but couldn't read the manufacturer's mark on the barrel in the dim light.

Cassidy said, "This is a Schmiesser MP40. If he'd pulled the trigger you'd have been cut in half." He looked at her. "You don't find this weapon in any of the villages."

"Somehow, I didn't think they were local. Here, is this the same thing?" She pushed the second weapon into his hands.

Do I need glasses? she wondered.

He looked at it for less than ten seconds. "Yeah, same model. I saw a lot of these in the past."

"Damn, I've really pissed off *somebody* with deep pockets."

"Whom *haven't* you pissed off?" Cassidy snorted.

"They used expensive Austrian weapons and admitted it wasn't personal, just a job," she said.

"Tell me everything that happened."

She related the event, and finished with, "I was on full alert, or they would have killed me. Who would pay to have me killed?"

"It could have been a family member of someone you killed in the past. It could also have been political revenge."

"My conquests are not advertised by me, nor admitted by my employers. They must be government." She nodded at the dead men bleeding in the snow. "But *which* one, and why?"

"Where was your last contract before going after Ferdinand Rochamboux?"

"British Canada, before that the Republic of California." She thought hard, trying to find anything back then that would warrant personal government assassins at this late date. "They were both sanctioned and clean. I left both clients on good terms."

"So," Cassidy scratched his chin, "they were hired by someone who didn't like how well you performed down south, or by someone local. If it was a local hire, I don't know how he did it, but I know who and why."

"Who?"

"Nathan Roubitaux is who. You interfered with his scheme that used Ferdinand as a go-between, and it cost him everything."

"Define *everything*."

"See, I don't know *how* he did it because he's in jail."

"Confederates?" she suggested.

"We thought we got all of them. Maybe Nathan is a very vindictive man."

"Can I talk to him?" She couldn't suppress an evil grin.

"I'd have to kick that one to the front office. Nathan is a political as well as criminal prisoner. I have no jurisdiction in the matter."

"So, I would have to ask Grisha?"

"And how would a *stupid* man know those answers?"

She winked at him. "I apologize for that remark. I thought you recognized me and were playing games."

"If you hadn't noticed before, I now invite you to look around. It's snowing heavily and visibility is all of six feet."

An ambulance with wailing siren and rotating red light that gave the falling snow a carnival effect came slowly down the street. Cassidy waved them to a stop and the noise died away. A man jumped out of the passenger door. The woman driver put the vehicle in neutral and jerked on the parking brake before following him.

Cassidy pointed to the two forms being slowly covered with new snow. "Please take them to the duty doctor. We need a full autopsy and have that forensics guy search their clothes and gear with a microscope. We want to know where they came from and everything else about them he can discover."

The two medics loaded the bodies with no more than a nod to Cassidy and Solare. In moments they vanished in the falling snow.

Cassidy glanced around. "Where the hell did Delcambré go?"

Solare stepped down into the street, took his arm and pulled Cassidy around, walked with him. "He went through that door," she nodded as they passed it. "I'm willing to bet he is extolling his admiration for a woman in there."

Cassidy grinned, put his hand over hers, and squeezed it. "I've never met anyone else quite like you," he said matching her measured pace.

"Like you, I am one of a kind," she said, wondering why she was being so chummy with this arrogant jerk.

"If you just weren't so arrogant–"

She jerked her hand away from his arm and hissed at him, "*You're* the arrogant jerk!"

He didn't lose his smile. "We really *are* a great deal alike, aren't we?"

Without responding she turned and hurried toward her little cabin. She had work to finish before calling Grisha tomorrow. Touching the lifted collection of papers under her vest, she smiled and knew her cheeks were warmer than normal considering the weather.

He's such an impossible man!

CHAPTER 88

TANANA
ALASKA REPUBLIK

"Mr. First Speaker, we have a response from French Canada," Captain Langbein announced and left the office. Pelagian rubbed his face, pushed his chair back, stood and followed his aide.

General Eluska stopped talking to two other officers when the First Speaker entered the communications room and came over to him, smiling. Pelagian grinned and returned the rough hug.

"Pelagian, I can't handle this sector in addition to Bridge. You gotta get Grisha back."

"And it's good to see you again, too, old friend."

"Sorry, I'm forgetting my manners. You're looking as tired as I feel. How are you?"

"I'm keeping up. How was your trip, Paul?"

"Exhausting. We need to pave that road."

"First we have to keep it." Pelagian looked at Captain Langbein. "Where's the message?"

Fred handed Pelagian a red folder. He opened it, read silently for a moment, and then looked up at the others

"The government of France in Canada has sent us an official apology. They will immediately withdraw all their agents and military personnel. They claim what happened was an exercise that got out of hand."

"It didn't seem like an exercise to me," Claude Adams said from where he sat by the window.

"But will they keep their word?" Grisha said, standing in the doorway. He still wore his snow-covered parka and mukluks.

"I am pleased you got here quickly, Grisha," Pelagian said. "I wish I knew the answer to your question. It is good you all are here. I value all your opinions."

Paul Eluska went over to Grisha and spoke too low for anyone else to hear. Pelagian had a pretty good idea what the conversation was about.

"Despite what the French wish us to believe, they did respond. That still leaves British Canada." He glanced around the room. "They have yet to respond, and their people have been in custody for the longest amount of time."

"Hang them," Grisha said. "They ambushed one of our patrols, killed a fine officer, and tried to kill a sergeant. They were out of uniform and had no identifying insignia on their clothing."

"We agreed to protect them as prisoners of war," Pelagian reminded him.

"You didn't. I did. I'll tell Rawls the news *and* lead him to the scaffold. The next day we hang the next highest rank in their group."

"How will their government find out what we did?"

"We show them, Mr. First Speaker. We send a message tonight of our intentions and give them twelve hours to respond. If they do not respond, we hang Rawls. A news reporter and a camera crew flew in this morning from California. I'm sure they will happily cover the event as well as air our grievances with the Brits."

Pelagian quickly surveyed the others. "Who agrees with Grisha?"

Everyone in the room raised their hand.

"Captain Langbein, format the message for my signature. Make sure the dispatch makes it clear the sentence will be carried out at dawn tomorrow. Grisha, I suggest you inform Rawls tonight. He might wish for clerical company."

"Right away, Mr. First Speaker." Grisha hesitated, and in a softer voice said, "Pelagian, don't waste any remorse on Rawls. He ordered his men to ambush a small patrol. He *killed* Captain Easthouse." Without further ado, he left the room.

Paul Eluska moved next to Pelagian and put his arm around his boss' shoulders.

"Yeah, he needs to be in charge of the army from here to the Canadas and the FPN."

Pelagian grinned. "Looks like Cassidy is going to get another challenge."

"Now you're talking!" Paul laughed.

CHAPTER 89

CHENA
ALASKA REPUBLIK

"How are we supposed to keep all these prisoners secured, fed, and guarded with just four of us?" Mack asked, waving her hands at the chilly stone walls of their office in the old Russian redoubt. "That poor Athabascan woman who does all the cooking needs an assistant, too."

"Corporal McKenzie, I have asked for more people and they're working on it. The Dená Rangers help a lot when they're not in the field. There's nothing more I can do. Now please get off my ass! Be thankful you even have a job."

"Thankful! I made more than this tending bar down in the Nation."

Lieutenant Alex Strom shook his head violently and pounded on his desk for over thirty seconds. Seething, he glared up at her. Mack's blue eyes resembled a startled doe, and she edged toward the door.

Alex lost the glare and dropped his face into his hands. "Dammit, Mack," he moaned. "If you keep pushing me all the time, I'm going to have to transfer you early. I don't want to do that. You're shaping up as a great Peacekeeper."

"Hell, Alex, I merely asked you a question and you bit my head off. It wasn't a personal query. It was professional." He could hear fear in her voice.

"I apologize for the outburst, Mack. I seriously do. I'm sweating blood over the same things you are, and I am responsible for the whole sector.

"So, when you said it all out loud, I boiled over, unfairly, at you. Please, rather than give me shit, help me figure out how we're going to handle this without outside help, okay?"

Her lips twitched. "You're forgiven, which I fully realize is not something a corporal should be saying to a lieutenant. I love the informality of this job, but sometimes I forget myself."

"You're good at knowing when not to be flippant and lax about titles. I need your mind to help me handle all this."

Her eyes softened with compassion, and she started to walk over to him.

The office door slammed open and two snow-covered figures stumbled into the office.

Mack had her pistol half out of the holster when Alex recognized the men and shouted, "At ease!"

Major Yukon Cassidy brushed snow off his parka and threw the hood back off his head. "Damn. How can it be snowing so heavily when it's this cold?"

Beside him, Roland Delcambré shook snow off his dark beard and watched Mack slide her weapon back where it belonged.

"You kinda surprised us, Major," Alex said.

"I told him to knock!" Delcambré snorted.

"Sorry. I didn't mean to startle anyone," Cassidy said with a grin. "That door opens more easily than I remembered."

"Corporal McKenzie cleaned and oiled the hinges. The door now opens beautifully," Alex said, feeling his heartbeat return to normal.

Cassidy looked at Mack. "Good work, Lieutenant."

Mack frowned. "He's the lieutenant. I'm the corporal."

"Not anymore. Since both of you have prior service in the Peacekeepers, you are a lieutenant and Alex is now a captain. We've restructured the organization and we need experienced people in leadership positions."

"Wow. If I stay in for another year, will I make general?" Alex asked with a wide grin. "I'm really a captain?"

Delcambré laughed. "I am now a major and he," he jabbed his thumb at Cassidy, "is our colonel."

"Sweet," Alex said. "What the hell is going on?"

"We have to increase the Peacekeeper force, as well as the army," Cassidy said.

"Why?" Alex asked. "We're not at war, are we? I thought we were just cleaning up mercenaries."

"Do you accept your promotions?"

"Hell, yes!" Mack said through a grin.

"Of course, we do, Ma–, uh, *Colonel* Cassidy. Now what's going on, *really*?"

"More than I think we can manage, but we're going to try like hell."

He told them about recent events. "We have to back up the army if it comes to that. We're all in this together. Dead or alive."

CHAPTER 90

CHENA
ALASKA REPUBLIK

"We really gotta let them go?" Captain Dexter Williams asked into the telephone. "Yes, *sir*," he said with a frown. "At once, *sir*."

He hung up the phone and glared at the stone wall of his office in the old Russian redoubt. Much of the damage from the war had been repaired and the structure now served again as a prison. It also served as the base of operations for the Dená Rangers and the Peacekeepers. The Imperial Russian double-headed eagle glowed red along with the rest of the firebox on the huge cast-iron stove heating the room.

Days like this made him wonder why he had accepted a commission. *They wanted me to be a Dená Ranger, that's why*, he thought. *And so did I.*

"Who the hell was that, Dexter?" Sergeant Charly Herring asked.

"Dammit. It's *Captain* Williams when you're in here. We have to release all the French prisoners."

"To whom?"

"Themselves. They're free. I just got the word from Grisha."

"You called Grisha, 'sir'?"

"I wanted him to know how much I didn't like the order. He's a smart man. He got the message."

"Dammit. They fired on us first!"

"Give yourself a minute to appreciate how much government does for us, then go release the prisoners. Get Corporal Wheeler and Trooper Conway to help you. Each prisoner is to be photographed from the front and side of their heads, their personal information put on a card, and delivered to me before they come in here.

"That will probably take a couple of hours. All of them have to check out with me *before* they are freed. One at a time."

An hour later the first prisoner emerged from the hallway and strutted up to the desk. "I am Minister Jacque Velade, of French Canada. I was just treated like a criminal and photographed against my wishes. I wish to file a formal complaint. I demand to be released."

Dexter said smoothly, "I ordered the photographs to be made so we may prove whom we released should the question ever arise." He pushed an ink pad and a card across the desk. "Is that card correct as to your identity and nationality?"

Now frowning, Velade leaned over and read the card, looked up with suspicion. *"Oui!"*

"Excellent! Please put your right thumb print there in the corner as verification."

"This is very unusual!"

Dexter grinned. "If you don't wish to verify your identity, we will be forced to keep you until we can do it on our own. That could take a few months."

Jacque Velade allowed Dexter to roll his inked thumb over the card.

"Thank you, sir. Send me the next person, Sergeant."

Velade frowned and held his thumb out. "Is there something on which I can clean my thumb?"

"Try the sergeant in front of you. But I must warn you. He's not really happy you're leaving us."

Velade looked over at a glowering Sgt. Herring and silently walked out the door.

Another man marched into the room and stood at attention.

"Who are you?" Dexter asked the trim man.

"Antoine Fenuere, Capitan of Infantry."

Dexter found his card and repeated the process.

Fenuere rolled his thumb without assistance. "I feel it only fair to tell you I shall return to have my revenge."

"Damn, Captain, we're letting you go free! What the hell else do you need?"

"You killed my brother out there on that joke of a highway."

"You have it backward, Captain. He, and you, participated in a military incursion into our nation, which we repelled at the cost of two troopers. If anyone is going to get revenge, it's me! At this point I have orders to give you your freedom."

"I would love another chance to fight you. Come on back whenever you want. If you feel *froggy*, just jump!"

Dexter stared him out of the room. "Next!"

CHAPTER 91

TANANA
ALASKA REPUBLIK

"Drummer," Grisha said, "start the knell."

Art Anderson, the Californian director, murmured into the microphone on his headset. The cameraman, Jeff Brown, also wearing a headset, focused on the drumhead as Tony Armlin, the sound man, lowered his boom mic to catch the tattoo.

The drummer rapped out the Death March as Captain Rawls, his hands manacled behind his back, stepped into the open air. The gallows stood darker than the sky in the faint early morning light. The sun would break the horizon at the appointed moment of his execution. Two Dená Rangers slow stepped on either side of him and an Anglican priest followed close behind. Rawls didn't hesitate, but stepped out in a military fashion.

Jeff slowly pulled the camera back from a close-up of Rawls' face and now framed the condemned along with the gallows. All Tony could capture was the reverberation of boots on stone.

Lined up in formation before the gallows, the twelve remaining prisoners stood at attention, each with their legs secured with a half-meter chain. All wore parkas with large, white PWs on their backs with a larger white X across the front. In rank for the last fifteen minutes, many were shivering as the temperature registered -30°F.

Jeff slowly panned across the witnesses, lingering to focus in on a young prisoner's eyes staring disbelievingly at his passing commander. Everyone's breath made instant, foggy wreaths around their faces before dissipating in the frigid air.

Without breaking stride, Rawls deliberately walked up the thirteen steps to the scaffold. He looked the hangman in the face, and then looked away. Sergeant First Class Ben Titus held the noose in his hand with determination in his face.

The camera moved to a close-up on the two men. The boom mic lowered to their heads.

"You lot really know how to twist a man's guts," Rawls said, "they told us the crown would deny us if captured. Now you bastards have to go and prove them right."

"It sounds to me that the bastards are the ones who are letting you die for them, Captain." He slipped the noose over Rawls' head and tightened it as he had been instructed.

The sky lightened in the east and a thin cobalt blue layer separated earth from sky. The obviously agitated priest leaned in to speak into Rawls' ear. "Is there anything you would like to say to me, my son?"

"Yeah; fuck off. I never believed your bullshite anyway."

The priest's face went chalky. He turned, and quickly descended the scaffold.

"Any last words?" Ben asked.

"Any other way out of this mess for me?"

"None that I know about."

"Then trip the fuckin–"

Ben jerked the lever down and he heard Rawls catch his last breath as his footing vanished.

A split second later Rawls' neck audibly snapped when the rope slightly rebounded.

The sun peeked over the edge of the horizon.

All Ben could see was Captain Easthouse dying next to him.

Art Anderson whispered into his mic, "Please tell me you got all of that."

CHAPTER 92

ST. ANTHONY, ALASKA REPUBLIK

"The last group checked in, Colonel Romanov," the radioman said. "Now they are all between us and the border."

"Therefore, we can breathe easier, yes, Fyodor?"

"Yes, Colonel, much easier."

"Please put me through to General Grigorievich."

"This is Suslov Field, St. Anthony. I have a call from Colonel Rom—"

"This is Grisha. What's the situation, Stephan?" His voice came over the new speaker loud and clear.

"We have all available units at, or enroute to Old Crow. All sapper work has been accomplished. Are you sure they're coming?"

"We're not positive, but we rank it as a high probability. Has the RCAF squadron arrived?"

"Yes, three hours ago. The ARAF got in an hour ago. It was good to see Jerry Yamato again."

"Has Yukon Cassidy arrived yet?"

"Yukon? No, I haven't seen or heard anything of him. I thought he was civilian police."

"He is, but the Peacekeepers are also there to help the military if needed. Yukon is a warrior. He has good instincts. Use him where he best fits—if he checks in with you at all."

"Noted."

"Good luck, Stephan." The line went dead.

CHAPTER 93

NEAR ST. ANTHONY, ALASKA REPUBLIK

"This is not part of my job précis, Colonel Cassidy," Roland Delcambré grumbled as they bounced along the RustyCan Highway. The utility swayed from side to side, making Cassidy grateful the day had remained windless. With the light gone hours ago the moonless night had narrowed down to the two shafts of illumination from his headlamps.

"We always add 'and other duties as required' in all of our contracts. Didn't you read yours?"

"I do not fear combat. You know this. However, this is a military operation, and we are but civilian Peacekeepers."

"Do you want me to stop and let you out, Roland?"

"Well–"

"You would never be able to face Solare again."

"What does–, is *she* down here also?"

"She left two hours before we did," Cassidy lied with a grin.

"Merde!" He stopped speaking and peered out his door window into the darkness.

Cassidy's grin endured and he wondered how much farther they would get before encountering a military checkpoint in the snow-blanketed expanse. As he crested a hill, he saw an APC blocking the road where Russian engineers had blasted away rock to permit passage.

"Very well done, Army!" he said aloud.

"That is a most effective checkpoint," Roland said in an approving tone. "I sincerely hope it's ours."

"Has to be," Cassidy said as he slowed the utility to a crawl. His grin withered.

"How would you know? You silenced our communications hours

ago."

"We'd know." *I hope!*

He started to sweat, wishing he had kept the radio live. He clicked off the safety on the .45-.70 hooked to the door next to him with quick-release clips.

Delcambré snickered and touched his boot knife. Recently he had acquired an automatic 10-gauge shotgun with a short barrel. The clip held six rounds and he had confided to Cassidy that by the time they were all expended any threat would be neutralized; *or* he would be dead.

Cassidy didn't want to test his companion's theory in this cold, dark, and lonely place.

A man carrying a red-tipped torch stepped from behind the rocks and a spotlight on the APC fastened on a point on the road just in front of them. The man made a wide swing with the torch and pointed it to the now illuminated patch of RustyCan.

"That APC has twin .50s machine guns centered on us," Delcambré muttered.

Cassidy glanced at his friend. Roland was sweating and coiled tight as a spring. The slightest trigger would snap him into ingrained action.

"I know," Cassidy said soothingly. "I was crew on one of those many years ago. Calm down, *oui*?"

"Your French is laughable." Delcambré slightly relaxed.

He brought the utility to a halt and cranked down the driver's window.

The officer stepped up to the window and blinked when he saw Cassidy.

"Colonel Cassidy! We were not alerted you would be out here," Captain Alex Strom said.

"Why not? You and a lot of other Peacekeepers are already here. I think this must be where all of us belong."

"Well said, Colonel." Alex blinked his torch twice and the spotlight winked out as the APC rolled behind the rocks. "About ten klicks ahead you'll contact the operations people. We'll let them know you're coming. You're the most excitement we've had in six hours."

"Thank you, Captain. I hope this spot remains unexciting," Cassidy said through a grin. As he drove on into the starlit night, he reflected that the checkpoint would make an excellent fallback position if things went to hell at Old Crow.

Delcambré snapped his shotgun into the clips on his door.

"Why did you do that, Roland?"

"I was tired of holding the weapon, obviously."

"No. Why did you put it into my head that those people might have been an enemy roadblock?"

"Because you didn't. You are contradiction of yourself in so many ways. Where you should cautiously approach, you charge, and also the other way about." Delcambré looked into the Cassidy's face in the glow of light from the instrument panel.

Cold air knifed in from around the sprung door. It seemed to carry more ozone than Cassidy remembered.

"You act like a man who doesn't know who he is any more," Roland said.

Cassidy looked back to his driving, throttled his glib, instant response, and said softly, "What would you have done differently back there?"

"I would have *worried* about it!"

"We would have ended up doing the same damn thing!"

Roland opened his mouth and then shut it, frowning into the night. "True, *mon ami*, and we both worried about it."

Cassidy laughed and a flash of light washed over them. He slammed on the brake pedal and grabbed his rifle at the same time. The light flickered. Roland leaned forward, tapped his shotgun barrel on the windscreen, and looked upward.

"Oh, how nice. The *Aurora Borealis* is out to light our way."

CHAPTER 94

TWENTY-FIVE KILOMETERS
EAST OF OLD CROW,
ALASKA REPUBLIK

"W<small>E HAVE ALL OUR PEOPLE IN PLACE</small>, Spotted Bird," Captain Four Arrows said while making *it is good* sign with his right hand.

"Dammit, Charley. How many times do I have to tell you to call me *General?*"

"Hell, Lawrence, we all know you're the boss!"

General Spotted Bird mentally shrugged. "Anything from the scouts?"

"They're due in right now."

A snow machine carrying two men roared up and stopped next to Spotted Bird's tank. The man riding on the back leaped off and snapped to attention.

The tank seemed to add to the numbing cold.

"Be at ease, Billy," Four Arrows said. "Whattya have for us?"

"There are twenty-four tanks and twenty troop carriers headed toward us on the Victoria Highway. They're four hours away, at most, if they don't stop."

"Have they crossed our border yet, Billy?" Spotted Bird asked.

"Yes, General. That's when we decided to report in."

"No air cover?" the general's tone seemed puzzled.

"None that we saw, sir. But it *is* dark."

Captain Four Feathers looked up at his kinsman and Spotted Bird nodded back. "Good work, warriors." The captain smiled. "Go get some food while you can."

The snow machine roared away with the two men.

"They are declaring war on us!" Four Arrows asked.

"Yeah, but that's not how they'll sing the story. They seem to think this sliver of the First People's Nation belongs to them because they built a road over it forty years ago. We didn't sell it. We leased it."

The general stared into the darkness, visualizing the tanks and artillery sitting out there, waiting. He wondered if the Brits would use air cover once the light returned.

CHAPTER 95

VICTORIA HIGHWAY,
ALASKA REPUBLIK

Percival Viscount Craddock, Colonel commanding Her Majesty's Own Canadian Armoured, rode next to the driver in a modified weapons carrier. Their stygian journey had taken a turn for the better with the advent of the Northern Lights. They reflected off the snow and improved visibility.

I would love to stop and view them properly, he thought. "Lovely display," he said to the driver.

"Yes, Milord." The driver suddenly grinned. "One of the Indian boys told me if one whistled at the lights they would come down and cut off your head. How can they believe such rubbish?"

"Did you try it for yourself, Corporal Lassiter?"

"As a matter of fact, sir, I did. As you can see, I suffered no harm."

Both men laughed.

Lassiter suddenly slowed the vehicle and snapped on the rear caution lights. "Approaching lights, Milord. It must be the scouts."

"I'm relieved I was the only one watching the sky," Craddock chuckled. "Sergeant Fowler, notify the column we will be stopping for fifteen minutes. I'm sure all the lads need a piss break as much as I do."

"Very good, sir," Fowler said from the space behind the driver's bench. He made the announcement over the radio as ordered.

The weapons carrier stopped on the edge of the snowy road. Corporal Lassiter shut down the engine per protocol. Engines needed relief and fuel consumption always nagged at one.

Craddock felt the cold begin to creep in immediately. He swung down off the vehicle, shivered in the brisk breeze that felt sharp enough to cut skin, and unzipped his fatigue trousers. By the time he finished voiding, the snow-goes came to a stop in front of the weapons carrier. He glanced back at the shadowy mass of machinery behind his vehicle and grinned.

Sergeant Horricks, the lead scout, stopped in front of Craddock, lifted his riding goggles off his face, stood at attention, and saluted. The viscount crisply returned the salute.

"What news?"

"We stopped when we saw the lights of Old Crow, Milord. We scanned the area with our binos and saw nothing moving other than a few small animals." His voice came strongly through his heavily frosted balaclava.

"You saw the lights of Old Crow. How big is the place?"

"Perhaps twenty cabins showing light, Milord. We were on the last rise prior to dropping down onto the floodplain. The temperature is dropping and the wind off the Porcupine River seems to be strengthening." Horricks looked off for a moment, and added, "It's bloody cold down there, sir."

"Nothing military to be seen, then?"

"Not that we saw, Milord. The snow on the highway is at least half a meter deep."

Craddock grinned. "Then we've got them where we want them. Excellent! You and Smith go get warmed up. Put the second squad on as scouts."

"Very good, Milord." He saluted and turned away as soon as possible. The wind slowed, giving the illusion of increased warmth in the sub-arctic night.

The snow-goes muttered past Percival, Viscount Craddock on their way to the rear of the kilometer-long column. Craddock recited the orders he had memorized six weeks ago in Victoria, the Capitol of British Canada.

"With utmost stealth and speed, neutralize the rebel capitol, and capture or annihilate the ringleaders," he said in a whisper.

The *Aurora Borealis* danced silently overhead. He looked up and whistled, then flinched when the shimmering band momentarily dipped toward him.

CHAPTER 96

TETLIN
ALASKA REPUBLIK

Cassidy and Delcambrè pulled into the crowded parking area at Tetlin Lodge. His utility seemed out of place among the APCs, scout cars, and tanks gathering snow as their engines idled.

"I hope we are not paying their petrol bills," Roland said as they walked toward the main entrance.

The path had been stomped to muddy slush. People in arctic combat gear passed them. On the lee side of the building a number of people stood around smoking and chatting.

Cassidy watched a FPN sergeant pass and bumped into someone.

"Colonel Cassidy! Wha–, uh, I didn't expect to see you and Major Delcambré here!"

"Why not, Lieutenant Casey? *You're* here."

Lieutenant Casey grinned. "True. We're *all* crazy."

"Did you leave anyone on duty in Fort Yukon?"

"Yes, sir. Sergeant Demientieff is plenty pissed about it, too."

"What are they having the Peacekeepers doing? Are they using us to advantage?"

Casey lost his smile before Cassidy finished.

"They're handling us like we're their kid sisters. They won't tell us what's going on, either. I admit to being a bit pissed off, sir."

"I don't blame you, Danny. Maybe they don't know what's going on, either. Let me see what I can find out." Cassidy entered the front door and wove through the crowded Tetlin Lodge. He spotted Captain Williams and moved next to him.

"Dexter, why is everyone in here and not out on the road?"

"We *were* out on the road," Dexter cut his eyes at Cassidy and then away. "Then a delegation from the First People's Nation showed up and wanted to talk strategy."

"So that was an FPN sergeant I saw. Strategy about what?"

"They haven't told me yet! Claude and Colonel Romanov are in there with three warriors."

"Who's here from the government besides Claude?"

"You are, Chief Peacekeeper. Get your butt in there." Dexter pushed him into a room containing a long table with five men facing each other across it.

Claude and Colonel Romanov made the shortest row and Cassidy sat down next to Claude.

"My apologies for being so late," he said to the men on the opposite side of the table. "I am honored to be here."

"Welcome, Cousin Cassidy," said the one-armed Cheyenne wearing a buffalo hide vest.

"Bear Tooth! How wonderful to see you!" They clasped wrists and beamed at each other.

"I love it," Claude said. "We're all family here. As Bear Tooth already knows, this is Colonel Yukon Cassidy, our Chief Peacekeeper."

Bear Tooth nodded. "Cousin, this is our Bannock brother, Benny Holds Fast, and Oglala brother, John Shadow Seeker."

As Cassidy nodded to the men, Claude said, "The FPN alerted us about a British Canadian armored group preparing to cross their territory without permission."

"Not much you can do about that, huh?" Cassidy said.

"Quite the contrary," Bear Tooth said with a grim smile. "We've dug in with our Northern Army and Western Army armored units as well as artillery. As soon as our unwelcome visitors cross our border, we're going to stop them one way or another."

"How large is their armored group?" Cassidy asked. The possible ramifications swirled in his head.

"At least two dozen heavy tanks, some artillery pieces, and about 400 infantry in troop transports." Bear Tooth glanced at Benny Holds Fast. "That's about it, huh?"

"And two snow machine scouts."

"Yeah. I ain't real worried about them."

All six men laughed.

"That's a lot of armor," Colonel Romanov said. "I think we could slow them down, but I don't believe we could stop them, Claude."

"Which is why we're here," John Shadow Seeker said. His voice held all the warmth of frosted steel plate. "We want to help you welcome our uninvited *Wasichu* guests in such a manner as they never come north again."

"Hokahey!" Cassidy said and grinned. "What do you have in mind?"

"We have General Spotted Bird and his Northern Army Armored in addition to the Western Army Armored also under his command," Shadow Seeker said. "If it was a fair fight, they would have the advantage."

He glanced around and made the evilest smile Cassidy had ever seen.

"They obviously have not studied our history. There will be many widows made in the next few hours. I don't know British Canadian customs, but bereft women all sound the same when they are wailing."

CHAPTER 97

TANANA
ALASKA REPUBLIK

"Pelagian, uh, Mr. First Speaker—"

He looked up from his desk at Grisha and Solare.

"Grisha, is there a problem?"

"Sorry, old habits and all that. This is Solare, one of our field agents."

Pelagian stood and bowed. "I am pleased to see you again, Solare. I wasn't aware of your exploits when our paths last crossed."

She nodded. "The pleasure is all mine, Mr. First Speaker."

"And now you address me as Pelagian, okay?"

"As you wish. I have found hard evidence that implicates Nathan Roubitaux with N'Go, or the Boss, the British Canadians, and the Empire of Austria."

"In what form is this hard evidence, Solare?" Pelagian's stomach started to roil, and he felt a frisson of fear steal down his spine.

She dropped a pile of documents on his desk.

"Invoices and letters. What looks like a treaty between the Alaska Republik and the British crown. Even more disturbing is this memorandum of agreement between Roubitaux and an attaché from the Austrian embassy in Victoria."

"I have to know where you found these documents."

"Nathan had a secret office in Lentnikoff's trading post. The safe was old and easy to access. I stole the documents. Does that matter?"

"We're still a wild frontier," Pelagian said with a laugh. "I sure don't have a problem with your methods. Besides, Nathan already pleaded guilty to treason."

"I understood that, sir," she said. "It was the British Canada and Austrian angles that surprised me."

"Right about now the British Canadian Army is making a huge mistake." He grinned. "We'll get to the Austrians later."

"If it's all the same to you, sir, may I question Nathan Roubitaux?"

"To what end? As I said, he's already pleaded guilty to treason."

"True, but he hasn't shown us all this cards yet. I think he still has one up his sleeve."

"By all means. Go down to Chena and visit him. Here let me write you a pass that even the most hard-assed army cop will honor."

"I like working with you, Pelagian," she said.

CHAPTER 98

NEAR OLD CROW, ALASKA REPUBLIK

"Colonel!" Sergeant Fowler blurted. "Scouts report a military roadblock on this side of the Porcupine River."

Viscount Craddock had been lulled by the engine, already become familiar with the road noise, and had dozed off during the night. He jerked awake, felt shocked at seeing the dark blue sky of morning rather than night's inky black, and thought about the sergeant's message.

"What nation? Can they tell?"

"Horricks says they're flying a FPN flag, sir."

"I distinctly remember telling him to take a respite! What's he doing out there?"

"Beggin' your pardon, Milord, but you've been asleep for nearly four hours. It was his turn again. We're nearly to the junction with the Russia-Canada Highway."

"Instruct Horricks to ask them their rationale for blocking the road to an armoured British Canadian column."

"Sir." Sergeant Fowler then spoke quietly over the radio. Silence reigned while Corporal Lassiter slowed the weapons carrier.

"Why are you slowing, Corporal?" Craddock's tone sounded peevish, even to him.

"I, I thought you might want to confer with the officers or something, Milord."

"I will tell you in advance when I wish for you to slow down. Maintain speed."

"Yes, sir. Sorry, sir."

"Milord," Sergeant Fowler said crisply, "the First People's Nation says we can't go through their land."

"We're not! We're in Russian, ah, Alaska Republik by all that's holy."

"Beggin' your pardon, Milord, but we *are* inside the FPN. Look at the map."

He handed a map and small torch forward and Craddock stared at the two-dimensional geography.

"Bloody hell! We negotiated for that passage *before* we helped build this bloody highway! We have every legal right to transit this dollop of land!" Craddock bellowed.

"According to the FPN major at the roadblock, the treaty does not include military equipment or supplies, Milord. Horricks reports the bloke has a facsimile of the treaty if you would care to inspect it."

"Lassiter, stop the convoy immediately." Craddock blushed and looked away from the driver. *It's pretty bad when a corporal is more prescient than the commanding officer.*

"It seems you have good instincts, George." Craddock looked at the driver whose chest immediately expanded.

"Sergeant Fowler, tell the column to prepare for battle. All officers forward at once. Have a windbreak constructed immediately."

"Sir!" Sergeant Fowler spoke quickly into his headset microphone.

A group of men in arctic gear appeared next to the weapons carrier and quickly erected a skeleton of aluminum tubing that attached to the vehicle. In minutes they tied down a heavy tarp complete with a burning oil heater inside. The entire operation took less than ten minutes.

Viscount Craddock hadn't noticed. He stared at the map trying desperately to remember what it was General Humphries had said about this piece of road.

Bloody hell, I had other things on my mind. If it had been important, he would have repeated it like he does everything else! I do wish I hadn't passed on air support.

"Milord," Sergeant Fowler said. "Sergeant Horricks requests an official response to the FPN representatives."

"Have him say we'll get back to them. I want him to return and make careful note of all military activity in the area."

"Very good, sir." Fowler's lowered voice became more background noise.

Two authoritative knocks on the door interrupted his thoughts and he looked up with a frown. Lieutenant Colonel Ornby, his second-in-command, raised his hand in a salute. The officers were assembled.

He squared his beret and stepped out of the warm vehicle into the still-cold dome. Wind rattled the canvas, causing the structure to shake constantly, and he could easily see his breath. All twenty officers snapped to attention.

"Be at ease, gentlemen," he felt grateful they were all out here with him. *Besides, I'm going to need every ally I can garner.*

"Here's the situation, gentlemen…" He explained about the FPN roadblock and the Natives' rationale. "As it turns out, we *are* in an uninhabited sliver of their nation. If we press on it could be construed as a declaration of war on them despite the fact we want nothing of the sort. Unfortunately, this is the only path to the Alaskan terrorists we have been charged with subduing. I fully realize I am responsible for anything this battalion does, and rightly so. But if anyone one of you has a better idea, I would jolly well love to hear it."

An officer raised his hand.

"Captain Reilly?"

"Would it be possible to request air support, milord?"

"Of course. Unfortunately, that would necessitate waiting for hours before we could continue, and no doubt give the rebels time to organize a proper defense."

"If I may, sir," Reilly pressed, "…perhaps we could request air support and then proceed with the assurance of potential aid in the very near future."

The memory of the staff officers exhibiting perplexity when he declined air cover in the first place came to his mind. That, obviously, had been his first mistake. At the time he had felt positive his armoured battalion could easily handle anything the savages could dish out, and said just that to the general's staff.

If he now called for help at the first blush of danger, they would all think him capricious, hubristic, and a bit of a coward. All of the officers stared at him intently.

They obviously approve of Reilly's request. Losing face is certainly better than losing my ass.

"I had hoped we could do this without using the BCAF, but so be it. I'll have Sergeant Fowler make the request as soon as I'm back in the weapons carrier."

"Very good, Milord," Captain Reilly said.

Viscount Craddock wondered if they all knew they had been holding their breath. He grinned.

"So we go through the roadblock, come what may! Back to your posts, gentlemen. We have a mission to complete."

He pulled himself into the cozy cabin of the weapons carrier while debating with himself about actually calling in the flyboys.

"Milord," Sergeant Fowler said, "yonder comes Horricks and Carruthers." He pointed out the windscreen at the approaching snow-goes.

"Very good, Sergeant."

"I heard your decision to use air cover, sir. I've already officially requested for same in your name."

His stomach sank enough that he tightened his sphincter.

"Well, let's just hope Horricks has good news."

Can this get any worse?

CHAPTER 99

CHENA REDOUBT, ALASKA REPUBLIK

Solare displayed her pass, chatted briefly with the guard at the door, and then followed the other Peacekeeper into the cold, massive prison.

My word! This place looks medieval at best, she thought. *I can tell the Russians built it.*

They stopped at a heavy iron door. Paul Wheeler, a former FI trooper, gave her a searching look. "You have an hour, but he doesn't know that."

"Thanks. I appreciate the leverage."

"I think we should have shot the son-of-a-bitch, myself." He opened the door.

Solare found herself in a cell adjacent to another cell. Nathan Roubitaux sat on a simple cot on the other side of the bars.

He gave her a disdainful once-over. "Who are you and why are you here?" he demanded.

"I would like to get some answers before they hang you. You have nothing to lose by talking to me."

"Who are you?"

"My name is Solare."

"You're the bitch who destroyed my empire. Why would I give you anything more?" He spat through the bars. "You've got a lot of brass to come in here wanting something from me."

"Yeah. I've heard that before. I can't offer you a damn thing other than the chance to get some weight off your mental shoulders. Unfortunately, I've already deduced you have no qualms about anything you did, right?"

"What a surprise! Yet another smart mouth woman trying to run my life."

"Maybe if you'd listened to the first one you wouldn't be in the mess you are now."

"Get out of here. I don't have to talk to you!"

"I'm not going anywhere. When did you sell your soul to the Austrians?"

He stood so quickly the cot fell on its side. The muscles in his face worked for a moment, and he said, "I have no idea what you are talking about."

"Wow. I can hardly wait to ask a question you do know about! What will you do, jump into the air?"

"I know nothing about any Austrians."

"They were killed by a man I killed mere minutes later. I was after their killer and had no use for his victims. Only later did I discover they were Austrians bearing gold and surface-to-air missiles superior to anything the Alaska Republik possessed.

"You are the reason all of those men died that day! Admit it!" she shouted.

His face twisted and she thought he was about to weep.

"You have no idea what a beautiful thing this Republik could have been! You meddled and made it all fall into chaos, you stupid slut! I want you to remember this day when the Austrian advisors help defeat this pitiful band of navel-gazing *individualists.*"

A growing thunder of footsteps in the passageway captured both their attention, and in Solare's case, brought alarm.

CHAPTER 100

VICTORIA HIGHWAY
FIRST PEOPLE'S NATION

Sergeant Horricks motored his snow-go slowly down the now faint trail he and Carruthers had made hours before. Even wearing a balaclava and goggles, his face felt frozen. The army didn't equip the big Enfield snow machines with windscreens, only tracks and skis.

Trying to reconnoiter while driving on windswept snow made for poor intelligence gathering. *Orders are orders*, he thought. He had seen enough back at the roadblock to convince himself this wasn't going to be the mad dash into Alaska and conquer all that Viscount Craddock had envisioned.

So far, nothing he promised us has transpired. It's going to take a real fight to get through that junction. All that bloody artillery...

Despite attempts at camouflage, the barrels of large artillery pieces were there if one knew what to look for. He felt sure he observed only a portion of what lay concealed in those forests. To cap it all off, he felt incredibly exposed to the enemy as well as the foul weather.

Damn Percy Craddock to hell!

He drove up to the cozy modified weapons carrier and stopped next to it.

No guard, no patrols, nothing military about this cock-up circus, he reflected.

Engulfed in a heavy parka, Colonel Craddock emerged from the vehicle in a cloud of heated air that dissipated instantly once he shut the door.

"What news?"

"They've dug in artillery all along the road on both sides. The roadblock at the junction is fortified with six heavy tanks and at least three weapons carriers. It will be a hard fight to breach that point with a frontal assault, Milord."

"How is it you saw none of this hours ago when you spied Old Crow?"

"We glassed the village from the last rise prior to going down into the flood plain, sir. This time we went all the way down to the Porcupine and encountered the roadblock. The artillery positions are difficult to spot until you're nearly on them."

"We've called for air support," Craddock said with a tinge of defeat. "Of course, the BCAF can't do damn all unless it's light out and that is three hours away." His tone had devolved into a whine.

"What would you do if you were in my place, Sergeant?"

Well, he asked. "I'd turn around and go home, Milord. We have lost the element of surprise if we ever had it. We're all sitting out here freezing our bums off while our machines wear out before our eyes–"

"I take your meaning, Sergeant," he snapped. "Load your machines onto the lorry and get warmed up. We'll be leaving soon."

"If you don't mind me asking, Colonel; in which direction?"

"I'll let you know." Craddock climbed back into his vehicle.

Horricks motored past the long line of idling machines, eager to get in out of the cold. At long last he reached the correct lorry and waved his crew out of their carryall. He put the snow machine in neutral and climbed off.

If Corporal Andersson hadn't caught his arm he would have fallen face down.

"Thanks, Nels," he muttered rubbing his numb legs. "Okay lads, stow both machines until the god of war changes his bleedin' mind again. Me 'n' Carruthers need warmth and large mugs of hot tea."

Carruthers already trudged toward the light shining from the windows of the mobile kitchen hooked to its own tractor. Horricks stumbled twice getting to the door and gratefully shut himself inside. The heat felt almost painful at first and he realized he had probably frostbit parts of his face and fingers. His feet burned and he really didn't wish to walk any more.

"Sit down before you fall down, Oscar!" boomed Commissary Sergeant John Hicks. He shoved a hot ceramic mug into Horricks' hands.

"Bless your heart, John. You put a dollop of rum in it."

Fox took off his motorcycle boots and groaned when he touched his feet. "Any chance of another cup of tea to pour on my feet, Commissary Sergeant?"

"Don't be daft. You'd only burn them." He went to a cupboard over the gas range and pulled out a stack of warm towels. He threw two at Carruthers and two at Horricks.

"Wrap your feet in these. Leave your stockings on. So, what's the word, mates?"

Both men reported what they had seen in minute detail. When they finished, Horricks looked up from nursing his feet.

"What's your outside thermometer read, John?"

Hicks glanced up at the dial. "Minus forty Celsius. It dropped thirty degrees in the past three hours. Who in his right mind would attack anyone in weather this bloody cold?"

The tannoy on the wall squawked. "Sergeant Hicks, we're pulling out in five."

"Someone who fights his war from a nice warm weapons carrier, that's who," Horricks grated.

CHAPTER 101

CHENA REDOUBT,
ALASKA REPUBLIK

Peacekeeper Corporal Paul Wheeler walked back to his desk after leading Solare to the prisoner. He glanced around for something to take his mind off the beer he'd be enjoying in an hour.

"What are you reading?"

Trooper Conway looked up from his book, and grinned. "It's one of those science fictional novels. It even has monsters from outer space."

"Spare me the details, please," Wheeler muttered.

Their office door swung open. Wheeler looked up at the man in the door, and blurted, "Major Riordan?" Another man stood behind Riordan, but Wheeler couldn't see his face. Riordan was carrying an automatic weapon that didn't quite point at Wheeler.

"I'm looking for recruits, Paul. Are you interested?"

"Recruits for what?"

"For the International Freekorps, what else?"

"Everyone went their own way, Major, right after you scarpered." He thought about how long it would take to unholster his pistol.

"So, you're not interested?"

"No, Major, I am not." He jerked his pistol from beneath its unfastened holster flap.

"Pity." Riordan lifted the muzzle of the automatic.

The fourth round went through Wheeler's throat, and everything stopped.

CHAPTER 102

VICTORIA HIGHWAY
FIRST PEOPLE'S NATION

"Somthing is moving out there, Captain," Corporal Ambrose said, peering through his binoculars. Their lookout position was inside the highest room in the Nations Junction Lodge. He was very grateful for the wonderful heat.

"Where?" Captain White Buffalo waited for the man to point before raising his glasses to his eyes. All light in the room had been extinguished hours ago. The large, double pane window offered a commanding view of the Victoria Highway and the slopes rising on either side.

The Russia-Canada Highway ran past the front of the lodge. The building sat in front of the junction and did a brisk trade with travelers. This was the first winter they would do better than the summer months. Everybody knew it.

"Look downslope from the farthest field gun out there. It coulda been a moose or something."

"In this weather? I thought all the animals up here hibernated in the winter."

Ambrose burst into laughter. After a minute he choked out, "You ain't from around here, are you?"

"No. I'm a Pawnee from the Platte River country, *Corporal*. I take it moose don't hibernate?"

"No, sir. They do not."

"Now I know. Can you still see movement?"

"Yes! There's a vehicle on the road, not showing lights."

A flash abruptly illuminated the field gun. The artillery piece rose into the air and crashed down into the forested slope. As if answering, three more pieces along the highway exploded.

The window creaked as the successive sound waves hit it.

"Sound the alarm!" White Buffalo shouted.

Corporal Ambrose flipped the switch and a siren ululated into the dark. "Hell, if they didn't hear those explosions, they won't hear this!"

The door opened and two men hurried in before slamming it behind them.

"Tell me!" General Lawrence Spotted Bird commanded. He peered out the window, binoculars ready in his hands.

"Less than five minutes ago we saw movement near the far emplacement," Captain White Buffalo fired his words like bullets. "While looking for further movement we saw a vehicle on the highway. Then the four artillery emplacements exploded."

Captain White Buffalo turned to his commander. "We thought the first movement might be a moose, but–"

"They hibernate, right?" Major Franklin Jones, the general's adjutant said.

Captain White Buffalo and Corporal Ambrose didn't look at each other.

"No, sir," Ambrose said woodenly. "They do not hibernate."

General Spotted Bird snorted. "Frank is an Otoe. They don't know shit about moose. No need."

While they spoke, a number of military vehicles, including two tanks in the lead, roared out of the compound, and raced down the Victoria Highway. The first tank fired, and an unseen vehicle became very visible when it exploded.

"Lieutenant Bison-in-the-Cloud is the best damn tank commander we've got." Spotted Bird nearly shook the window with his vehemence. "He just instigated an *incident*, or we're at war with the damn Brits. How long we got till daylight?"

"Between an hour and an hour-and-a-half, General," Major Jones said while peering at his wristwatch. "Should I alert the anti-aircraft unit?"

"I'll bet you five dollars Canadian that they're already manning their weapons and ready to fight." Spotted Bird ginned.

"No, thank you, General. I've served with you long enough to know you don't bluff worth a damn."

"Gentlemen, I don't think three minutes would change events here this morning." General Spotted Bird raked White Buffalo and Ambrose with his gimlet eyes. "But the next time you even see a moose, I want to know about it. That aside, good reporting."

The senior officers swept out of the room.

"So…" Captain White Buffalo said, "…are we in trouble, or not?"

"I think we broke even, sir. But I don't think we would a second time."

"Noted. Thank you."

CHAPTER 103

CHENA REDOUBT, ALASKA REPUBLIK

Solare dropped her hand within touching distance of the .45 in her shoulder bag. Voices filled the passageway outside the cell. The door burst open and a man she didn't recognize strutted in as if he owned the place.

Shit, maybe he does, she thought.

Before she could form a question, Nathan spoke.

"It's about damn time, Riordan! Open this damn door."

Riordan frowned at Solare. "Who the hell are you? His girlfriend?"

Despite herself, she laughed out loud. *That was stupid, but I couldn't help it. For that matter, who the hell is Riordan?*

Another man armed with a pistol went to Nathan's cell and unlocked the door. She saw other men in the passageway behind Riordan, but couldn't determine their number.

Nathan flung the barred door open and grinned.

"By God, we can make this work yet!" He began to push past the man with the keys, then stopped. He pointed at Solare. "Kill her before you leave this cell."

The man's eyes slowly moved over her, and he grinned. "Do I have to kill her immediately?"

"That's up to you. But I want her dead."

Riordan and Nathan went out the door and down the passageway. The men all followed them. Except one.

Solare hadn't taken her eyes off the man with the pistol who had watched her since Nathan issued his order. The overwhelming lust in his face reassured her. *None of them know I'm armed.*

He glanced at the door.

Probably wants to make sure we're alone, she decided.

She used that moment of inattention to pull out her .45 and shoot him through the head.

CHAPTER 104

VICTORIA HIGHWAY
FIRST PEOPLE'S NATION

Major Roger Allenby, officer commanding Squadron Alfa, Special Air Service, grinned into the night. His lads had achieved their goal.

And beautifully done! he thought. His breath sent rapidly dissipating little puffs of fog into the night.

Squadron Sergeant Major Lannister slid up next to him on the knoll. The position commanded an excellent view of the highway as well as the junction.

"Our lads are retreating in good order, Major. We have two prisoners and no casualties. Some of the FPN people are getting close. You saw what they did to the decoy unit."

"Have everyone fall back to the insertion point."

"Sir!" The squadron sergeant disappeared.

"Back to the insertion point!" he said to the corporal next to him. They both moved out into the snow-bright night.

If I had sat there another five minutes, I would have frozen my ass to the earth, the major thought.

Allenby moved quickly but cautiously down the slope toward the byway where they had deployed, and the heated trucks waited.

✪

Sergeant Tanaka motioned for his rangers to spread out as they slowly advanced thorough the freezing forest. Moving inside the tree line proved easier than breaking trail in open areas. The snow wasn't as uniformly deep. When he breathed in heavily through his nose his nostrils wanted to stick together.

He suddenly recollected visiting a huge commercial freezer with his uncle. It smelled the same. The Athabascans had told them they shouldn't exercise too much, or they would freeze their lungs.

It has to be forty below! We need to rethink our tactics. He motioned for the radioman.

"Yeah, Sarge?" Corporal Tony Eluska asked.

"Put me through to General Spotted Bird."

"Wait one." He muttered into his headset then pulled off and handed it to Tanaka. "Here he is, Sarge."

General Spotted Bird sounded like he was standing in front of him. "Whatcha got, Sergeant Tanaka?"

"I want to call off pursuit and establish a secure perimeter. They have to go through us. We don't need to waste energy chasing them. That's my assessment, General."

"Your C.O. just finished telling me the same thing. Good thinking on both your parts. We agreed the perimeter should be a thousand meters out."

"Copy that, General. Tanaka out."

He handed the headset back to Corporal Eluska. "Thanks. C'mon, we got work to do."

CHAPTER 105

VICTORIA HIGHWAY
FIRST PEOPLE'S NATION

Colonel Yukon Cassidy liked the camouflaged parka the FPN had given him. He just wished the balaclava were as effective. He carefully examined the 105 mm cannon where it had landed fifteen-plus meters from its previous position.

"Whattya think, Cassidy?" Major Roland Delcambré asked. "You know more about artillery than I do."

"You don't know *anything* about artillery!"

"That's what I just said. Weren't you listening?"

"Nothing's damaged. The Yanks make these things damn near indestructible. The Brits only knocked the support out from under it. We just have to put it back where it belongs."

"Give me a few minutes," Delcambré said and flashed his torch up the slope.

Two men pulled a large hook and attached cable down from the massive winch secured to two large trees. One of the men dragged a large loop of cable in his other hand.

"Here you, are, sir," one man puffed.

"Thanks Thiessen. Hook this thing up so we can put it back where it's needed."

"Yes, sir," he mumbled and waved his helper over.

They rigged a harness around the cannon while a group of men fashioned a rude sled using the trees knocked down in the assault. Cassidy considered himself handy in the bush, but these fellows proved amazing. Wearing parkas and without breaking a sweat they had the piece restored to the slope and in firing position in twenty-five minutes.

The Brits had knocked down four cannons of which only one was too damaged for further action. With four crews working on the other three field pieces, they were ready for duty within two hours. Working steadily against the clock, they all knew the ball would go up once daylight arrived, and the sky continued to brighten.

The camouflage had been completed when the first British Canadian jet shrieked overhead.

"Everybody stay down," Cassidy said over the artillery frequency, "...the tanks will be along directly."

CHAPTER 106

RUSTYCAN HIGHWAY, ALASKA REPUBLIK

Riordan felt euphoric as he and the others moved through the night. His plan had worked perfectly so far. The weeks of hiding and scheming finally bore fruit.

After scraping at the stone wall beneath the window of his cell with a small knife for the better part of a year, the mortar bonding the stones finally loosened, and they could be pulled out at will. The hole faced the forest behind the town and few people ever visited the area. During the months of incarceration, he had stolen every scrap of fabric he could lay hands on.

The material had been braided and knotted to provide a safe descent to the ground outside the wall of his cell. He wasn't about to attempt a ten meter drop without knowing the nature of the landing zone in advance. Not knowing how long it would be until his next meal he had also hoarded the rough bread provided.

Three of his stolen towels became a pouch for his slim provisions to hang off his back. He begged another blanket to fight off the cold radiating from the walls of Chena Redoubt. The guards easily believed him, and the blanket also went into the pouch.

He had been an exemplary prisoner for his entire nine month stay. Four months ago, the warders ceased doing bed checks after the final meal of the day. Riordan had become routine and therefore nullified in their minds. One hour after the evening meal of stew, he had dropped the spoon into his pouch and tied it securely to his body. He wore every article of clothing he owned.

He secured one end of his escape rope to the iron bed built into the wall opposite the window. After quietly removing the loose stones and setting them on the stone floor he had thrown the cloth rope through the opening. After waiting a full five minutes for any alarms he grasped the rope and backed out the hole into the cold night.

Once on the ground he headed for the seedy part of town. The greatest stroke of luck had been coming across Oskar Nilsson, one of his former troopers. The man had intended to rob him until they recognized each other.

They got drunk in Oskar's shack and plotted their next move. Not long after Riordan's escape they heard through the mukluk telegraph that N'Go had been apprehended.

"Wasn't he your best mate?" Oskar drunkenly asked one night.

"I thought so. I actually hoped so," Riordan said.

"I sense a tear in that sheet."

"He's a man, not a piece of sailcloth. I kept waiting for him to break me out. But he never did."

"Maybe he couldn't."

"Nah. If he'd wanted to get me out, he woulda done it, and elegantly at that."

"So, what are you going to do about him?"

"Nothing. I'm going to leave him there to rot. Maybe they'll hang him."

✪

That had been six weeks ago. Now Riordan, Nilsson, and his new band of recently freed British SAS escapees followed Nathan to a large warehouse near the Chena River.

Nathan pointed to a large lock on the immense sliding door. "Break that. I no longer have the key."

Once inside, Nathan located a fuse box and snapped the handle up with an electric crackle. Overhead lights blazed on, and Riordan and his men beheld crates of weapons and ammunition. Off to the side sat two U.S. M113 armored personnel carriers.

"I believe we can all fit into these," Nathan said. "Make sure the petrol is topped off and all ammunition reserves are full. Can any of your people drive one of these machines?"

"All of us can," Riordan said with a wide grin.

"Excellent. Are any of you a trained radio operator?" Nathan swept his cold glance over them.

Without hesitation four men raised their hands.

"Excellent. You, and you, get in there and get the sets warmed up. We need to know what is happening out there in the world."

"Why do you think something is happening?" Riordan asked.

"Because nobody is here. Because we all escaped so easily. That was a skeleton crew you bested. All the others are somewhere else, and we need to know where and why."

In moments the radio operators picked up the traffic from Old Crow and reported same.

Riordan smiled. "They won't anticipate anyone attacking them from the rear. We can hit them in the ass and then link up with the Brits!"

Nathan slowly nodded and said, "We're wasting time. Saddle up."

In moments the two APCs roared down the RustyCan Highway.

✪

Safe in her utility, Solare clicked over to the Peacekeeper frequency.

"Hello, I need to speak to someone at Old Crow."

"This is Captain Strom. How may I help you?"

"Alex, this is Solare. Where exactly are you?"

"Manning a roadblock ten klicks west of Old Crow, why?"

"How many people do you have with you?"

"Four, do you have something to tell me or are we just passing time? This is a mil–"

"Riordan, Nathan, and a dozen escaped SAS cutthroats are headed your way. Riordan broke them out of prison and killed two Peacekeepers in the process."

"Is N'Go with them?"

"I didn't see him. But I couldn't see all of them, either."

"Thanks for the heads up, Solare. We'll be ready for them."

"I'm following a mile behind them. Please don't shoot me."

CHAPTER 107

VICTORIA HIGHWAY
FIRST PEOPLE'S NATION

Viscount Craddock kept his eyes on the road ahead. The reconnaissance aircraft reported seeing armored units at the junction. That was, unfortunately, in front of the bridge over the Porcupine River and they had no option other than to take it.

He had kept his snow-go scouts with the column. It would be far too derelict to subject his men to -35°C temperatures. Besides, Sergeant Horricks was looking much worse for wear. *Perhaps a younger man was needed?*

The weapons carrier came to a stop and Craddock looked over at the driver.

"Lassiter?"

"This is the last high point before we drop into the valley, Colonel. You said you wished to see where Sergeant Horricks first saw the lights of Old Crow. This is the precise location, sir."

"Very good, Lassiter. You remember orders longer than I do, ha, ha."

Corporal Lassiter looked off to his right. "Amazing view from here, sir."

"More bloody land good for nothing profitable. A useless river, bleak landscape, and cold as a well digger's arse. Why anyone would live here voluntarily is far beyond me."

"It isn't for everyone," Lassiter said, "...that's for sure.

"Where were the artillery emplacements we neutralized?" He held his binoculars to his eyes.

"Off to the left there, Milord," Sergeant Fowler said from behind him. "You can see where the field pieces scoured the trees when they fell."

"Why don't I see the cannons themselves?"

"Perhaps they fell into the trees below them." Fowler's tone reeked of hope.

"How long ago were they eliminated?"

"Three or four hours ago, Milord."

Craddock felt relief sweep through him. "Oh, jolly good. Even the Royal Engineers couldn't have repositioned them in that amount of time."

"Gawd, I hope not!" Lassiter mumbled.

"Do you have something to say, *Corporal* Lassiter?"

"No, Milord. Sorry, Milord. Didn't realize I was speaking out loud, sir."

"For the record; I share your concern. Where the hell is our air cover?"

Sergeant Fowler cleared his throat. "They should be–"

A thunderous roar swept over them, blotting out his words and nearly their collective minds.

Five Meteor jet aircraft flew down the valley in V formation, splitting to each side when they passed over the junction.

"Why didn't they bomb them?" Craddock blurted.

"No provocation, Milord," Sergeant Fowler said. "Neither were they challenged by the First People's Nation. They have no reason to fire, yet."

"Even though we destroyed their artillery. Very well. Let's be more provocative! Drive on, Corporal Lassiter!"

Lassiter kept his speed down until the lead tank closed on his tailgate and then speeded up.

"Colonel Craddock, may I offer a suggestion?" Lassiter said.

"Of course, Corporal."

"Wouldn't it be better if a tank was the first vehicle to reach the roadblock? Especially if there will be armed resistance?"

"Excellent point, Corporal! Sergeant, radio the lead tank to go around us when we slow down, and Lassiter moves us off to the side. They will have the honor of being the spear point of the column."

Fowler lowered his voice and mumbled into his headset.

"Pull over when you wish, Lassiter," Fowler said.

Almost immediately Lassiter pulled over on a wide spot in the rough, gravel road. A Centurion tank roared past close enough for one tread to tap a bit of paint off the weapons carrier's front fender.

"Bastard!" Lassiter snapped.

"Think of him as an eager shield, Corporal," Craddock said with a chuckle.

They roared down the road behind the tank. Lassiter dropped back enough from the behemoth so the rocks its treads threw up in its wake didn't hit their vehicle or smash their windscreen. Lassiter glanced up at the scarred hillside.

"Don't worry, Corporal," Colonel Craddock said. "All the firepower is in front of that tank."

Sergeant Fowler interrupted, "Colonel, the FPN is advising the column to halt a thousand meters from the roadblock, or we will be fired on."

"Tell them if they do not move aside, we will go through them."

"Sir, they say if we do not halt, we are at war with the FPN and their allies."

Who the hell are their allies? he wondered. *I don't remember ignoring anything about this!* "Tell them to parse it as they will. We are coming through!"

CHAPTER 108

RUSTYCAN HIGHWAY, ALASKA REPUBLIK

"Shit!" Alex said with emphasis. "Two of theirs against one of ours."

"What are you talking about, Captain?" Lieutenant MacDonald asked, her eyes wide and searching his face for nonverbal answers.

"We have hostiles coming up from the north."

"How soon will they be here?"

"About five hours. They just left Chena."

She grinned. "So, we call down to Old Crow for reinforcements, and then kick their asses!"

"I hope Old Crow can spare us the people. They're pretty busy down there."

"How many hostiles we talking about?"

"Two APCs full of SAS troopers, Nathan, and Riordan." Alex returned her quick grin. "You have no idea how much I am looking forward to this!"

"Captain Strom," Mack said in a pleading voice. "Please don't do anything stupid."

"Not to worry. Riordan and Nathan are handling that end of things. C'mon, we got lots to do before our guests arrive."

CHAPTER 109

BATTLE OF THE JUNCTION
FIRST PEOPLE'S NATION

"They aren't slowing down, *mon ami!*" Delcambré said over their closed communications circuit.

Cassidy, walking in slow steady circles to keep his blood moving, stopped, and looked down at the Victoria Highway.

"Emplacement Four, target the twelfth tank in the column. That will be our plug. Emplacement Three, target the eighth tank. Emplacement One, Target the fourth tank.

"Everyone got that?" He received three affirmatives. "Great. Don't fire until I give the command."

Overhead, the British Meteor fighters flew in great circles, maintaining station.

"How many of our people are down there at the junction?" Cassidy asked.

"At least six of our Peacekeepers," Delcambré said. "Probably more. Once the word got out that we were here I'm sure they avoided contact so we couldn't order them back to their posts."

"Don't they know me better than that?"

"Not yet. This night will tell us all a great deal about each other."

"You're such a romantic, Roland."

"Ah, look, *mon ami*. The *merde* is about to hit the fan!"

Below them the leading British tank passed the thousand-meter mark, and was promptly fired on by three artillery pieces hidden in the forest surrounding the road. The Centurion lost a tread, began smoking, and shuddered to a stop. The hatches flew open and three of the crew cleared the machine before the ammo inside exploded, jarring the machine a meter to the right.

The weapons carrier immediately behind the tank swerved off the edge of the road and slid down to a stop on the long embankment bearing the highway up out of the tundra. The fighter squadron shrieked down at the junction.

"Fire!" Cassidy said crisply over the artillery network. All three cannons fired.

Three tanks in the column went into their death throes.

"Now work backward from your initial targets!" Cassidy said, trying not to yell over the connection.

✪

At the junction two antiaircraft batteries threw thousands of rounds at the diving planes. The aircraft launched missiles and pulled up to climb away. The last Meteor caught more rounds than it could withstand, burst into flames, and roared into an antiaircraft battery at full speed, destroying the emplacement and killing five FPN soldiers.

The four remaining Meteors regained altitude and were attacked by six Swordmaster jets of the Republic of California Air Force. Taken by surprise, the Meteor flight lost a bird immediately. The other three went in different directions and gained altitude.

As the jets gained altitude for maneuvering space, six Eureka P-61s curved in over the junction and roared down the British column, strafing.

✪

Cassidy kept the artillery firing. The Brits were in a chaotic traffic jam. Eight of their tanks were out of action and burning.

The tank commanders fired into the trees far below the actual gun emplacements obviously in the belief the weapons couldn't have regained their previous elevation. Smoke drifted over the valley. British Canadian infantry advanced toward the junction but hesitated to pass through an artillery duel to reach their goal.

The snow had ceased, and the infantry stood out starkly on the ground cover. Many went down to stay. Some fired missiles at the attacking aircraft: the heat-seeking type.

✪

"Missiles! Evasive action!" Jerry yelled into his microphone and threw *Satori* into an upward spiral. A rocket burned past his cockpit, and he pulled hard to the right. He breathed a quick sigh of relief.

The missile twisted back around and detonated just behind the exhaust, blowing *Satori*, and Lieutenant Colonel Jerry Yamato, to pieces.

⭐

"That was one of ours!" Cassidy screamed. "Take out those bastards with the missiles!"

Seconds later three high explosive rounds enveloped the British Canadian ground forces. Another volley followed almost instantly.

Cassidy watched where the pieces of the aircraft fell. *People will want to know.*

White flags appeared on the remaining tanks and lorries.

Cassidy changed frequencies. "Lawrence, they're surrendering! The whole damn column is surrendering!"

"You positive about that, Yukon?"

"Yes, General. I am positive."

CHAPTER 110

TANANA
ALASKA REPUBLIK

Bodecia and Magda were folding bandages for combat medic supplies at the hospital. She had been envying Magda's quick fingers and total absorption in the task. Her daughter's hands suddenly stopped and trembled.

Magda's eyes focused somewhere far away. She frowned and calmly said, "Jerry just died. I hope he didn't suffer pain."

"How do you know this?" Bodecia asked as gently as she could. She feared for her daughter's mind.

"This thing happened in me the moment I first met him. A part of me filled that I hadn't known was empty. I knew it was him completing me." She sniffed.

"It just went away. That part is gone." Tears streamed down her face. "I knew we would never have children."

The phone on the wall rang and Bodecia picked it up. Pelagian was sobbing on the other end.

"I, I need to talk to Magda, my love."

"She already knows. Thank you, my husband." She hung up the phone and her own tears started as she hugged her daughter.

CHAPTER 111

OLD CROW
ALASKA REPUBLIK

"I demand to speak with someone in authority," Viscount Craddock said, exuding massive hubris. He kept his hands clasped together and resting on the desk between him and his captor.

Captain Dexter Williams grinned. "I've got a bunch of authority. Talk away." He leaned back in his chair and put both of his feet on the table, nearly touching Craddock's hands.

Someone behind Dexter laughed and he turned to see General Spotted Bird of the FPN Army. The general grinned at him and nodded.

"I like you, Captain. You'll go places. If you don't mind, I'll take it from here."

Dexter slowly straightened to his feet. "Thank you, General. I do have a lot of other things on my list. Good luck with the right hand of God, here."

✪

It had been hours since the FPN soldiers had pulled him from his vehicle. What passed for daylight had long since faded into more stygian darkness. Still, Craddock felt emboldened. Surely even an aboriginal general officer would be able to understand his point of view.

The general sat down and leaned back in his chair. "Why did you attack my country with no provocation or declaration of war? Are you a bandit?"

"I am a colonel in the British Canadian Army carrying out a police action that has nothing to do with the First People's Nation!"

The general pulled a pack of cigarettes from his shirt pocket, went through the elaborations of lighting one, and offered the pack to Craddock who shook his head. "No thank you."

"You are wrong. You violated our border with military aircraft and armored units. You killed over a score of our people, and destroyed a great deal of our defensive equipment. How the hell didn't this escapade have anything to do with us?"

"We were traversing a road we helped construct and have used since the day it was completed. How can you *legally* stop us now?"

Spotted Bird held his hand up and a lieutenant moved up behind him and placed a document in it. The general tossed it on the desk between them. "Read the underlined part on the first page."

Craddock read the whole page, wincing inside. *How could they have not told me about this?* He regarded the general.

"I was following orders from my commanding officer."

"To attack us?"

"No! We were to go into the zone of rebellion called the Alaska Republik, and arrest, or eliminate the ringleaders. You placed your people in our way. Therefore, you have as much responsibility about this misconstrued battle as I do."

"You're an *idiot*, Viscount Craddock. There must be some vengeful people back in Victoria who wanted to see you make a criminal fool of yourself. Both of our nations signed the original of that document, and your boss *knew* it."

Spotted Bird took a long drag on his cigarette.

Craddock flushed scarlet and opened his mouth, but Spotted Bird held up his hand.

"Allow me to finish!" He blew smoke at Craddock, who flinched. "We have tried to contact your government for the past twenty hours. They have not responded.

"We sent an urgent diplomatic letter through your embassy in the Republic of California. No response. This is all very reminiscent of how the recent war between the Empire of Japan and the Republic of California began—and we all know how *that* ended.

"We have captured over 300 of your troops. I got no idea how many we killed out there in the cold. But it's all *your* fault."

Craddock felt starkers. He could only see one option that would leave him with any honor at all.

"May I be given a revolver with one round and placed in an empty room?"

"Oh, *fuck* no! You are a political pawn." Spotted Bird grinned widely.

"We are going to utilize you as much as we can. You will get the little room to yourself, but no weapon, or shoestrings, or belts. Well, you get my drift."

Percival Viscount Craddock burst into tears.

General Spotted Bird laughed.

CHAPTER 112

RUSTYCAN HIGHWAY, ALASKA REPUBLIK

"I see two sets of headlights, Captain!" the look-out shouted from her perch at the top of the ridge. "They're moving fast."

"Thanks, Boesser! When you think they're a mile out, get down out of sight."

"Yes, sir."

It's not every day you get to order around a librarian!

"Lieutenant MacDonald, are all of your people in place?"

"Yes, sir. I've got a squad of Dená Rangers on each side of the cut, and six more camouflaged about a hundred and fifty meters back down the road. They're dug in and protected."

"Excellent. Let's hope Riordan isn't completely stupid and surrenders without a fight."

"You'd hate that, wouldn't you?" Mack asked, and grinned.

"Yeah, I would. He'll fight, just wait and see. Turn on the light and get to your position."

Mack entered the APC and a moment later the powerful spotlight illuminated the road ten meters from the vehicle.

"Positions!" Alex yelled. "Remember, the challenge is 'owl', and the answer is 'feather'."

✪

"Major Riordan, someone just turned on a bright light ahead of us." The SAS trooper glanced over his shoulder. "D'ya want me to stop?"

"No, don't stop. Reduce your speed to twenty klicks." He threw back the overhead hatch and climbed two steps up the ladder into the incredibly frigid wind. Despite his hands shaking from the bitter cold, the binoculars showed a quiet roadblock and no undue activity. He quickly glassed the ridge in both directions but saw nothing.

It's the middle of a bloody cold night and all the action is south of them. Riordan had been in the same situation more than once. *They'll think we are more reinforcements.*

He dropped back into the warm cabin and pushed forward to the driver.

"Stop about three meters this side of the ring of light."

"Piece of cake, sir."

Riordan turned to the men crowded into the machine with him. "Be ready to deploy if I give you a thumbs up. Don't forget to kill the spotlight over the hatch before you exit."

✪

The lead APC stopped right where Alex knew it would. Riordan always played things the same way.

He must not have N'Go with him.

The engine noise died down to an idle and the headlights went dark. Figures moved out from behind both APCs, keeping a minimum of two meters between them.

Time to play.

"Who are you?" Strom shouted.

"Reinforcements!" Riordan yelled.

Alex grinned. "For who?"

"The Alaska Republik Army."

"Then why did you already deploy troopers?"

"I know that voice," Riordan said. "Is that you, Lieutenant Strom? I heard you had gone into other employ."

"I need for you and all your people to drop your weapons and move into the light with your hands clasped behind your heads. It's too fucking cold out here to mess around. Get to it."

"Fuck it, lads," Riordan said conversationally. "Fire at will."

The spotlight burst as hundreds of rounds smashed into it and ricocheted off the APC. Alex ducked and shouted, "Let 'em have it!"

Automatic rifle fire blazed from the top and face of the rock wall on both sides of the road. The twin .50s on all three APCs roared to life. Two *panzerfaust* rockets roared into Riordan's idling APCs and both machines exploded. The resulting shrapnel and debris took out those who hadn't taken adequate cover as well as damaging the Alaska Republik vehicle.

"Oh, God! I'm hit, I'm hit!" someone shrieked beyond the burning APCs.

Fire gouted out of the machines and lent a hellish glow to the landscape. Figures rushed a few yards and then took cover or were hit and dropped in their tracks. A constant stream of bullets came from the SAS position.

Alex knew they were using the traditional infantry advance technique of three small units working together. Two would fire and the third would advance. Unfortunately for them the Dená Rangers up in the rocks could see all of them and the attrition continued unabated.

Alex peered into the burning twilight, trying to figure out Riordan's position. A round splanged off the APC next to his face and he dropped down. Weapons fire filled the night, and he didn't know who was friend and who was foe any more.

He knew he had people out there on the far side of Riordan's men. *I won't do that again*, he thought ruefully.

Someone sprinted past the APC and was hit three times before they could get through the rock cut.

The gunfire died away. Someone slithered toward Alex from behind.

"Owl," he harshly whispered.

"Feather," Mack answered softly.

"Are you wounded?"

"No. Are you?"

"No, and I want to keep it that way. Why did you leave your position?"

"Two of the guys are covering my spot. I don't know about you, but I am really feeling the cold."

"Thanks," he said. "I was trying to ignore it."

"How can we press the issue? I know all of our people are freezing."

"We sure as hell can't call a truce," Alex snapped. "And it's too dark to call in the air force."

"Maybe we could talk them into surrendering."

"They are all facing a rope, Mack. They ain't gonna just give up," he said with more asperity than he wanted to exhibit.

Something landed between them. Alex looked down and immediately kicked the object as hard as he could.

"Grenade!" he bellowed and dropped to the ground.

Mack dropped down to her knees.

The grenade hit the rocks and ricocheted off toward the enemy and exploded. Shrapnel went in all directions.

"Augg!" Mack screamed, and grabbed her left shoulder as she fell flat.

"Medic!" Alex bellowed as he grabbed her. He rolled her onto her back and opened her parka enough to rip away the blood-soaked shirt fabric. Someone rushed up.

He looked up into the face of Sergeant Helen Anton.

"Doc, she got hit in the shoulder, I–"

"Did great," she said with a quick smile. "I have her now."

"Thanks Doc!" He grabbed his Kalashnikov and jumped up to his post. Sara Boesser hurried over and helped carry Mack away on a stretcher.

Those are two strong women! he thought. *Mack ain't light.*

He became aware of people running at him. Instantly he fired an arc of bullets across their charge. Four went down, and five more behind them fired their weapons as they continued their advance.

Alex's Kalashnikov ran out of ammo.

"Shit! He pulled out his pistol and shot the closest man. The others went down under a fusillade of rounds from the two closest rangers in the rocks.

He smelled cordite, burning rubber, and fear. He could hear the crackle of the burning APCs and realized all gunfire had ceased. Sweat poured off Alex.

"Is anyone alive out there?" he shouted.

Two people stumbled toward him.

"Owl," he said.

"Feathers," the two men said at the same time.

"You guys need help?"

"Yeah, I do," one said as the other fell on his face.

"Medic!"

"I think we got them all, Captain," the first ranger said. "We checked every person we came across."

"Do you know what Tim Riordan looks like?"

"Who?"

"Never mind. I got this." Alex put a fresh clip in his weapon and eased out into the bloody landscape. With the flickering red glow from the fires, and the blood splattered snow, he felt he was entering the frozen part of Hades.

"Now where is that son of a bitch?" Alex began examining the faces of the dead.

CHAPTER 113

NEAR OLD CROW
ALASKA REPUBLIK

Major Timothy Riordan, late of the International Freekorps, hurried through the night. He knew as long as he kept moving, he would not freeze to death. Therefore, he did his best to ignore his fatigue.

"What pisses me off the most," he muttered as he trudged down the snowy road. "Is the fact I am being hunted by men I trained. That just isn't fair."

The Northern Lights whirled and danced over him. He appreciated the illumination but had no time to observe the ionic ballet. He kept his eyes constantly moving over the frigid landscape.

The lights danced over the frost crusted snow. He didn't relish the abrasions his clothing would suffer from the hardened snow. He moved out of the APC tracks and struck out cross country at an angle to the road

As soon as he ordered his men to shoot, he had moved out the rear of the machine and taken cover. When both of the APCs were hit with panzerfaust the blasts knocked him flat on his face. As he got to his knees, a man he didn't recognize to his immediate right had risen up toward him. After two steps the fire from the roadblock cut the man down.

Riordan appreciated irony more than most. He crawled over to the dead man and relieved him of his weapon and ammo. Keeping low, he hurried into the dark and away from the firefight.

Screams and weapons fire hurried him through the darkness. He circled around to the rocky up-cropping and carefully climbed over. He hugged the icy-cold rocks as closely as possible, the dense, frozen boulders of stone chilled him further.

They're all engaged elsewhere, but it only takes one pair of eyes to ruin your whole day. He grinned and slowly made his way down the other side of the rocky ridge. British Canada beckoned in the distance where something in the sky exploded as he watched.

Poor bastard. I'm glad I'm far away from that.

CHAPTER 114

OLD CROW
ALASKA REPUBLIK

Yukon Cassidy trudged across the snow thankful for the snowshoes he had taken off a British Canadian lorry. A number of other Peacekeepers and a squad of Dená Rangers searched through the forest with him. They searched for any sign of Lieutenant Colonel Jerry Yamato.

Cassidy knew they wouldn't find any part of Jerry. He had been the most vulnerable part of the aircraft. Thus far they had found pieces of metal from the P-61 Eureka and put them on a sled two of the rangers pulled behind them.

Roland moved over next to Cassidy. The daylight would be gone again in an hour. The temperature had risen to -20°F.

"I fear we will have to wait for spring to complete this sad search."

"Unfortunately, I agree with you." Cassidy said. "We're all exhausted and my adrenaline ran out hours ago. I think I could sleep right here."

"Let us return to the road, Colonel. There was talk of mobile kitchens captured from the invaders."

"I hope they have coffee as well as tea."

Delcambré tripped and fell in the snow.

"Damn!" he bellowed as he went down.

Cassidy looked where he had tripped and plucked a broken strip of aluminum out of the snow. An oval of metal had been driven into the larger piece. He wrenched the pieces apart and examined the smaller one.

"I'll be damned. Look at this, Roland." He helped the smaller man to his feet and handed him the shiny oval.

Roland stared at it for a long moment and his eyes filled. "His identity tag." He motioned at the piece of aluminum Cassidy still held.

"That must have been part of the cockpit." Delcambré dabbed at his eyes.

"I think we can all go home now," Cassidy said. He pulled a whistle from his pocket and blew two sharp blasts.

All of the men and women searching the area turned toward the road and continued searching as they went.

The Victoria Highway bustled with organized chaos. Crews of captured British Canadian soldiers directed by armed FPN troopers cleared the destroyed tanks and lorries from the road. Other groups of prisoners retrieved the bodies of their fallen mates.

Wounded men were placed in the backs of lorries staffed by medics. The lucky ones had a doctor attending, but those were few and far between. A BC tank rumbled past, fresh from pushing damaged units into the ditch. There was more to clear farther back down the road.

"Cassidy!" a familiar voice bellowed. He looked up to see General Spotted Bird, grinned, and walked toward him. The older man looked as wrung out as Cassidy felt.

Cassidy saluted and Spotted Bird waved it off. "Don't worry about that military crap right now."

"What can I do for you, Lawrence?"

"Have you heard from all of your Peacekeepers yet?"

"No. A few are in my group. We were hoping to recover some of Colonel Yamato's bird."

"Any luck?"

Cassidy handed him the identity tag. After a long moment of examining it, Spotted Bird handed it back.

"He was a good man from all I hear."

"Yeah. Why did you ask about my people?"

The general related the roadblock battle. "Some of your people are dead, some are wounded. Your Captain Strom deserves a medal for his handling of that mess."

"Hell, Lawrence, you deserve a medal for handling this part of it."

"I felt we had to make up for allowing the French to enter Alaska Republik unannounced. Besides, I'm still pissed at the Brits for the way they used us in the Austrian War."

"I'll drink to that," Cassidy said grimly. "Did my people capture Riordan?"

"I don't think so. That bastard has more lives than a cat."

"Even cats run out of lives, and Riordan isn't even a cat. Hell, I like cats."

CHAPTER 115

NEAR OLD CROW
ALASKA REPUBLIK

"Aha," Solare said softly to herself. "There's where he came down out of the rocks."

She had followed Riordan and Nathan's escape in her utility. Giving them a half mile lead she had kept her distance. When the firefight broke out, she turned around and retreated a mile.

Bullets could be deadly even at a distance. Once the gunfire ceased, she approached the area with her headlights on. Dená Rangers stopped her and took her on foot to Captain Strom.

"Solare!" Alex said when he saw her. "They tell me you have a utility out there. What's in the back?"

"Camping gear, a sleeping bag, and a small mattress, why?"

"We have wounded that need to be driven to Tetlin for air evacuation to Tanana."

She tossed him the keys. "All yours. Did you get Riordan and Nathan?"

"Nathan is one of the severely wounded. No sign of Riordan. That son-of-a-bitch can get out of anything."

"Are you sure he didn't get past you here on the road?"

"Positive. I don't know where he went, and I don't have time to look for him."

"Can you give me some rations? I'm going to track him down."

"Hell, yeah. I heard how you tracked down Ferdinand Rochamboux. Well done, by the way."

✪

She found where Riordan had struck out across country wearing only boots. She pulled out her compass, read the heading and then noted the particulars in her little field book. She had brought her snowshoes with her and knew Riordan had to break trail and couldn't go as fast as she could in deep snow. Within a mile he had turned and headed for the rock ridge.

She followed over the ridge and found where he had come down. His tracks went straight out toward the Victoria Highway. Solare grinned, carefully laid down her rifle, and slipped out of her backpack.

She made notes. After untying the cord holding the snowshoes she reached into her pack and found some dried salmon strips Alex had given her. While she ate, she scanned the horizon with binoculars.

If Riordan thought someone was following him, he would certainly set up an ambush, she thought.

According to Alex there had been a big fight near Old Crow with the British Canadian Army. Tanks, jets, the whole thing.

"If he gets to them before I get to him, I'll lose him in the mess," she muttered.

Within minutes she had donned her snowshoes. With weapon in hand, she continued tracking her quarry.

CHAPTER 116

TANANA
ALASKA REPUBLIK

"Mr. First Speaker, there is an urgent telephone call for you," Captain Langbein said from the hall outside Pelagian's office.

"Urgent call from who, Fred?"

"Somebody in the British Canada government, sir."

"This should be good. Put it through, please."

"Yes, sir."

His handset buzzed and Pelagian picked up the phone. "This is the First Speaker of the Alaska Republik. To whom am I speaking?"

"Thank you for taking my call, Mr. First Speaker. I am Charles Winslow, Minister for War for British Canada. I would like you to release Viscount Craddock at your earliest opportunity, else our nations will be at war."

The man's matter-of-fact tone of condescension enraged Pelagian.

"*Will be?* We *have* been at war since your armored column roared over the thousand-meter line outside Old Crow. Are your communications with your armored assassins so poor that you didn't get the word?"

"There was a lamentable lapse in judgment on the parts of some individuals in our government, but–"

"Tell that to my daughter, whose husband was blown out of the sky by your troops. We all have blood in this game, and we're not about to accept anything from you people other than a total surrender."

"Don't be absurd! Why would *we* surrender to an upstart nation with no standing army?"

"Look up the little rebellion King George III had on his watch. Then consider that our allies, the Republic of California, the First

People's Nation, and the United States of America, have all pledged to stand with us if invaded. You *invaded* us!"

"You are blowing this all out of proportion, sir. That was merely an exercise that—"

"Please, you're only making it worse. Unless you wish to negotiate terms, we are finished here."

"I, I need to speak to my government."

"You do that. Don't take too long." Pelagian slammed the phone onto its cradle. He stabbed the intercom button for his secretary.

"Irene, please find Claude and ask him to come see me."

He dropped into his chair as anger laden with grief swirled through him. His temper had always lurked under the thin veneer of what balance he possessed. At this point he needed a trusted, calmer mind.

His phone buzzed and he picked up the receiver. "Pelagian here."

"Mr. First Speaker. This is Minister for State–"

"Where are you, Claude?"

"I'm in Old Crow. What do you need?"

"I need your counsel. How soon can you get here?"

"I'm taking a British Canadian surrender at the moment. Can I get back to you?"

"The whole country is surrendering?"

"No. Just the commander of the invading military."

"I want the whole damned country to surrender, Claude. They killed Jerry, and I want to make them pay."

Claude's voice softened. "I didn't know that was Jerry. I saw him die." Claude hesitated and for a moment Pelagian thought the call had ended. "I'll twist their nuts as hard as I can, Mr. First Speaker, I promise."

"Thank you, Claude."

"At your service, sir. Good night."

"Good night."

CHAPTER 117

TANANA
ALASKA REPUBLIK

Magda wondered when she would feel the pain others were experiencing over Jerry's death.

How can I grieve if the man I love died doing what he loved best, flying to the aid of his comrades? He and she both knew the potential threat could become manifest at any moment. Now it had. *No surprise there*, she thought.

A light knock sounded, and she looked at the door and smiled.

"Come in, Mother."

Bodecia closed the door softly behind her and stared at her daughter with wide, beseeching eyes. Magda could see the pain and loss in those two bottomless depths. She opened her arms and Bodecia rushed, sobbing, into her embrace.

"He was such a good man," Bodecia sobbed into her shoulder.

"Yes, he was," Magda said. "I never knew a finer person and I told him that often."

"How can you be so serene after such a loss, daughter?"

"Jerry and I had talked many times about his potential death in an aircraft. He knew his profession could be unforgiving, and chance always ruled. I know I'll always love him, and I will never meet his equal. That's not something to grieve. It is something to celebrate."

"You're *celebrating* the death of your husband?" Bodecia said wonderingly, and pulled away.

"Yes, to the point that he died doing what he loved. Doing what he felt he had to do, and that he was facing the enemy. I rejoice in his honorable warrior passing because it's what he would have wanted."

Bodecia, now dry-eyed, asked, "What will you do now? Will you stay here in the capitol?"

"Probably not. I am very much pulled to the Peacekeepers. I love the concept and know that there is a need for compassion as well as guaranteed retribution."

"Yukon would give you any role you wished."

"We'll see. He's not a very forgiving man."

"What have you done he needs to forgive?"

"Not me. The rest of the world. Cassidy's challenged when the situation requires compassion."

The phone rang and Magda grabbed it.

"Tanana Hospital. Okay, yes. We'll be ready. Thank you." She stared at her mother as she hung up the phone.

"We have a helicopter inbound with wounded from Old Crow. One of them is Nathan Roubitaux and he's critical. I'll alert Doctor Woodruff."

"I'll get people moving and prepare the operating room. I would rather that Nathan died at the end of a rope than from being wounded in a fight."

"Agreed." Magda hurried off to find the doctor.

CHAPTER 118

NEAR VICTORIA HIGHWAY
FIRST PEOPLE'S NATION

Timothy Riordan neary sobbed with exhaustion and hunger. For twenty-four hours or more he had been running on empty. His lungs ached and the outside of his wool trousers were frozen from the knees down.

The small creek he thought nothing of crossing had contained a weak spot where the not-yet-frozen current flowed fastest. It wasn't all that deep, but his boots and pants were instantly soaked. Wet wool retains heat. Soaked boot leather does not. It freezes.

Knowing that winter never granted mercy, Riordan stumbled through the forest on numbed feet he hadn't felt for over an hour. He also didn't have any way of making a fire.

I've got to find a medic, or at least shelter.

He had never before in his life felt so frightened. It had always been easy to fool men and women. He had met his match when it came to fooling nature.

The exhilaration of escaping the firefight had worn off before he reached the rocky ridge. Already tired he knew if he stopped, he would freeze to death. Always before in his life he knew he could go until it was safe to stop.

That's when he encountered the damned creek and the odds against his survival rose to daunting heights. He cursed himself for not grabbing more gear when he exited the APC. But as always, he had allowed bloodlust to dominate his actions.

The air temperature in the clear, dark subarctic night slid inexorably further downward. He strangled the whimper that tried to rise in his throat and woodenly trudged onward.

✪

Solare easily followed Riordan's path. Even before she reached the stream, she knew he didn't believe anyone followed him. She read the trail accurately and even winced when she spied where he went through the ice.

"Dammit, he's making this too easy for me!" she blurted out loud. Immediately she crouched down and carefully surveyed all within her sight. If she had suffered the same mishap, she would have made a fire as soon as possible to dry out her footgear.

She neither saw nor smelled smoke.

Maybe he doesn't have matches or flint? She found that nearly impossible to believe. Everyone in the north carried the means to make fire at all times. One's life could depend on it.

She continued following his tracks. After the creek she noticed his path ceased to be straight. It veered from large tree to large tree, not that they grew to any height in a land dominated by permafrost.

"His feet are freezing," she said in a worried tone. "Damn it. I want him to be a worthy quarry. Not some damn wounded beast needing to be put down!"

She quickened her step, thinking hard. A quick look at the rough map from Captain Strom told her which way was the most direct route to the highway. Solare felt she was close to catching Riordan but couldn't hurry too much. He was still a desperate man with a weapon.

The cold cut into her lungs and she immediately slowed. *Slow down, Solare,* she thought. *You have more time than he does.*

Darkness prevailed and the new moon hid its face behind the shadow of Earth. She pulled out her small torch and tied it to a sturdy sapling she cut. After switching it on, she extended the sapling out, so the light was a meter and a half in front of her.

Following the sometimes erratic trail of Riordan, she continued on. The air grew noticeably colder, and she pulled the flaps of her fur hat down over her ears. The icy darkness seemed to magnify sound and she clearly heard large machines and hints of voices in the distance.

A quick red flare of light winked ahead of her, and something *cracked* between the torch and her hand before she heard the gunshot.

"Oh!" she blurted loudly. The torch dropped into the snow. She froze in place, wishing she could extinguish the light.

Okay, she decided, *this is an even fight again.*

She grinned and awkwardly jumped to her left behind a black spruce no larger than her arm. Nothing. She circled out to her left and tried desperately to reconstruct the red flash in her mind's eye.

How far away was he? She decided on a number and then doubled it. Slowly, as absolutely quietly as possible, she moved back to the heading she had followed.

The modified safety on her rifle didn't make a sound when she pushed it off. Solare was betting her life she was ahead of Riordan. Time would tell.

She didn't relax, she merely waited, all senses fully alert. Her nostrils tried to stick together when she inhaled. That told her the temperature was at minus forty Fahrenheit or colder.

Can't work up a sweat or I'm dead. The thought ran through her mind automatically. Her woodcraft tended to interrupt her when she was in the field, and she never ignored it.

She heard him before she saw his dark form move across the snow field behind him. He grunted in pain with every step, and as her finger caressed the rifle's trigger. She sighed.

"God damn it, Riordan! Give up or you're a dead man!" she shouted.

He fell to his knees and wildly fired an automatic weapon in her direction.

She shot him once in what she thought was his chest. He dropped into the snow. Again, she quietly crept up on him.

No movement came from the dark crumpled form. She reached out with her weapon and pushed his weapon off to the side with a quick thrust.

"I have you covered. Can you speak?"

"Wh–who?" he said in a liquid tone. "Are, you?"

"Solare. The woman in the cell, you arrogant bastard."

"No." His labored breathing interfered with his speech. "She's dead. I heard, the shot."

"Yeah. That was my .45. You're going to die on me, aren't you?"

"Not, *yet!*" He raised up wildly in the snow with a pistol in his hand.

She shot him with the .45 she held in her left hand.

He flopped back silently, and his heels drummed weakly in the snow.

"You just couldn't surrender, could you, you arrogant ass?"

Solare said to his silent form.

She trudged back up his trail and retrieved the torch and stick. Back at Riordan's body she tied the stick crossways in the spruce. She finally turned and moved off toward the lights flickering through the trees.

I hope they have hot coffee and something warm to eat.

Stoney Compton

(Leonard Wayne Compton)

Stoney Compton lives north of Farmington, New Mexico with his wife, Colette, two dogs, and an ever-changing number of cats. He is a Navy veteran, and a past Writers of the Future Contest winner. He still holds Alaska and Alaskans near and dear.